EMMA VIECELI ~ MALIN RYDÉN

A love story... but a bit broken.

Cover coloured by Christina Strain

SOARING PENGUIN
PRESS

LONDON UK

BREAKS

By Emma Vieceli and Malin Rydén

Published by Soaring Penguin Press
4 Florence Terrace
London
SW15 3RU
www.soaringpenguinpress.com

This edition © 2017 Soaring Penguin Press

ISBN 978-1-908030-21-4

Printed in Ukraine.

To Pud, Elle and the DAH posse.x

- Emma

To Aleph and CJ for making me a better writer.
To Elle and the DAH crew for sparking these shenanigans.

- Malin

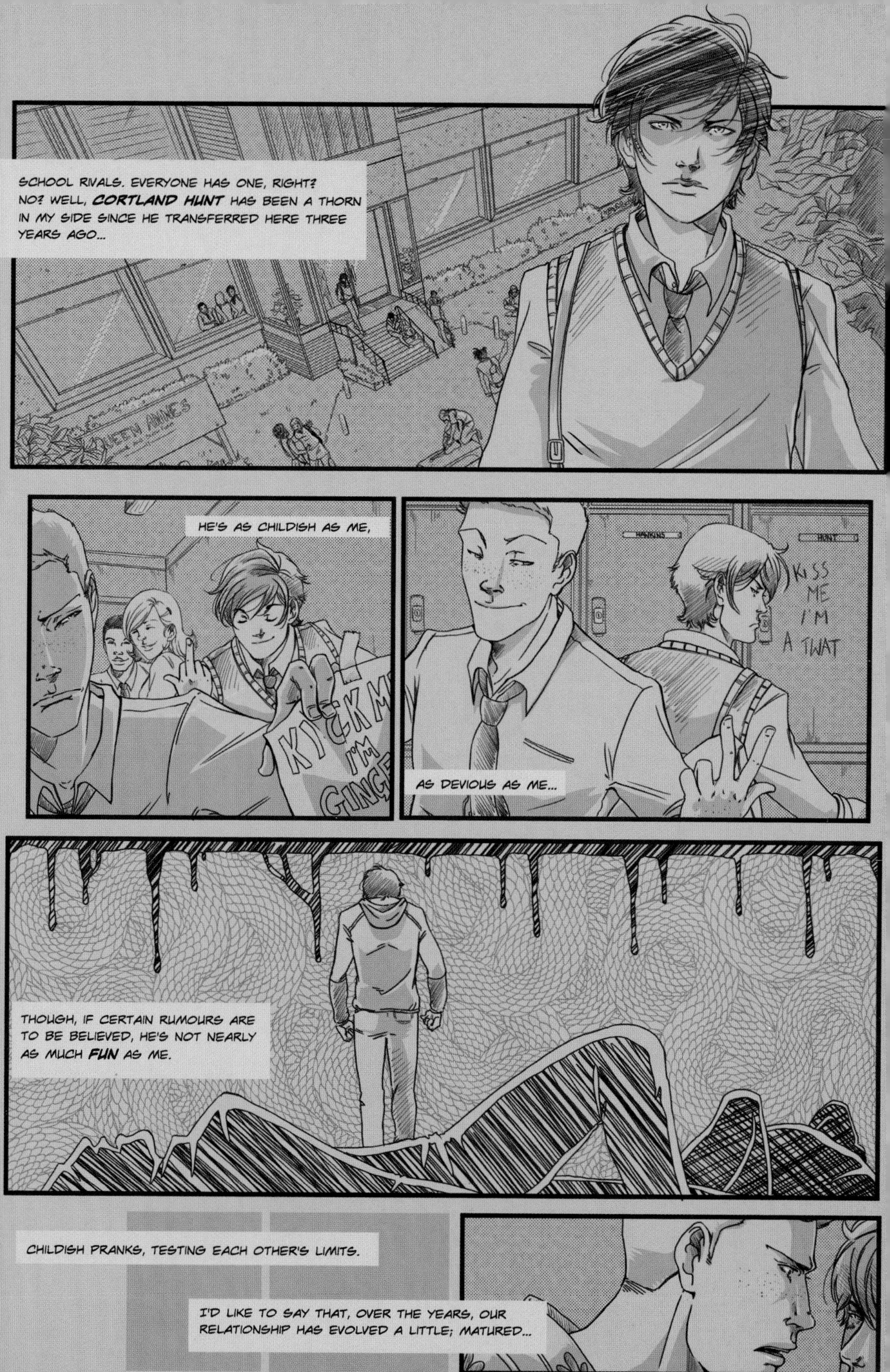
SCHOOL RIVALS. EVERYONE HAS ONE, RIGHT? NO? WELL, CORTLAND HUNT HAS BEEN A THORN IN MY SIDE SINCE HE TRANSFERRED HERE THREE YEARS AGO...
QUEEN ANNE'S
HE'S AS CHILDISH AS ME,
KICK ME I'M GINGE
HAWKINS
HUNT
KISS ME I'M A TWAT
AS DEVIOUS AS ME...
THOUGH, IF CERTAIN RUMOURS ARE TO BE BELIEVED, HE'S NOT NEARLY AS MUCH FUN AS ME.
CHILDISH PRANKS, TESTING EACH OTHER'S LIMITS.
I'D LIKE TO SAY THAT, OVER THE YEARS, OUR RELATIONSHIP HAS EVOLVED A LITTLE; MATURED...

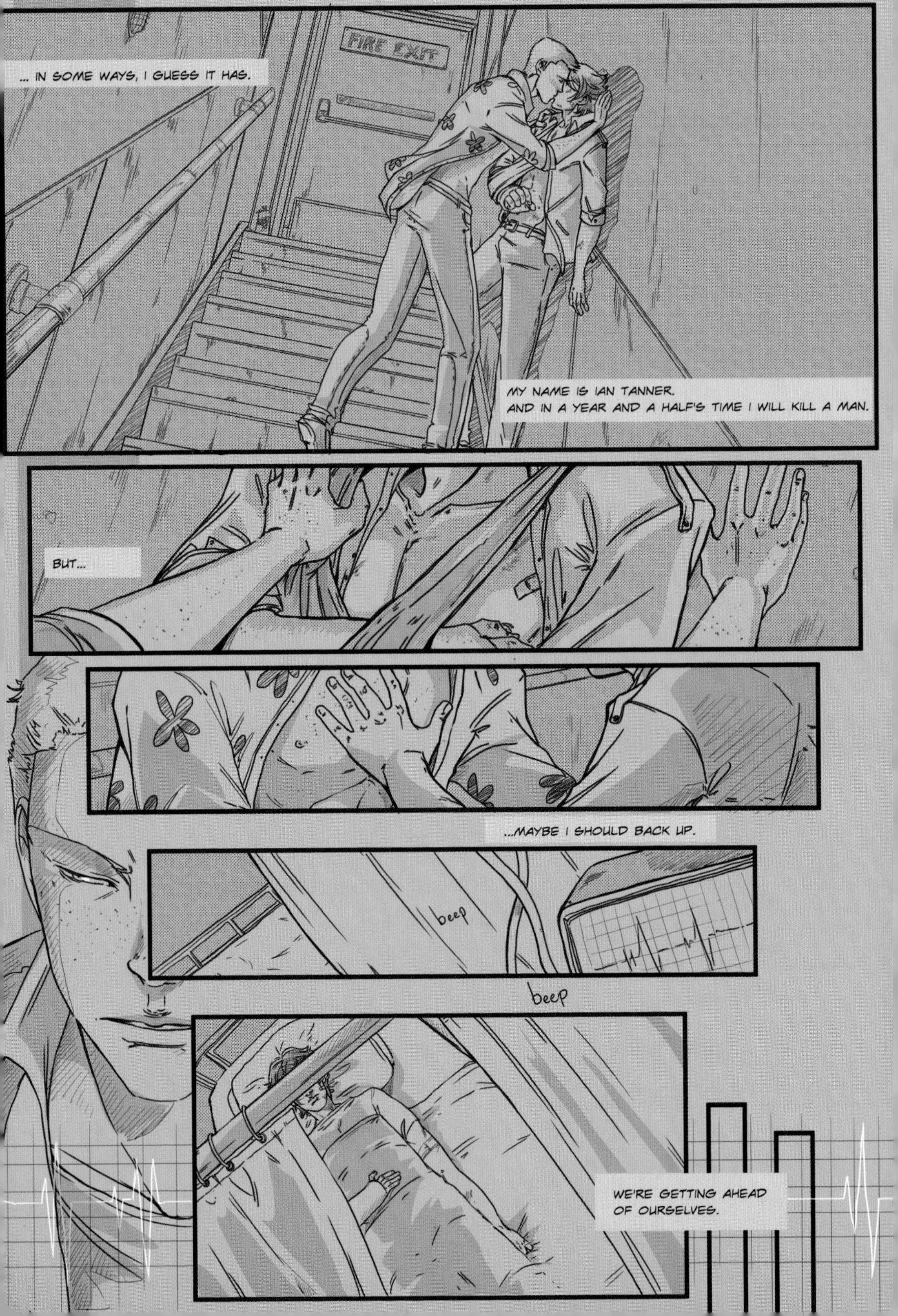
... IN SOME WAYS, I GUESS IT HAS.
FIRE EXIT
MY NAME IS IAN TANNER.
AND IN A YEAR AND A HALF'S TIME I WILL KILL A MAN.
BUT...
...MAYBE I SHOULD BACK UP.
beep
beep
WE'RE GETTING AHEAD OF OURSELVES.

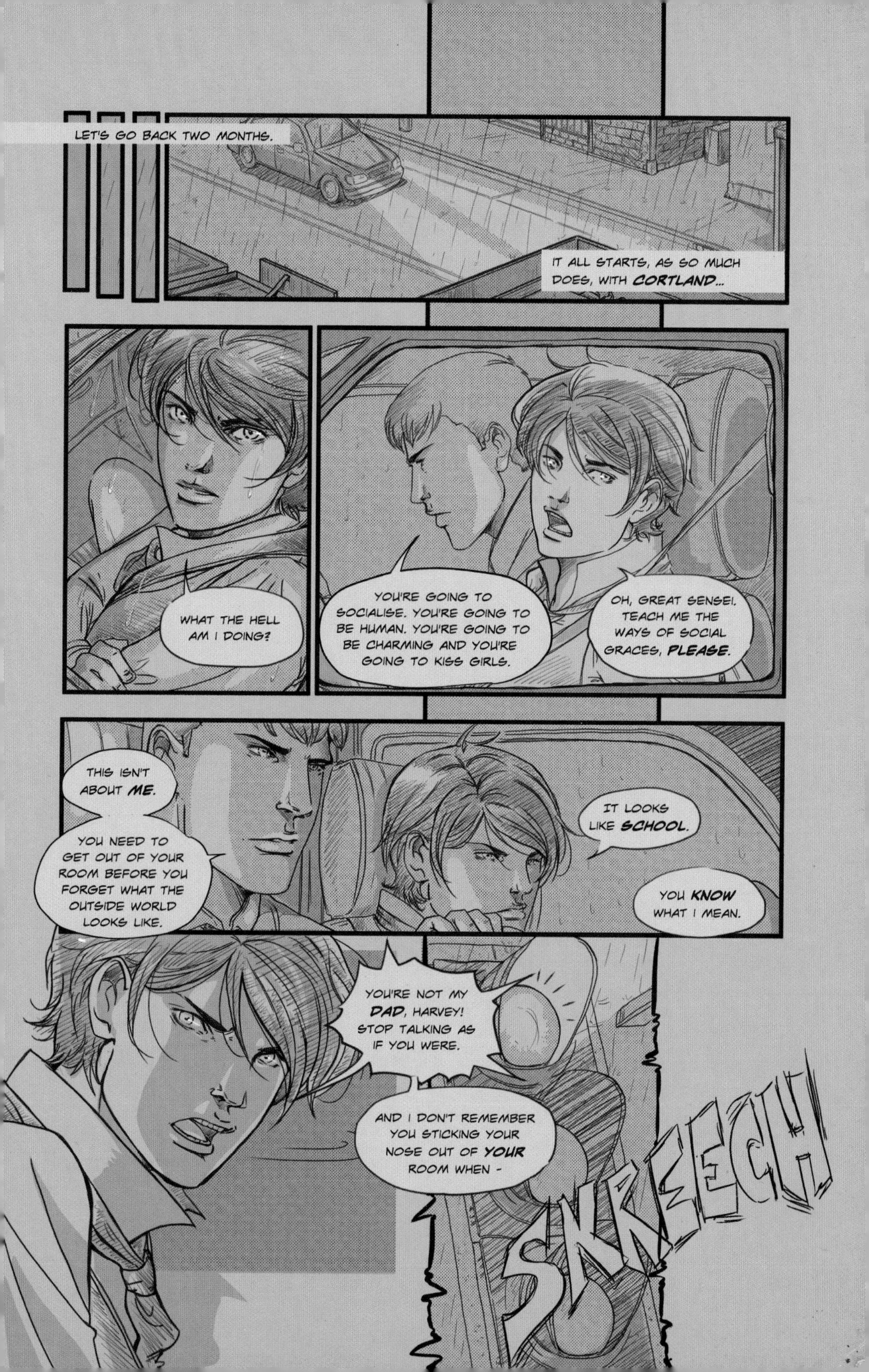
LET'S GO BACK TWO MONTHS.
IT ALL STARTS, AS SO MUCH DOES, WITH CORTLAND...
WHAT THE HELL AM I DOING?
YOU'RE GOING TO SOCIALISE. YOU'RE GOING TO BE HUMAN. YOU'RE GOING TO BE CHARMING AND YOU'RE GOING TO KISS GIRLS.
OH, GREAT SENSEI. TEACH ME THE WAYS OF SOCIAL GRACES, PLEASE.
THIS ISN'T ABOUT ME.
YOU NEED TO GET OUT OF YOUR ROOM BEFORE YOU FORGET WHAT THE OUTSIDE WORLD LOOKS LIKE.
IT LOOKS LIKE SCHOOL.
YOU KNOW WHAT I MEAN.
YOU'RE NOT MY DAD, HARVEY! STOP TALKING AS IF YOU WERE.
AND I DON'T REMEMBER YOU STICKING YOUR NOSE OUT OF YOUR ROOM WHEN -
SKREECH!

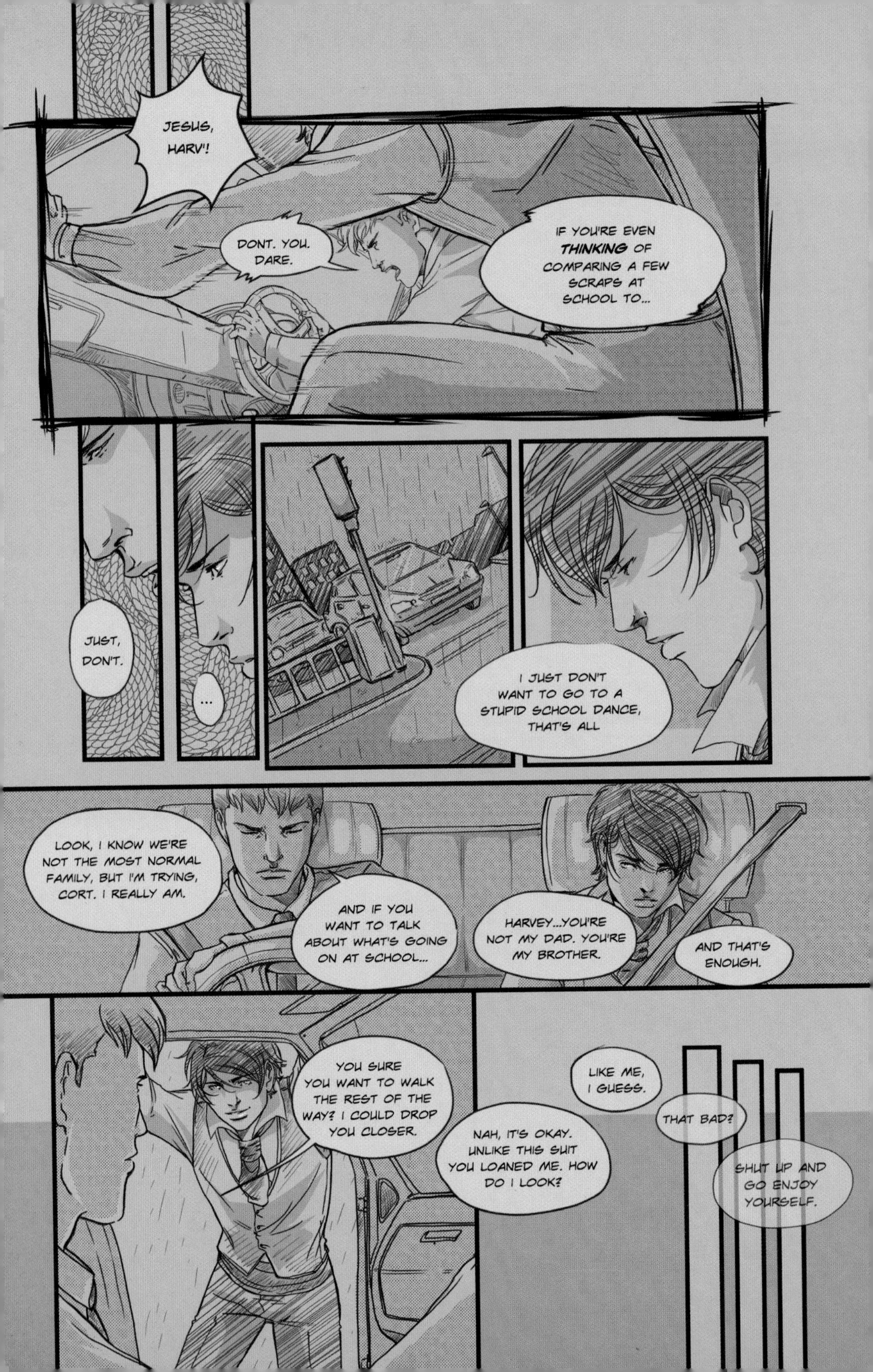
JESUS, HARV'!
DONT. YOU. DARE.
IF YOU'RE EVEN ***THINKING*** OF COMPARING A FEW SCRAPS AT SCHOOL TO...
JUST, DON'T.
...
I JUST DON'T WANT TO GO TO A STUPID SCHOOL DANCE, THAT'S ALL
LOOK, I KNOW WE'RE NOT THE MOST NORMAL FAMILY, BUT I'M TRYING, CORT. I REALLY AM.
AND IF YOU WANT TO TALK ABOUT WHAT'S GOING ON AT SCHOOL...
HARVEY...YOU'RE NOT MY DAD. YOU'RE MY BROTHER.
AND THAT'S ENOUGH.
YOU SURE YOU WANT TO WALK THE REST OF THE WAY? I COULD DROP YOU CLOSER.
NAH, IT'S OKAY. UNLIKE THIS SUIT YOU LOANED ME. HOW DO I LOOK?
LIKE ME, I GUESS.
THAT BAD?
SHUT UP AND GO ENJOY YOURSELF.

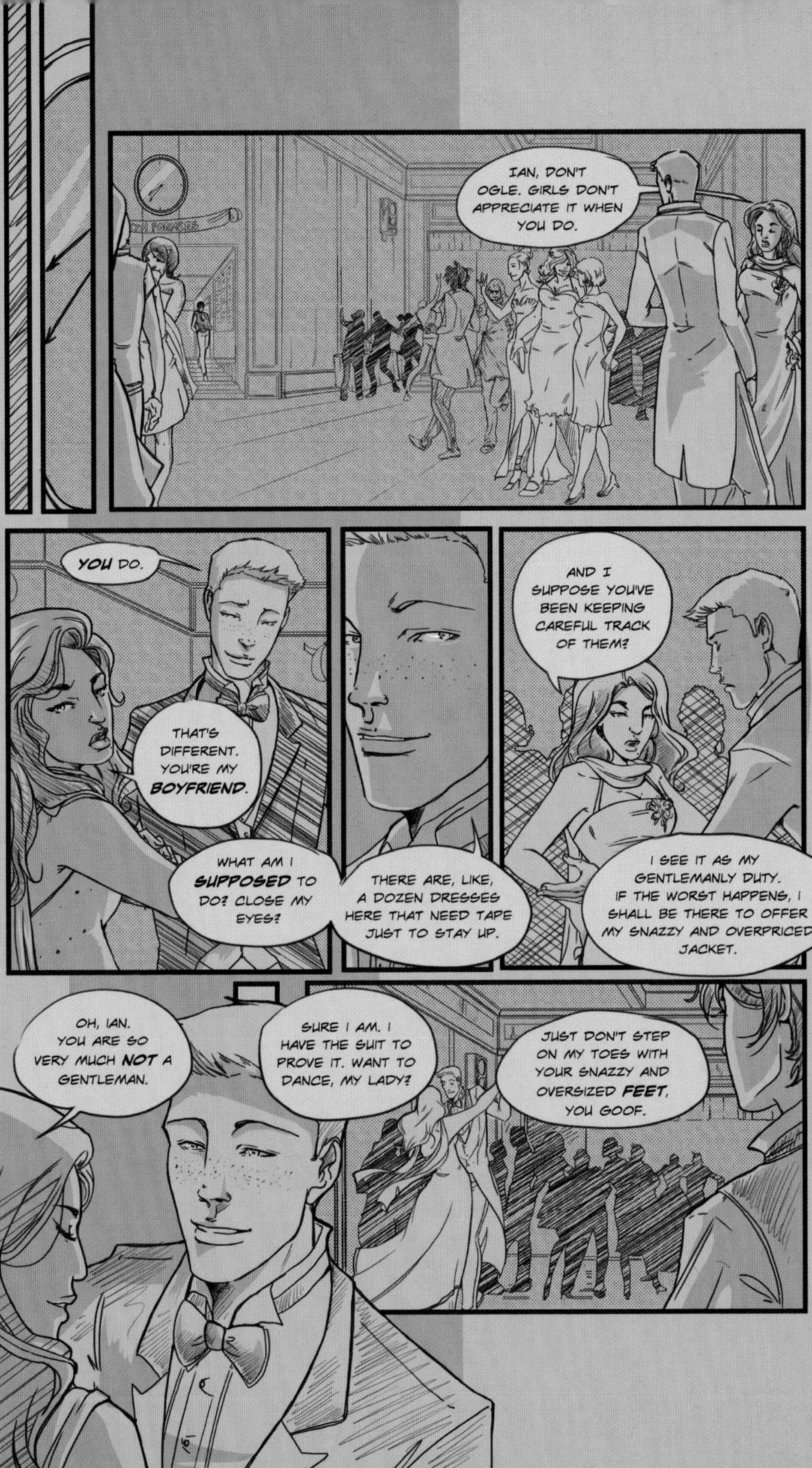
IAN, DON'T OGLE. GIRLS DON'T APPRECIATE IT WHEN YOU DO.
YOU DO.
THAT'S DIFFERENT. YOU'RE MY BOYFRIEND.
WHAT AM I SUPPOSED TO DO? CLOSE MY EYES?
THERE ARE, LIKE, A DOZEN DRESSES HERE THAT NEED TAPE JUST TO STAY UP.
AND I SUPPOSE YOU'VE BEEN KEEPING CAREFUL TRACK OF THEM?
I SEE IT AS MY GENTLEMANLY DUTY. IF THE WORST HAPPENS, I SHALL BE THERE TO OFFER MY SNAZZY AND OVERPRICED JACKET.
OH, IAN. YOU ARE SO VERY MUCH NOT A GENTLEMAN.
SURE I AM. I HAVE THE SUIT TO PROVE IT. WANT TO DANCE, MY LADY?
JUST DON'T STEP ON MY TOES WITH YOUR SNAZZY AND OVERSIZED FEET, YOU GOOF.

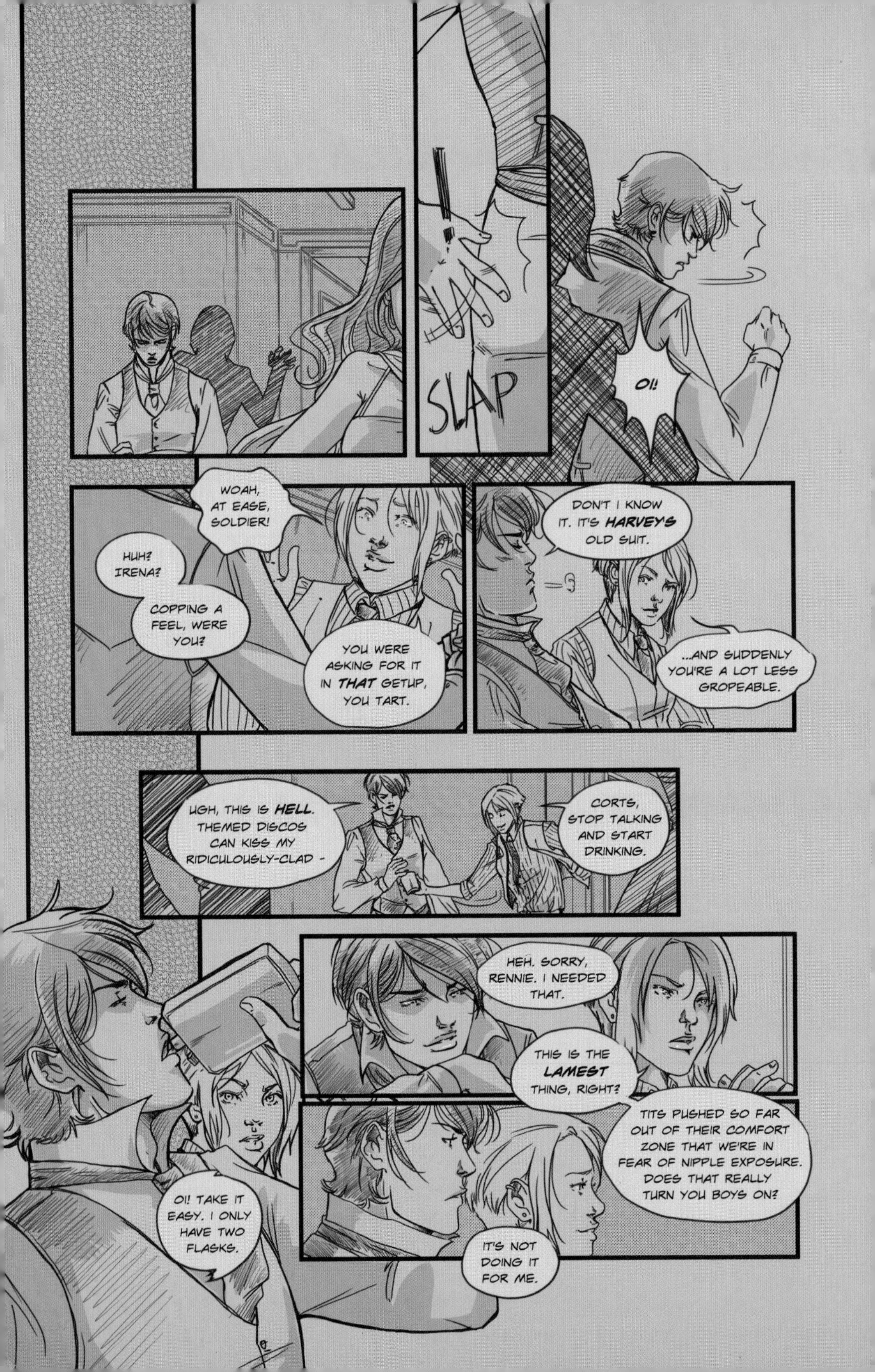
SLAP
OI!
WOAH, AT EASE, SOLDIER!
HUH? IRENA?
COPPING A FEEL, WERE YOU?
YOU WERE ASKING FOR IT IN THAT GETUP, YOU TART.
DON'T I KNOW IT. IT'S HARVEYS OLD SUIT.
...AND SUDDENLY YOU'RE A LOT LESS GROPEABLE.
UGH, THIS IS HELL. THEMED DISCOS CAN KISS MY RIDICULOUSLY-CLAD -
CORTS, STOP TALKING AND START DRINKING.
HEH. SORRY, RENNIE. I NEEDED THAT.
THIS IS THE LAMEST THING, RIGHT?
TITS PUSHED SO FAR OUT OF THEIR COMFORT ZONE THAT WE'RE IN FEAR OF NIPPLE EXPOSURE. DOES THAT REALLY TURN YOU BOYS ON?
OI! TAKE IT EASY. I ONLY HAVE TWO FLASKS.
IT'S NOT DOING IT FOR ME.

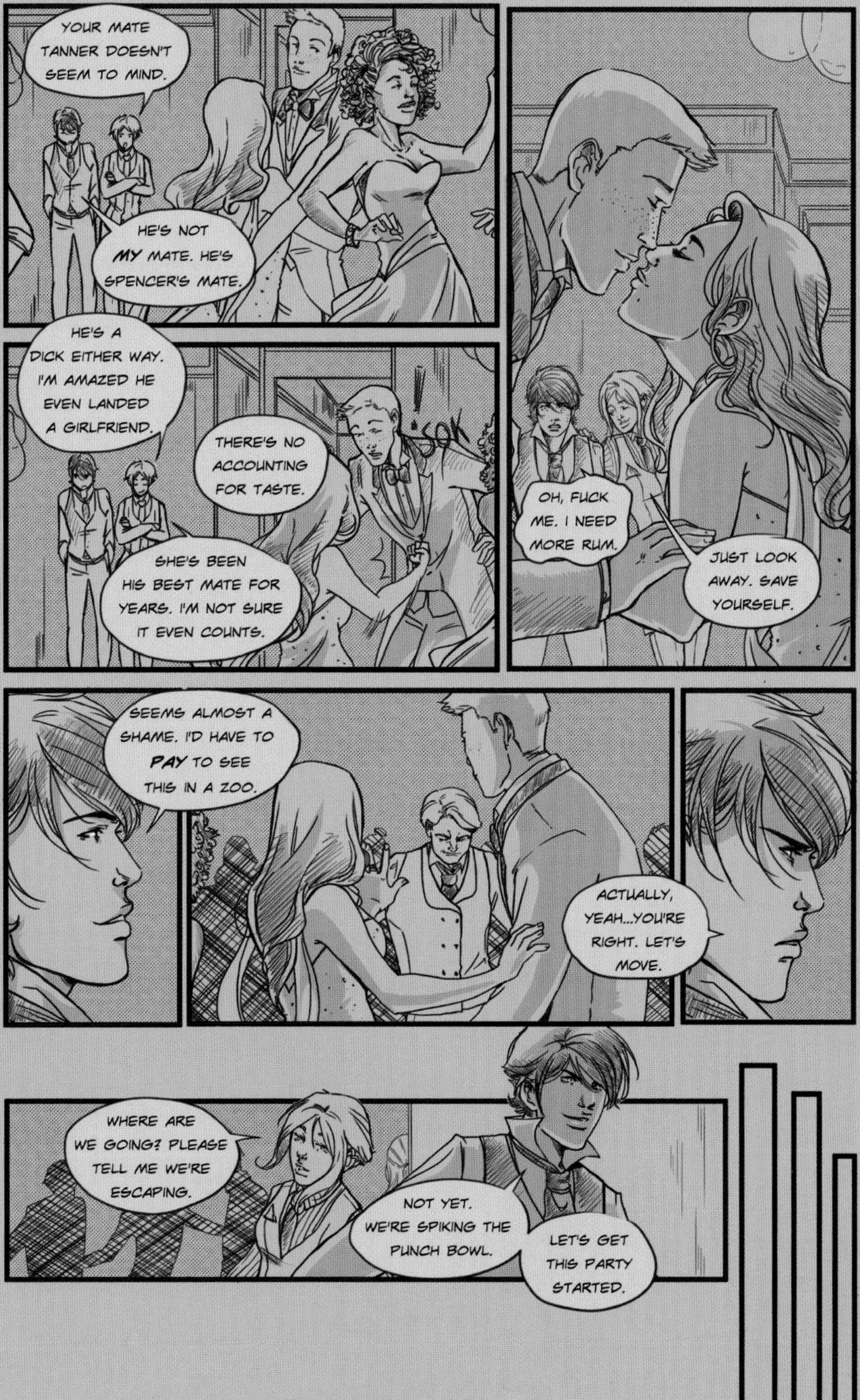
YOUR MATE TANNER DOESN'T SEEM TO MIND.
HE'S NOT MY MATE. HE'S SPENCER'S MATE.
HE'S A DICK EITHER WAY. I'M AMAZED HE EVEN LANDED A GIRLFRIEND.
THERE'S NO ACCOUNTING FOR TASTE.
SHE'S BEEN HIS BEST MATE FOR YEARS. I'M NOT SURE IT EVEN COUNTS.
OH, FUCK ME. I NEED MORE RUM.
JUST LOOK AWAY. SAVE YOURSELF.
SEEMS ALMOST A SHAME. I'D HAVE TO PAY TO SEE THIS IN A ZOO.
ACTUALLY, YEAH...YOU'RE RIGHT. LET'S MOVE.
WHERE ARE WE GOING? PLEASE TELL ME WE'RE ESCAPING.
NOT YET. WE'RE SPIKING THE PUNCH BOWL.
LET'S GET THIS PARTY STARTED.

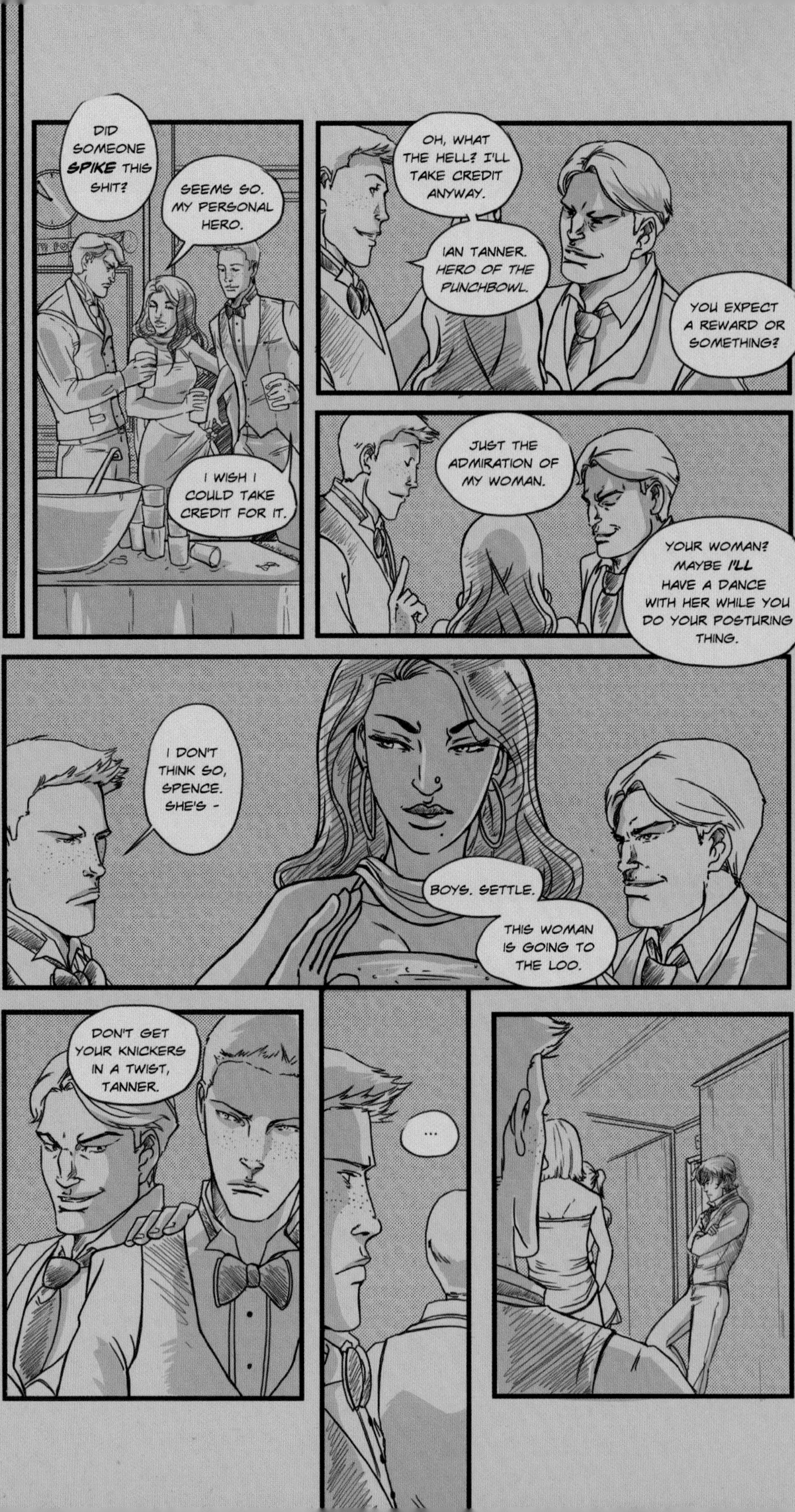
DID SOMEONE SPIKE THIS SHIT?
SEEMS SO. MY PERSONAL HERO.
I WISH I COULD TAKE CREDIT FOR IT.
OH, WHAT THE HELL? I'LL TAKE CREDIT ANYWAY.
IAN TANNER. HERO OF THE PUNCHBOWL.
YOU EXPECT A REWARD OR SOMETHING?
JUST THE ADMIRATION OF MY WOMAN.
YOUR WOMAN? MAYBE I'LL HAVE A DANCE WITH HER WHILE YOU DO YOUR POSTURING THING.
I DON'T THINK SO, SPENCE. SHE'S -
BOYS. SETTLE.
THIS WOMAN IS GOING TO THE LOO.
DON'T GET YOUR KNICKERS IN A TWIST, TANNER.
...

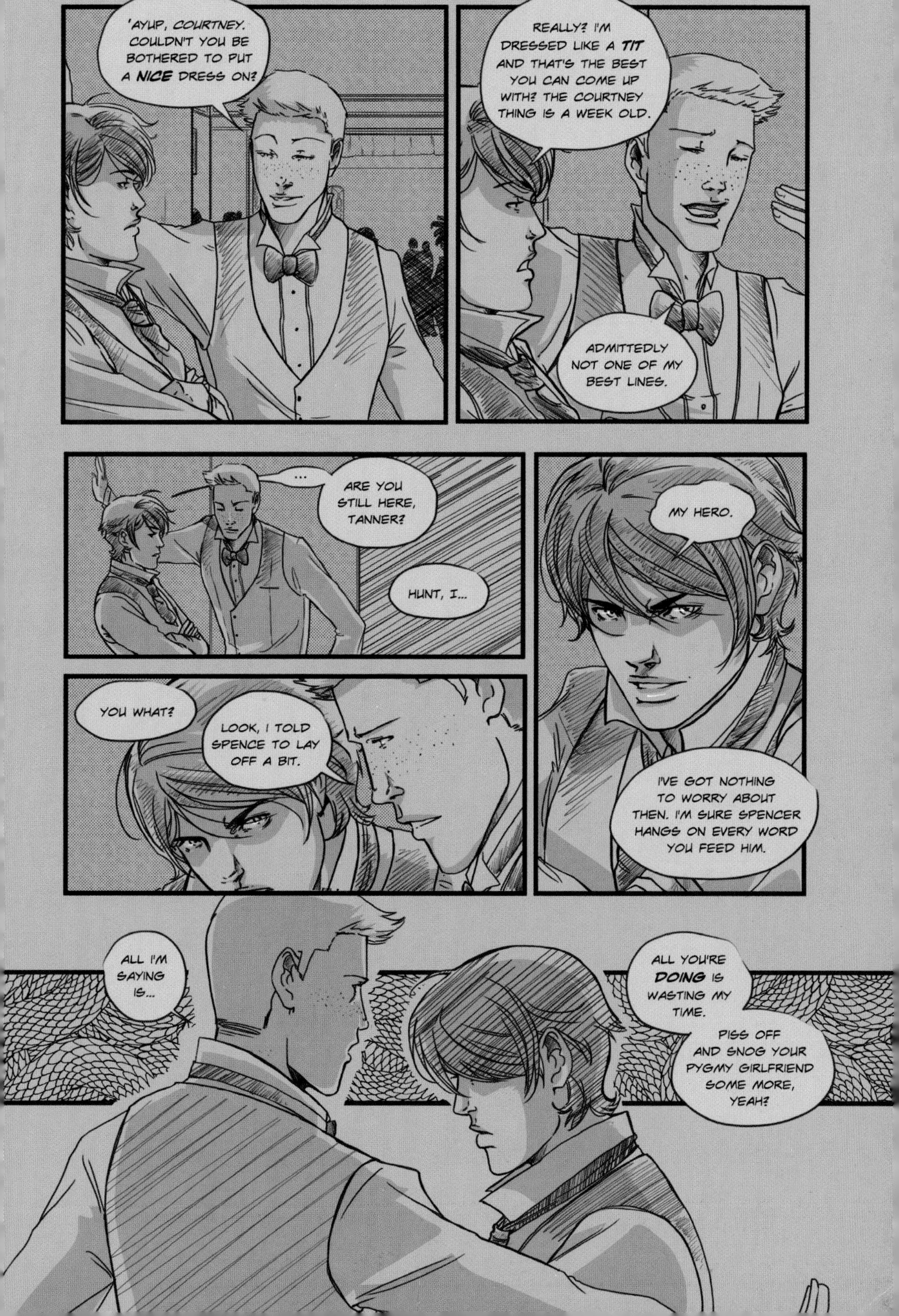
'AYUP, COURTNEY. COULDN'T YOU BE BOTHERED TO PUT A NICE DRESS ON?
REALLY? I'M DRESSED LIKE A TIT AND THAT'S THE BEST YOU CAN COME UP WITH? THE COURTNEY THING IS A WEEK OLD.
ADMITTEDLY NOT ONE OF MY BEST LINES.
...
ARE YOU STILL HERE, TANNER?
HUNT, I...
YOU WHAT?
LOOK, I TOLD SPENCE TO LAY OFF A BIT.
MY HERO.
I'VE GOT NOTHING TO WORRY ABOUT THEN. I'M SURE SPENCER HANGS ON EVERY WORD YOU FEED HIM.
ALL I'M SAYING IS...
ALL YOU'RE DOING IS WASTING MY TIME.
PISS OFF AND SNOG YOUR PYGMY GIRLFRIEND SOME MORE, YEAH?

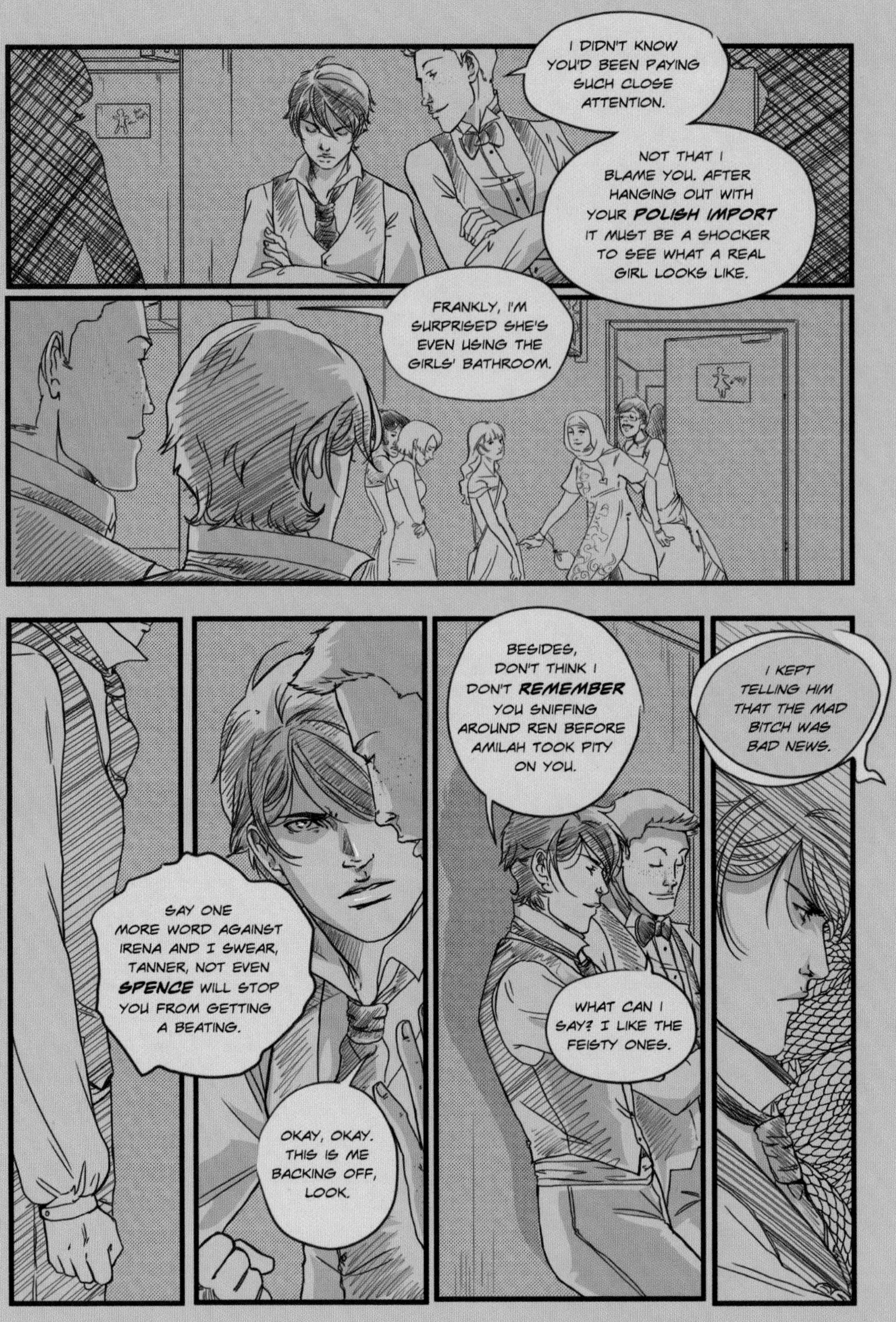
I DIDN'T KNOW YOU'D BEEN PAYING SUCH CLOSE ATTENTION.
NOT THAT I BLAME YOU. AFTER HANGING OUT WITH YOUR POLISH IMPORT IT MUST BE A SHOCKER TO SEE WHAT A REAL GIRL LOOKS LIKE.
FRANKLY, I'M SURPRISED SHE'S EVEN USING THE GIRLS' BATHROOM.
SAY ONE MORE WORD AGAINST IRENA AND I SWEAR, TANNER, NOT EVEN SPENCE WILL STOP YOU FROM GETTING A BEATING.
OKAY, OKAY. THIS IS ME BACKING OFF, LOOK.
BESIDES, DON'T THINK I DON'T REMEMBER YOU SNIFFING AROUND REN BEFORE AMILAH TOOK PITY ON YOU.
WHAT CAN I SAY? I LIKE THE FEISTY ONES.
I KEPT TELLING HIM THAT THE MAD BITCH WAS BAD NEWS.

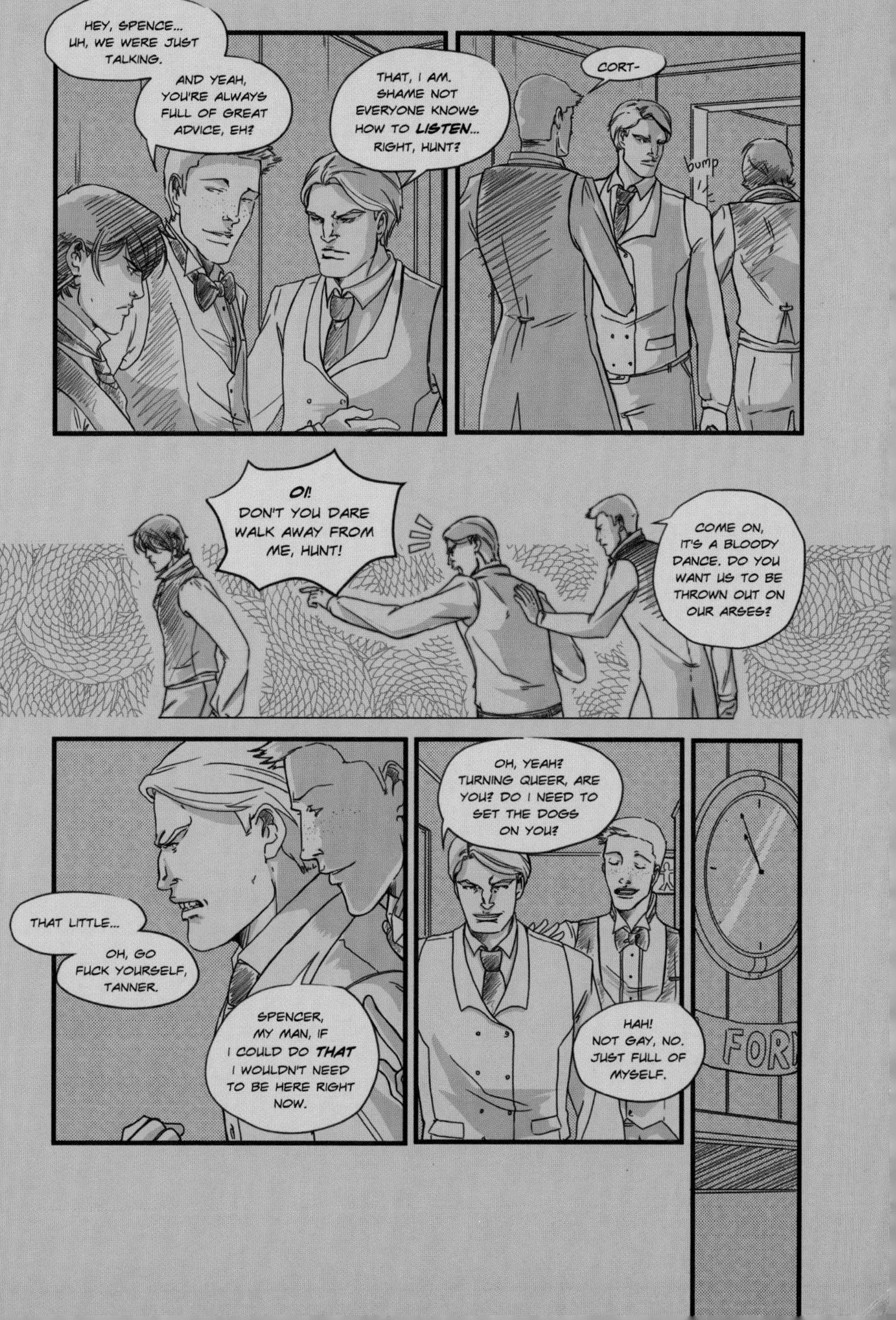
HEY, SPENCE... UH, WE WERE JUST TALKING.
AND YEAH, YOU'RE ALWAYS FULL OF GREAT ADVICE, EH?
THAT, I AM. SHAME NOT EVERYONE KNOWS HOW TO LISTEN... RIGHT, HUNT?
CORT-
bump
OI! DON'T YOU DARE WALK AWAY FROM ME, HUNT!
COME ON, IT'S A BLOODY DANCE. DO YOU WANT US TO BE THROWN OUT ON OUR ARSES?
THAT LITTLE...
OH, GO FUCK YOURSELF, TANNER.
SPENCER, MY MAN, IF I COULD DO THAT I WOULDN'T NEED TO BE HERE RIGHT NOW.
OH, YEAH? TURNING QUEER, ARE YOU? DO I NEED TO SET THE DOGS ON YOU?
HAH! NOT GAY, NO. JUST FULL OF MYSELF.
FOR

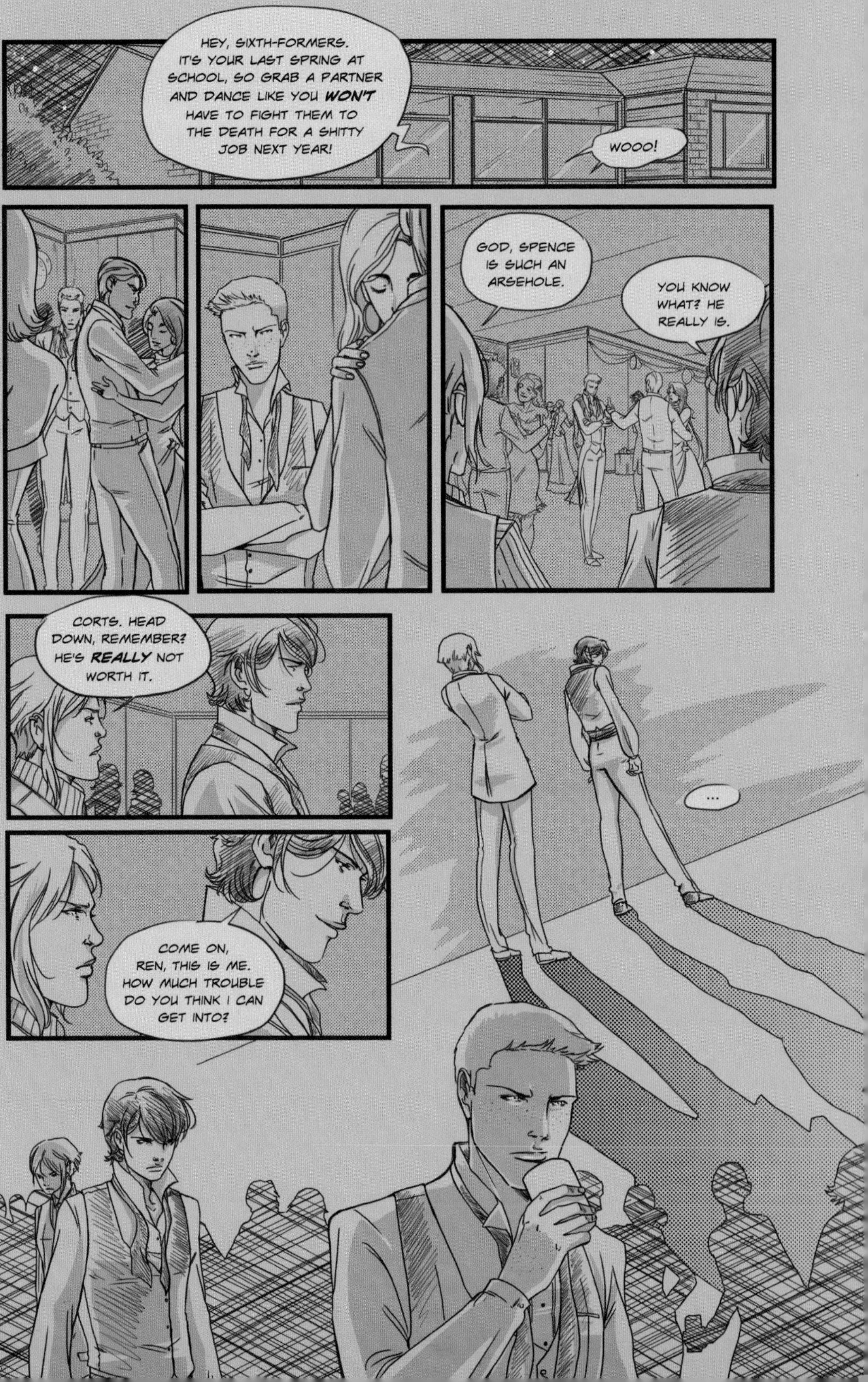
HEY, SIXTH-FORMERS. IT'S YOUR LAST SPRING AT SCHOOL, SO GRAB A PARTNER AND DANCE LIKE YOU *WON'T* HAVE TO FIGHT THEM TO THE DEATH FOR A SHITTY JOB NEXT YEAR!
WOOO!
GOD, SPENCE IS SUCH AN ARSEHOLE.
YOU KNOW WHAT? HE REALLY IS.
CORTS. HEAD DOWN, REMEMBER? HE'S *REALLY* NOT WORTH IT.
COME ON, REN, THIS IS ME. HOW MUCH TROUBLE DO YOU THINK I CAN GET INTO?
...

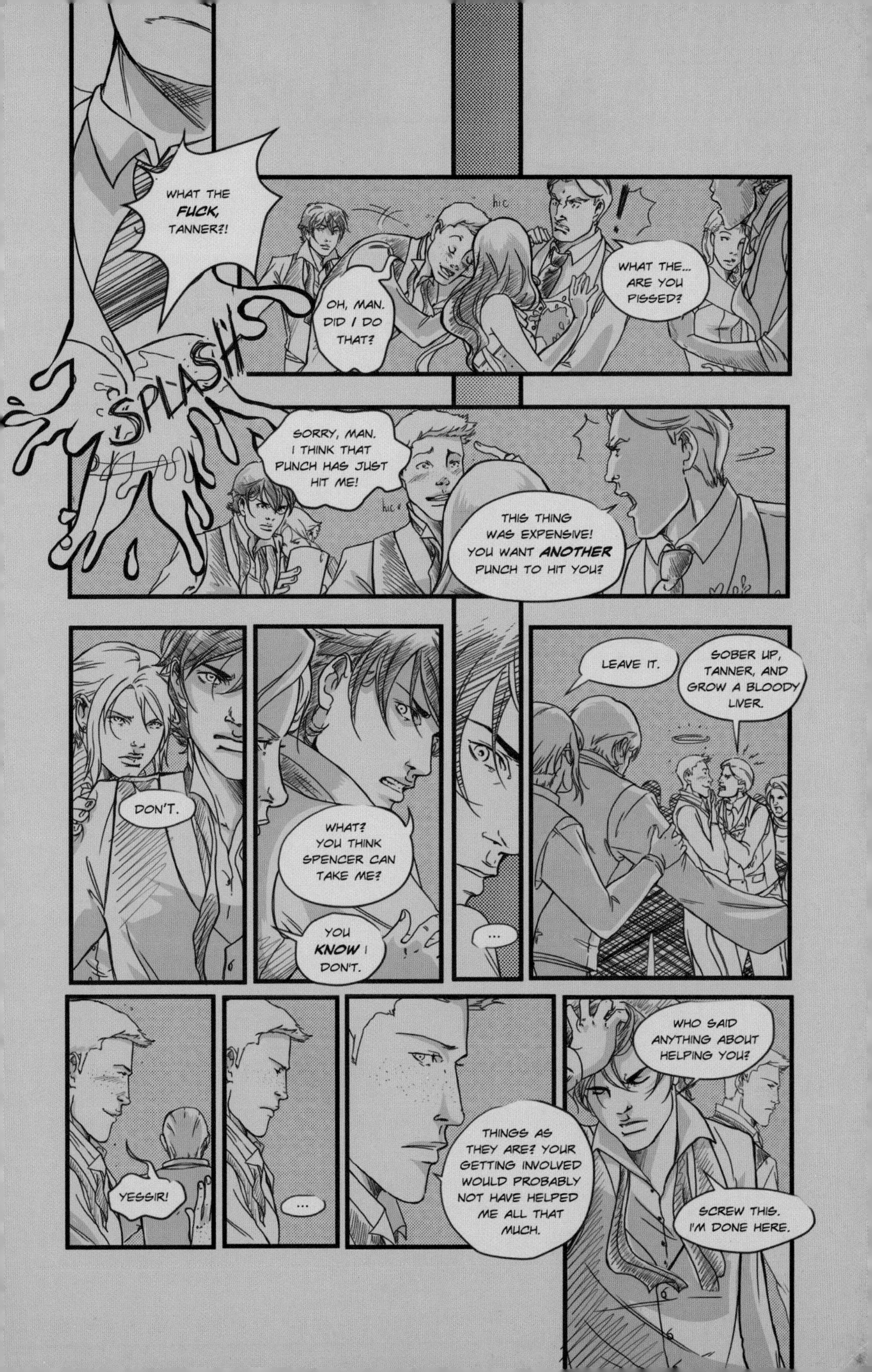
WHAT THE FUCK, TANNER?!
SPLASH
hic
OH, MAN. DID I DO THAT?
WHAT THE... ARE YOU PISSED?
SORRY, MAN. I THINK THAT PUNCH HAS JUST HIT ME!
hic
THIS THING WAS EXPENSIVE! YOU WANT ANOTHER PUNCH TO HIT YOU?
DON'T.
WHAT? YOU THINK SPENCER CAN TAKE ME?
YOU KNOW I DON'T.
...
LEAVE IT.
SOBER UP, TANNER, AND GROW A BLOODY LIVER.
YESSIR!
...
THINGS AS THEY ARE? YOUR GETTING INVOLVED WOULD PROBABLY NOT HAVE HELPED ME ALL THAT MUCH.
WHO SAID ANYTHING ABOUT HELPING YOU?
SCREW THIS. I'M DONE HERE.

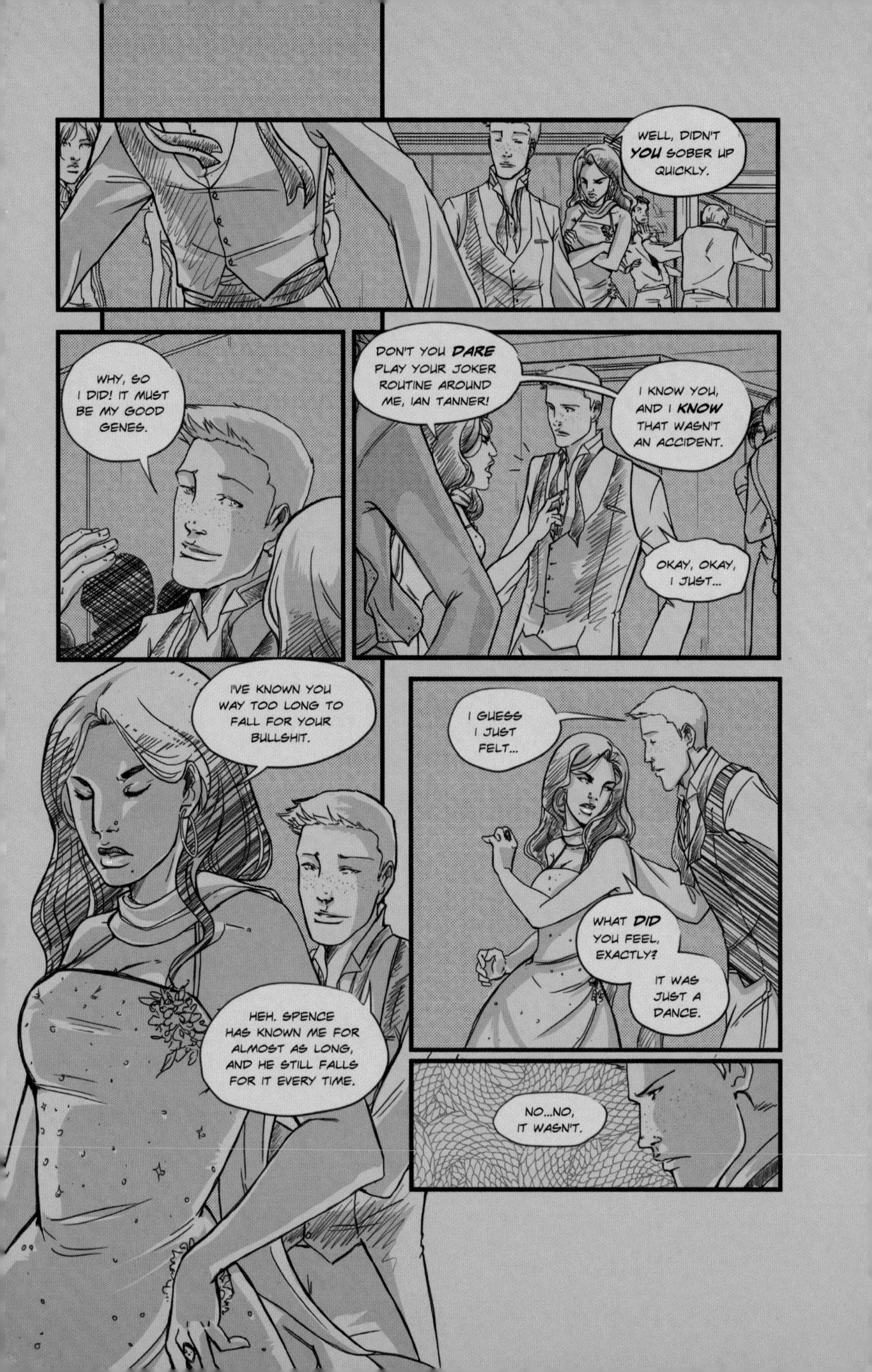
WELL, DIDN'T YOU SOBER UP QUICKLY.
WHY, SO I DID! IT MUST BE MY GOOD GENES.
DON'T YOU DARE PLAY YOUR JOKER ROUTINE AROUND ME, IAN TANNER!
I KNOW YOU, AND I KNOW THAT WASN'T AN ACCIDENT.
OKAY, OKAY, I JUST...
I'VE KNOWN YOU WAY TOO LONG TO FALL FOR YOUR BULLSHIT.
HEH. SPENCE HAS KNOWN ME FOR ALMOST AS LONG, AND HE STILL FALLS FOR IT EVERY TIME.
I GUESS I JUST FELT...
WHAT DID YOU FEEL, EXACTLY?
IT WAS JUST A DANCE.
NO...NO, IT WASN'T.

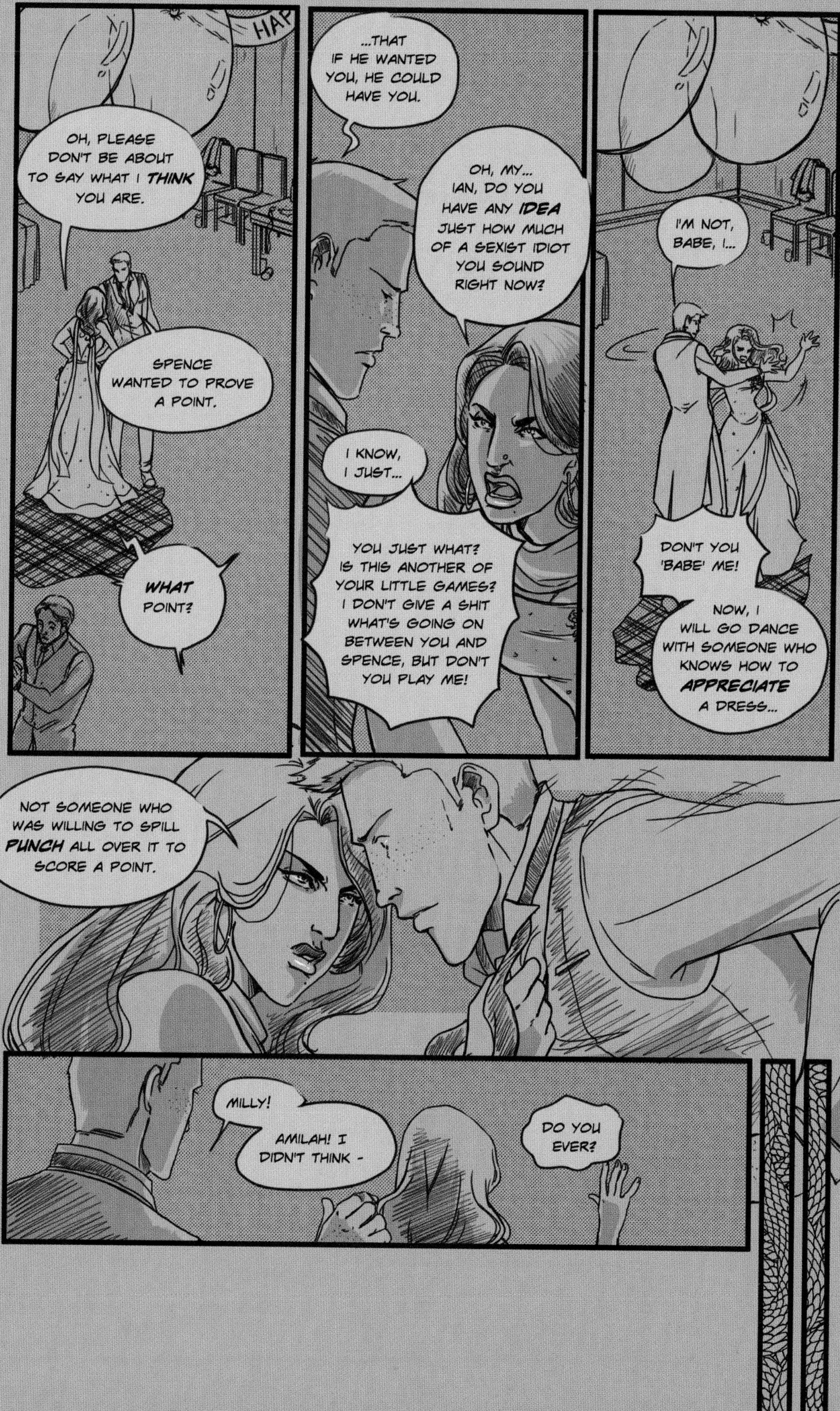
HAP
OH, PLEASE DON'T BE ABOUT TO SAY WHAT I THINK YOU ARE.
SPENCE WANTED TO PROVE A POINT.
WHAT POINT?
...THAT IF HE WANTED YOU, HE COULD HAVE YOU.
OH, MY... IAN, DO YOU HAVE ANY IDEA JUST HOW MUCH OF A SEXIST IDIOT YOU SOUND RIGHT NOW?
I KNOW, I JUST...
YOU JUST WHAT? IS THIS ANOTHER OF YOUR LITTLE GAMES? I DON'T GIVE A SHIT WHAT'S GOING ON BETWEEN YOU AND SPENCE, BUT DON'T YOU PLAY ME!
I'M NOT, BABE, I...
DON'T YOU 'BABE' ME!
NOW, I WILL GO DANCE WITH SOMEONE WHO KNOWS HOW TO APPRECIATE A DRESS...
NOT SOMEONE WHO WAS WILLING TO SPILL PUNCH ALL OVER IT TO SCORE A POINT.
MILLY!
AMILAH! I DIDN'T THINK -
DO YOU EVER?

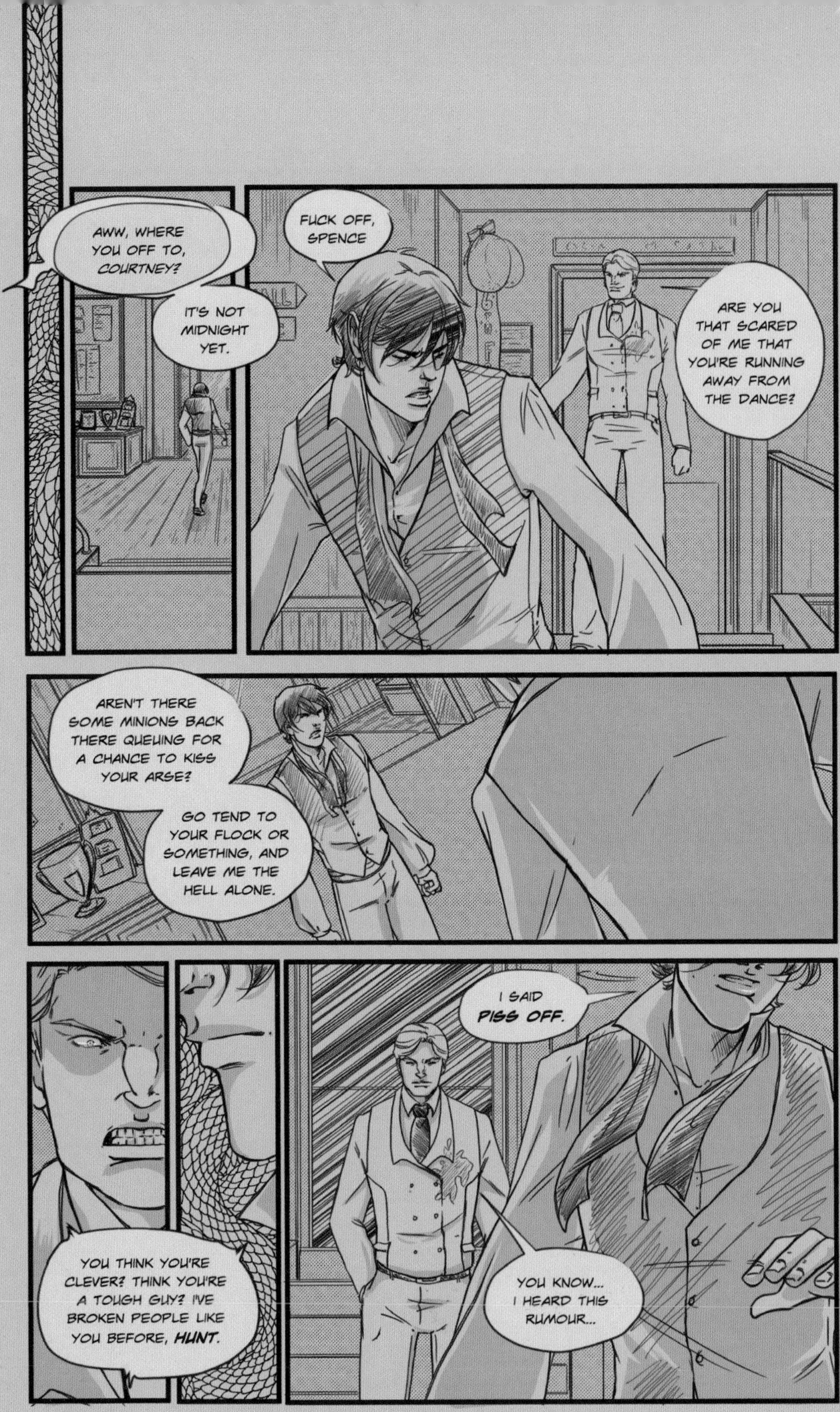
AWW, WHERE YOU OFF TO, COURTNEY?
IT'S NOT MIDNIGHT YET.
FUCK OFF, SPENCE
ARE YOU THAT SCARED OF ME THAT YOU'RE RUNNING AWAY FROM THE DANCE?
AREN'T THERE SOME MINIONS BACK THERE QUEUING FOR A CHANCE TO KISS YOUR ARSE?
GO TEND TO YOUR FLOCK OR SOMETHING, AND LEAVE ME THE HELL ALONE.
YOU THINK YOU'RE CLEVER? THINK YOU'RE A TOUGH GUY? I'VE BROKEN PEOPLE LIKE YOU BEFORE, HUNT.
I SAID PISS OFF.
YOU KNOW... I HEARD THIS RUMOUR...

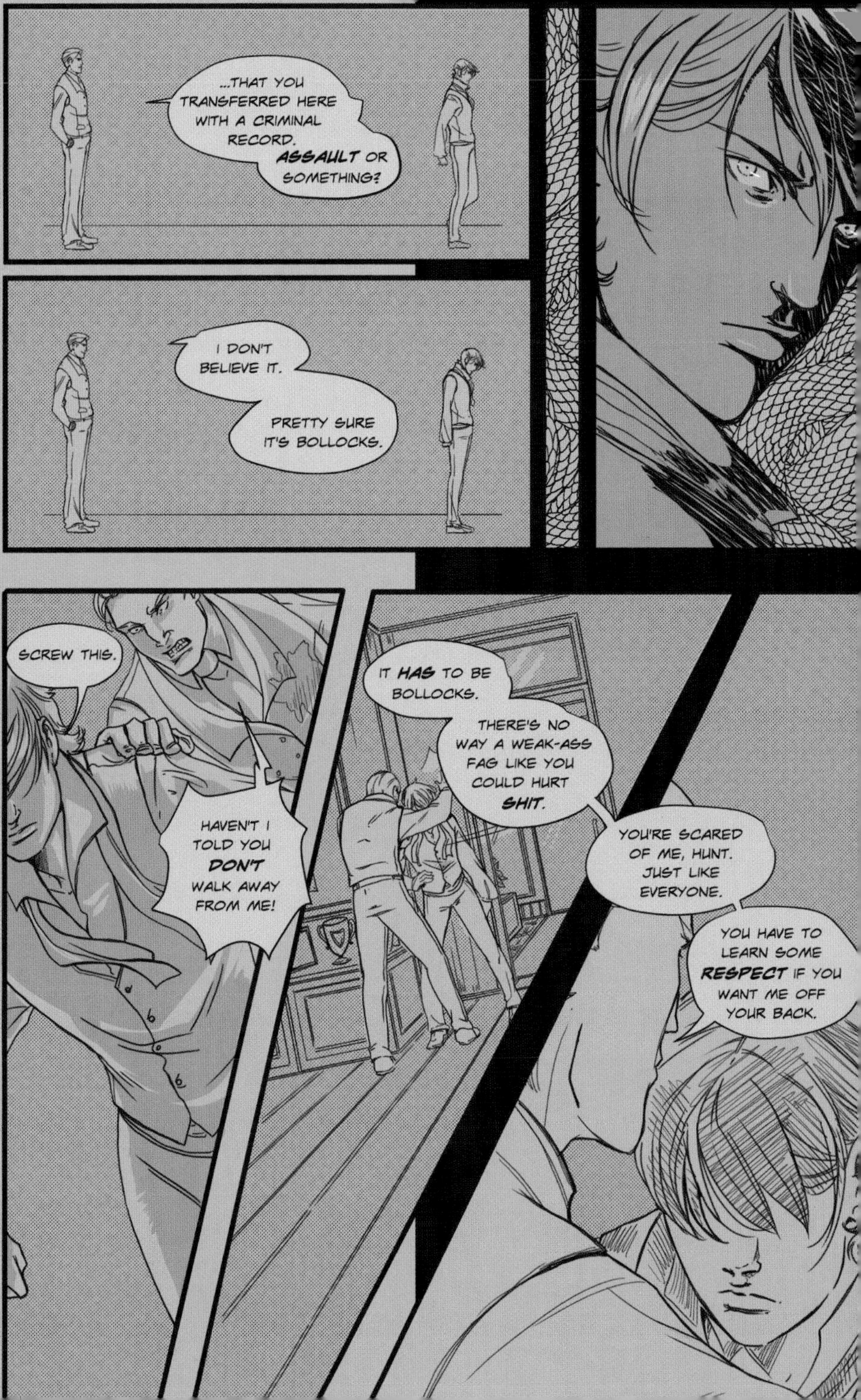
...THAT YOU TRANSFERRED HERE WITH A CRIMINAL RECORD. ASSAULT OR SOMETHING?
I DON'T BELIEVE IT.
PRETTY SURE IT'S BOLLOCKS.
SCREW THIS.
HAVEN'T I TOLD YOU DON'T WALK AWAY FROM ME!
IT HAS TO BE BOLLOCKS.
THERE'S NO WAY A WEAK-ASS FAG LIKE YOU COULD HURT SHIT.
YOU'RE SCARED OF ME, HUNT. JUST LIKE EVERYONE.
YOU HAVE TO LEARN SOME RESPECT IF YOU WANT ME OFF YOUR BACK.

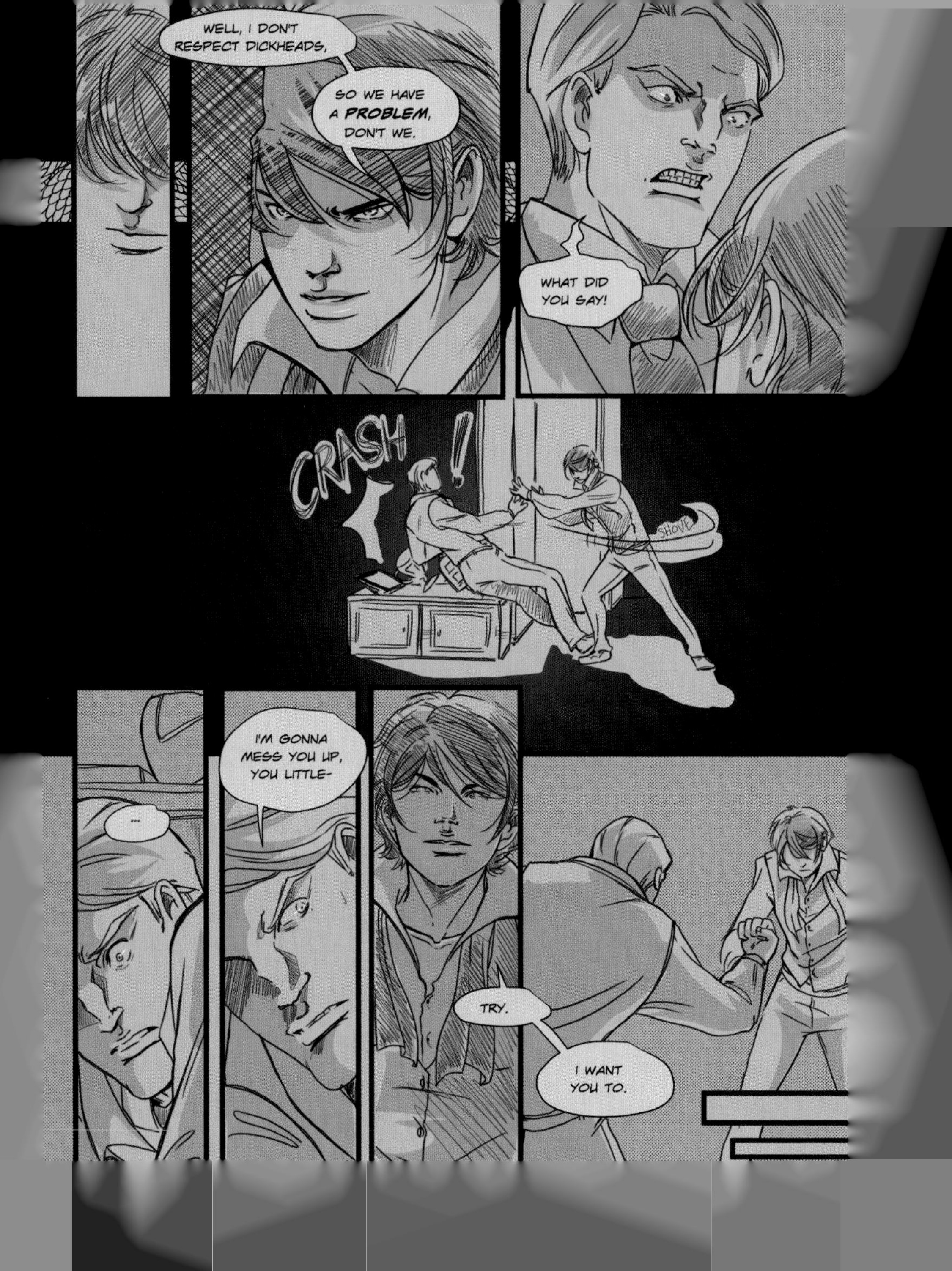
WELL, I DON'T RESPECT DICKHEADS,
SO WE HAVE A **PROBLEM**, DON'T WE.
WHAT DID YOU SAY!
CRASH!
SHOVE
...
I'M GONNA MESS YOU UP, YOU LITTLE-
TRY.
I WANT YOU TO.

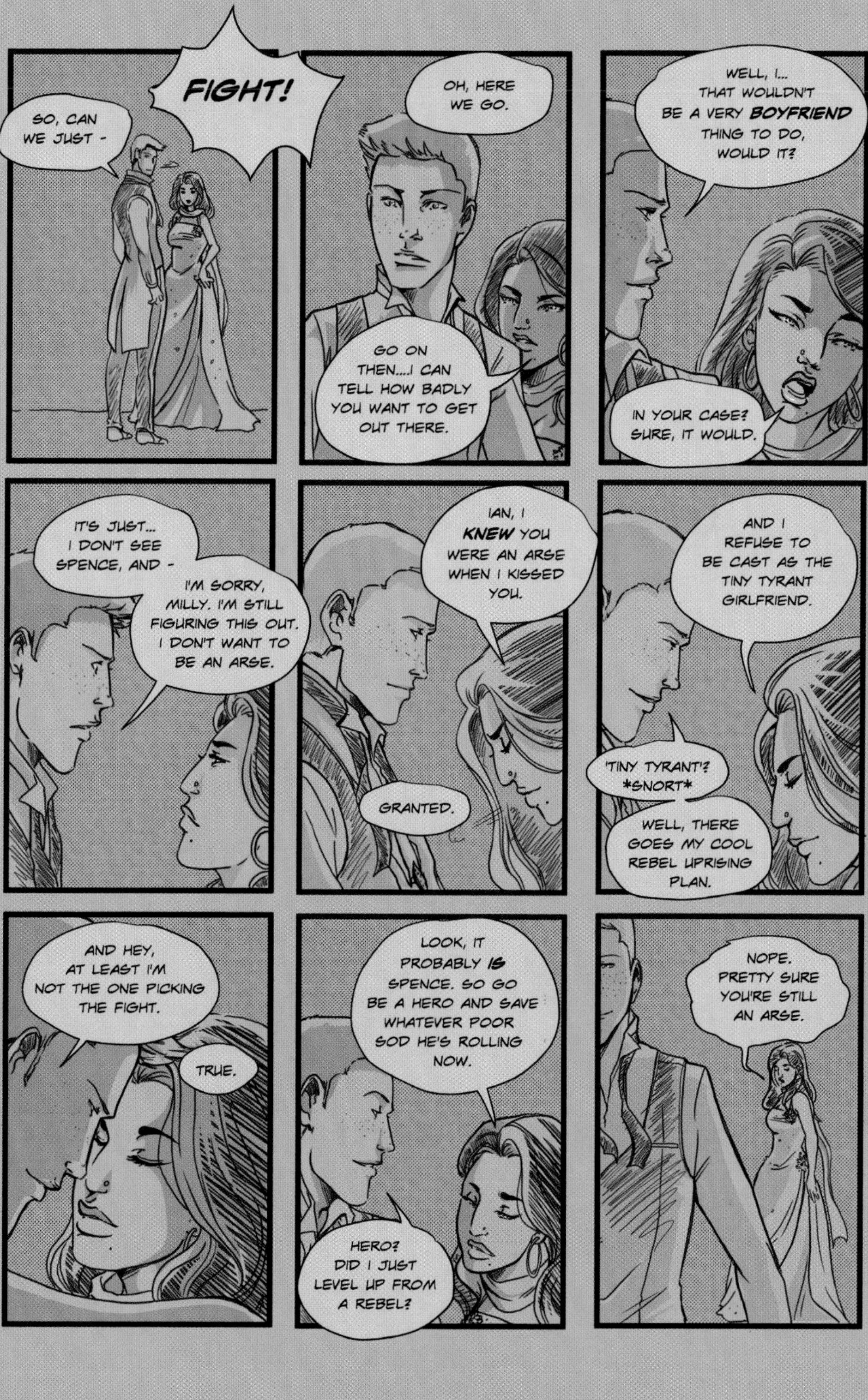
SO, CAN WE JUST -
FIGHT!
OH, HERE WE GO.
GO ON THEN....I CAN TELL HOW BADLY YOU WANT TO GET OUT THERE.
WELL, I... THAT WOULDN'T BE A VERY BOYFRIEND THING TO DO, WOULD IT?
IN YOUR CASE? SURE, IT WOULD.
IT'S JUST... I DON'T SEE SPENCE, AND -
I'M SORRY, MILLY. I'M STILL FIGURING THIS OUT. I DON'T WANT TO BE AN ARSE.
IAN, I KNEW YOU WERE AN ARSE WHEN I KISSED YOU.
GRANTED.
AND I REFUSE TO BE CAST AS THE TINY TYRANT GIRLFRIEND.
'TINY TYRANT'? *SNORT*
WELL, THERE GOES MY COOL REBEL UPRISING PLAN.
AND HEY, AT LEAST I'M NOT THE ONE PICKING THE FIGHT.
TRUE.
LOOK, IT PROBABLY IS SPENCE. SO GO BE A HERO AND SAVE WHATEVER POOR SOD HE'S ROLLING NOW.
HERO? DID I JUST LEVEL UP FROM A REBEL?
NOPE. PRETTY SURE YOU'RE STILL AN ARSE.

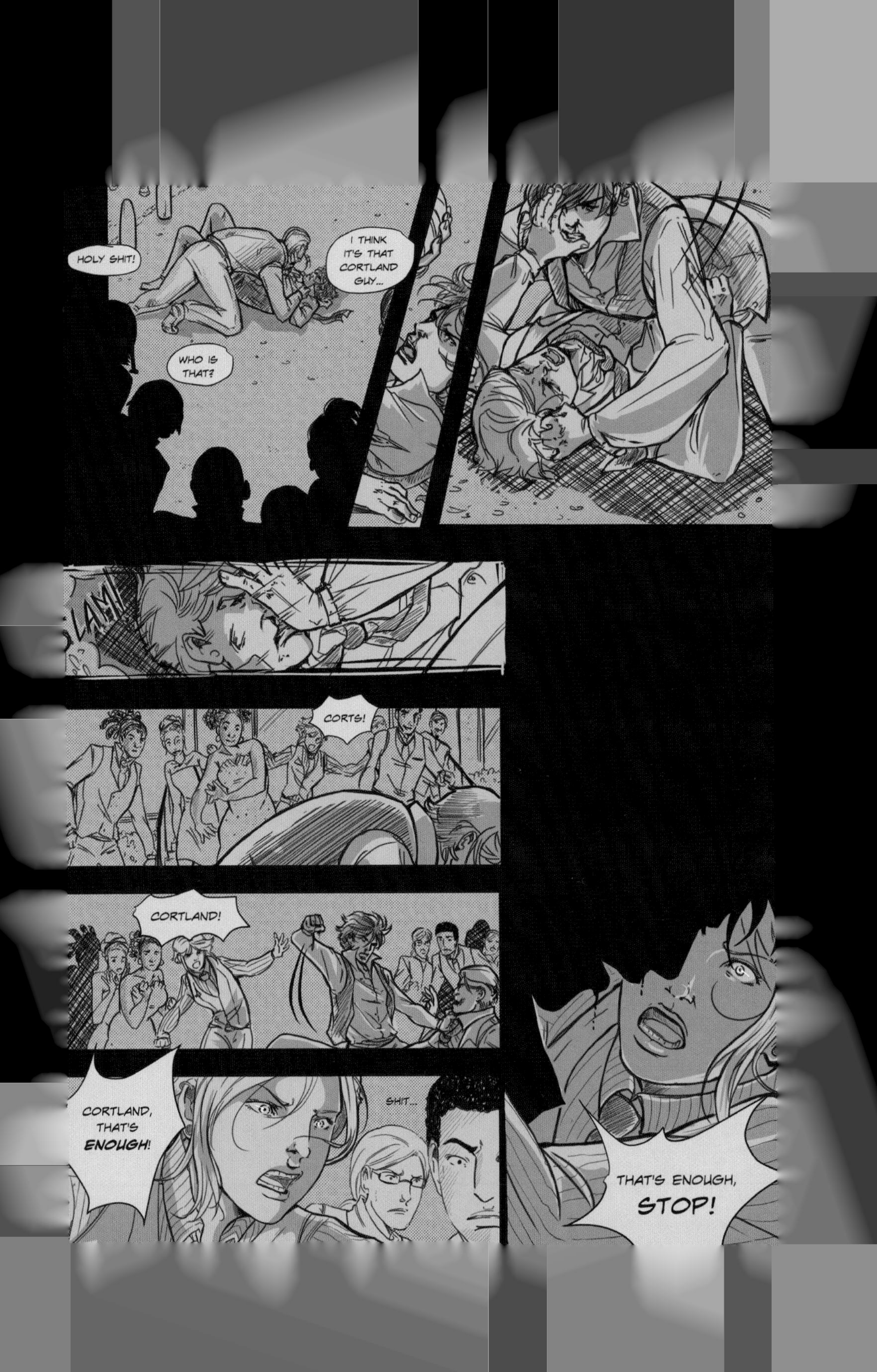

HOLY SHIT!
I THINK IT'S THAT CORTLAND GUY...
WHO IS THAT?
SLAM!
CORTS!
CORTLAND!
CORTLAND, THAT'S ENOUGH!
SHIT...
THAT'S ENOUGH, STOP!

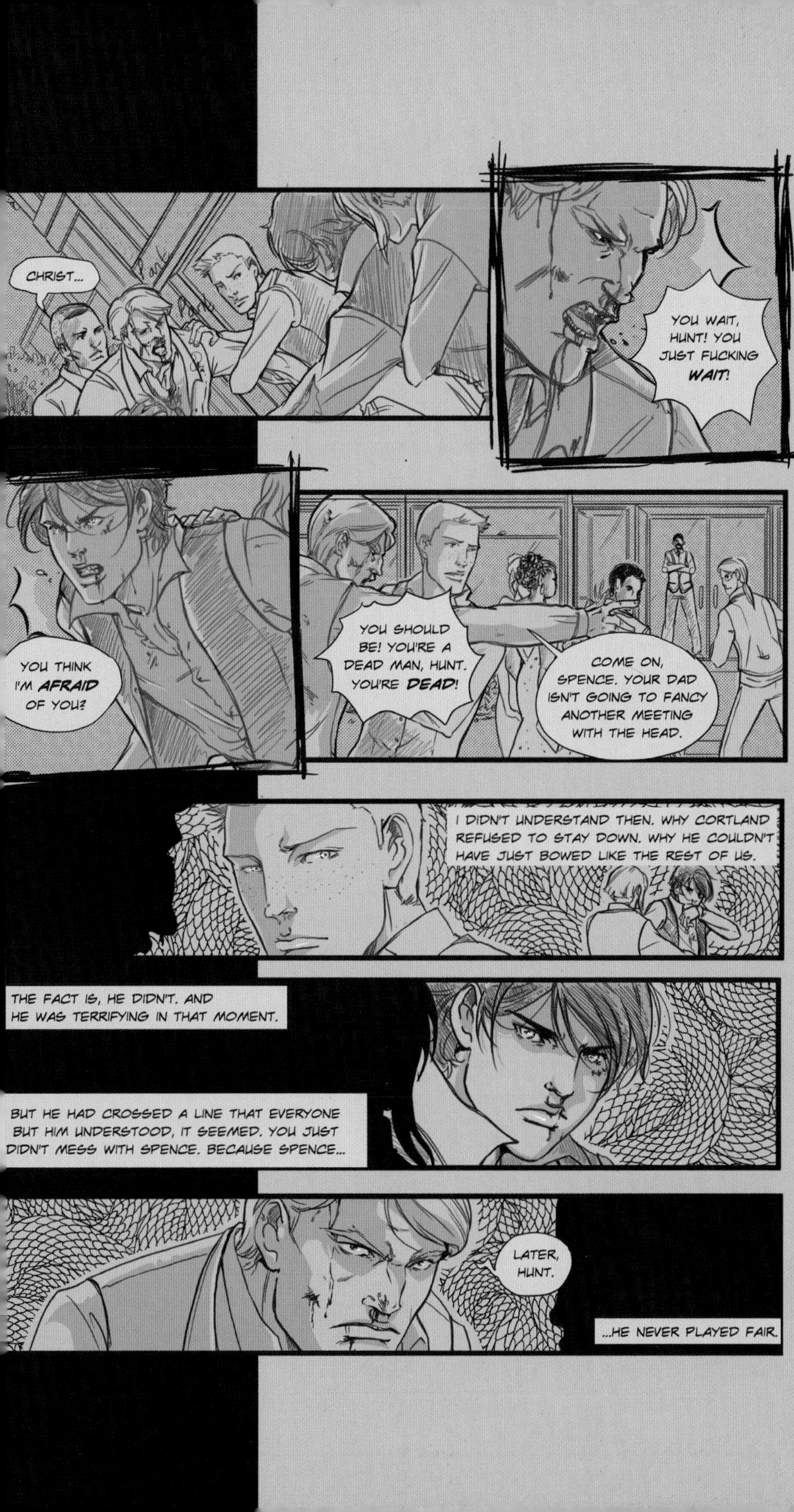
CHRIST...
YOU WAIT, HUNT! YOU JUST FUCKING WAIT!
YOU THINK I'M AFRAID OF YOU?
YOU SHOULD BE! YOU'RE A DEAD MAN, HUNT. YOU'RE DEAD!
COME ON, SPENCE. YOUR DAD ISN'T GOING TO FANCY ANOTHER MEETING WITH THE HEAD.
I DIDN'T UNDERSTAND THEN. WHY CORTLAND REFUSED TO STAY DOWN. WHY HE COULDN'T HAVE JUST BOWED LIKE THE REST OF US.
THE FACT IS, HE DIDN'T. AND HE WAS TERRIFYING IN THAT MOMENT.
BUT HE HAD CROSSED A LINE THAT EVERYONE BUT HIM UNDERSTOOD, IT SEEMED. YOU JUST DIDN'T MESS WITH SPENCE. BECAUSE SPENCE...
LATER, HUNT.
...HE NEVER PLAYED FAIR.

ISSUE 2

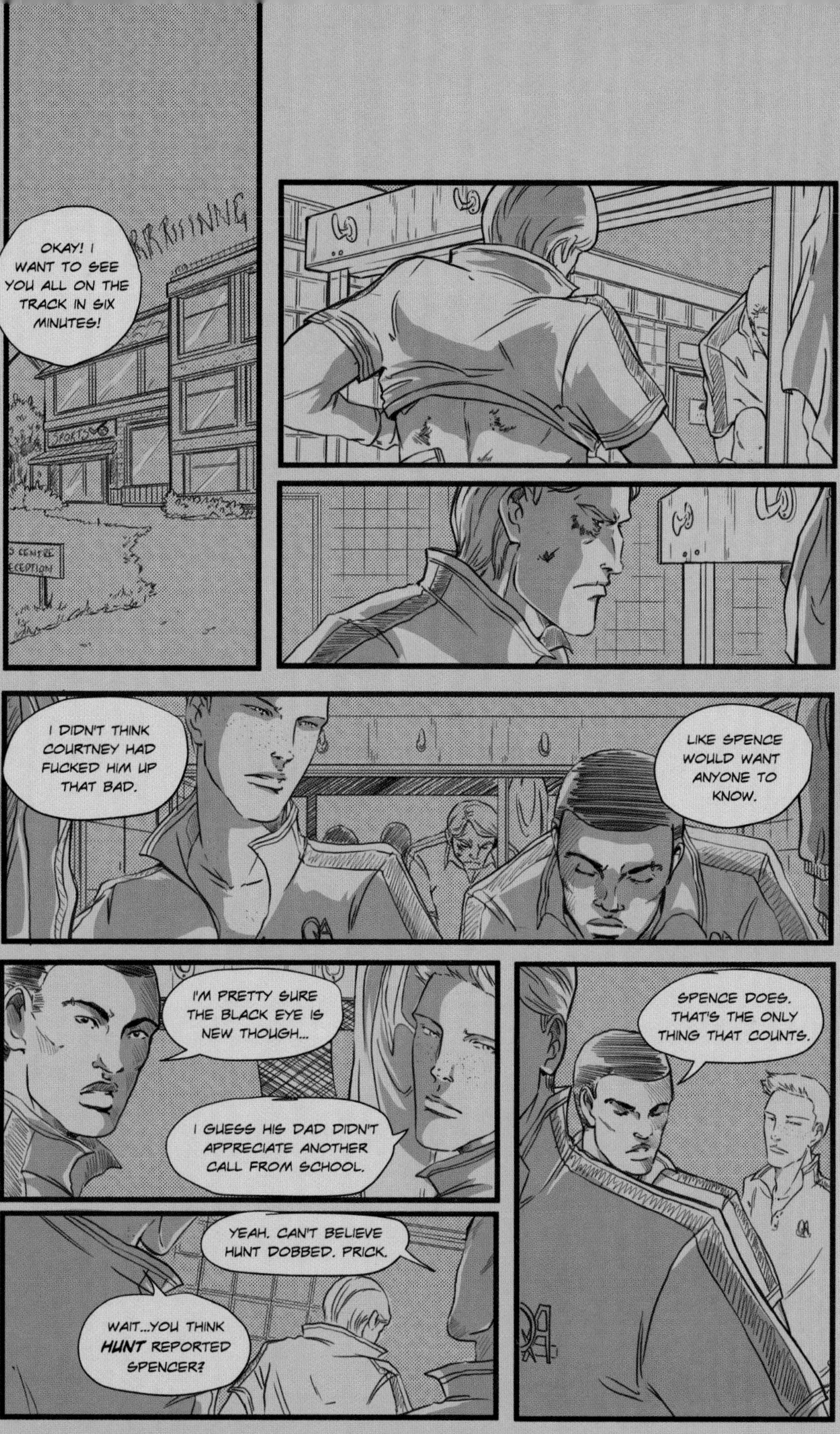
RRRiiiiNNG
OKAY! I WANT TO SEE YOU ALL ON THE TRACK IN SIX MINUTES!
I DIDN'T THINK COURTNEY HAD FUCKED HIM UP THAT BAD.
LIKE SPENCE WOULD WANT ANYONE TO KNOW.
I'M PRETTY SURE THE BLACK EYE IS NEW THOUGH...
I GUESS HIS DAD DIDN'T APPRECIATE ANOTHER CALL FROM SCHOOL.
SPENCE DOES. THAT'S THE ONLY THING THAT COUNTS.
YEAH. CAN'T BELIEVE HUNT DOBBED. PRICK.
WAIT...YOU THINK **HUNT** REPORTED SPENCER?

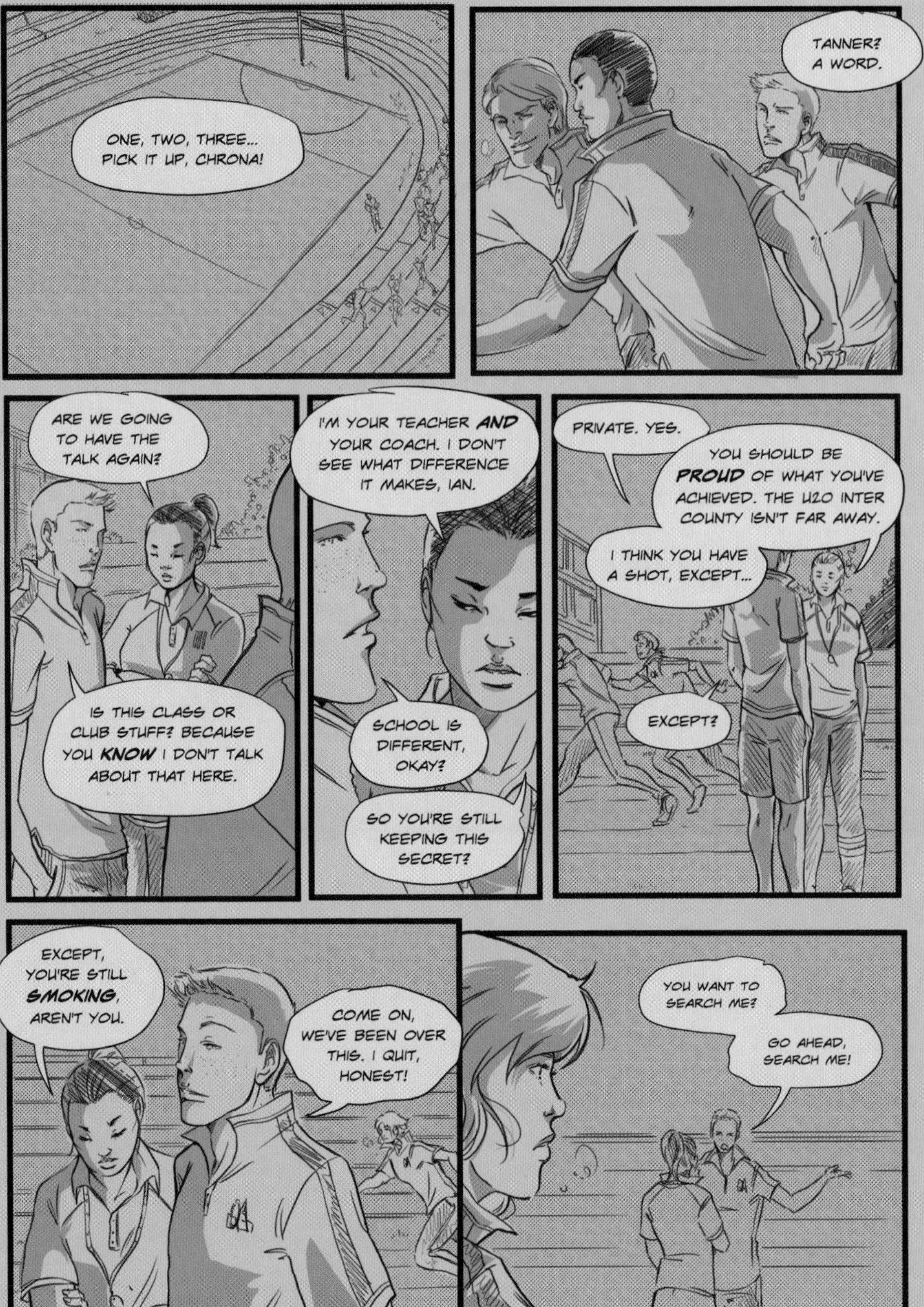
ONE, TWO, THREE... PICK IT UP, CHRONA!
TANNER? A WORD.
ARE WE GOING TO HAVE THE TALK AGAIN?
IS THIS CLASS OR CLUB STUFF? BECAUSE YOU KNOW I DON'T TALK ABOUT THAT HERE.
I'M YOUR TEACHER AND YOUR COACH. I DON'T SEE WHAT DIFFERENCE IT MAKES, IAN.
SCHOOL IS DIFFERENT, OKAY?
SO YOU'RE STILL KEEPING THIS SECRET?
PRIVATE. YES.
YOU SHOULD BE PROUD OF WHAT YOU'VE ACHIEVED. THE U20 INTER COUNTY ISN'T FAR AWAY.
I THINK YOU HAVE A SHOT, EXCEPT...
EXCEPT?
EXCEPT, YOU'RE STILL SMOKING, AREN'T YOU.
COME ON, WE'VE BEEN OVER THIS. I QUIT, HONEST!
YOU WANT TO SEARCH ME?
GO AHEAD, SEARCH ME!

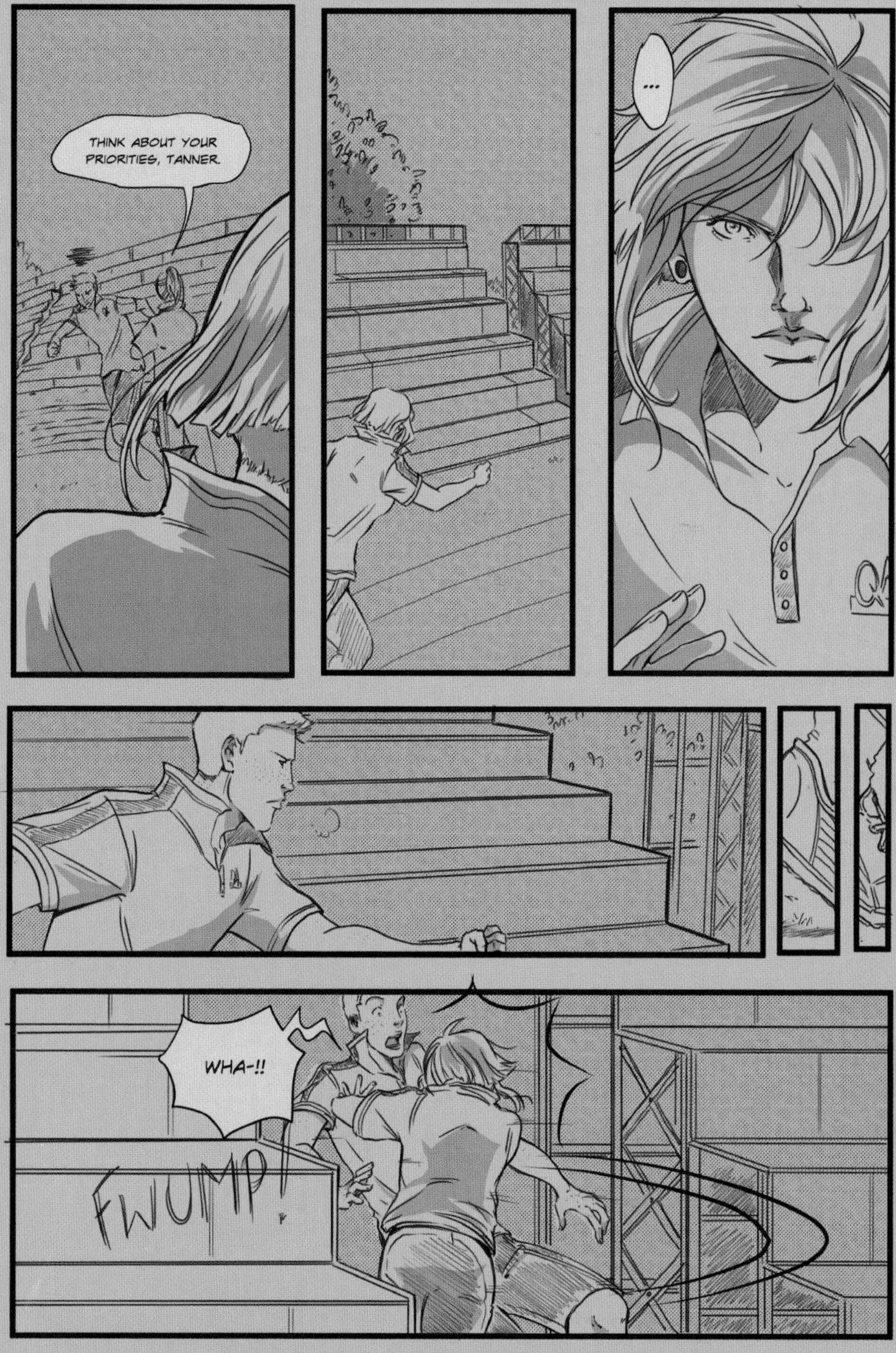
THINK ABOUT YOUR PRIORITIES, TANNER.
...
WHA-!!
FWUMP!

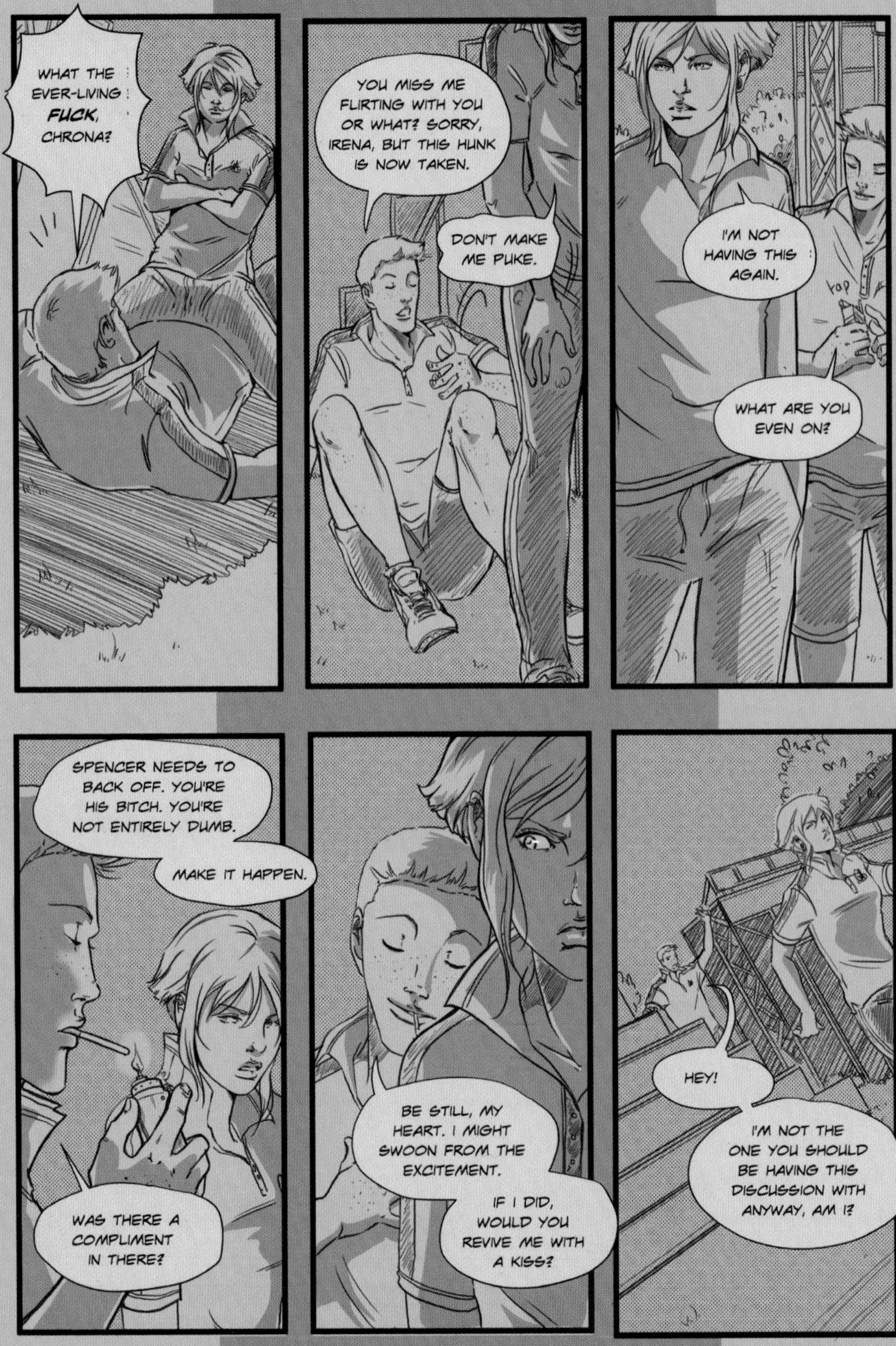
WHAT THE EVER-LIVING **FUCK**, CHRONA?
YOU MISS ME FLIRTING WITH YOU OR WHAT? SORRY, IRENA, BUT THIS HUNK IS NOW TAKEN.
DON'T MAKE ME PUKE.
I'M NOT HAVING THIS AGAIN.
tap
WHAT ARE YOU EVEN ON?
SPENCER NEEDS TO BACK OFF. YOU'RE HIS BITCH. YOU'RE NOT ENTIRELY DUMB.
MAKE IT HAPPEN.
WAS THERE A COMPLIMENT IN THERE?
BE STILL, MY HEART. I MIGHT SWOON FROM THE EXCITEMENT.
IF I DID, WOULD YOU REVIVE ME WITH A KISS?
HEY!
I'M NOT THE ONE YOU SHOULD BE HAVING THIS DISCUSSION WITH ANYWAY, AM I?

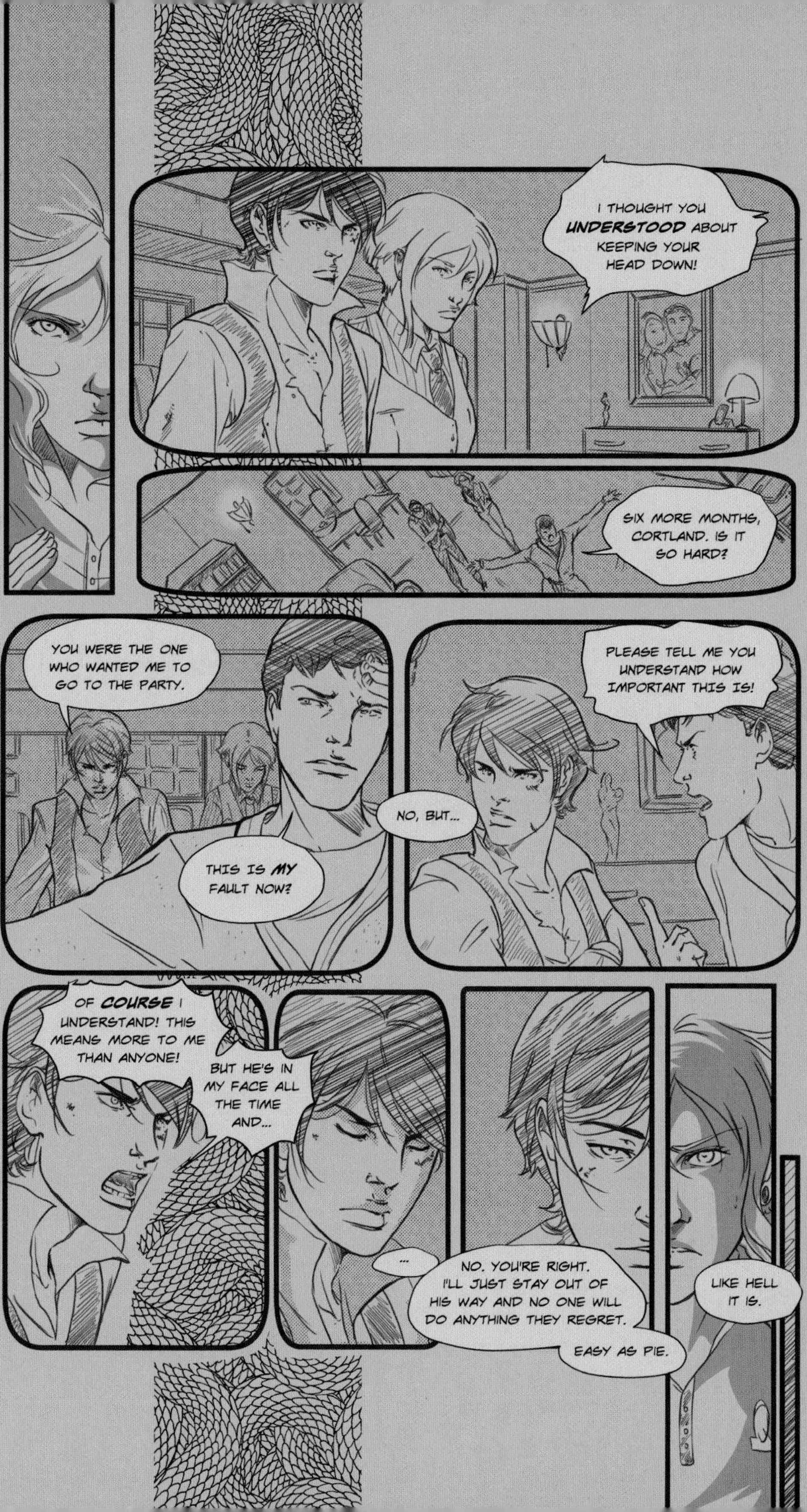
I THOUGHT YOU UNDERSTOOD ABOUT KEEPING YOUR HEAD DOWN!
SIX MORE MONTHS, CORTLAND. IS IT SO HARD?
YOU WERE THE ONE WHO WANTED ME TO GO TO THE PARTY.
THIS IS MY FAULT NOW?
NO, BUT...
PLEASE TELL ME YOU UNDERSTAND HOW IMPORTANT THIS IS!
OF COURSE I UNDERSTAND! THIS MEANS MORE TO ME THAN ANYONE!
BUT HE'S IN MY FACE ALL THE TIME AND...
...
NO. YOU'RE RIGHT. I'LL JUST STAY OUT OF HIS WAY AND NO ONE WILL DO ANYTHING THEY REGRET.
EASY AS PIE.
LIKE HELL IT IS.

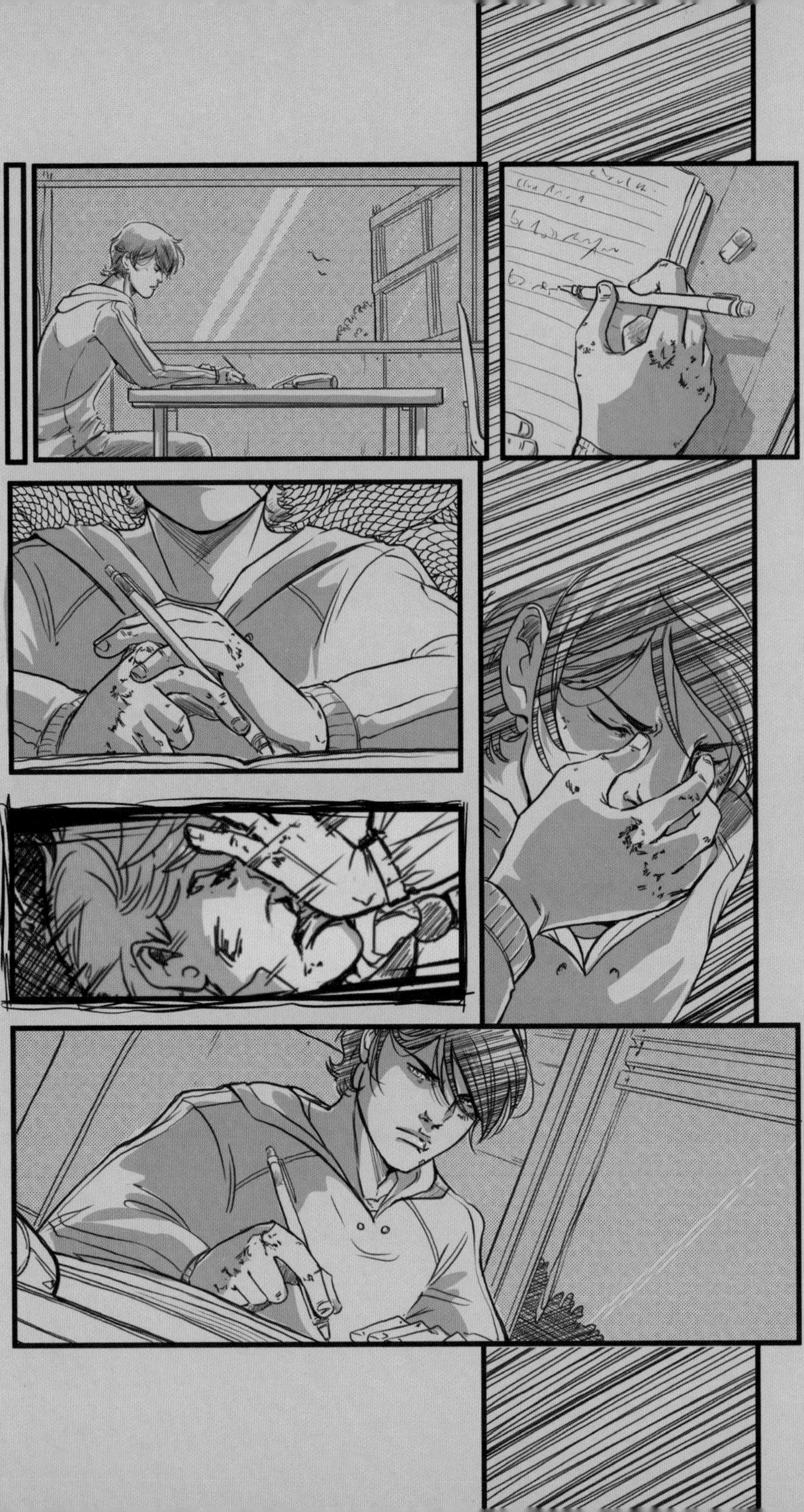

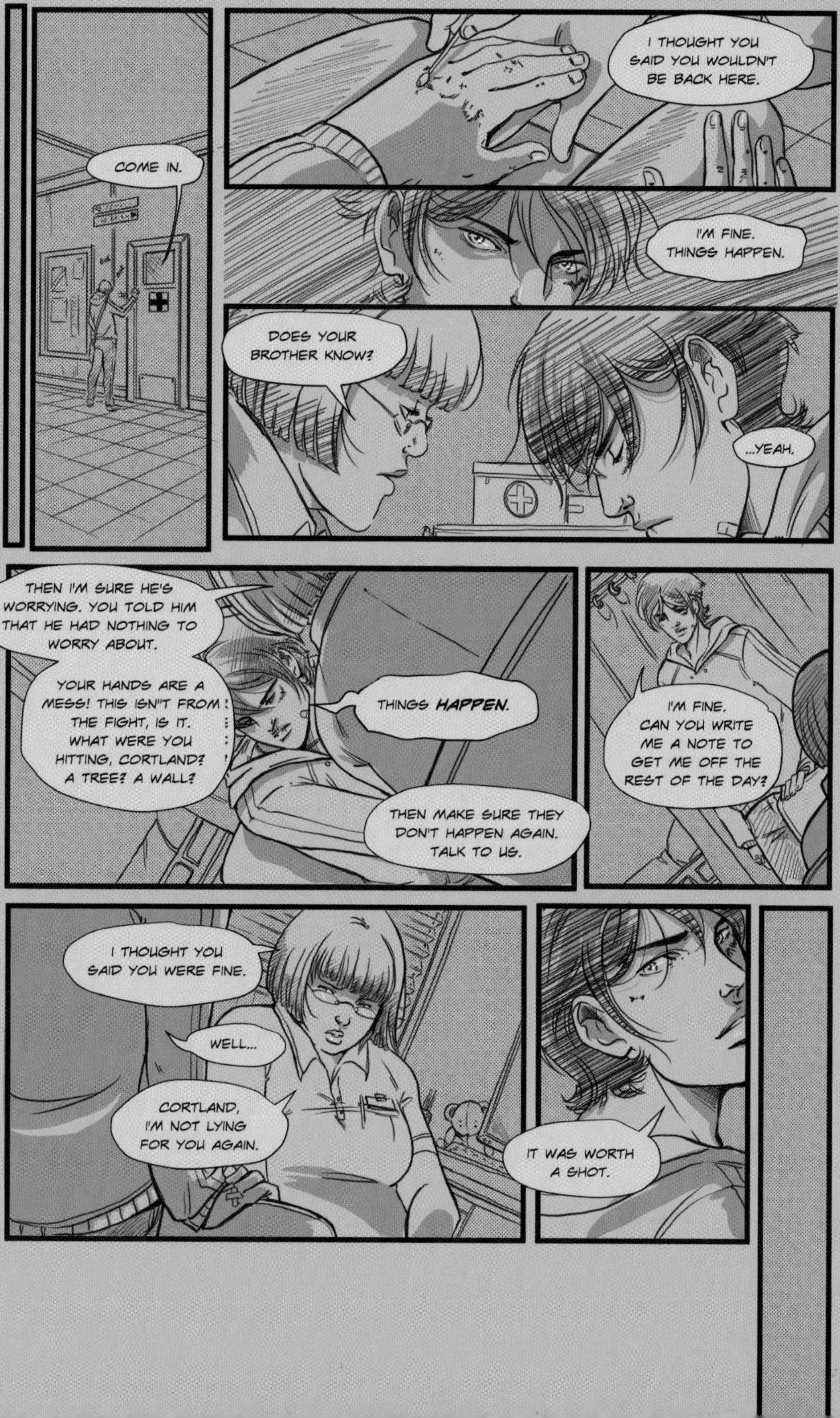
COME IN.
I THOUGHT YOU SAID YOU WOULDN'T BE BACK HERE.
I'M FINE. THINGS HAPPEN.
DOES YOUR BROTHER KNOW?
...YEAH.
THEN I'M SURE HE'S WORRYING. YOU TOLD HIM THAT HE HAD NOTHING TO WORRY ABOUT.
YOUR HANDS ARE A MESS! THIS ISN"T FROM THE FIGHT, IS IT. WHAT WERE YOU HITTING, CORTLAND? A TREE? A WALL?
THINGS **HAPPEN.**
THEN MAKE SURE THEY DON'T HAPPEN AGAIN. TALK TO US.
I'M FINE. CAN YOU WRITE ME A NOTE TO GET ME OFF THE REST OF THE DAY?
I THOUGHT YOU SAID YOU WERE FINE.
WELL...
CORTLAND, I'M NOT LYING FOR YOU AGAIN.
IT WAS WORTH A SHOT.

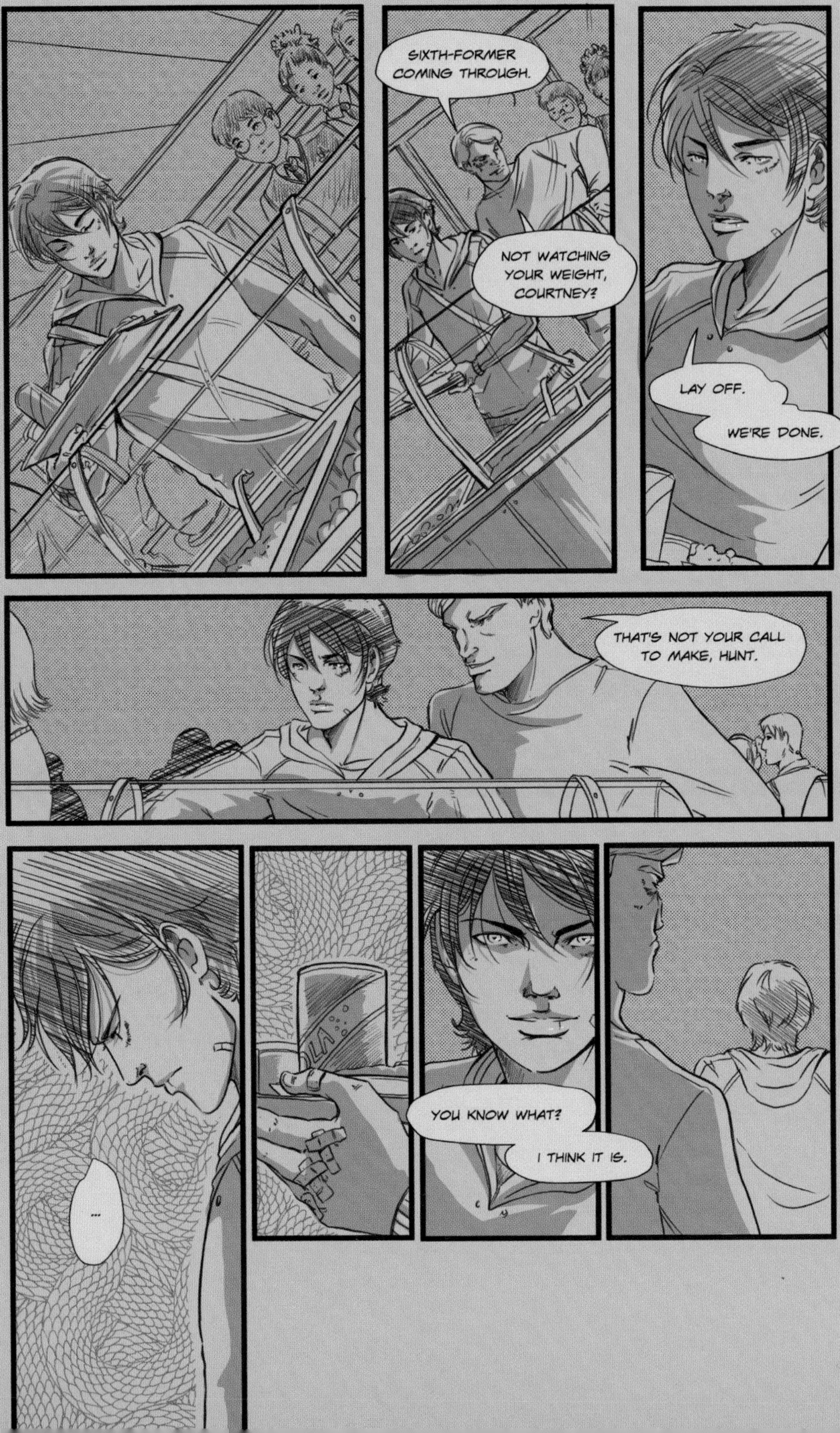
SIXTH-FORMER COMING THROUGH.
NOT WATCHING YOUR WEIGHT, COURTNEY?
LAY OFF.
WE'RE DONE.
THAT'S NOT YOUR CALL TO MAKE, HUNT.
...
YOU KNOW WHAT?
I THINK IT IS.

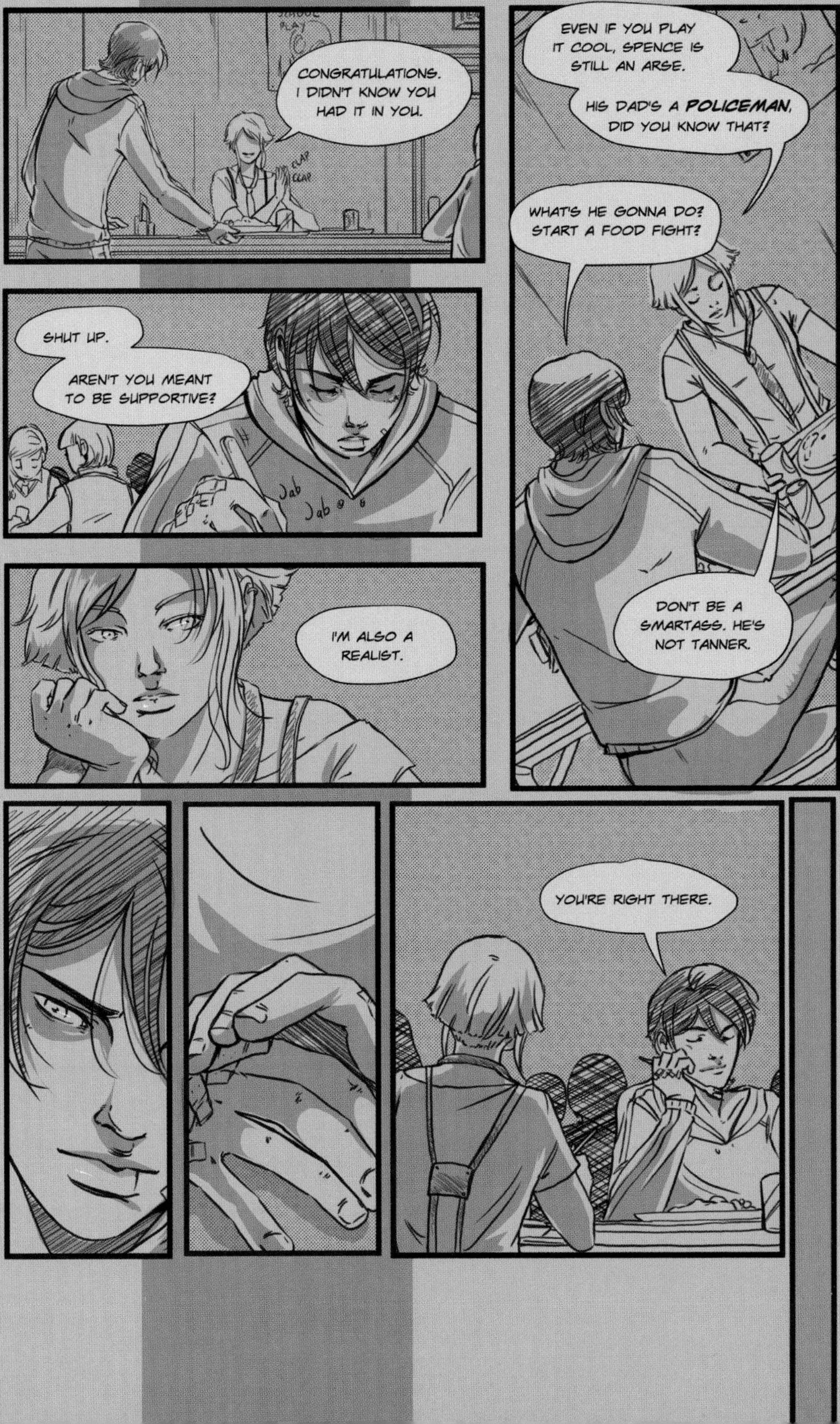
CONGRATULATIONS. I DIDN'T KNOW YOU HAD IT IN YOU.
CLAP CLAP
SHUT UP.
AREN'T YOU MEANT TO BE SUPPORTIVE?
Jab Jab
I'M ALSO A REALIST.
EVEN IF YOU PLAY IT COOL, SPENCE IS STILL AN ARSE.
HIS DAD'S A **POLICEMAN**, DID YOU KNOW THAT?
WHAT'S HE GONNA DO? START A FOOD FIGHT?
DON'T BE A SMARTASS. HE'S NOT TANNER.
YOU'RE RIGHT THERE.

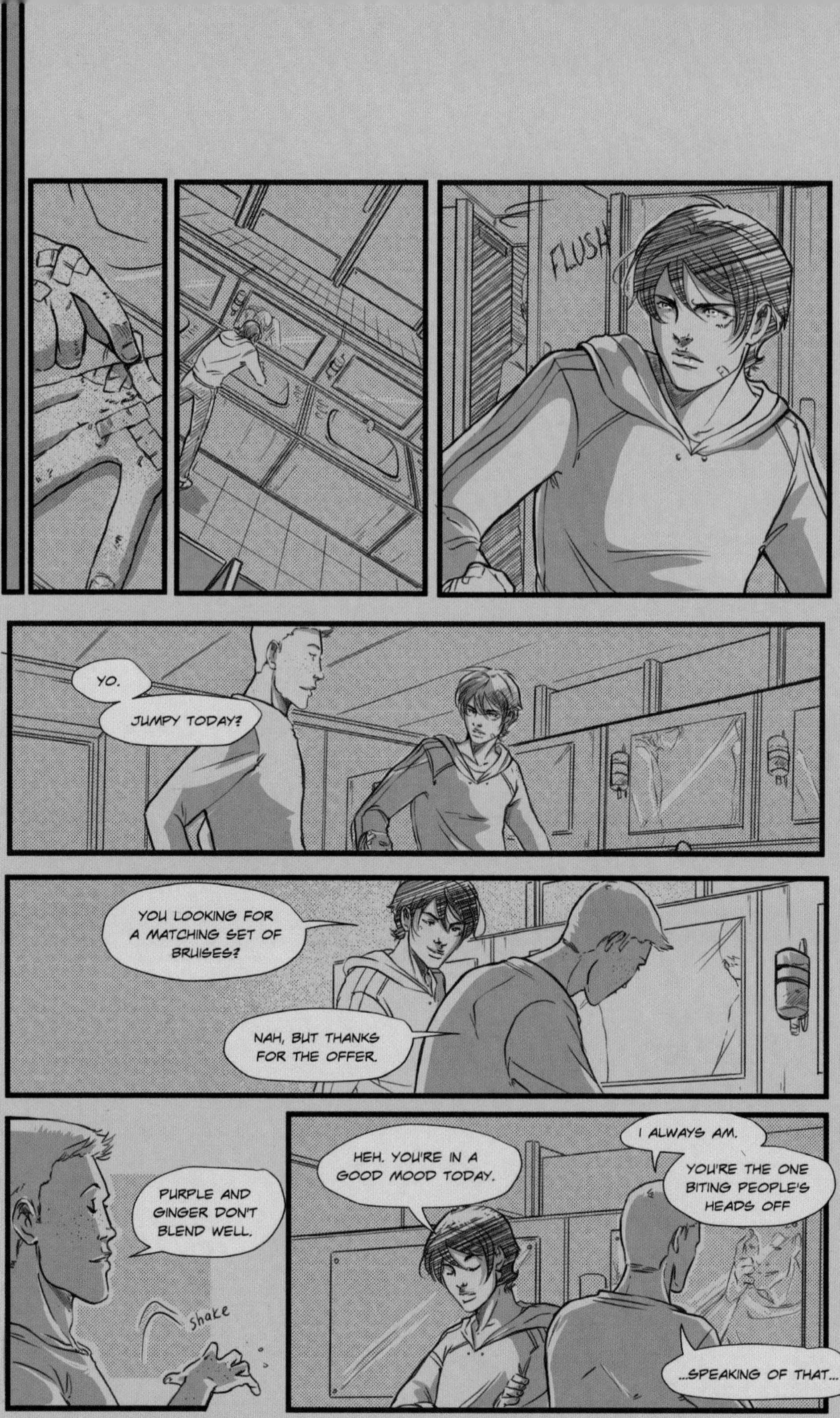
FLUSH
YO.
JUMPY TODAY?
YOU LOOKING FOR A MATCHING SET OF BRUISES?
NAH, BUT THANKS FOR THE OFFER.
PURPLE AND GINGER DON'T BLEND WELL.
shake
HEH. YOU'RE IN A GOOD MOOD TODAY.
I ALWAYS AM.
YOU'RE THE ONE BITING PEOPLE'S HEADS OFF
...SPEAKING OF THAT...

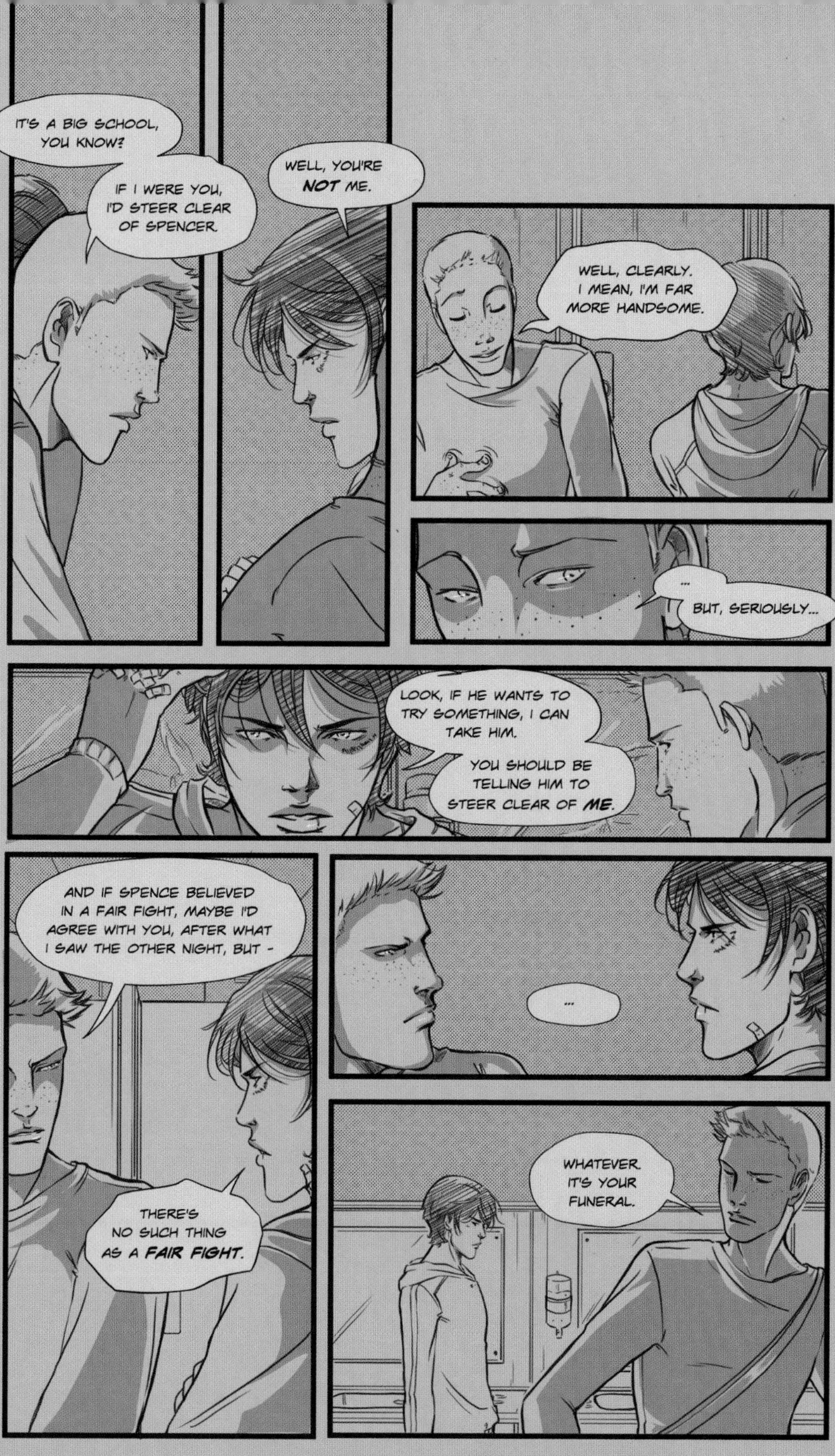

IT'S A BIG SCHOOL, YOU KNOW?
IF I WERE YOU, I'D STEER CLEAR OF SPENCER.
WELL, YOU'RE NOT ME.
WELL, CLEARLY. I MEAN, I'M FAR MORE HANDSOME.
...
BUT, SERIOUSLY...
LOOK, IF HE WANTS TO TRY SOMETHING, I CAN TAKE HIM.
YOU SHOULD BE TELLING HIM TO STEER CLEAR OF ME.
AND IF SPENCE BELIEVED IN A FAIR FIGHT, MAYBE I'D AGREE WITH YOU, AFTER WHAT I SAW THE OTHER NIGHT, BUT -
THERE'S NO SUCH THING AS A FAIR FIGHT.
...
WHATEVER. IT'S YOUR FUNERAL.

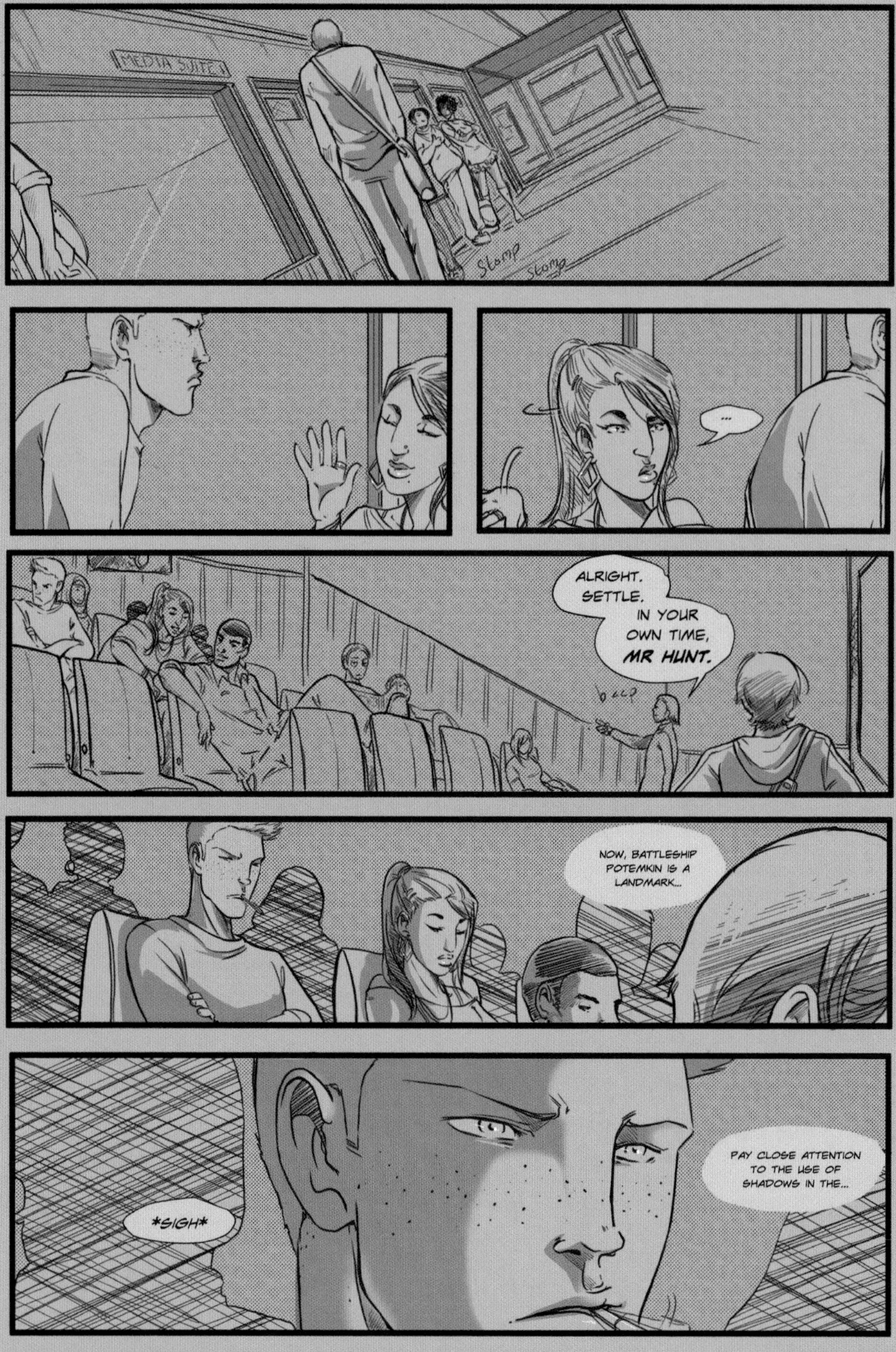
MEDIA SUITE
Stomp
stomp
...
ALRIGHT. SETTLE. IN YOUR OWN TIME, MR HUNT.
NOW, BATTLESHIP POTEMKIN IS A LANDMARK...
PAY CLOSE ATTENTION TO THE USE OF SHADOWS IN THE...
SIGH

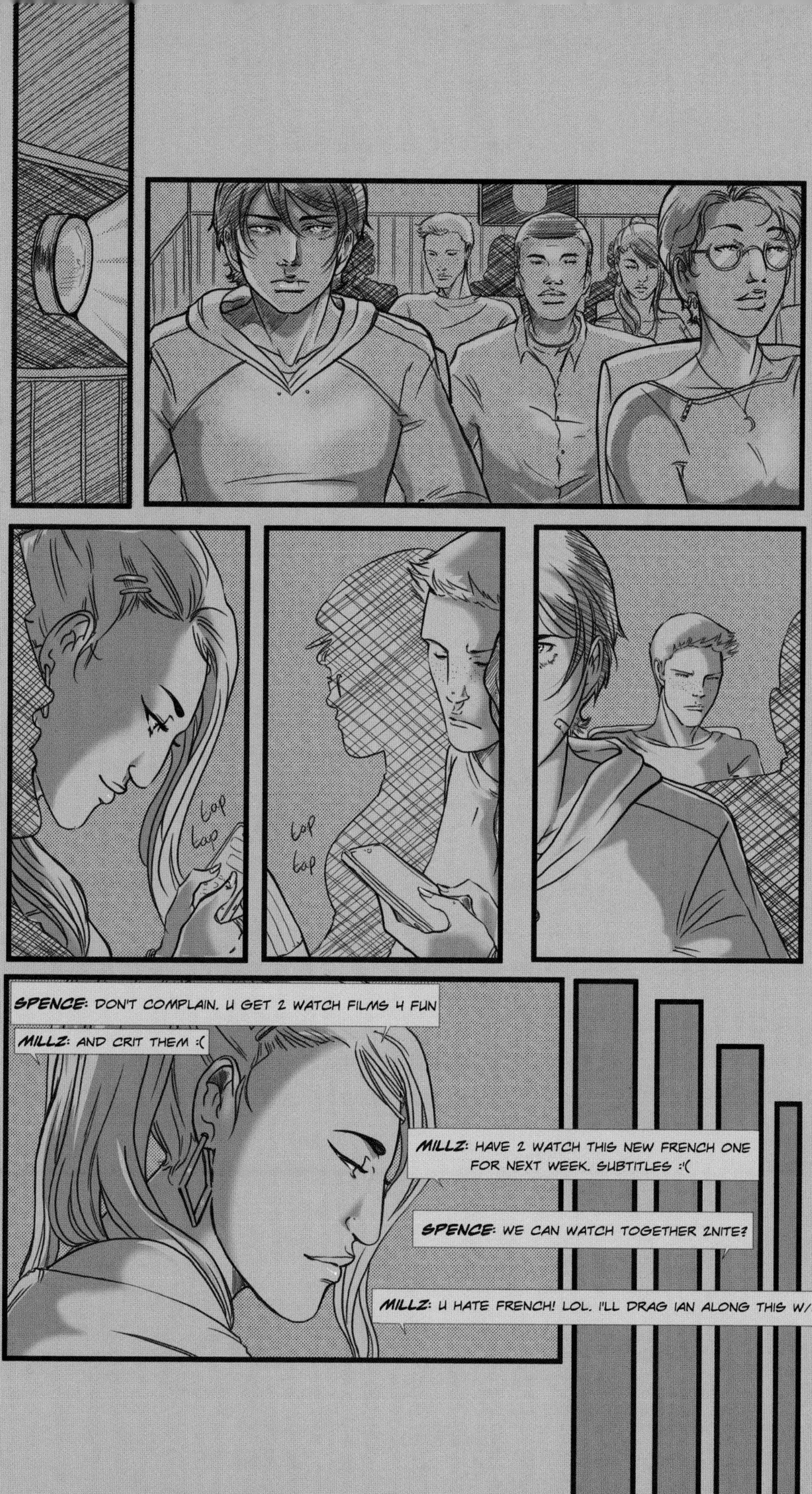
tap
tap
tap
tap
SPENCE: DON'T COMPLAIN. U GET 2 WATCH FILMS 4 FUN
MILLZ: AND CRIT THEM :(
MILLZ: HAVE 2 WATCH THIS NEW FRENCH ONE FOR NEXT WEEK. SUBTITLES :'(
SPENCE: WE CAN WATCH TOGETHER 2NITE?
MILLZ: U HATE FRENCH! LOL. I'LL DRAG IAN ALONG THIS W/E

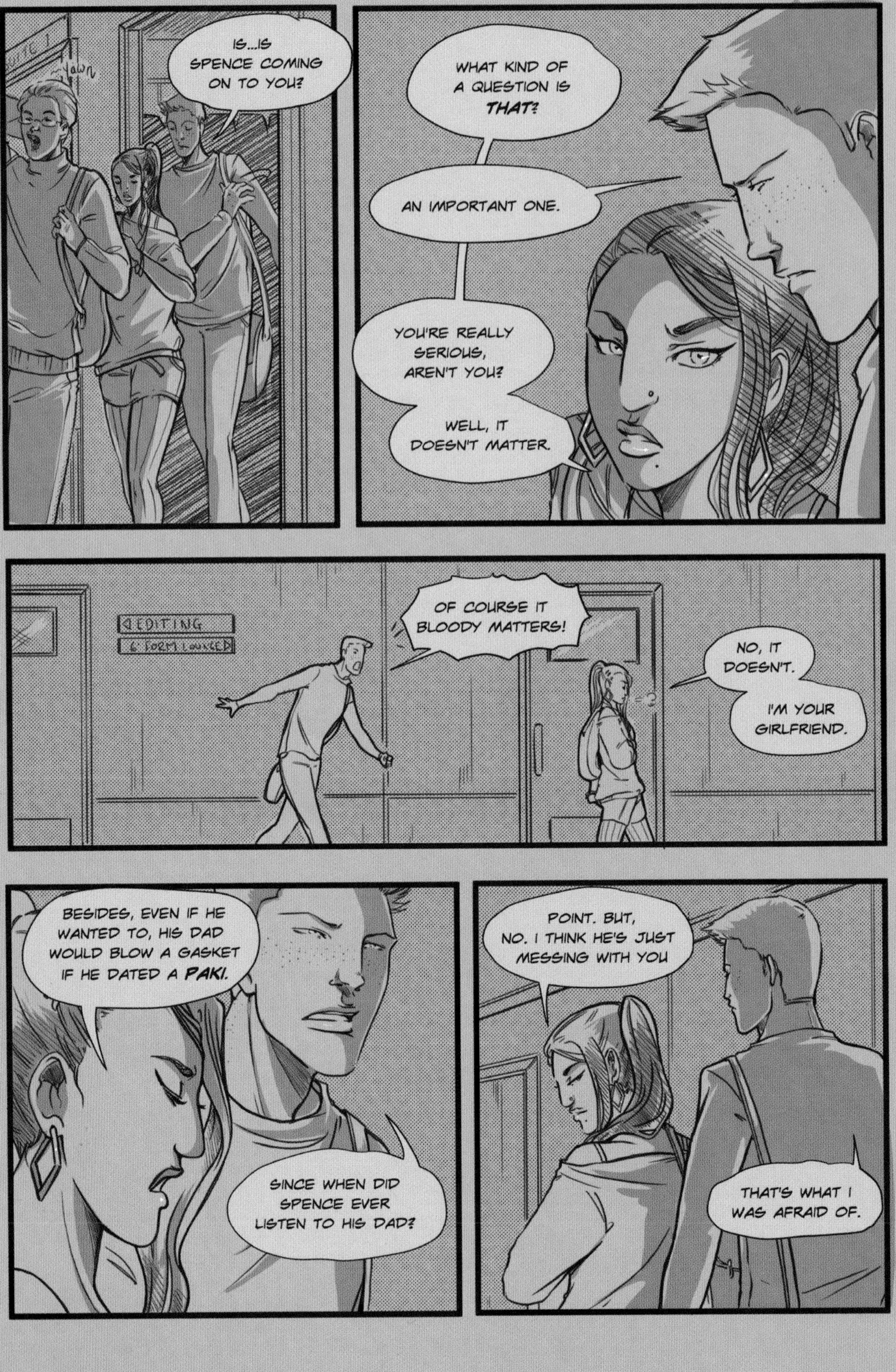
Yawn
IS...IS SPENCE COMING ON TO YOU?
WHAT KIND OF A QUESTION IS *THAT?*
AN IMPORTANT ONE.
YOU'RE REALLY SERIOUS, AREN'T YOU?
WELL, IT DOESN'T MATTER.
EDITING
6 FORM LOUNGE
OF COURSE IT BLOODY MATTERS!
NO, IT DOESN'T.
I'M YOUR GIRLFRIEND.
BESIDES, EVEN IF HE WANTED TO, HIS DAD WOULD BLOW A GASKET IF HE DATED A *PAKI.*
SINCE WHEN DID SPENCE EVER LISTEN TO HIS DAD?
POINT. BUT, NO. I THINK HE'S JUST MESSING WITH YOU
THAT'S WHAT I WAS AFRAID OF.

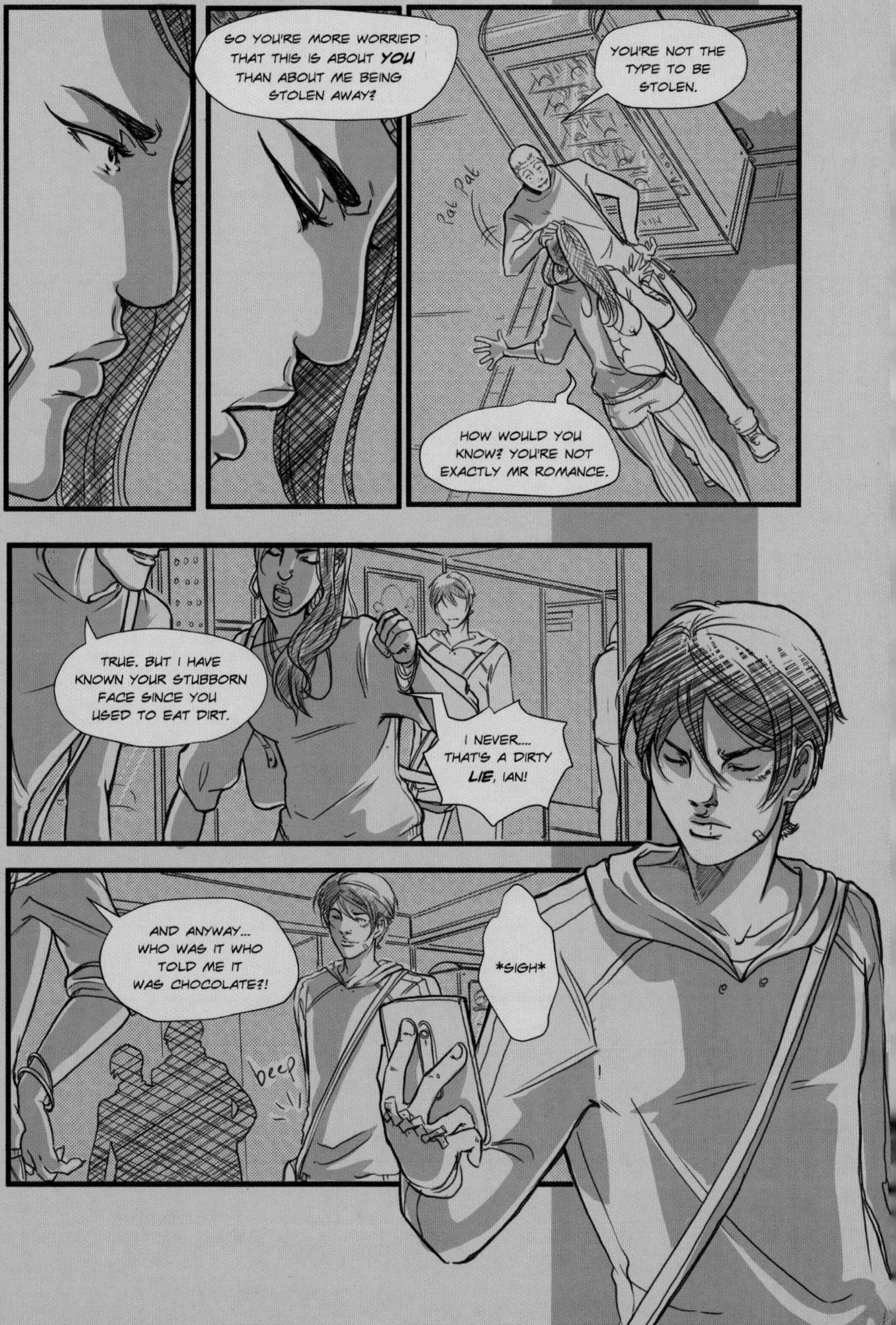
SO YOU'RE MORE WORRIED THAT THIS IS ABOUT YOU THAN ABOUT ME BEING STOLEN AWAY?
YOU'RE NOT THE TYPE TO BE STOLEN.
Pat Pat
HOW WOULD YOU KNOW? YOU'RE NOT EXACTLY MR ROMANCE.
TRUE. BUT I HAVE KNOWN YOUR STUBBORN FACE SINCE YOU USED TO EAT DIRT.
I NEVER.... THAT'S A DIRTY LIE, IAN!
AND ANYWAY... WHO WAS IT WHO TOLD ME IT WAS CHOCOLATE?!
beep
SIGH

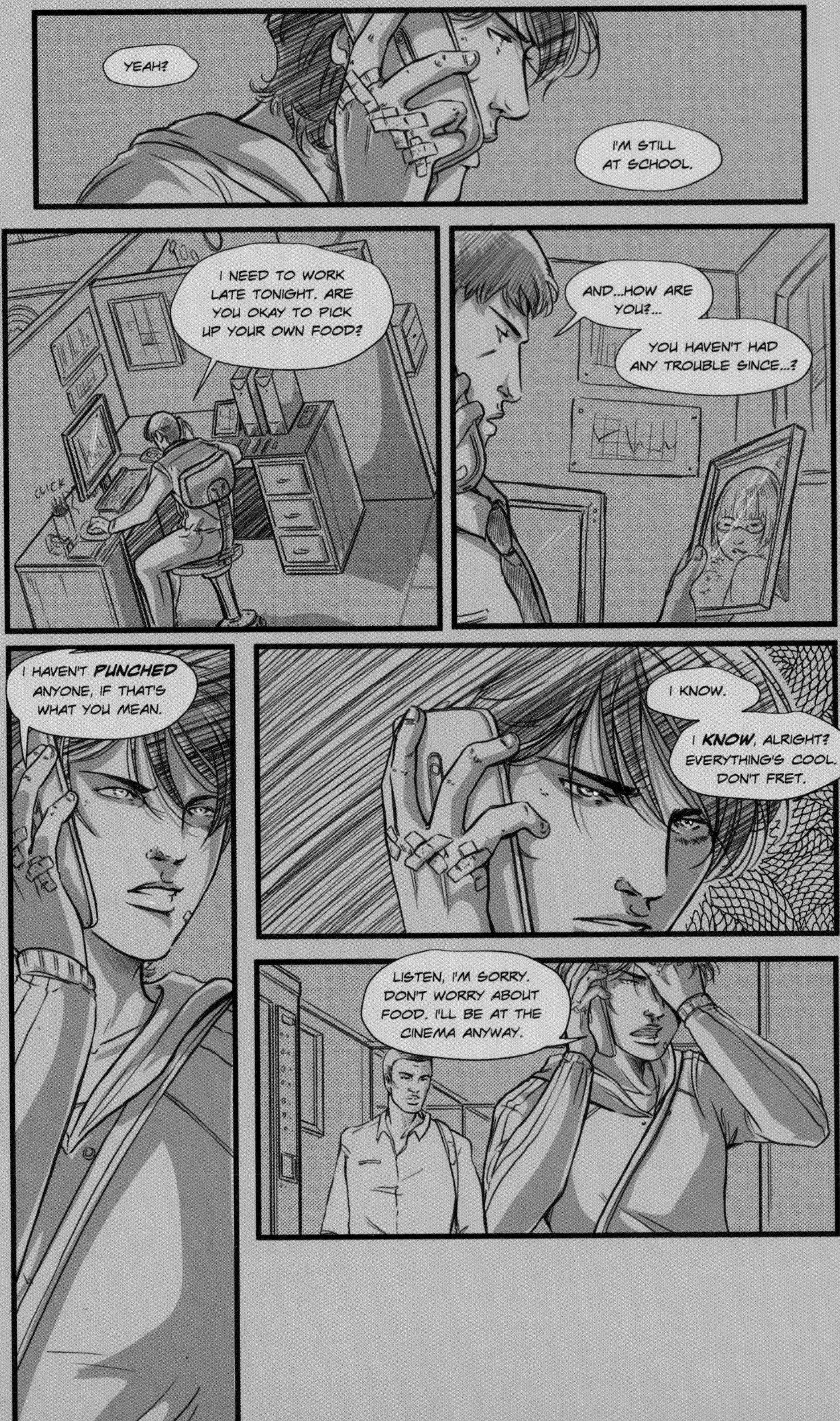
YEAH?
I'M STILL AT SCHOOL.
I NEED TO WORK LATE TONIGHT. ARE YOU OKAY TO PICK UP YOUR OWN FOOD?
CLICK
AND...HOW ARE YOU?...
YOU HAVEN'T HAD ANY TROUBLE SINCE...?
I HAVEN'T **PUNCHED** ANYONE, IF THAT'S WHAT YOU MEAN.
I KNOW.
I **KNOW**, ALRIGHT? EVERYTHING'S COOL. DON'T FRET.
LISTEN, I'M SORRY. DON'T WORRY ABOUT FOOD. I'LL BE AT THE CINEMA ANYWAY.

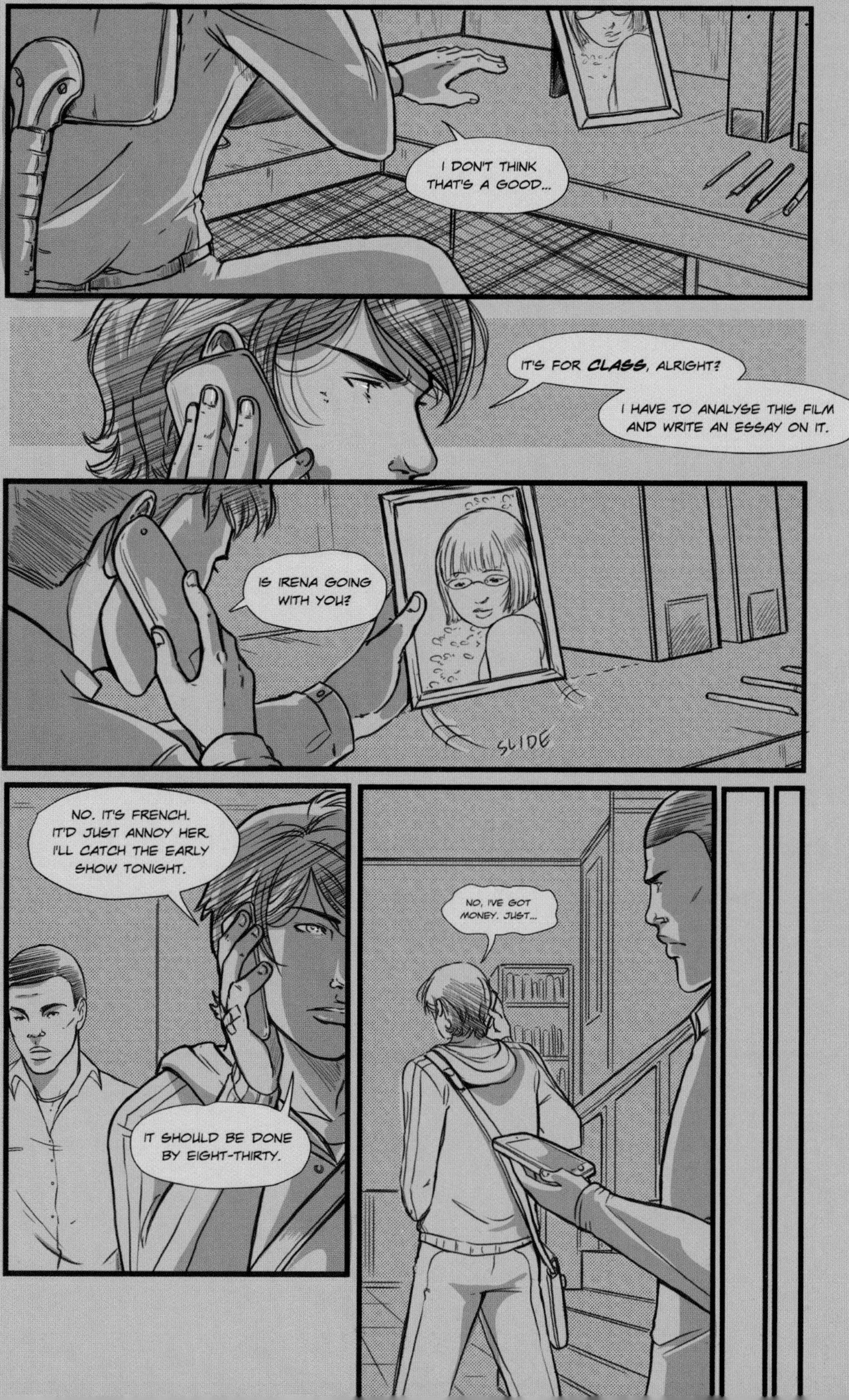
I DON'T THINK THAT'S A GOOD...
IT'S FOR **CLASS**, ALRIGHT?
I HAVE TO ANALYSE THIS FILM AND WRITE AN ESSAY ON IT.
IS IRENA GOING WITH YOU?
SLIDE
NO. IT'S FRENCH. IT'D JUST ANNOY HER. I'LL CATCH THE EARLY SHOW TONIGHT.
IT SHOULD BE DONE BY EIGHT-THIRTY.
NO, I'VE GOT MONEY. JUST...

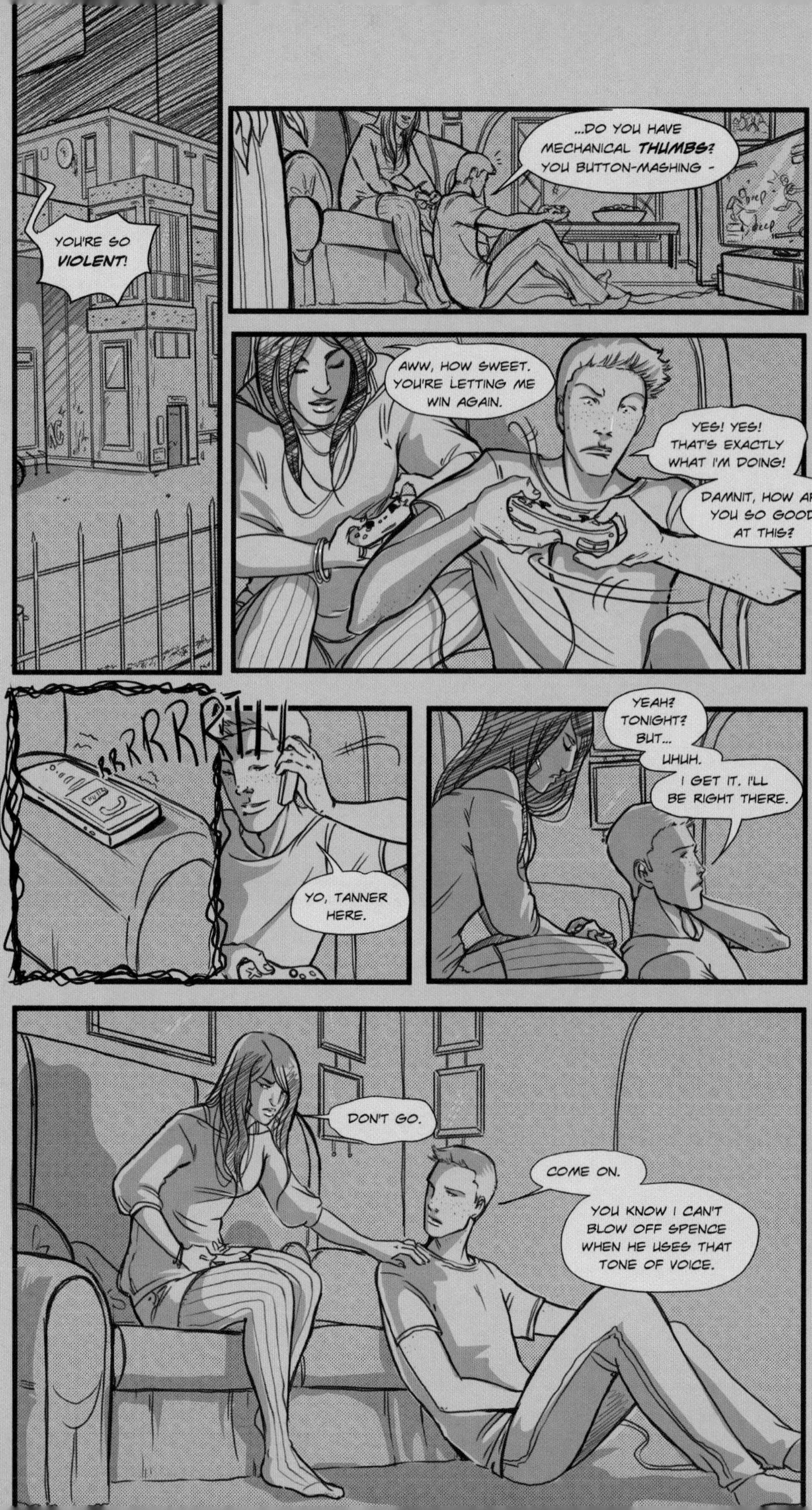
YOU'RE SO VIOLENT!
...DO YOU HAVE MECHANICAL THUMBS? YOU BUTTON-MASHING -
AWW, HOW SWEET. YOU'RE LETTING ME WIN AGAIN.
YES! YES! THAT'S EXACTLY WHAT I'M DOING!
DAMNIT, HOW ARE YOU SO GOOD AT THIS?
RRRRRRR!!!
YO, TANNER HERE.
YEAH? TONIGHT? BUT...
UHUH.
I GET IT. I'LL BE RIGHT THERE.
DON'T GO.
COME ON.
YOU KNOW I CAN'T BLOW OFF SPENCE WHEN HE USES THAT TONE OF VOICE.

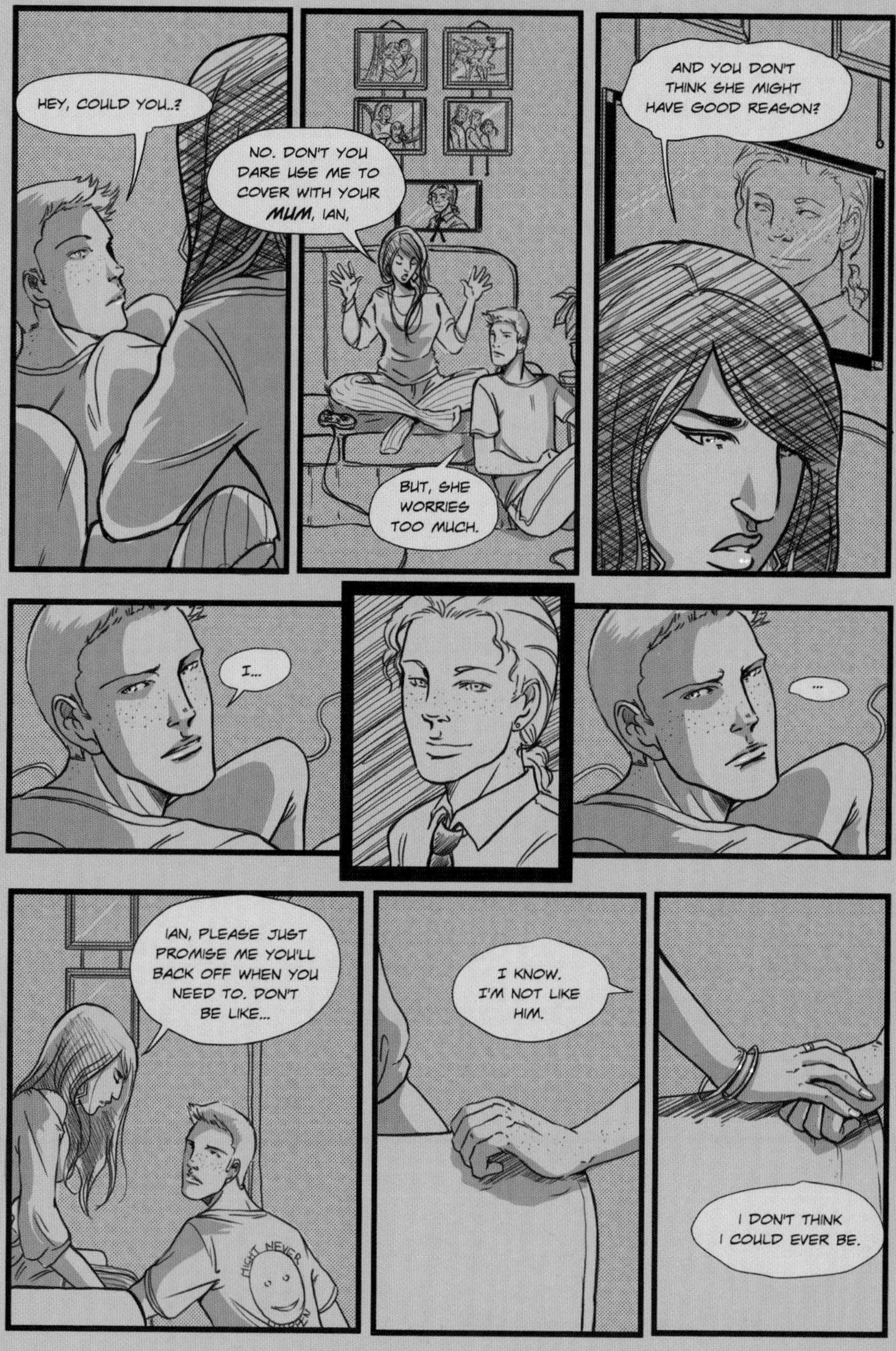
HEY, COULD YOU..?
NO. DON'T YOU DARE USE ME TO COVER WITH YOUR *MUM*, IAN,
BUT, SHE WORRIES TOO MUCH.
AND YOU DON'T THINK SHE MIGHT HAVE GOOD REASON?
I...
...
IAN, PLEASE JUST PROMISE ME YOU'LL BACK OFF WHEN YOU NEED TO. DON'T BE LIKE...
I KNOW. I'M NOT LIKE HIM.
I DON'T THINK I COULD EVER BE.

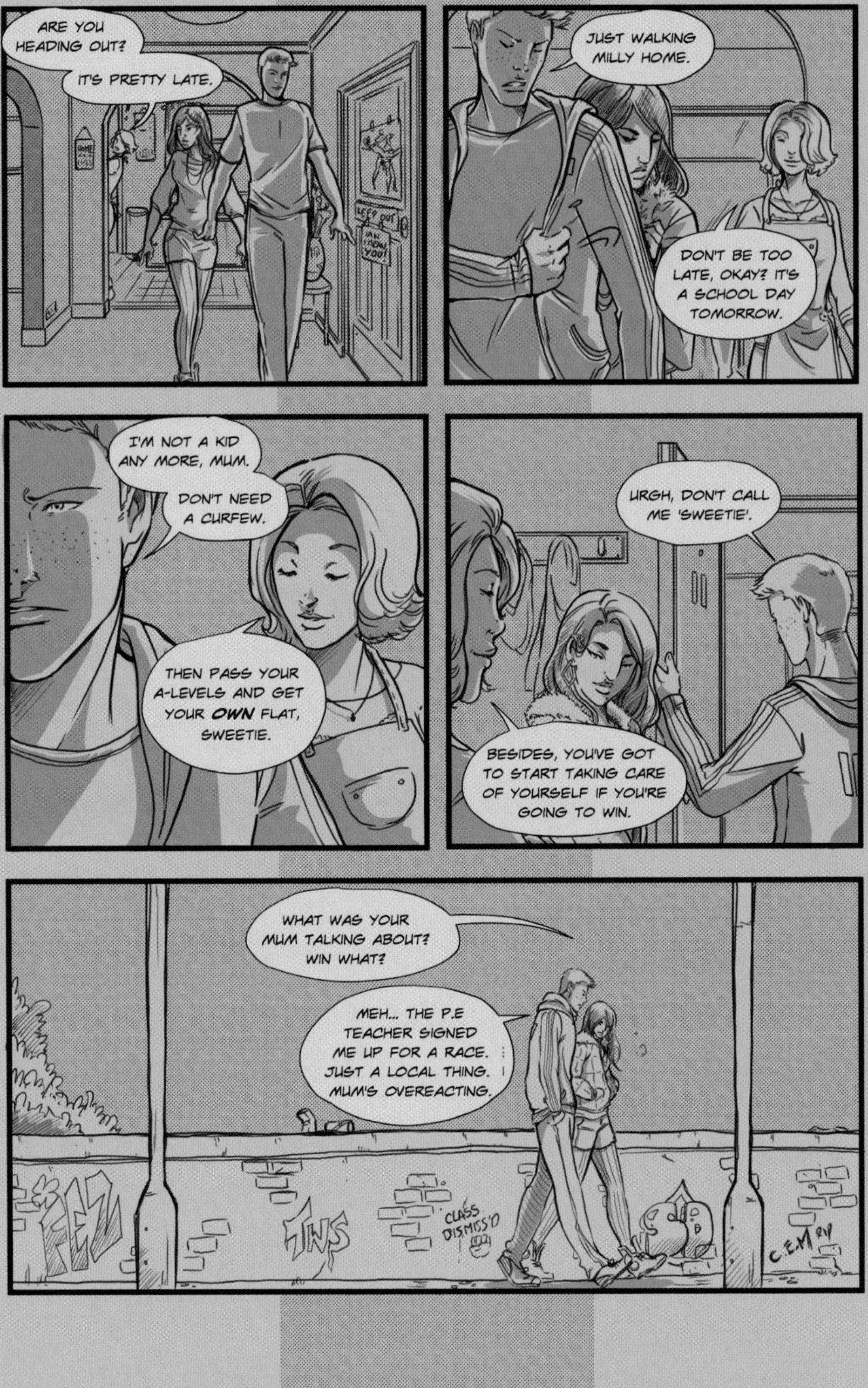
ARE YOU HEADING OUT?
IT'S PRETTY LATE.
JUST WALKING MILLY HOME.
DON'T BE TOO LATE, OKAY? IT'S A SCHOOL DAY TOMORROW.
I'M NOT A KID ANY MORE, MUM.
DON'T NEED A CURFEW.
THEN PASS YOUR A-LEVELS AND GET YOUR OWN FLAT, SWEETIE.
URGH, DON'T CALL ME 'SWEETIE'.
BESIDES, YOU'VE GOT TO START TAKING CARE OF YOURSELF IF YOU'RE GOING TO WIN.
WHAT WAS YOUR MUM TALKING ABOUT? WIN WHAT?
MEH... THE P.E TEACHER SIGNED ME UP FOR A RACE. JUST A LOCAL THING. MUM'S OVEREACTING.
CLASS DISMISS'D
C.E.M

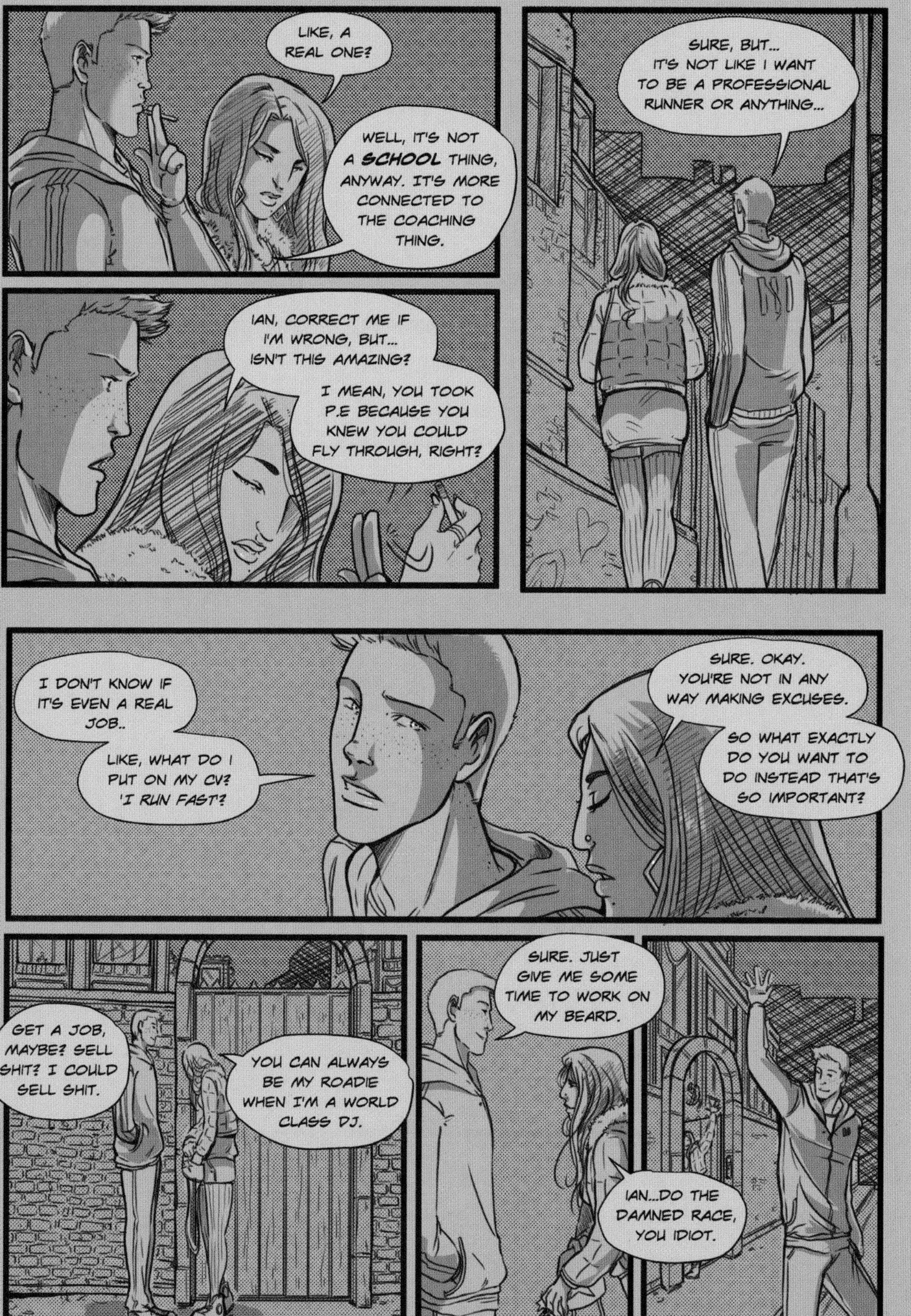
LIKE, A REAL ONE?
WELL, IT'S NOT A SCHOOL THING, ANYWAY. IT'S MORE CONNECTED TO THE COACHING THING.
IAN, CORRECT ME IF I'M WRONG, BUT... ISN'T THIS AMAZING?
I MEAN, YOU TOOK P.E BECAUSE YOU KNEW YOU COULD FLY THROUGH, RIGHT?
SURE, BUT... IT'S NOT LIKE I WANT TO BE A PROFESSIONAL RUNNER OR ANYTHING...
I DON'T KNOW IF IT'S EVEN A REAL JOB..
LIKE, WHAT DO I PUT ON MY CV? 'I RUN FAST'?
SURE. OKAY. YOU'RE NOT IN ANY WAY MAKING EXCUSES.
SO WHAT EXACTLY DO YOU WANT TO DO INSTEAD THAT'S SO IMPORTANT?
GET A JOB, MAYBE? SELL SHIT? I COULD SELL SHIT.
YOU CAN ALWAYS BE MY ROADIE WHEN I'M A WORLD CLASS DJ.
SURE. JUST GIVE ME SOME TIME TO WORK ON MY BEARD.
IAN...DO THE DAMNED RACE, YOU IDIOT.

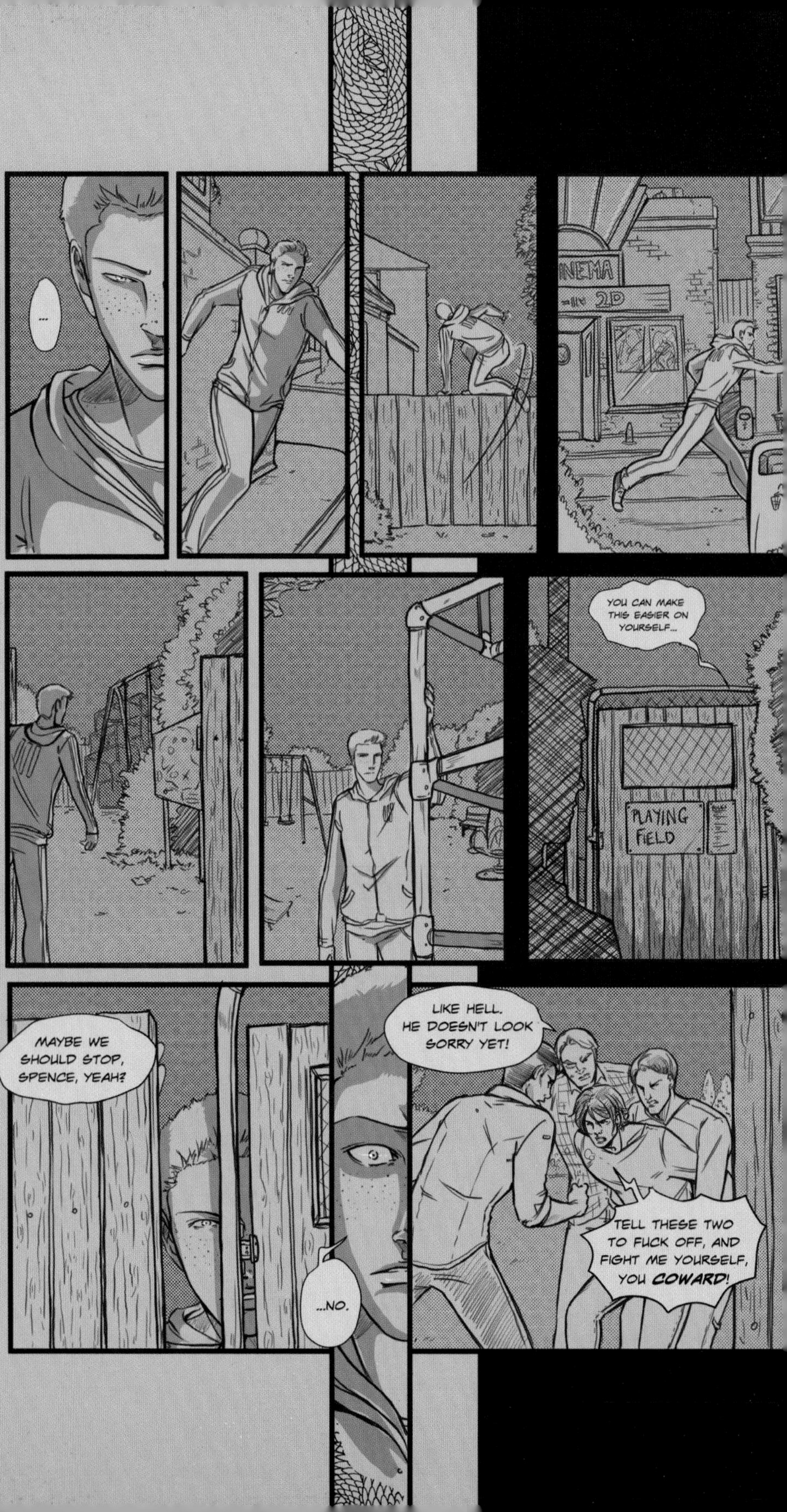
...
NEMA
2D
YOU CAN MAKE THIS EASIER ON YOURSELF...
PLAYING FIELD
MAYBE WE SHOULD STOP, SPENCE, YEAH?
...NO.
LIKE HELL. HE DOESN'T LOOK SORRY YET!
TELL THESE TWO TO FUCK OFF, AND FIGHT ME YOURSELF, YOU COWARD!

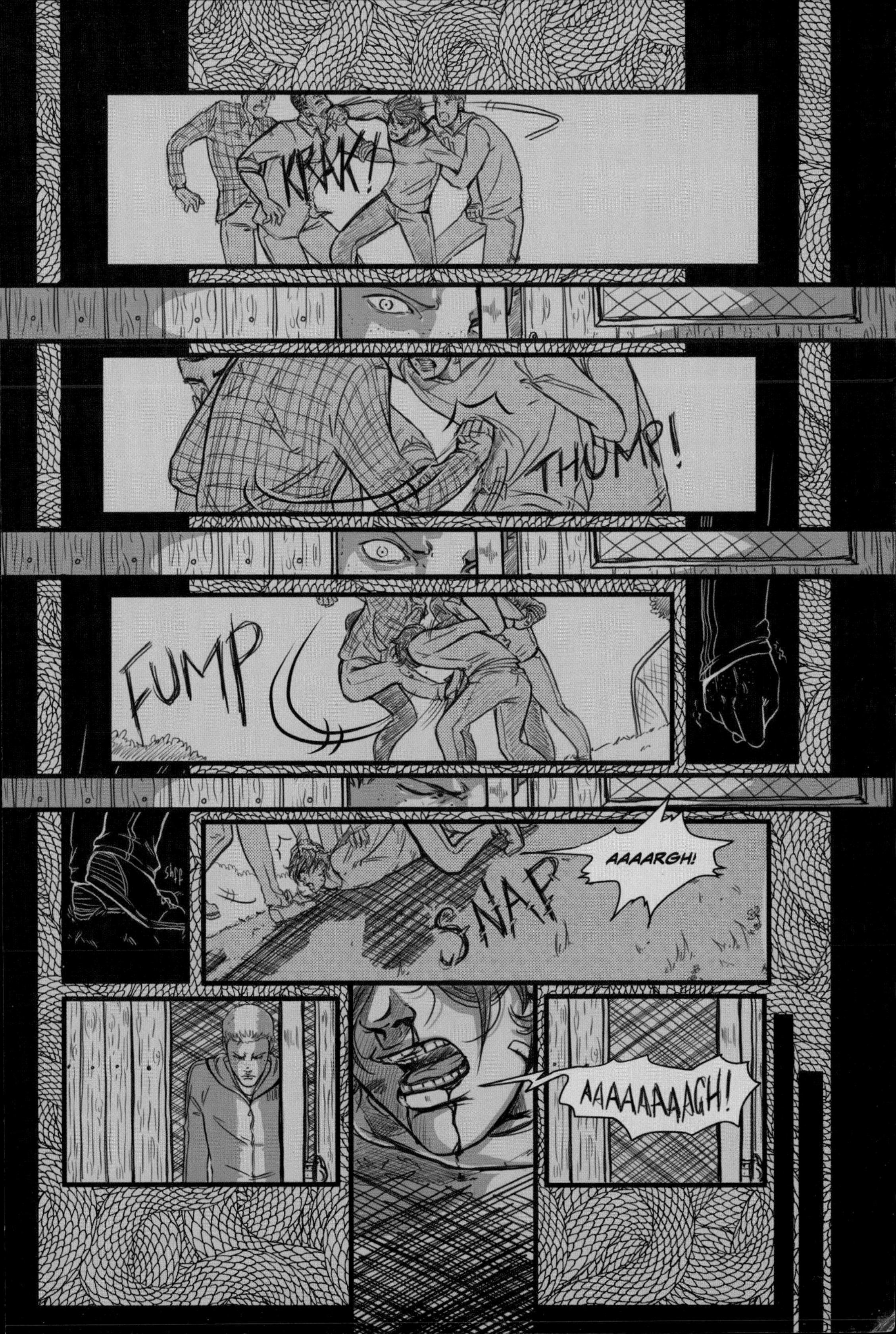
KRAK!
THUMP!
FUMP
SNAP
AAAARGH!
AAAAAAAAGH!

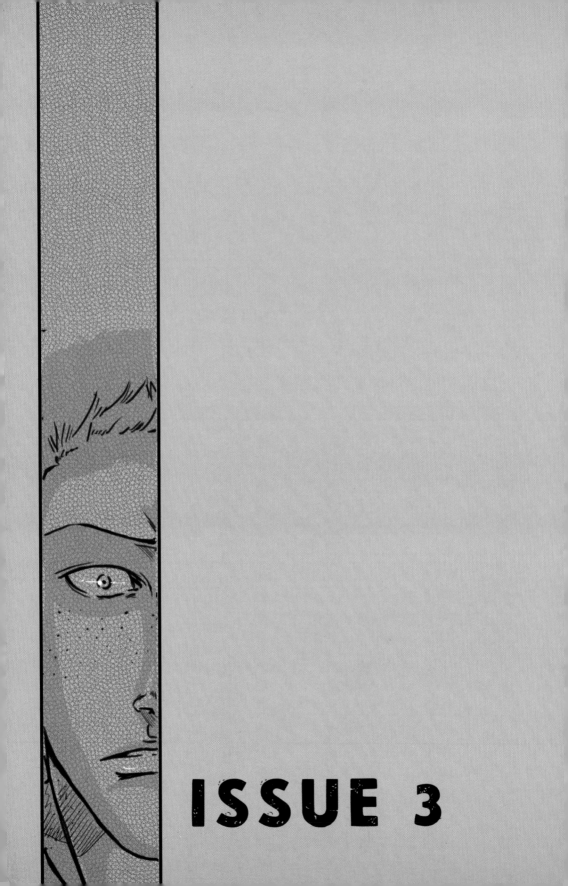

ISSUE 3

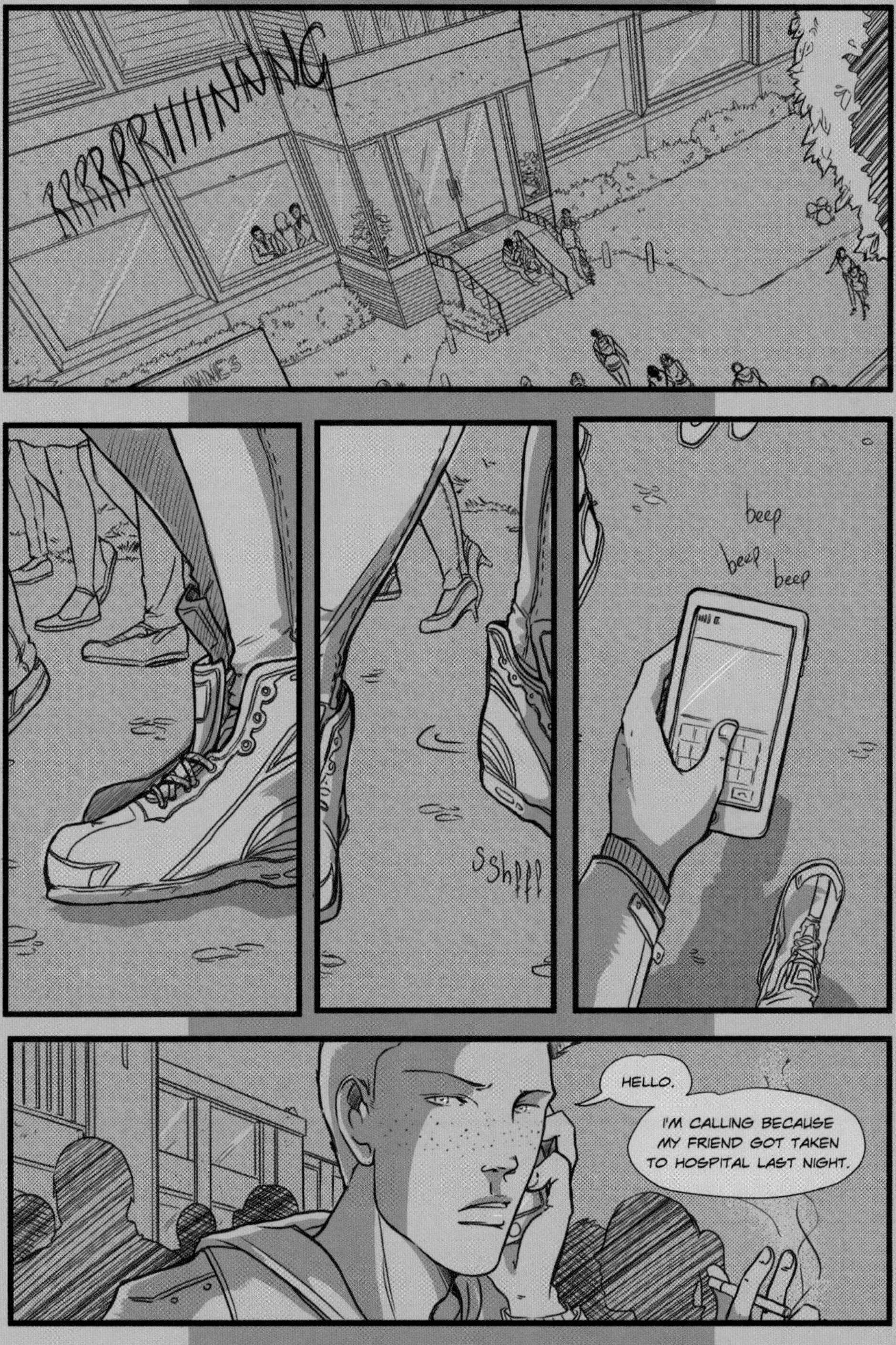
KRRRRRIIIINNNNG
beep
beep
beep
SShhhh
HELLO.
I'M CALLING BECAUSE MY FRIEND GOT TAKEN TO HOSPITAL LAST NIGHT.

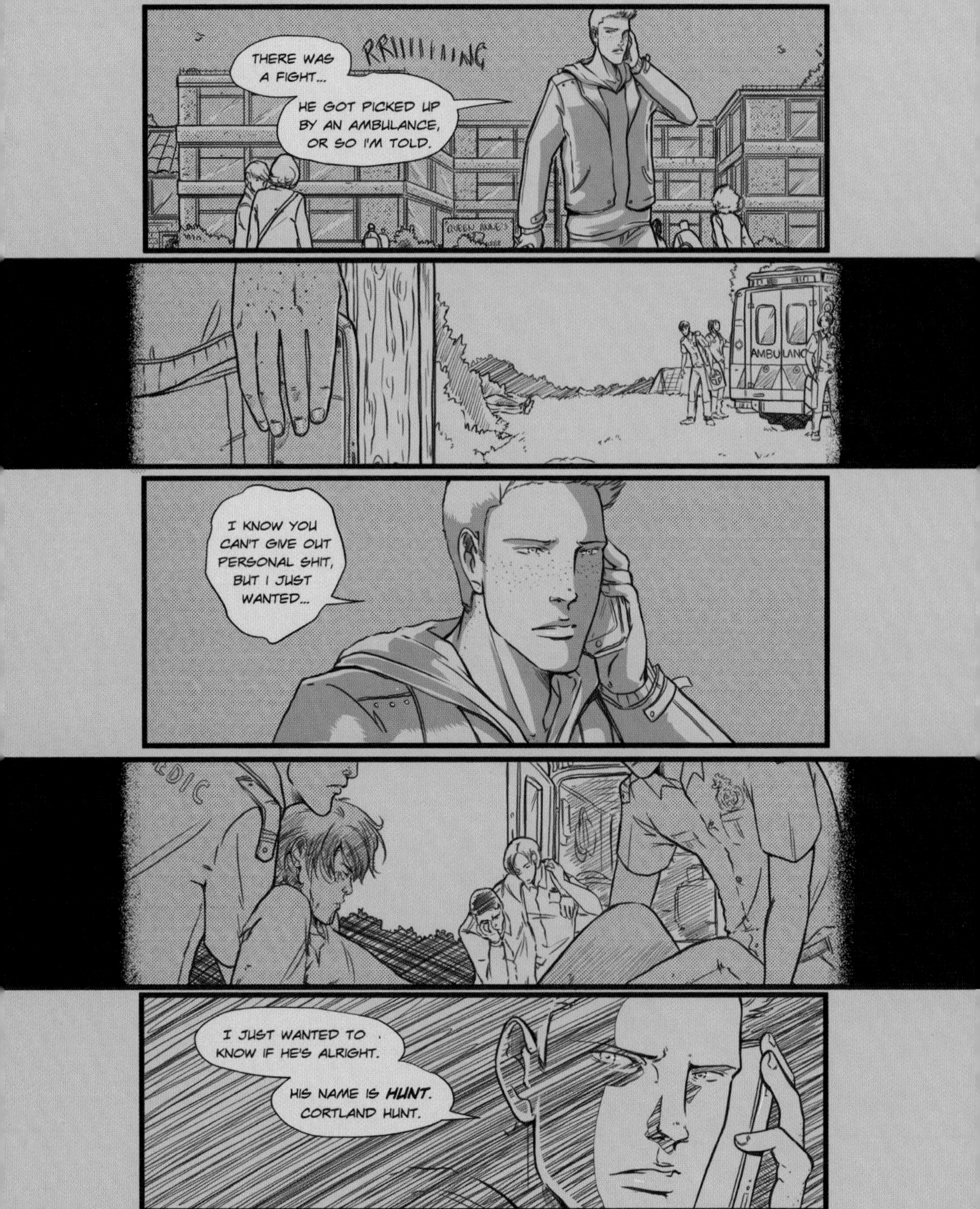
THERE WAS A FIGHT...
RRIIIIIING
HE GOT PICKED UP BY AN AMBULANCE, OR SO I'M TOLD.
AMBULANCE
I KNOW YOU CAN'T GIVE OUT PERSONAL SHIT, BUT I JUST WANTED...
I JUST WANTED TO KNOW IF HE'S ALRIGHT.
HIS NAME IS **HUNT**. CORTLAND HUNT.

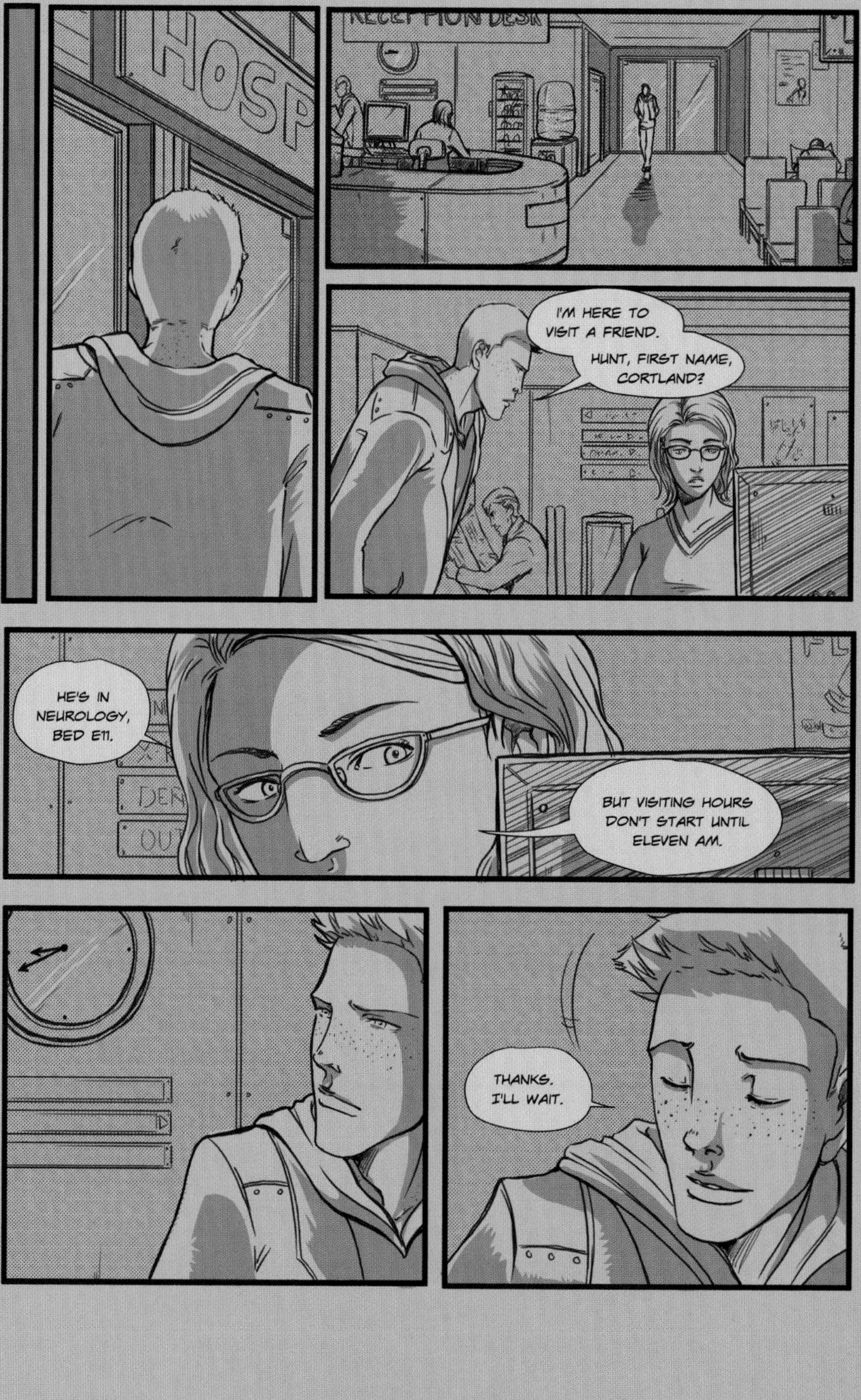
HOSP
RECEPTION DESK
I'M HERE TO VISIT A FRIEND.
HUNT, FIRST NAME, CORTLAND?
HE'S IN NEUROLOGY, BED E11.
BUT VISITING HOURS DON'T START UNTIL ELEVEN AM.
THANKS. I'LL WAIT.

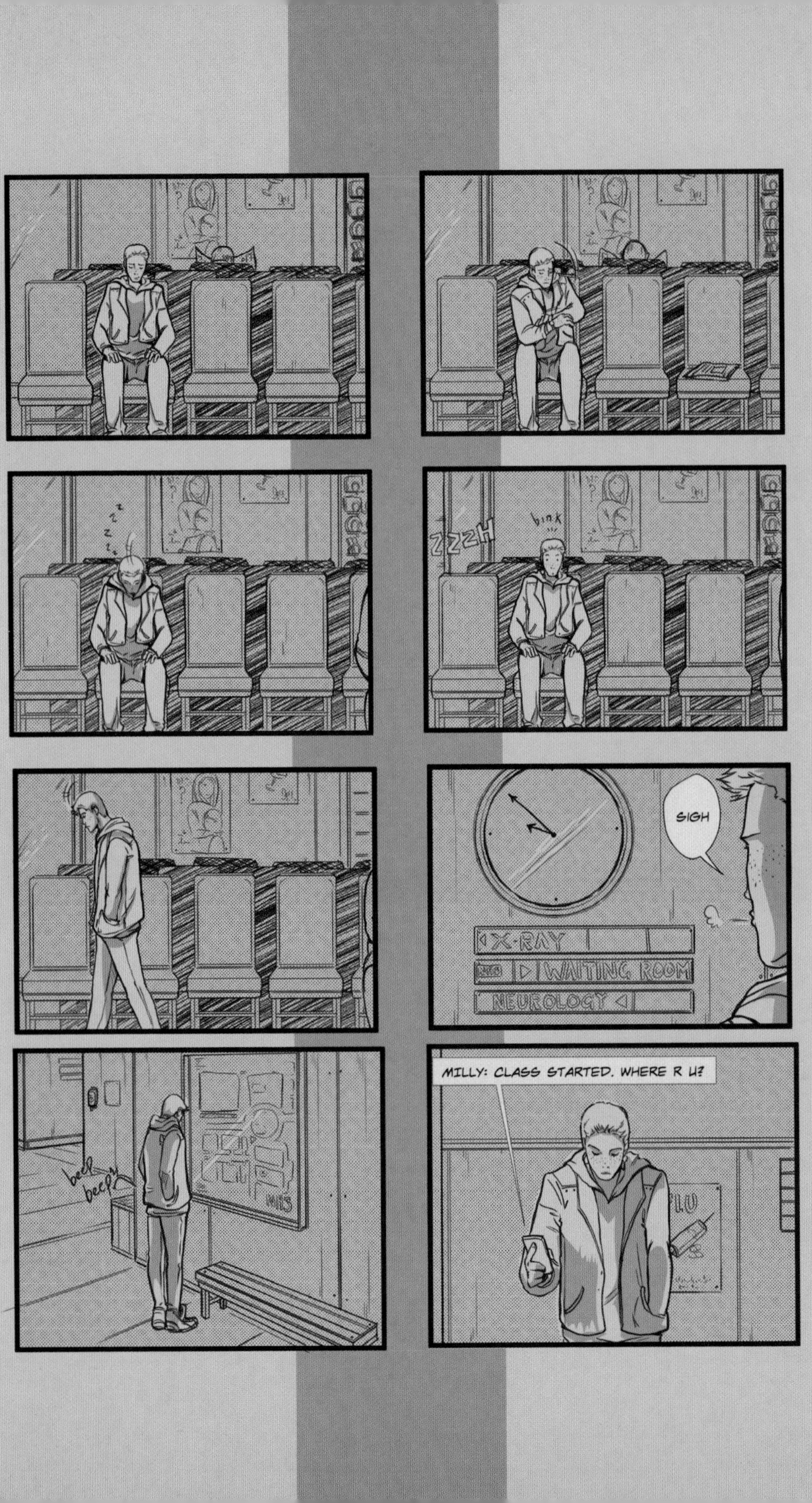
ZZZH
bink
SIGH
X-RAY
WAITING ROOM
NEUROLOGY
beep beep
MILLY: CLASS STARTED. WHERE R U?
FLU

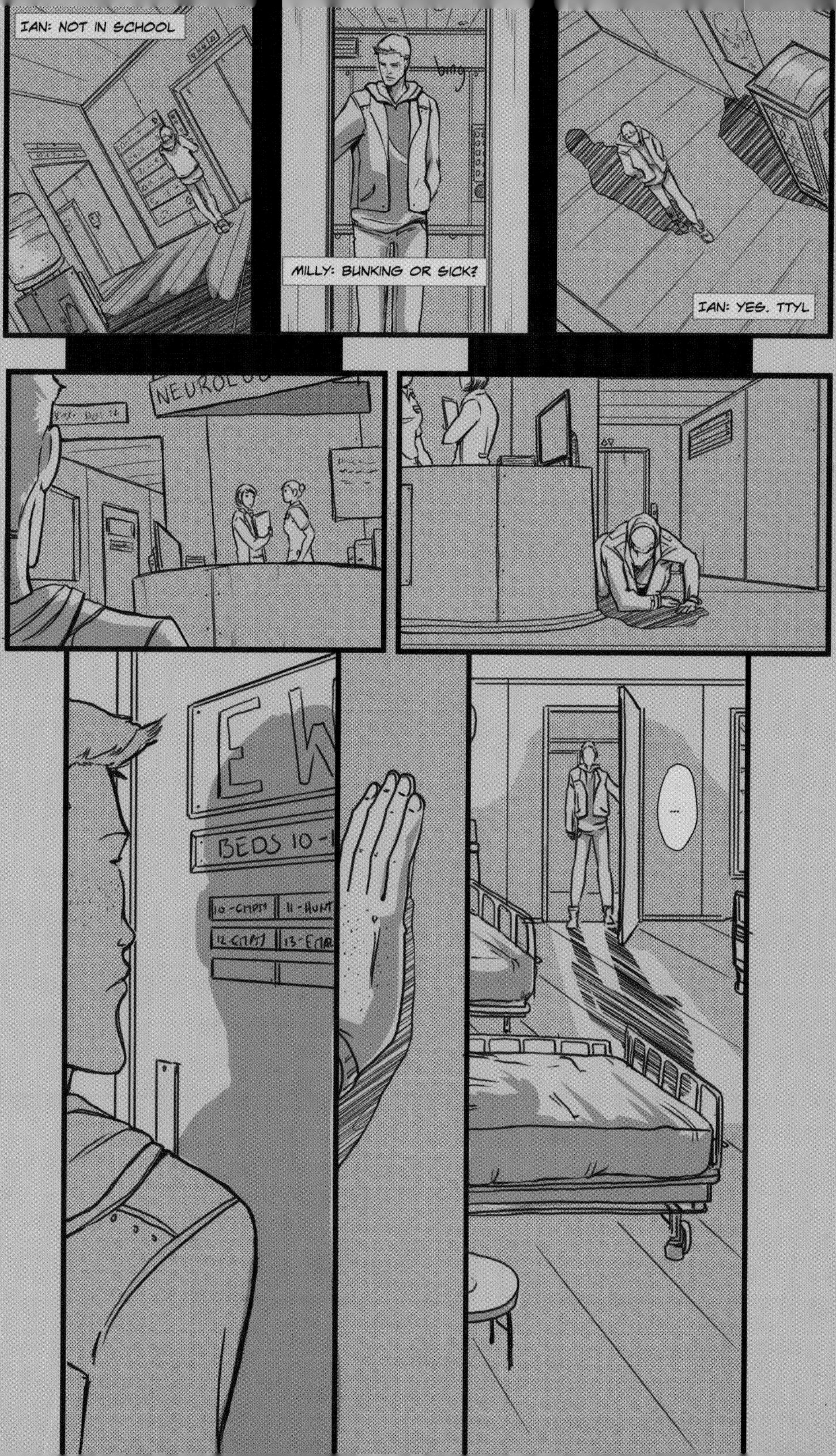
IAN: NOT IN SCHOOL
bing
MILLY: BUNKING OR SICK?
IAN: YES. TTYL
BEDS 10-
...

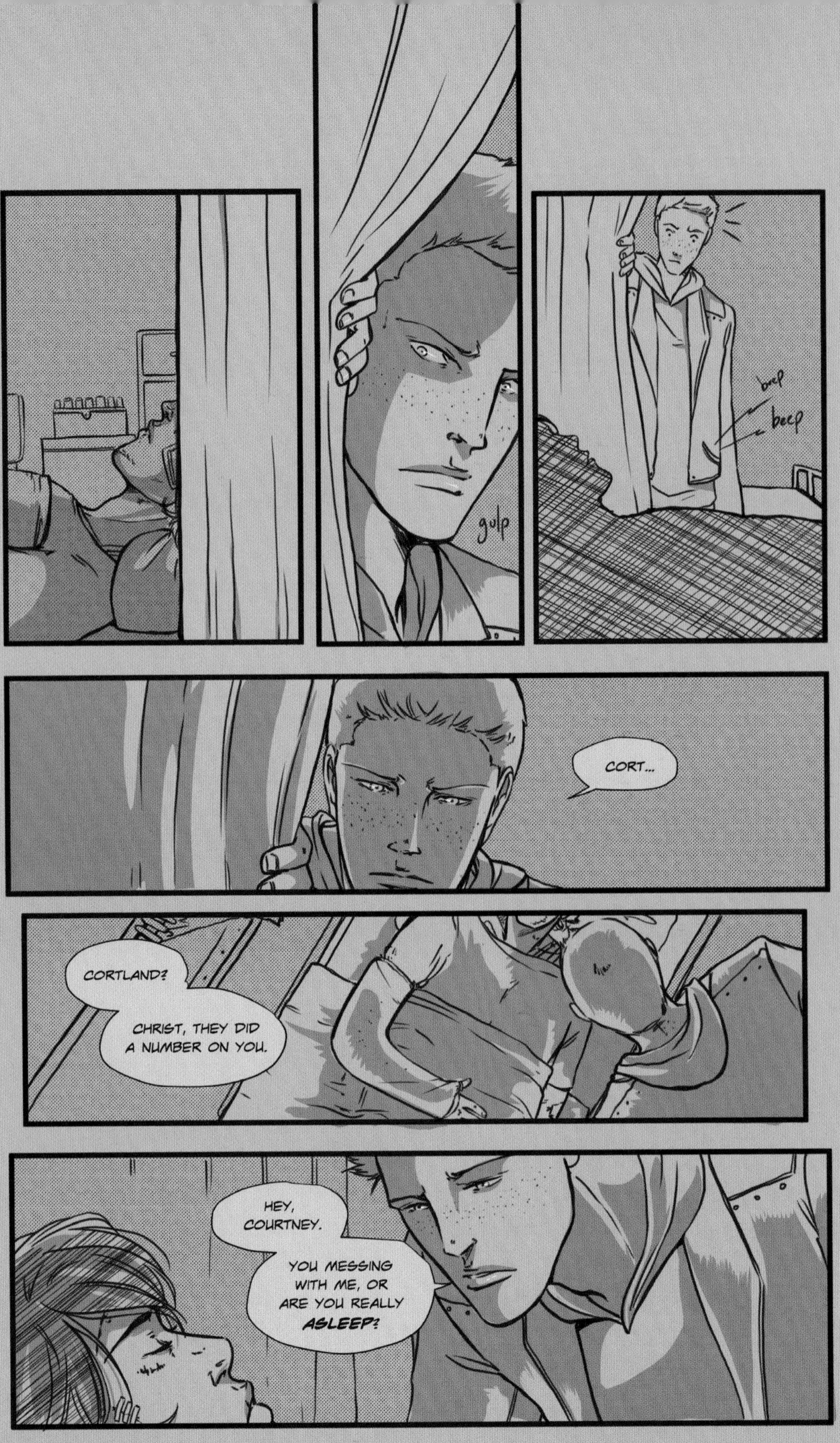
gulp
beep
beep
CORT...
CORTLAND?
CHRIST, THEY DID A NUMBER ON YOU.
HEY, COURTNEY.
YOU MESSING WITH ME, OR ARE YOU REALLY *ASLEEP*?

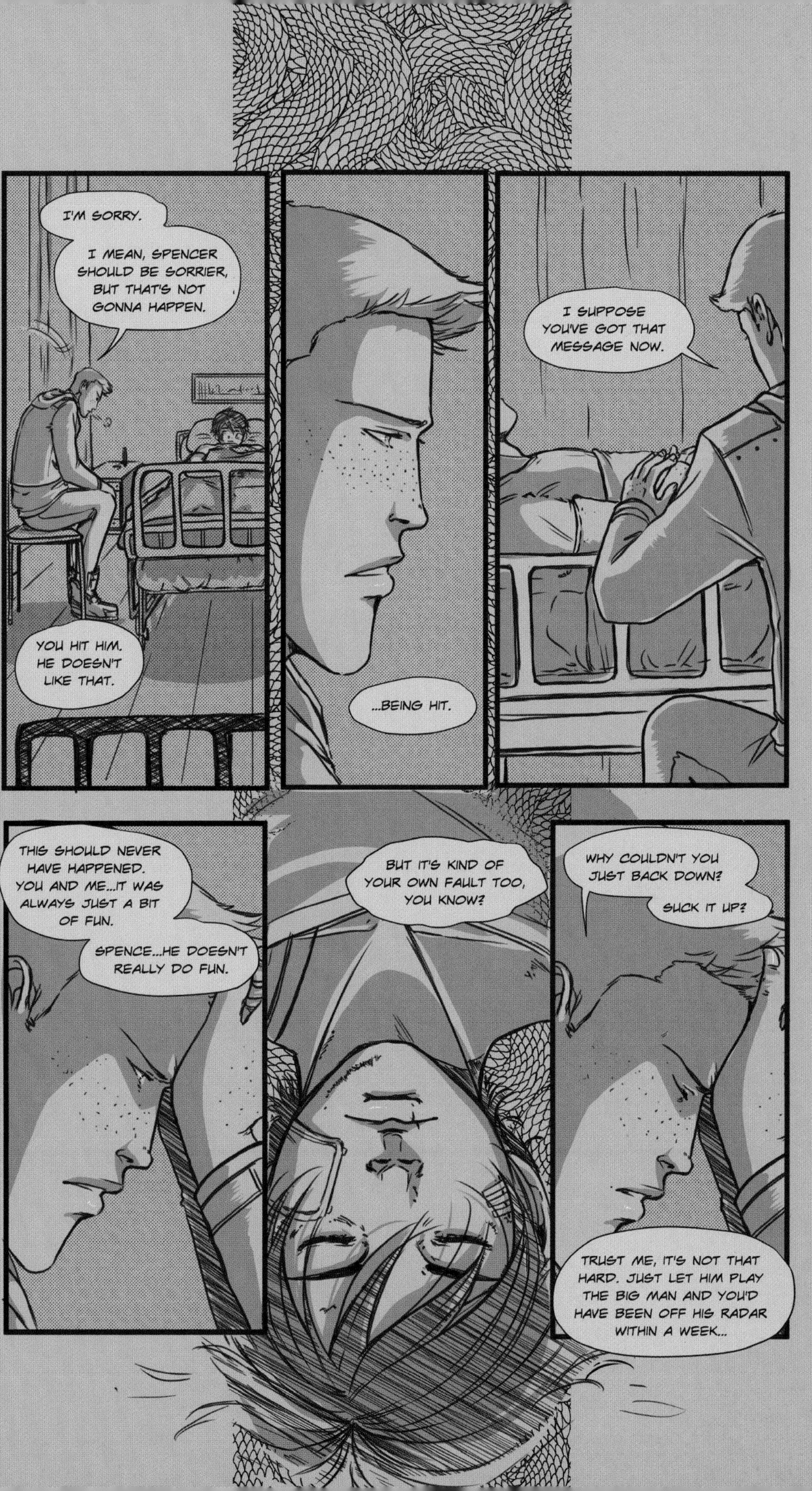
I'M SORRY.
I MEAN, SPENCER SHOULD BE SORRIER, BUT THAT'S NOT GONNA HAPPEN.
YOU HIT HIM. HE DOESN'T LIKE THAT.
...BEING HIT.
I SUPPOSE YOU'VE GOT THAT MESSAGE NOW.
THIS SHOULD NEVER HAVE HAPPENED. YOU AND ME...IT WAS ALWAYS JUST A BIT OF FUN.
SPENCE...HE DOESN'T REALLY DO FUN.
BUT IT'S KIND OF YOUR OWN FAULT TOO, YOU KNOW?
WHY COULDN'T YOU JUST BACK DOWN?
SUCK IT UP?
TRUST ME, IT'S NOT THAT HARD. JUST LET HIM PLAY THE BIG MAN AND YOU'D HAVE BEEN OFF HIS RADAR WITHIN A WEEK...

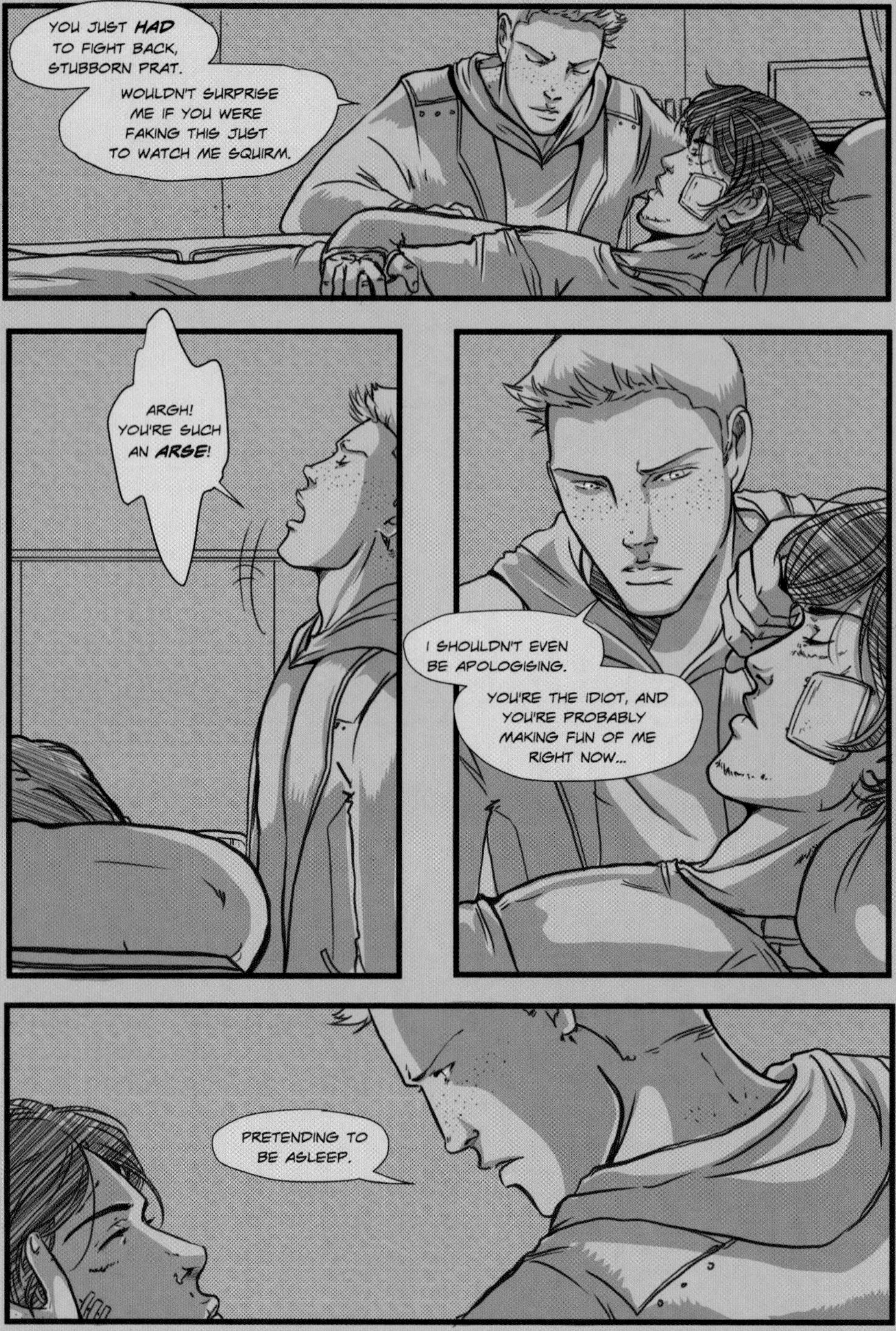
YOU JUST HAD TO FIGHT BACK, STUBBORN PRAT.
WOULDN'T SURPRISE ME IF YOU WERE FAKING THIS JUST TO WATCH ME SQUIRM.
ARGH! YOU'RE SUCH AN ARSE!
I SHOULDN'T EVEN BE APOLOGISING.
YOU'RE THE IDIOT, AND YOU'RE PROBABLY MAKING FUN OF ME RIGHT NOW...
PRETENDING TO BE ASLEEP.

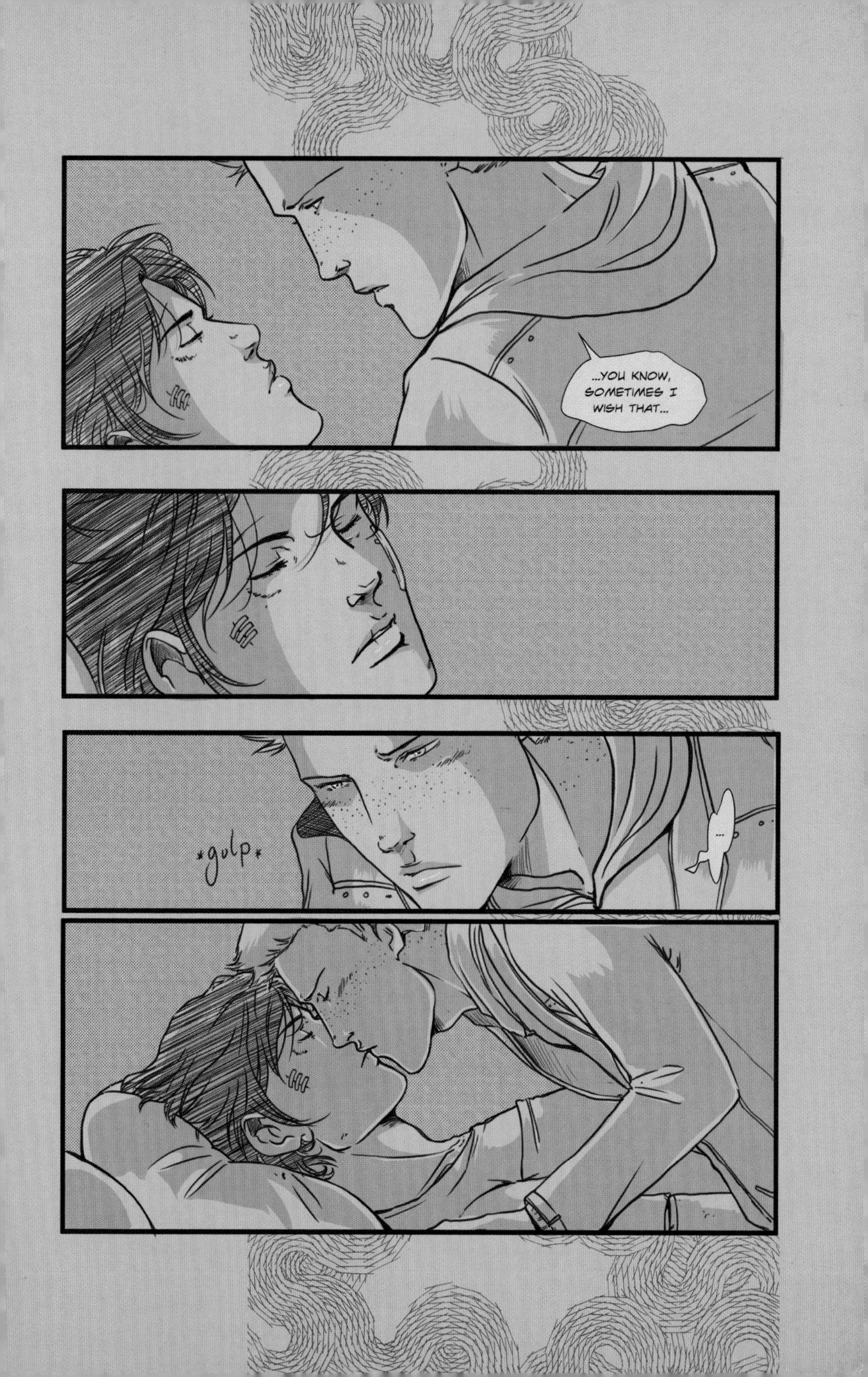
...YOU KNOW, SOMETIMES I WISH THAT...
gulp
...

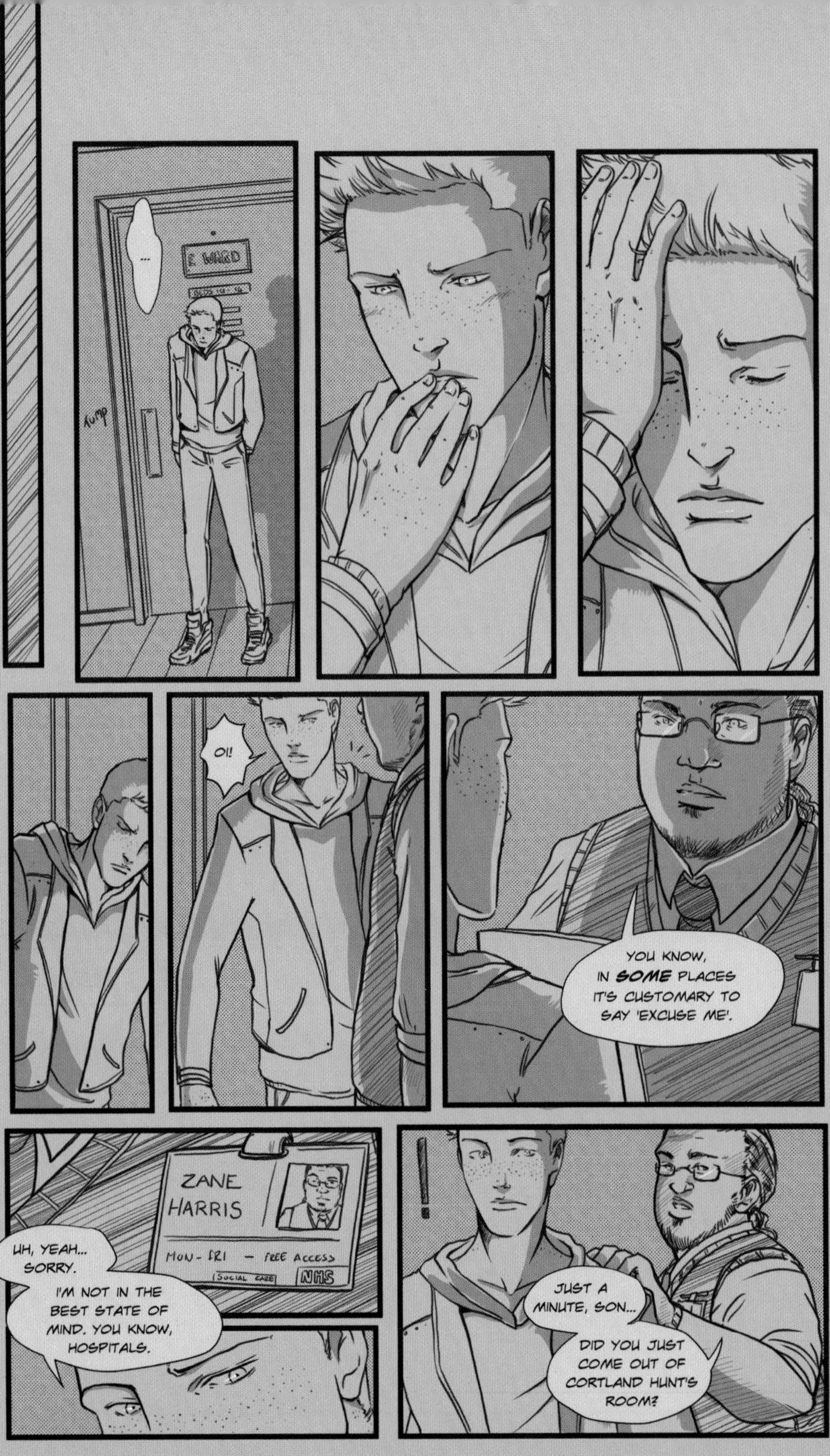
...
E WARD
OI!
YOU KNOW, IN SOME PLACES IT'S CUSTOMARY TO SAY 'EXCUSE ME'.
ZANE HARRIS
MON - FRI - FREE ACCESS
SOCIAL CARE
NHS
UH, YEAH... SORRY.
I'M NOT IN THE BEST STATE OF MIND. YOU KNOW, HOSPITALS.
!
JUST A MINUTE, SON...
DID YOU JUST COME OUT OF CORTLAND HUNT'S ROOM?

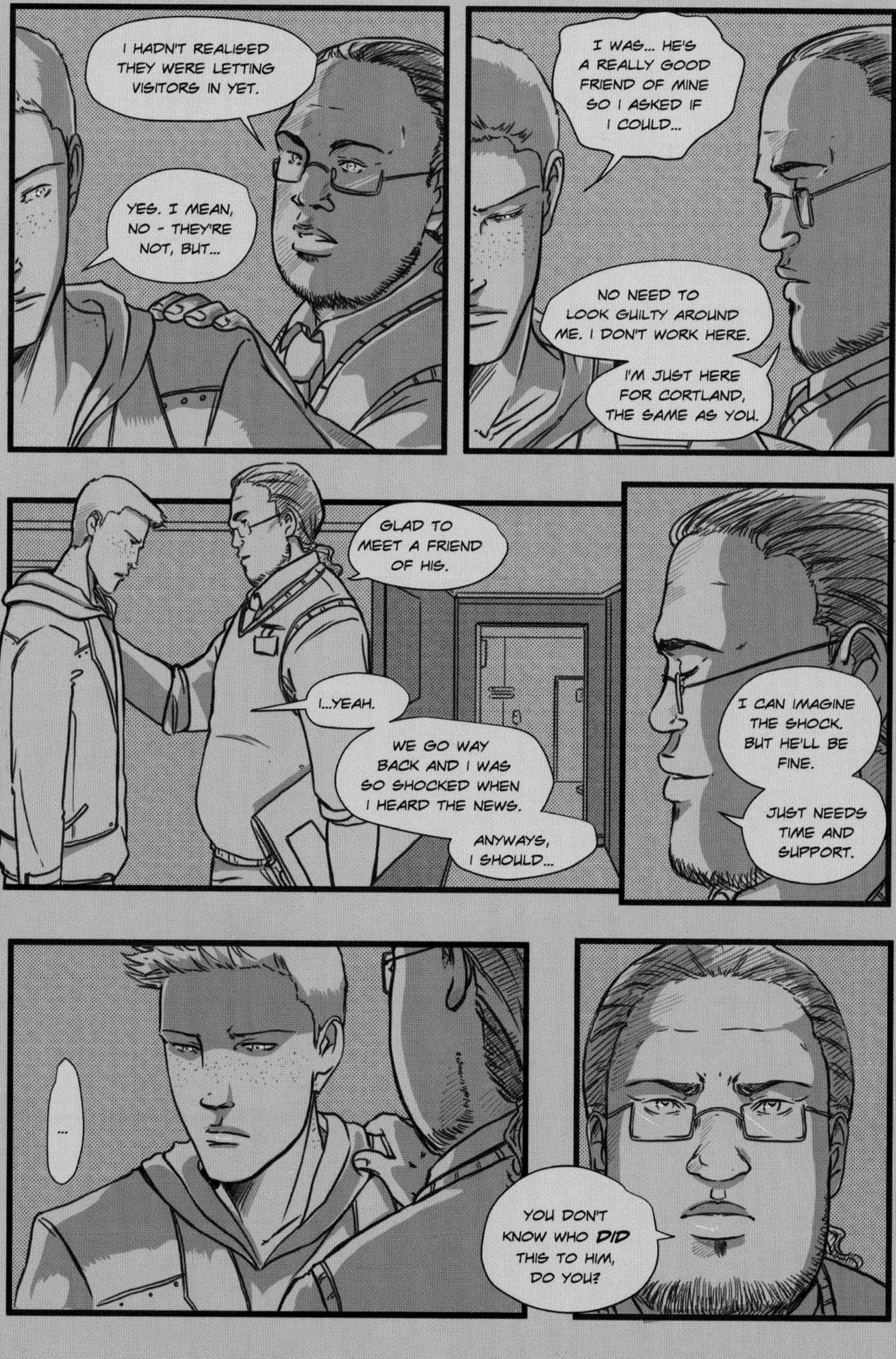
I HADN'T REALISED THEY WERE LETTING VISITORS IN YET.
YES. I MEAN, NO - THEY'RE NOT, BUT...
I WAS... HE'S A REALLY GOOD FRIEND OF MINE SO I ASKED IF I COULD...
NO NEED TO LOOK GUILTY AROUND ME. I DON'T WORK HERE.
I'M JUST HERE FOR CORTLAND, THE SAME AS YOU.
GLAD TO MEET A FRIEND OF HIS.
I...YEAH.
WE GO WAY BACK AND I WAS SO SHOCKED WHEN I HEARD THE NEWS.
ANYWAYS, I SHOULD...
I CAN IMAGINE THE SHOCK. BUT HE'LL BE FINE.
JUST NEEDS TIME AND SUPPORT.
...
YOU DON'T KNOW WHO **DID** THIS TO HIM, DO YOU?

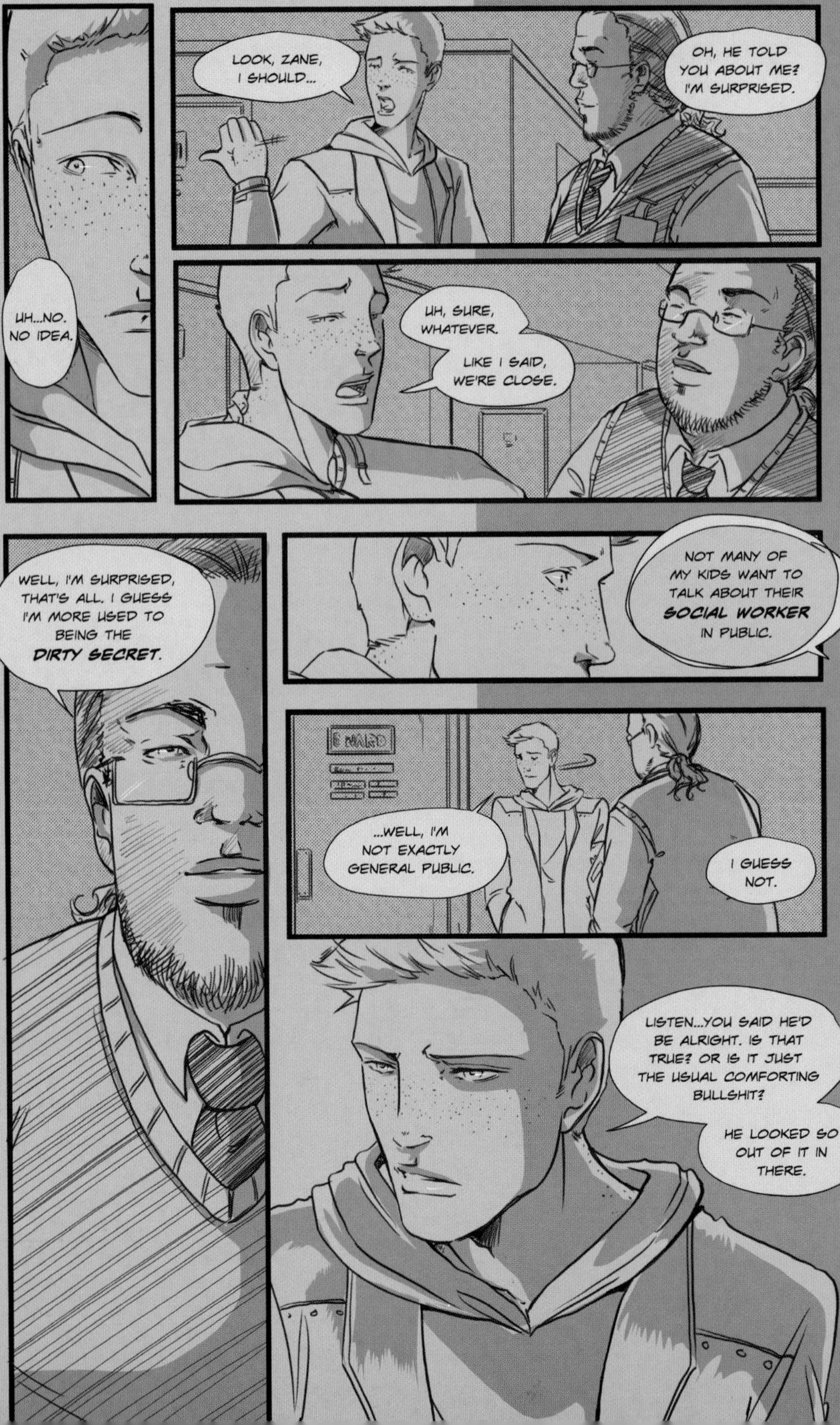
LOOK, ZANE, I SHOULD...
OH, HE TOLD YOU ABOUT ME? I'M SURPRISED.
UH...NO. NO IDEA.
UH, SURE, WHATEVER.
LIKE I SAID, WE'RE CLOSE.
WELL, I'M SURPRISED, THAT'S ALL. I GUESS I'M MORE USED TO BEING THE DIRTY SECRET.
NOT MANY OF MY KIDS WANT TO TALK ABOUT THEIR SOCIAL WORKER IN PUBLIC.
...WELL, I'M NOT EXACTLY GENERAL PUBLIC.
I GUESS NOT.
LISTEN...YOU SAID HE'D BE ALRIGHT. IS THAT TRUE? OR IS IT JUST THE USUAL COMFORTING BULLSHIT?
HE LOOKED SO OUT OF IT IN THERE.

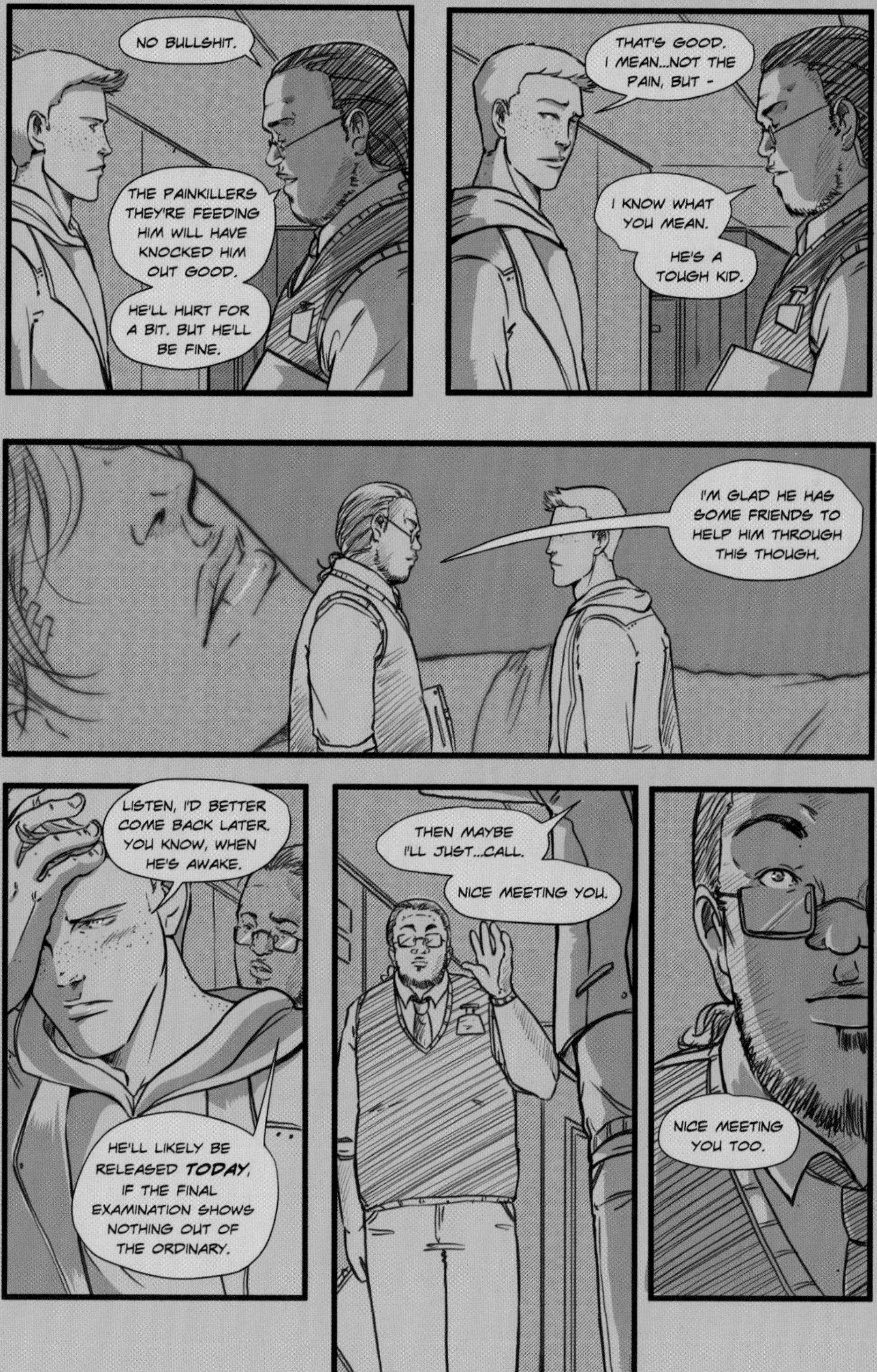
NO BULLSHIT.
THE PAINKILLERS THEY'RE FEEDING HIM WILL HAVE KNOCKED HIM OUT GOOD.
HE'LL HURT FOR A BIT. BUT HE'LL BE FINE.
THAT'S GOOD. I MEAN...NOT THE PAIN, BUT -
I KNOW WHAT YOU MEAN.
HE'S A TOUGH KID.
I'M GLAD HE HAS SOME FRIENDS TO HELP HIM THROUGH THIS THOUGH.
LISTEN, I'D BETTER COME BACK LATER. YOU KNOW, WHEN HE'S AWAKE.
HE'LL LIKELY BE RELEASED TODAY, IF THE FINAL EXAMINATION SHOWS NOTHING OUT OF THE ORDINARY.
THEN MAYBE I'LL JUST...CALL.
NICE MEETING YOU.
NICE MEETING YOU TOO.

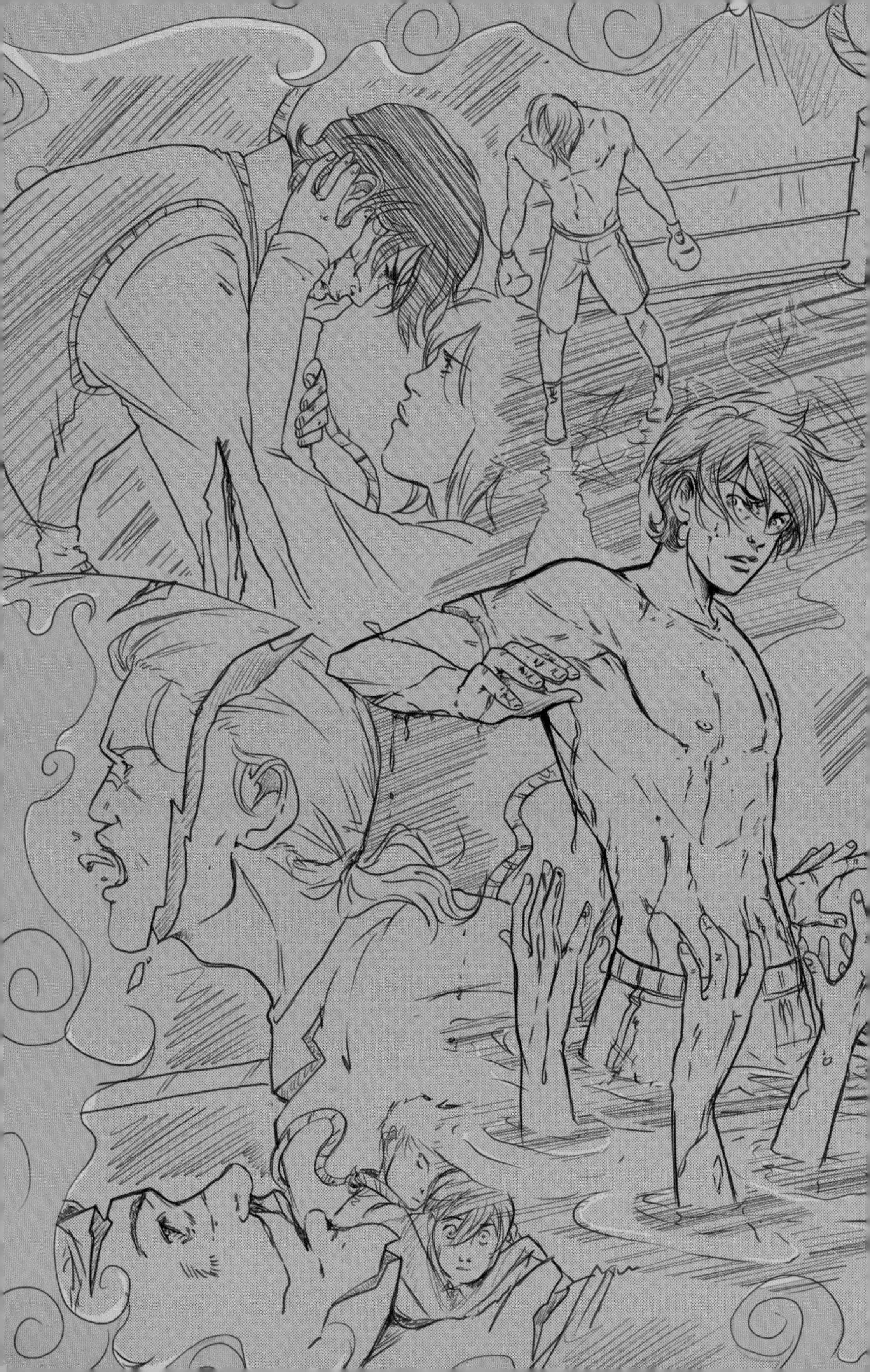

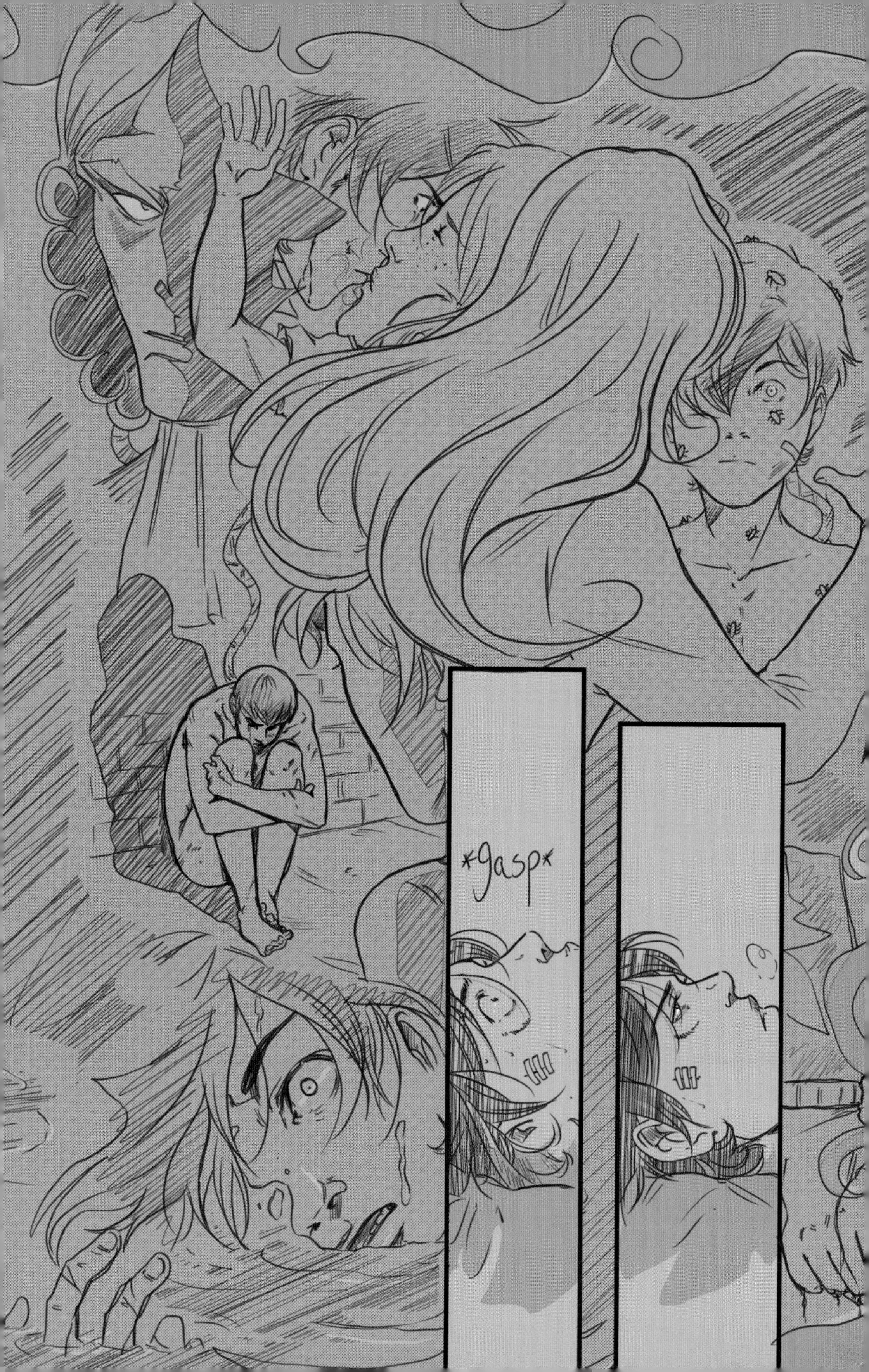
gasp

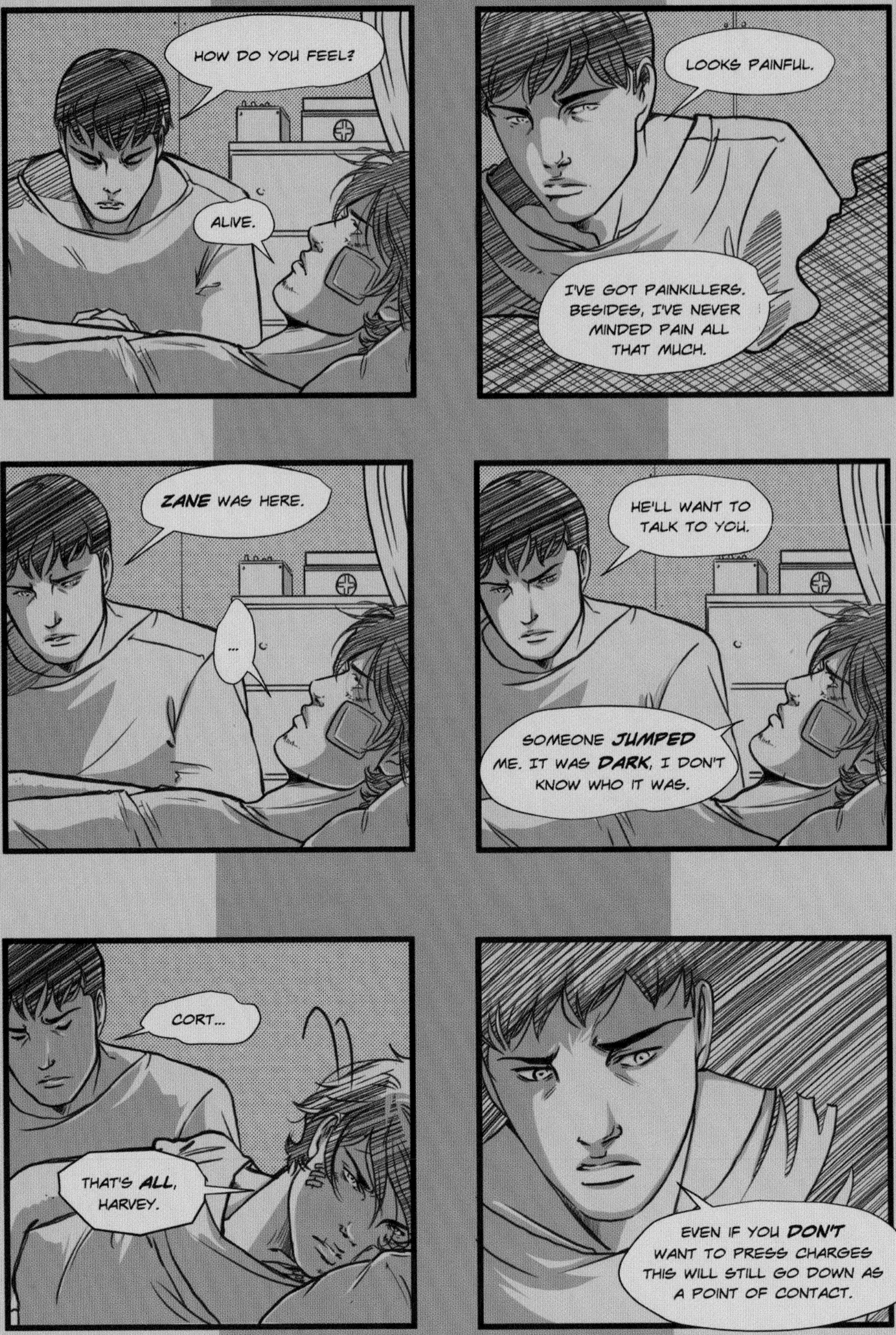
HOW DO YOU FEEL?
ALIVE.
LOOKS PAINFUL.
I'VE GOT PAINKILLERS. BESIDES, I'VE NEVER MINDED PAIN ALL THAT MUCH.
ZANE WAS HERE.
...
HE'LL WANT TO TALK TO YOU.
SOMEONE JUMPED ME. IT WAS DARK, I DON'T KNOW WHO IT WAS.
CORT...
THAT'S ALL, HARVEY.
EVEN IF YOU DON'T WANT TO PRESS CHARGES THIS WILL STILL GO DOWN AS A POINT OF CONTACT.

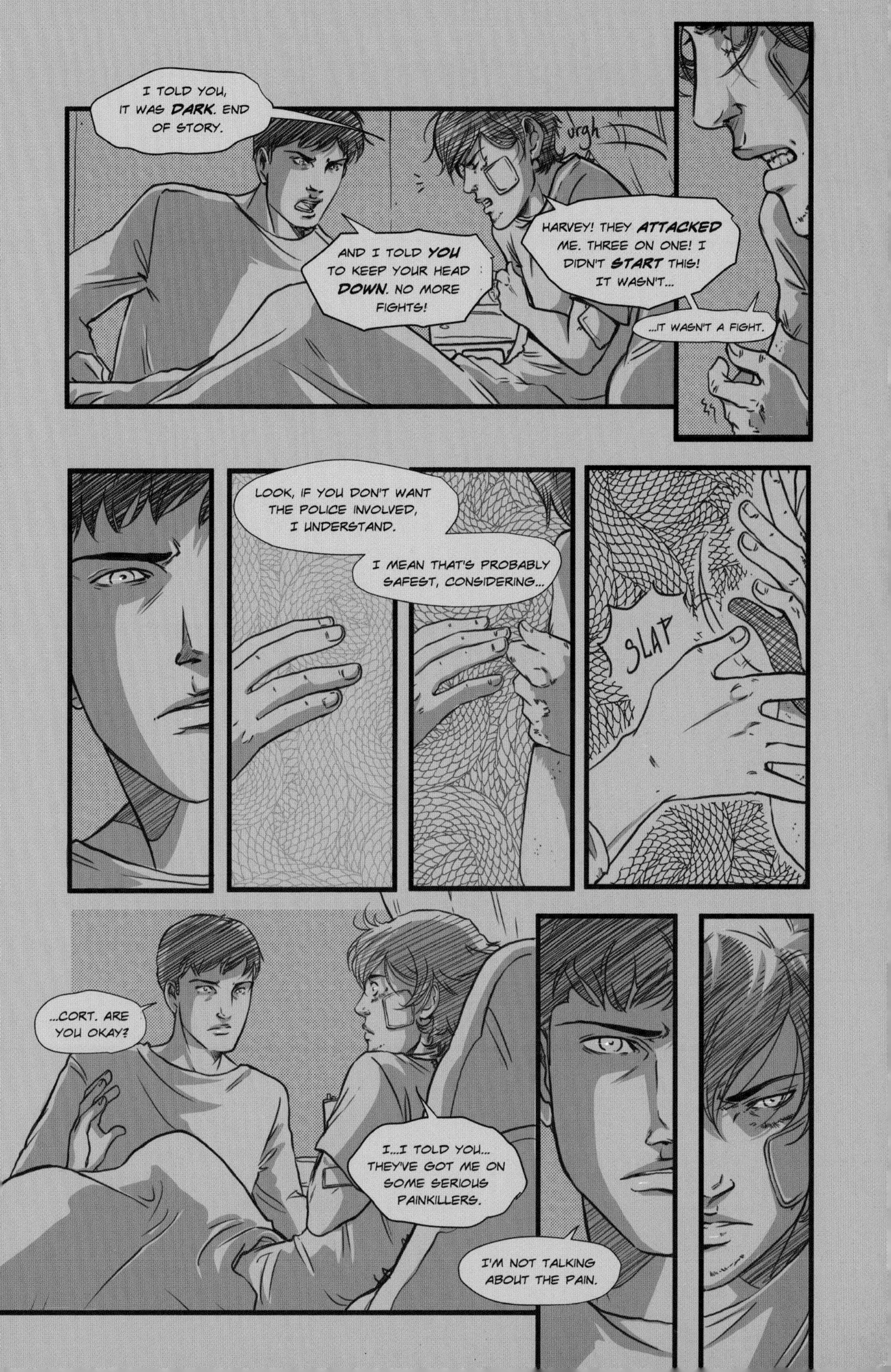
I TOLD YOU, IT WAS DARK. END OF STORY.
AND I TOLD YOU TO KEEP YOUR HEAD DOWN. NO MORE FIGHTS!
urgh
HARVEY! THEY ATTACKED ME. THREE ON ONE! I DIDN'T START THIS! IT WASN'T...
...IT WASN'T A FIGHT.
LOOK, IF YOU DON'T WANT THE POLICE INVOLVED, I UNDERSTAND.
I MEAN THAT'S PROBABLY SAFEST, CONSIDERING...
SLAP
...CORT. ARE YOU OKAY?
I...I TOLD YOU... THEY'VE GOT ME ON SOME SERIOUS PAINKILLERS.
I'M NOT TALKING ABOUT THE PAIN.

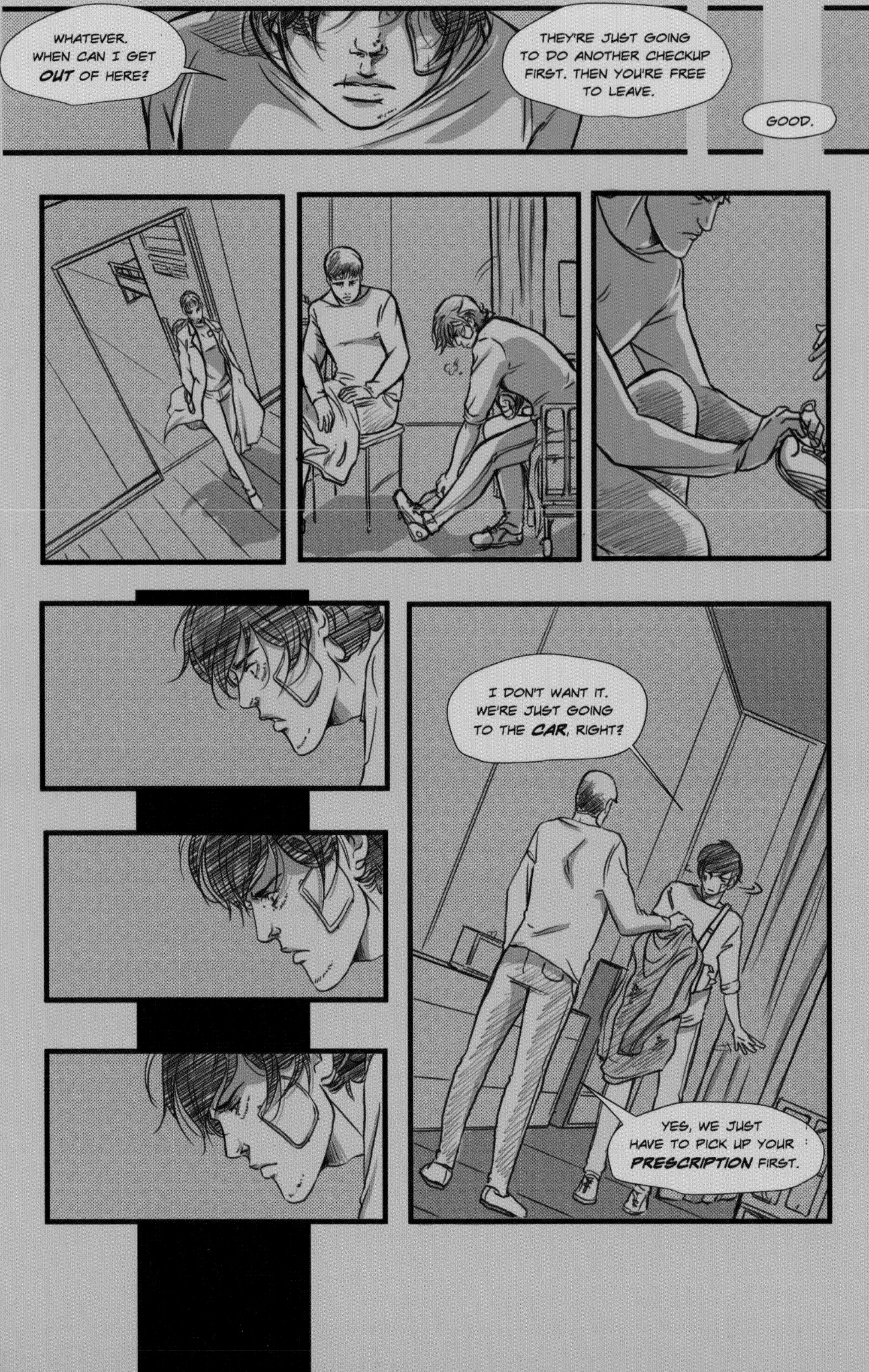
WHATEVER. WHEN CAN I GET OUT OF HERE?
THEY'RE JUST GOING TO DO ANOTHER CHECKUP FIRST. THEN YOU'RE FREE TO LEAVE.
GOOD.
I DON'T WANT IT. WE'RE JUST GOING TO THE CAR, RIGHT?
YES, WE JUST HAVE TO PICK UP YOUR PRESCRIPTION FIRST.

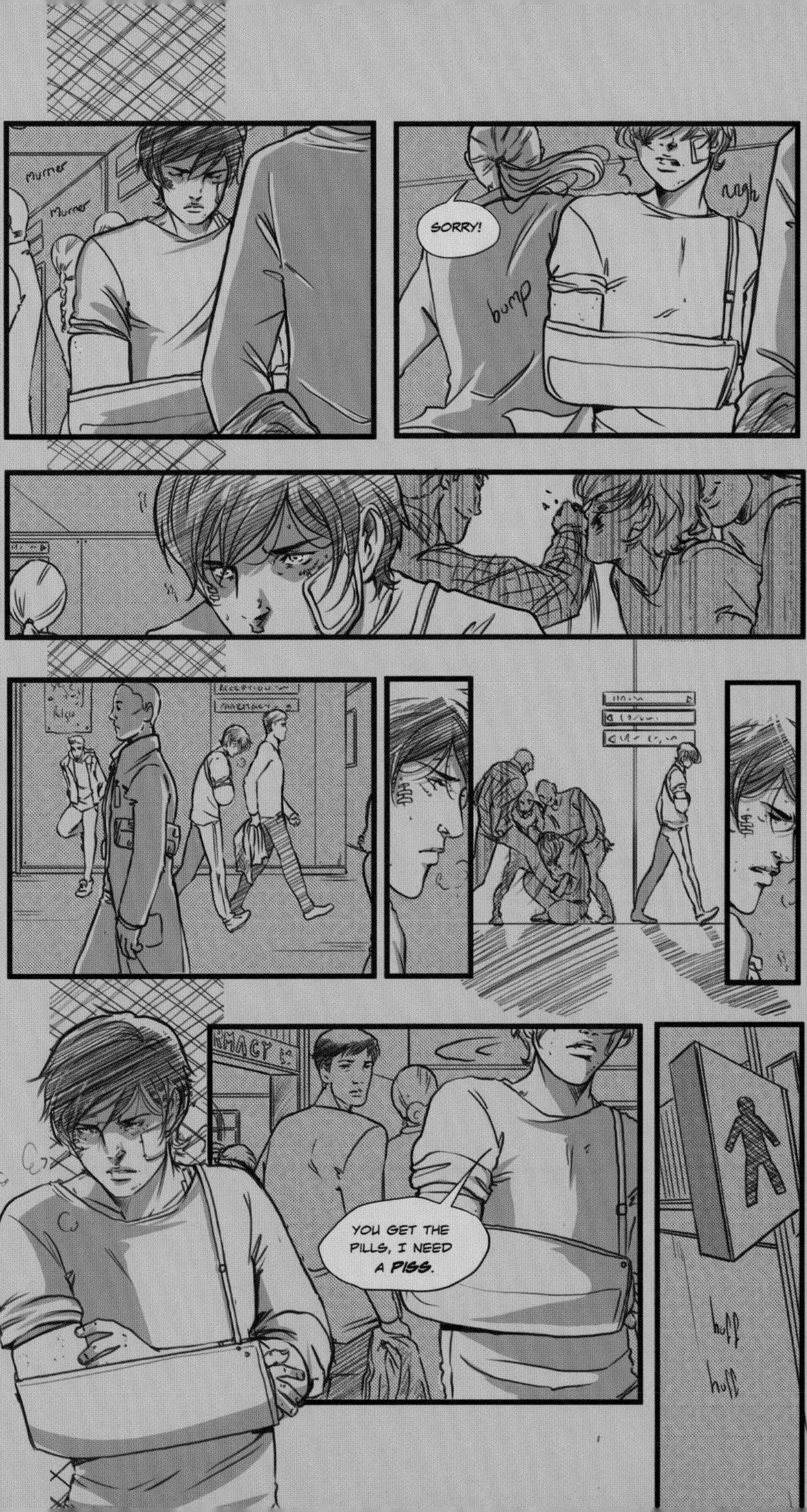
Murmer
Murmer
SORRY!
bump
nngh
YOU GET THE PILLS, I NEED A PISS.
huff
huff

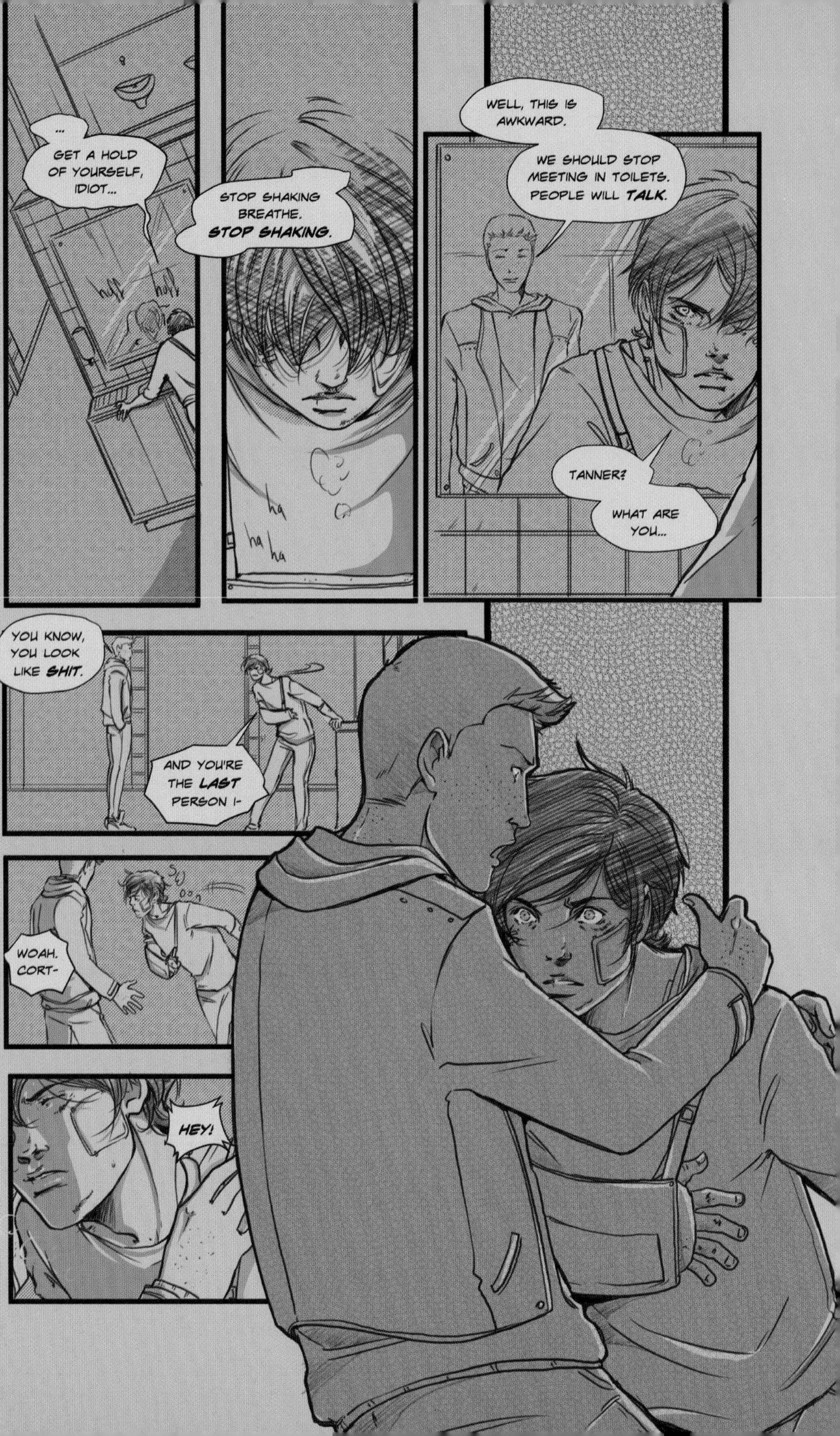

...
GET A HOLD OF YOURSELF, IDIOT...
huff huff
STOP SHAKING BREATHE. STOP SHAKING.
ha ha ha ha
WELL, THIS IS AWKWARD.
WE SHOULD STOP MEETING IN TOILETS. PEOPLE WILL TALK.
TANNER?
WHAT ARE YOU...
YOU KNOW, YOU LOOK LIKE SHIT.
AND YOU'RE THE LAST PERSON I-
WOAH. CORT-
HEY!

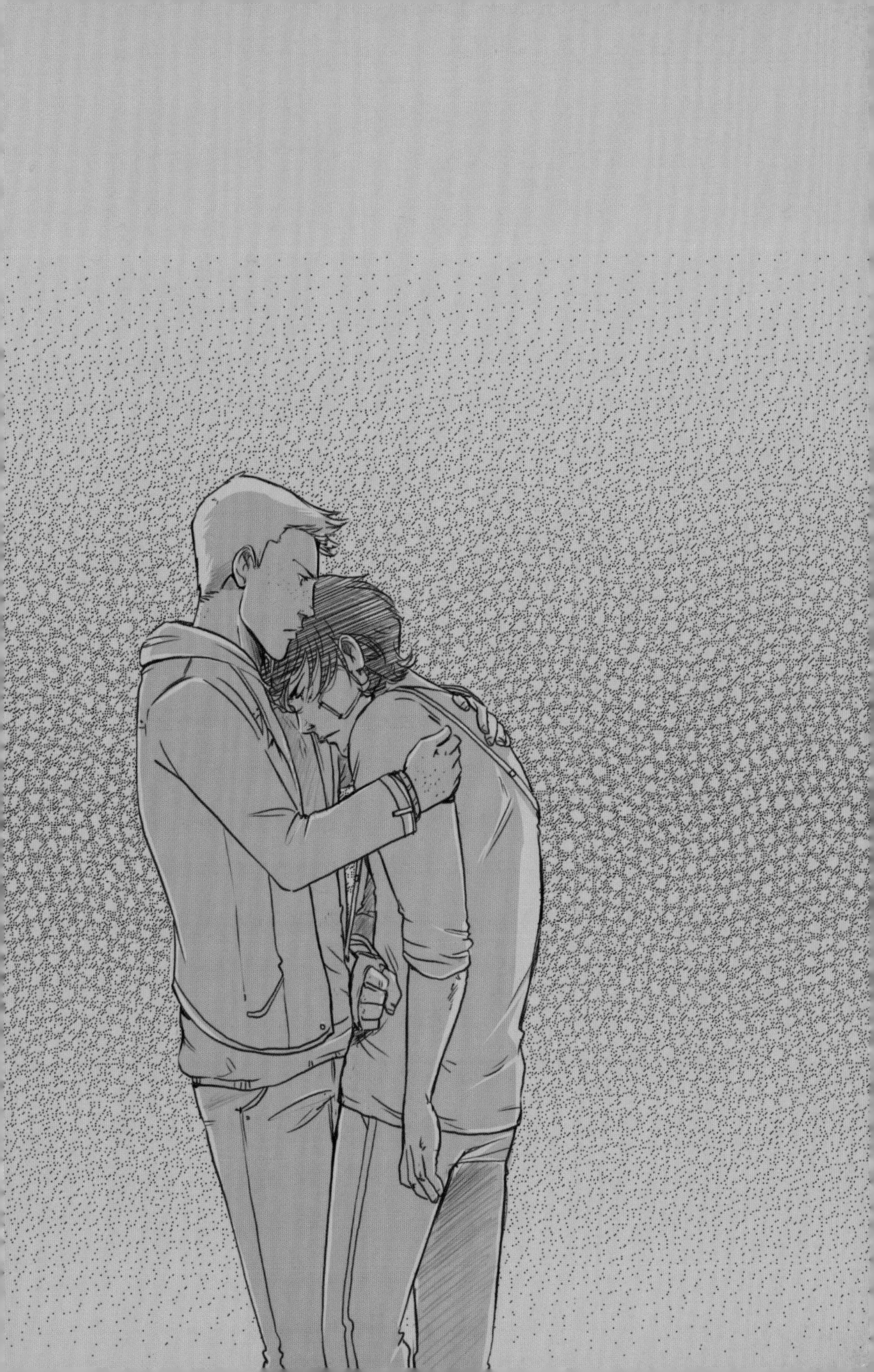

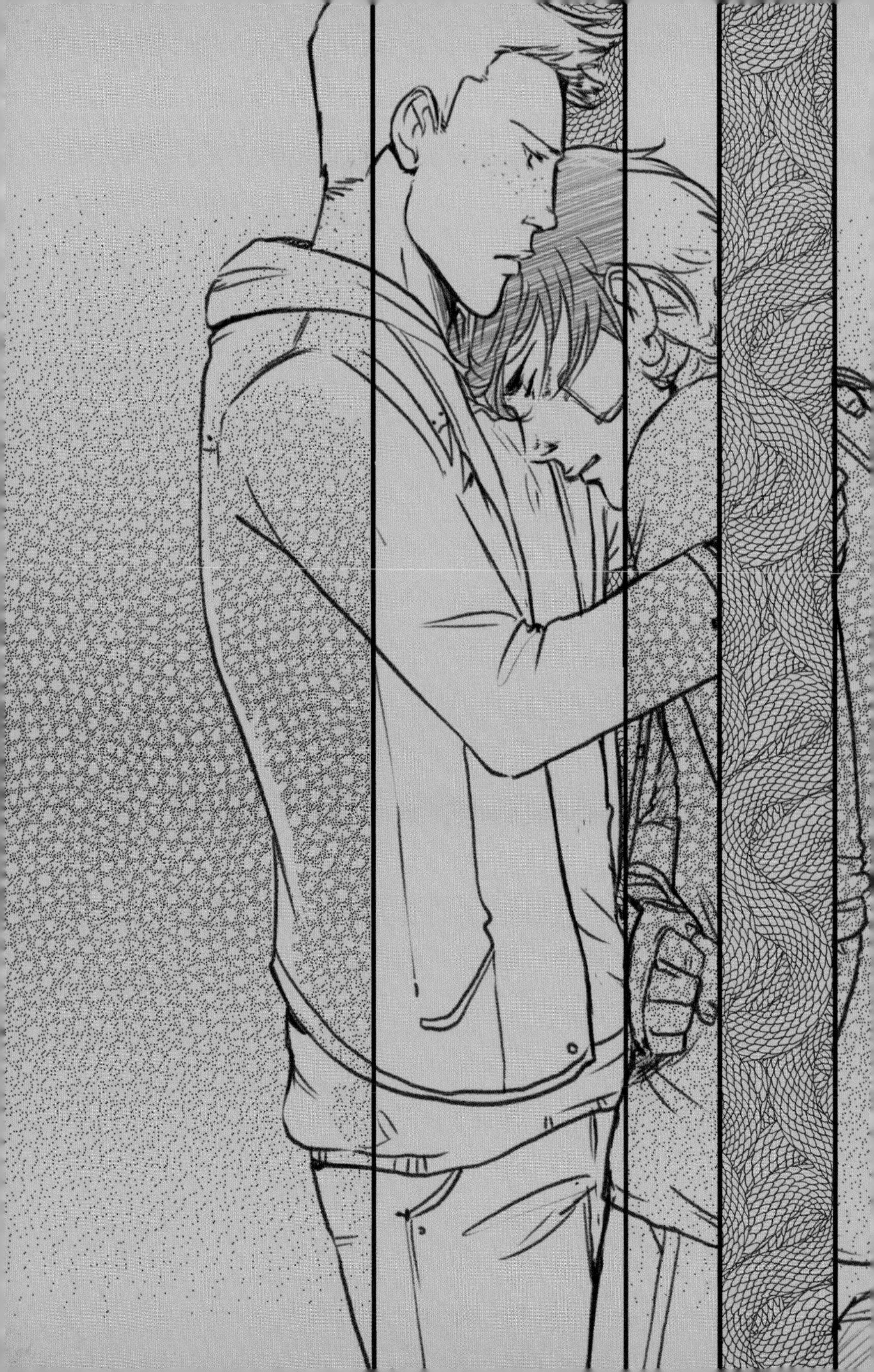

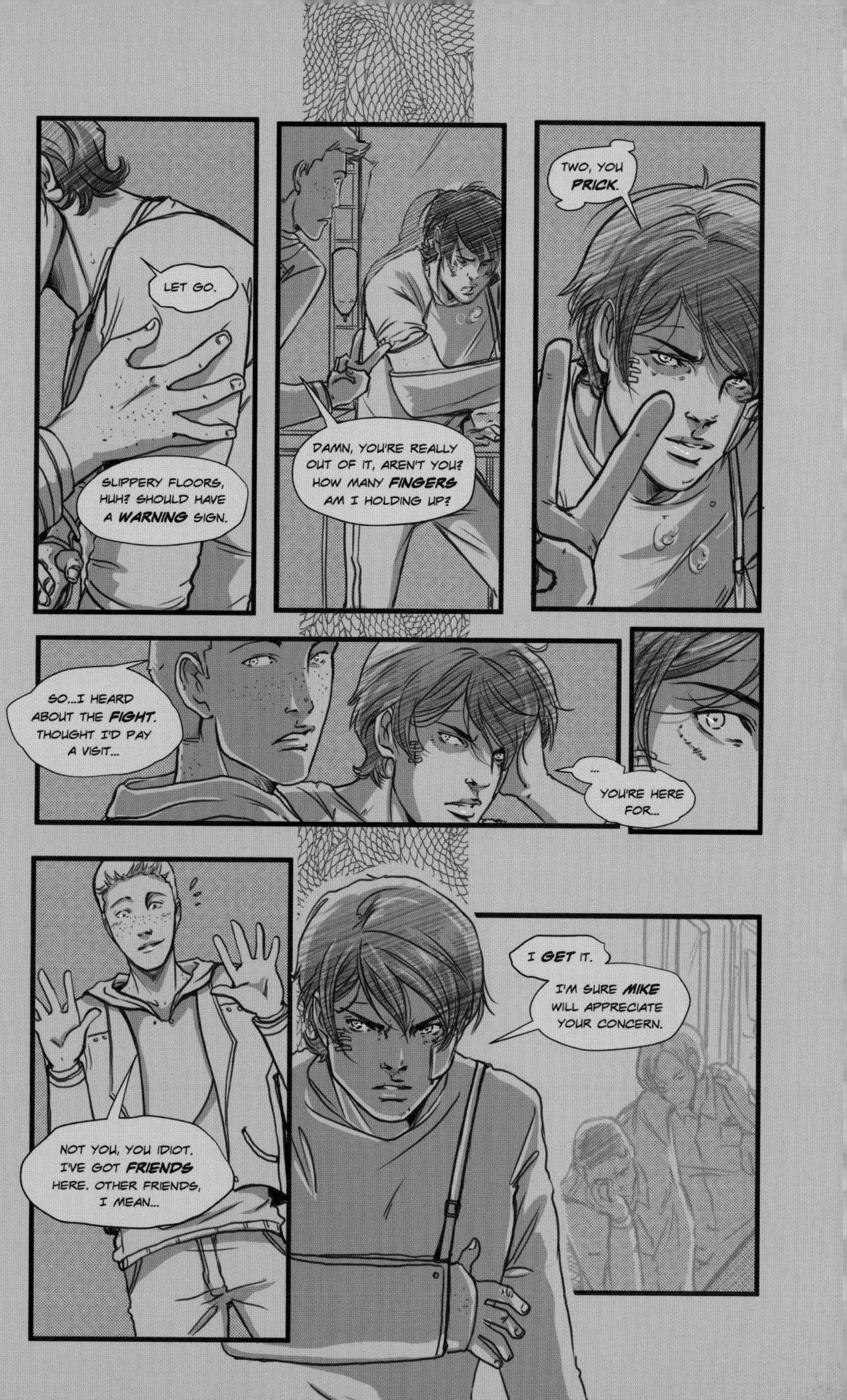
LET GO.
SLIPPERY FLOORS, HUH? SHOULD HAVE A WARNING SIGN.
DAMN, YOU'RE REALLY OUT OF IT, AREN'T YOU? HOW MANY FINGERS AM I HOLDING UP?
TWO, YOU PRICK.
SO...I HEARD ABOUT THE FIGHT. THOUGHT I'D PAY A VISIT...
... YOU'RE HERE FOR...
I GET IT.
I'M SURE MIKE WILL APPRECIATE YOUR CONCERN.
NOT YOU, YOU IDIOT. I'VE GOT FRIENDS HERE. OTHER FRIENDS, I MEAN...

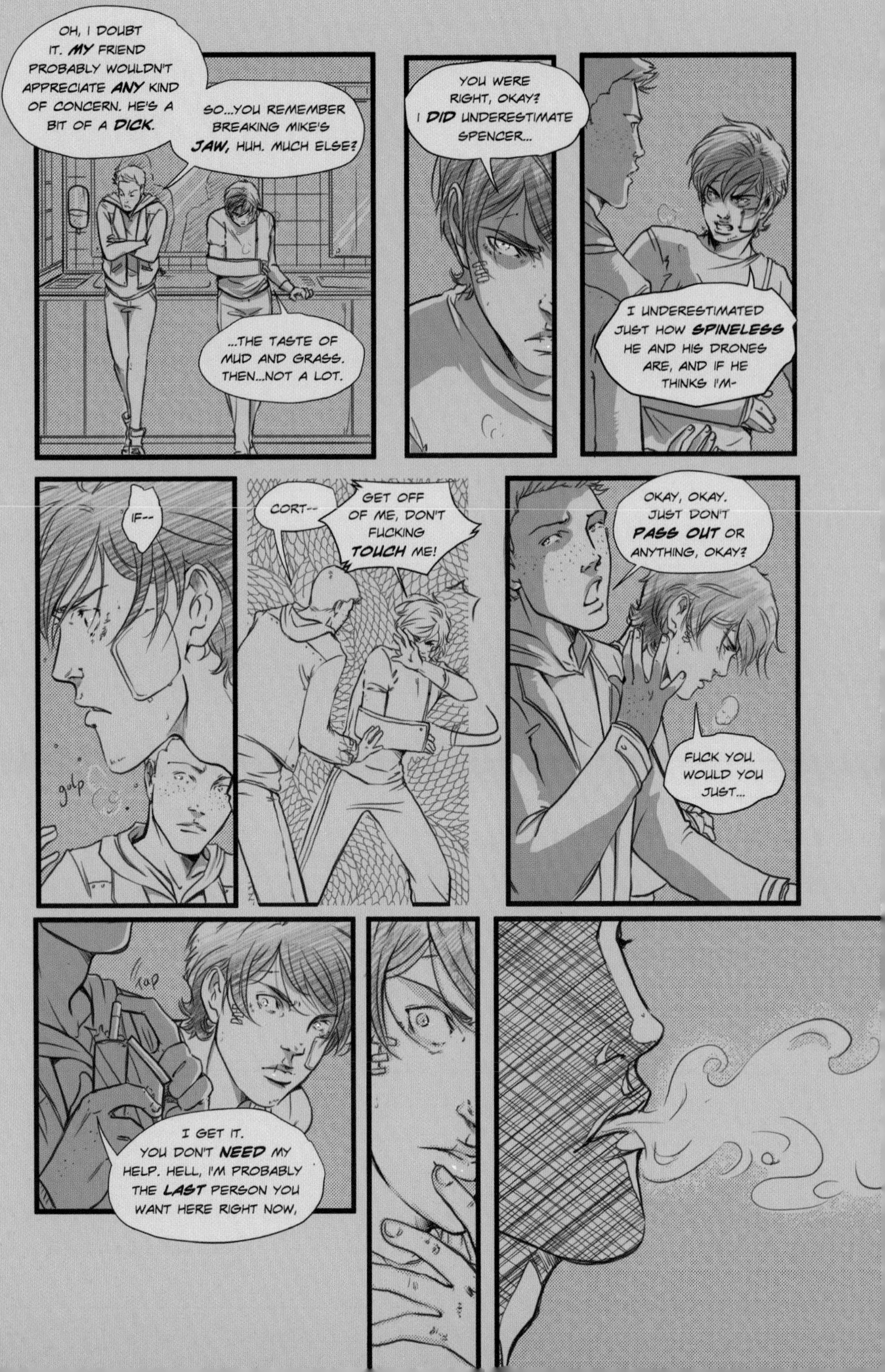
OH, I DOUBT IT. MY FRIEND PROBABLY WOULDN'T APPRECIATE ANY KIND OF CONCERN. HE'S A BIT OF A DICK.
SO...YOU REMEMBER BREAKING MIKE'S JAW, HUH. MUCH ELSE?
...THE TASTE OF MUD AND GRASS. THEN...NOT A LOT.
YOU WERE RIGHT, OKAY? I DID UNDERESTIMATE SPENCER...
I UNDERESTIMATED JUST HOW SPINELESS HE AND HIS DRONES ARE, AND IF HE THINKS I'M-
IF--
gulp
CORT--
GET OFF OF ME, DON'T FUCKING TOUCH ME!
OKAY, OKAY. JUST DON'T PASS OUT OR ANYTHING, OKAY?
FUCK YOU. WOULD YOU JUST...
tap
I GET IT. YOU DON'T NEED MY HELP. HELL, I'M PROBABLY THE LAST PERSON YOU WANT HERE RIGHT NOW,

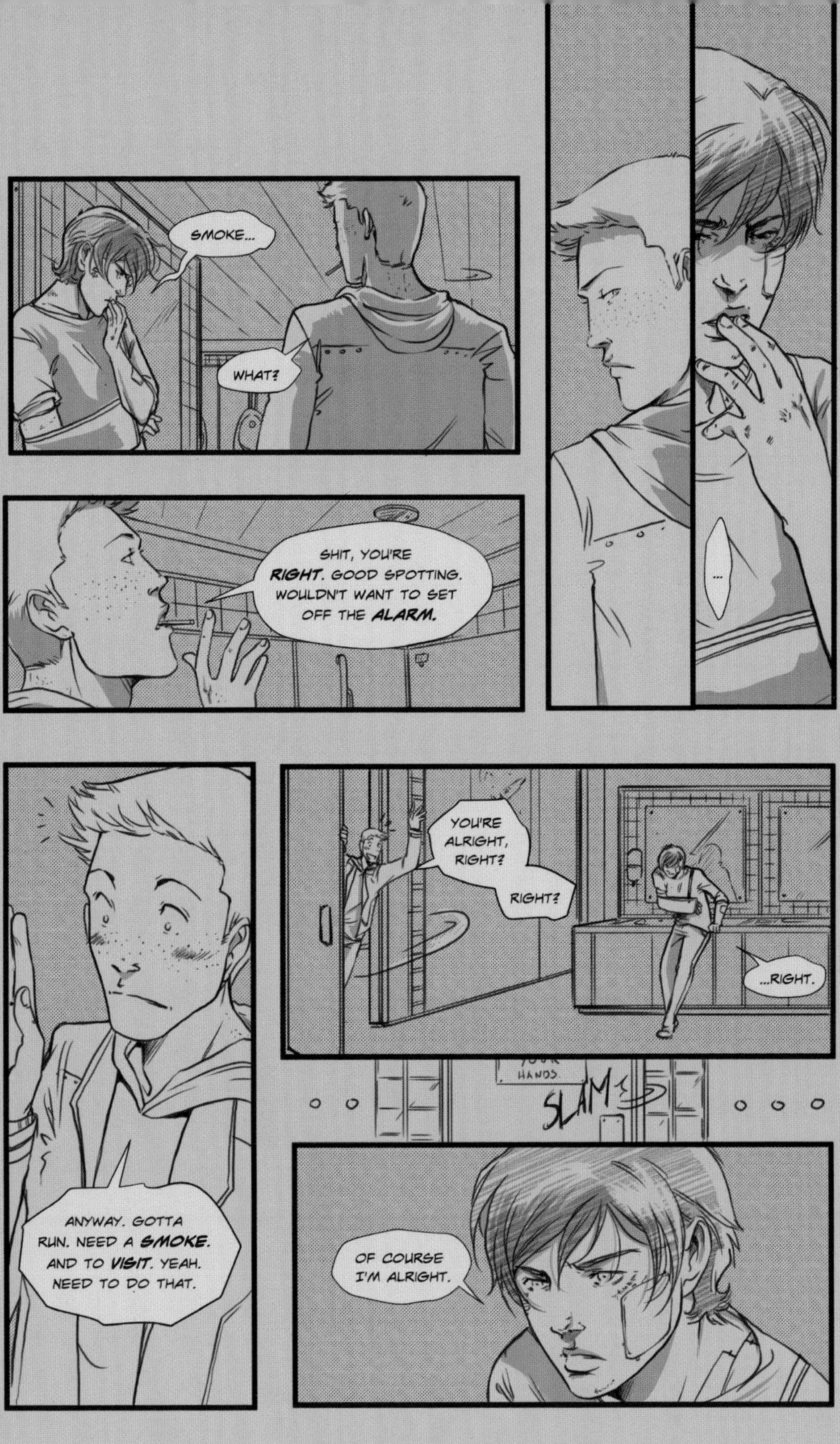
SMOKE...
WHAT?
SHIT, YOU'RE RIGHT. GOOD SPOTTING. WOULDN'T WANT TO SET OFF THE ALARM.
...
ANYWAY. GOTTA RUN. NEED A SMOKE. AND TO VISIT. YEAH. NEED TO DO THAT.
YOU'RE ALRIGHT, RIGHT?
RIGHT?
...RIGHT.
HANDS.
SLAM
OF COURSE I'M ALRIGHT.

ISSUE 4

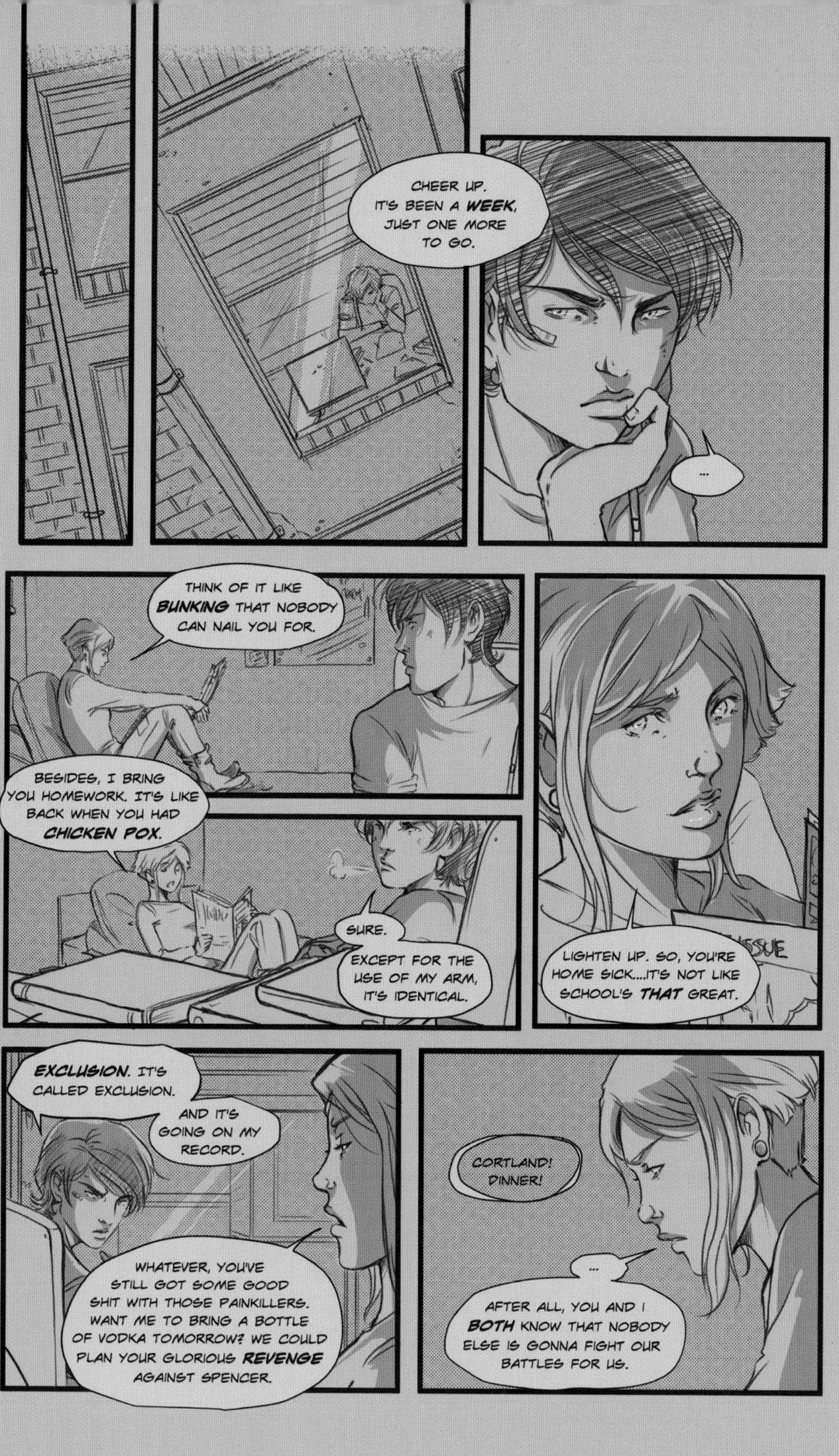
CHEER UP. IT'S BEEN A WEEK, JUST ONE MORE TO GO.
...
THINK OF IT LIKE BUNKING THAT NOBODY CAN NAIL YOU FOR.
BESIDES, I BRING YOU HOMEWORK. IT'S LIKE BACK WHEN YOU HAD CHICKEN POX.
SURE.
EXCEPT FOR THE USE OF MY ARM, IT'S IDENTICAL.
LIGHTEN UP. SO, YOU'RE HOME SICK....IT'S NOT LIKE SCHOOL'S THAT GREAT.
EXCLUSION. IT'S CALLED EXCLUSION.
AND IT'S GOING ON MY RECORD.
WHATEVER, YOU'VE STILL GOT SOME GOOD SHIT WITH THOSE PAINKILLERS. WANT ME TO BRING A BOTTLE OF VODKA TOMORROW? WE COULD PLAN YOUR GLORIOUS REVENGE AGAINST SPENCER.
CORTLAND! DINNER!
...
AFTER ALL, YOU AND I BOTH KNOW THAT NOBODY ELSE IS GONNA FIGHT OUR BATTLES FOR US.

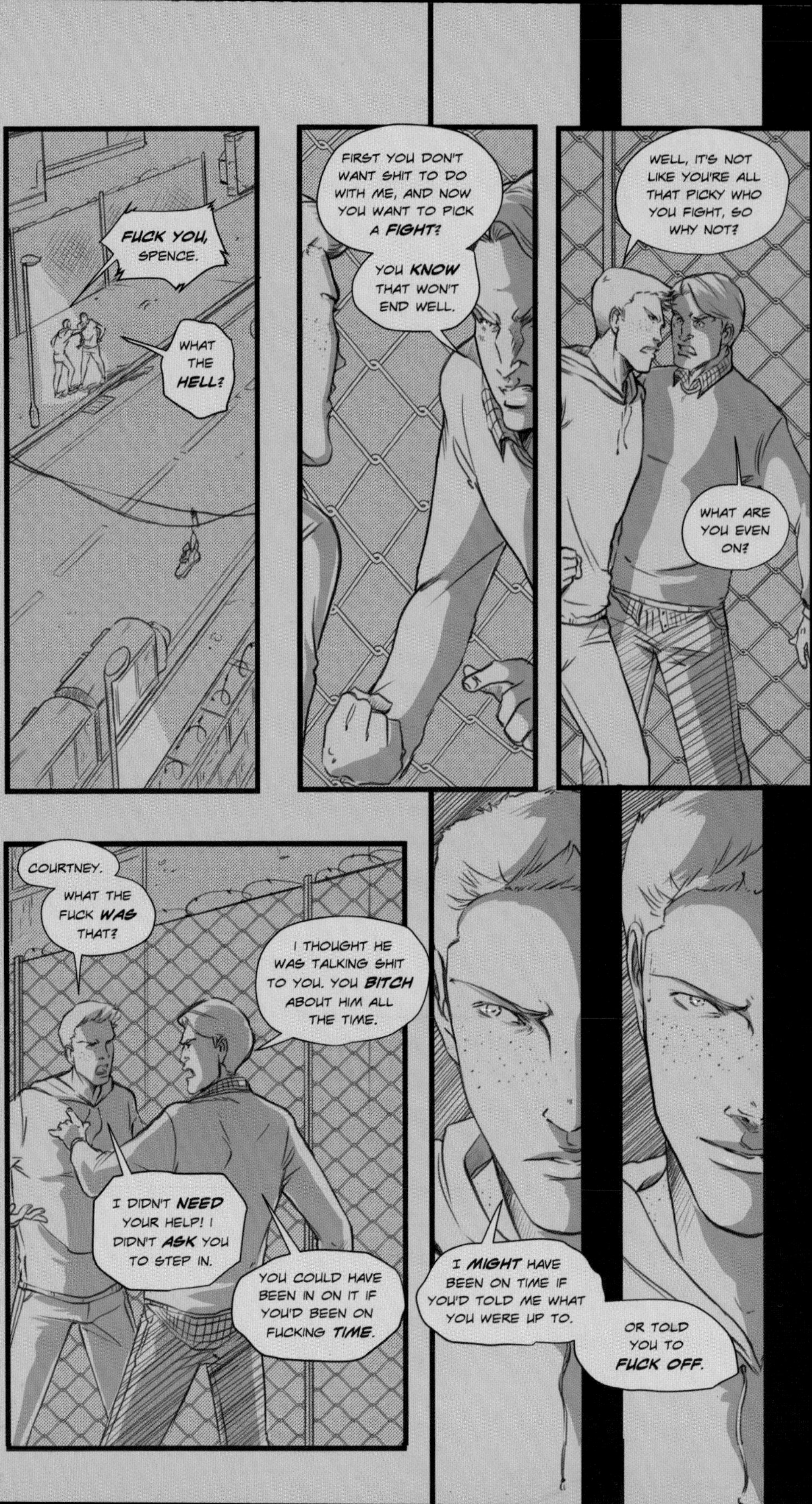

FUCK YOU, SPENCE.
WHAT THE HELL?
FIRST YOU DON'T WANT SHIT TO DO WITH ME, AND NOW YOU WANT TO PICK A FIGHT?
YOU KNOW THAT WON'T END WELL.
WELL, IT'S NOT LIKE YOU'RE ALL THAT PICKY WHO YOU FIGHT, SO WHY NOT?
WHAT ARE YOU EVEN ON?
COURTNEY.
WHAT THE FUCK WAS THAT?
I THOUGHT HE WAS TALKING SHIT TO YOU. YOU BITCH ABOUT HIM ALL THE TIME.
I DIDN'T NEED YOUR HELP! I DIDN'T ASK YOU TO STEP IN.
YOU COULD HAVE BEEN IN ON IT IF YOU'D BEEN ON FUCKING TIME.
I MIGHT HAVE BEEN ON TIME IF YOU'D TOLD ME WHAT YOU WERE UP TO.
OR TOLD YOU TO FUCK OFF.

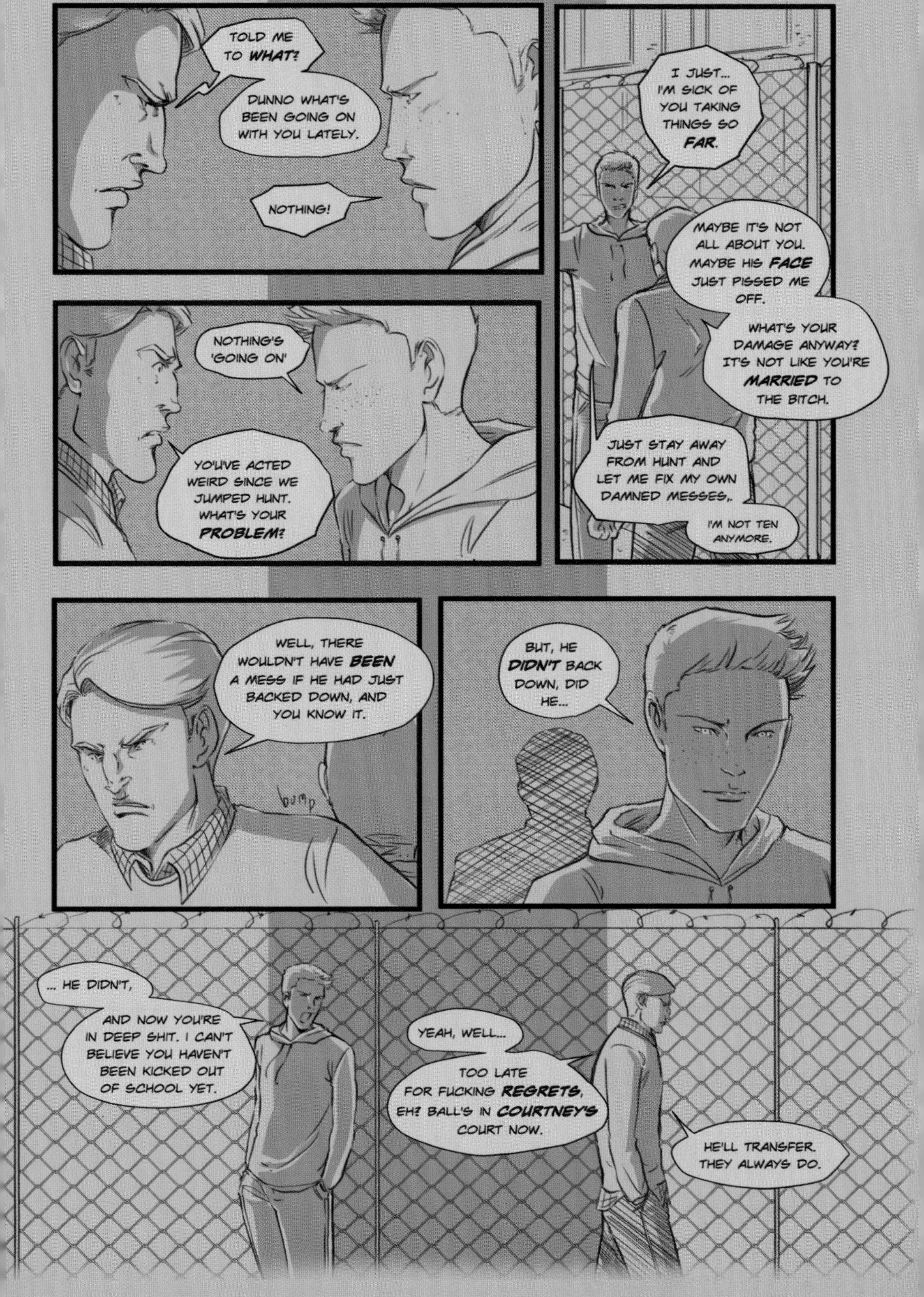
TOLD ME TO WHAT?
DUNNO WHAT'S BEEN GOING ON WITH YOU LATELY.
NOTHING!
NOTHING'S 'GOING ON'
YOU'VE ACTED WEIRD SINCE WE JUMPED HUNT. WHAT'S YOUR PROBLEM?
I JUST... I'M SICK OF YOU TAKING THINGS SO FAR.
MAYBE IT'S NOT ALL ABOUT YOU. MAYBE HIS FACE JUST PISSED ME OFF.
WHAT'S YOUR DAMAGE ANYWAY? IT'S NOT LIKE YOU'RE MARRIED TO THE BITCH.
JUST STAY AWAY FROM HUNT AND LET ME FIX MY OWN DAMNED MESSES,.
I'M NOT TEN ANYMORE.
WELL, THERE WOULDN'T HAVE BEEN A MESS IF HE HAD JUST BACKED DOWN, AND YOU KNOW IT.
bump
BUT, HE DIDN'T BACK DOWN, DID HE...
... HE DIDN'T,
AND NOW YOU'RE IN DEEP SHIT. I CAN'T BELIEVE YOU HAVEN'T BEEN KICKED OUT OF SCHOOL YET.
YEAH, WELL...
TOO LATE FOR FUCKING REGRETS, EH? BALL'S IN COURTNEY'S COURT NOW.
HE'LL TRANSFER. THEY ALWAYS DO.

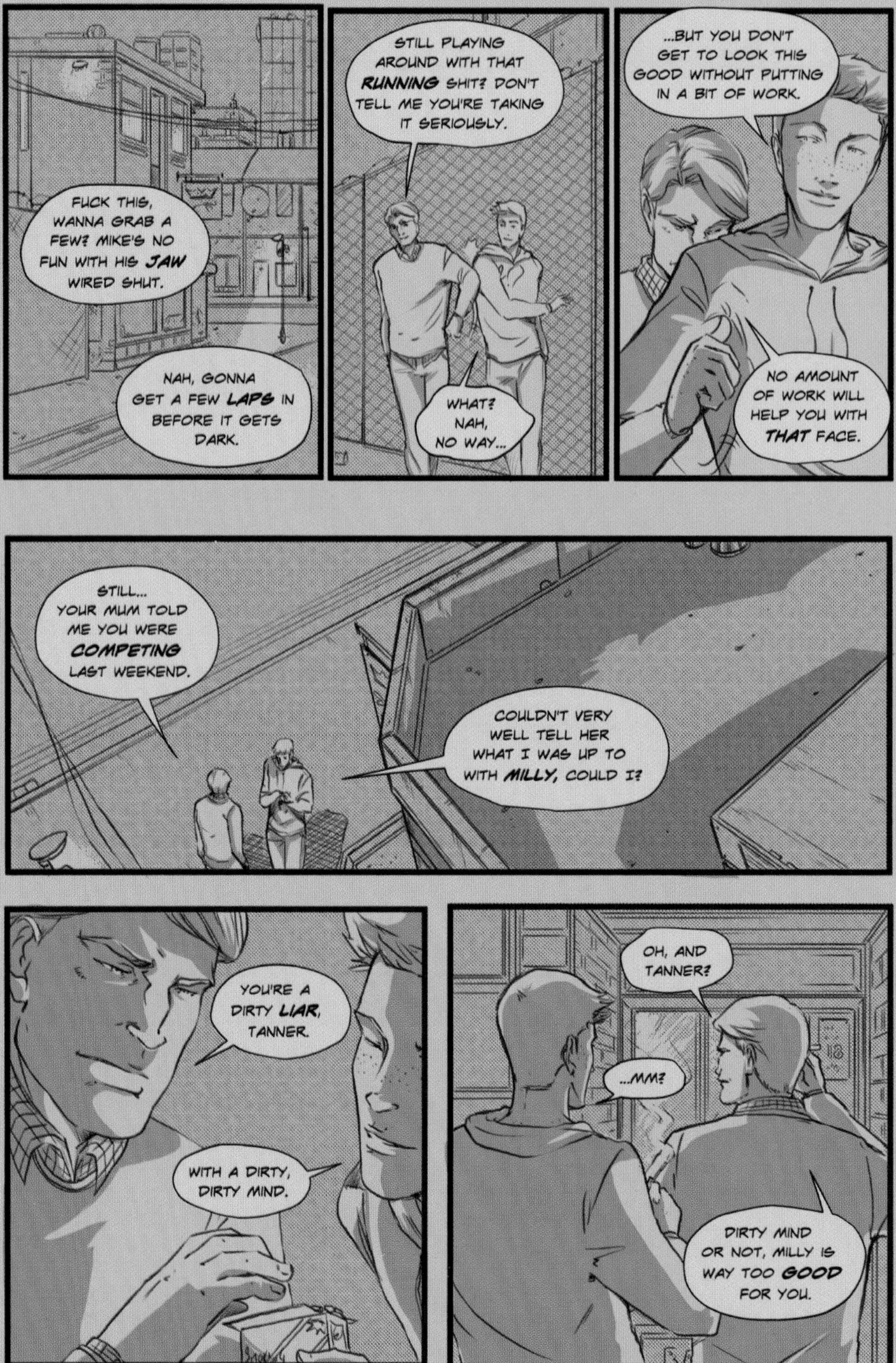
FUCK THIS, WANNA GRAB A FEW? MIKE'S NO FUN WITH HIS JAW WIRED SHUT.
NAH, GONNA GET A FEW LAPS IN BEFORE IT GETS DARK.
STILL PLAYING AROUND WITH THAT RUNNING SHIT? DON'T TELL ME YOU'RE TAKING IT SERIOUSLY.
WHAT? NAH, NO WAY...
...BUT YOU DON'T GET TO LOOK THIS GOOD WITHOUT PUTTING IN A BIT OF WORK.
NO AMOUNT OF WORK WILL HELP YOU WITH THAT FACE.
STILL... YOUR MUM TOLD ME YOU WERE COMPETING LAST WEEKEND.
COULDN'T VERY WELL TELL HER WHAT I WAS UP TO WITH MILLY, COULD I?
YOU'RE A DIRTY LIAR, TANNER.
WITH A DIRTY, DIRTY MIND.
OH, AND TANNER?
...MM?
DIRTY MIND OR NOT, MILLY IS WAY TOO GOOD FOR YOU.

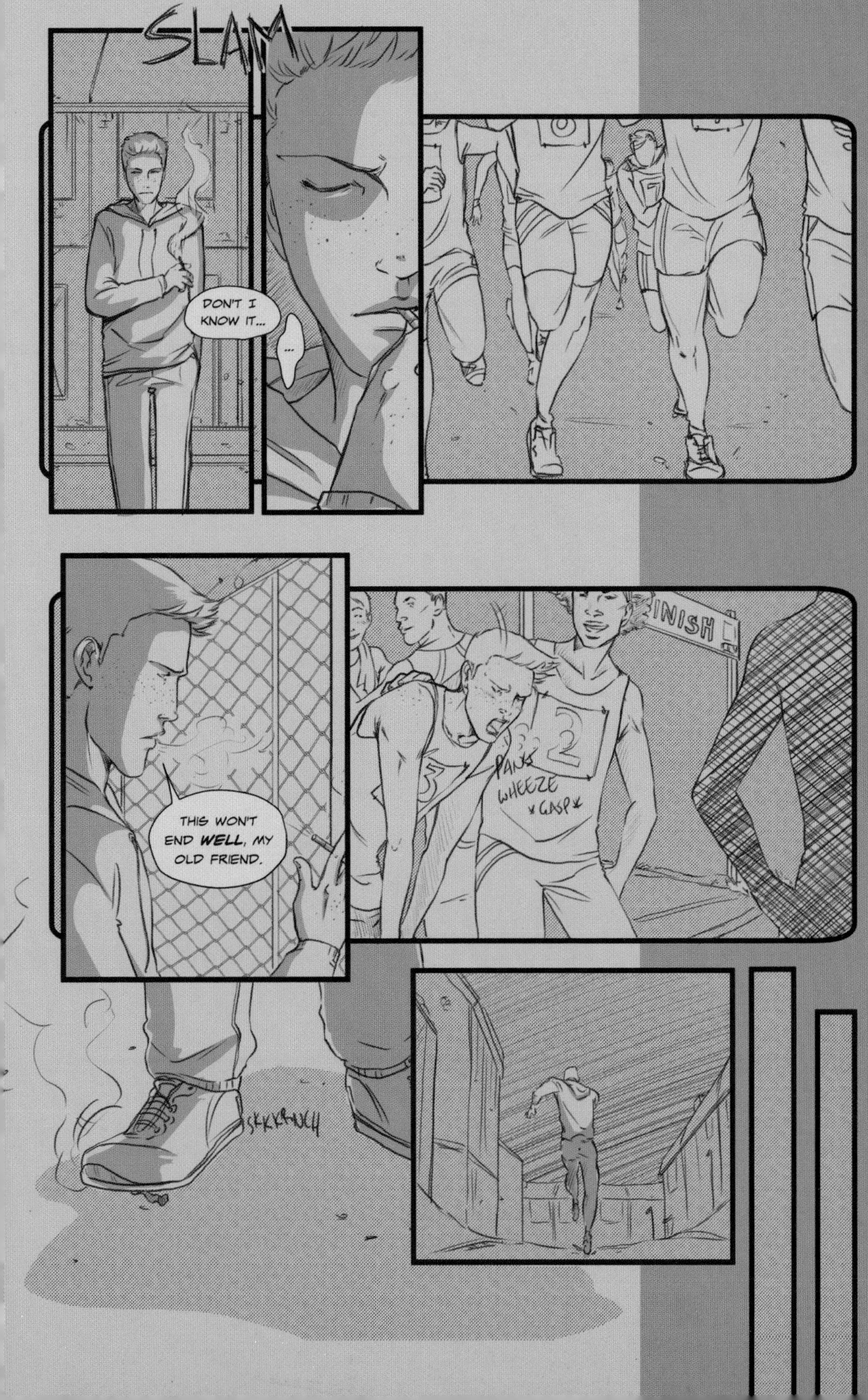
SLAM
DON'T I KNOW IT...
...
INISH
WHEEZE
GASP
THIS WON'T END **WELL**, MY OLD FRIEND.

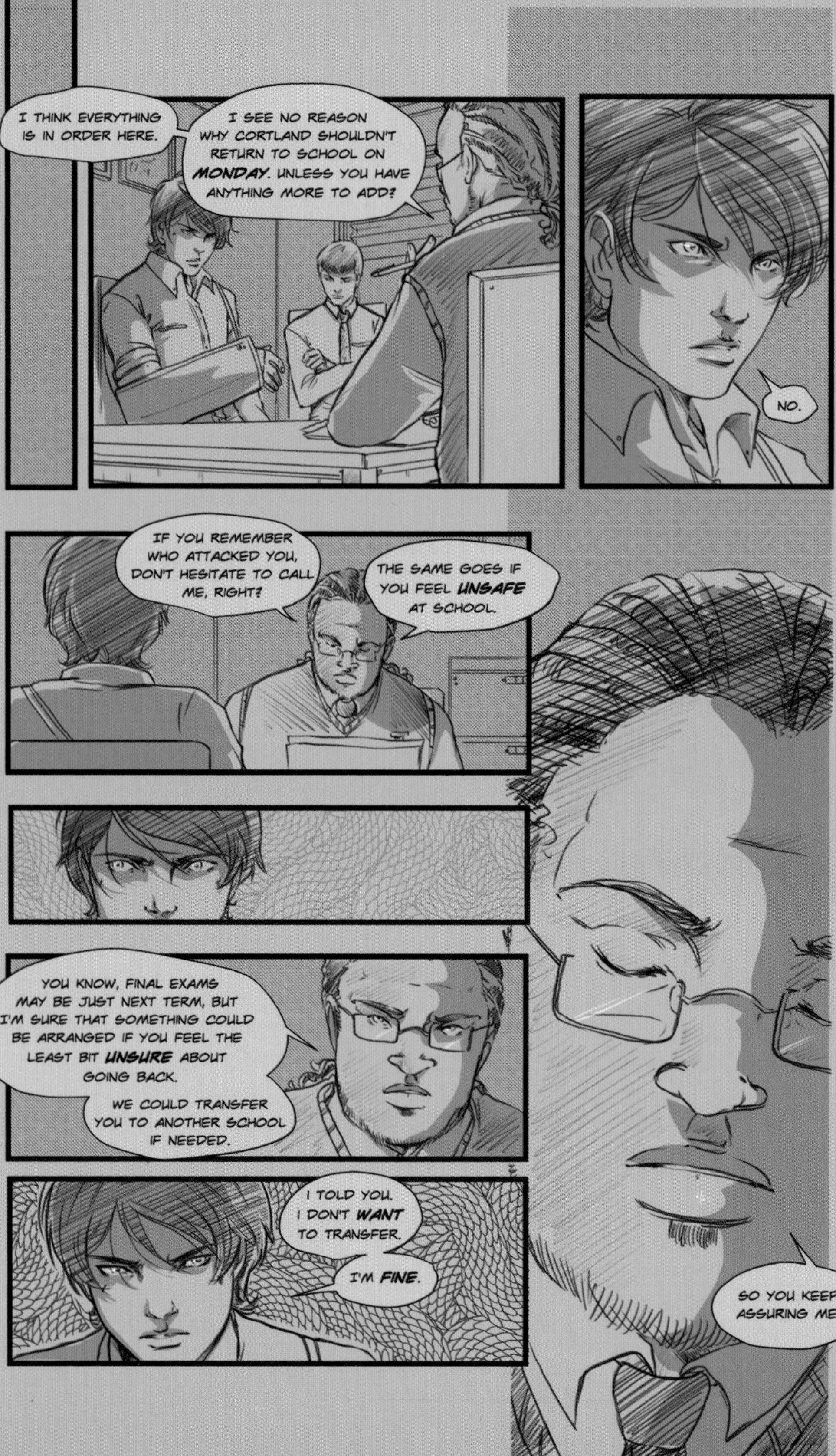
I THINK EVERYTHING IS IN ORDER HERE.
I SEE NO REASON WHY CORTLAND SHOULDN'T RETURN TO SCHOOL ON MONDAY. UNLESS YOU HAVE ANYTHING MORE TO ADD?
NO.
IF YOU REMEMBER WHO ATTACKED YOU, DON'T HESITATE TO CALL ME, RIGHT?
THE SAME GOES IF YOU FEEL UNSAFE AT SCHOOL.
YOU KNOW, FINAL EXAMS MAY BE JUST NEXT TERM, BUT I'M SURE THAT SOMETHING COULD BE ARRANGED IF YOU FEEL THE LEAST BIT UNSURE ABOUT GOING BACK.
WE COULD TRANSFER YOU TO ANOTHER SCHOOL IF NEEDED.
I TOLD YOU. I DON'T WANT TO TRANSFER.
I'M FINE.
SO YOU KEEP ASSURING ME.

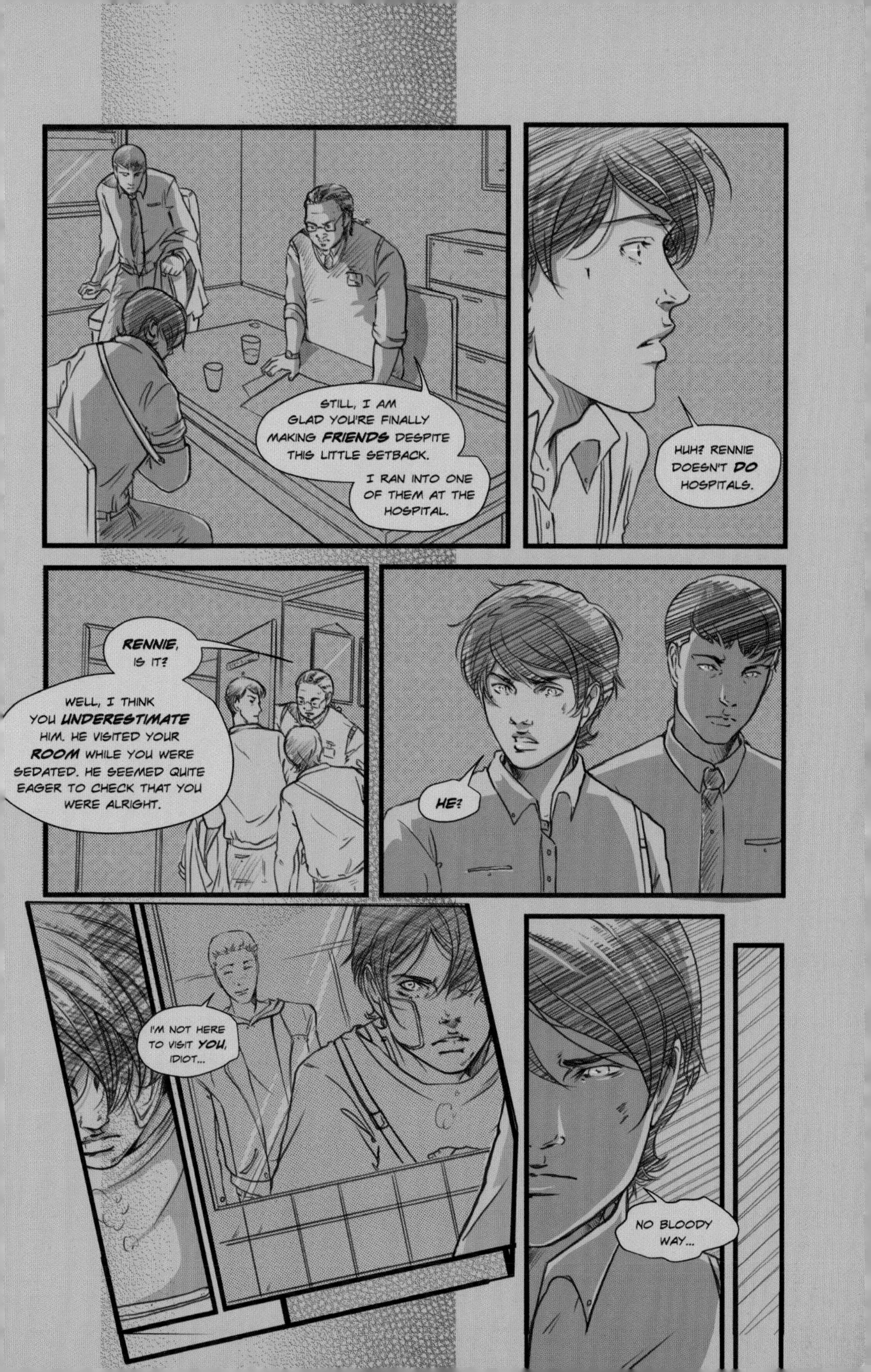
STILL, I AM GLAD YOU'RE FINALLY MAKING FRIENDS DESPITE THIS LITTLE SETBACK.
I RAN INTO ONE OF THEM AT THE HOSPITAL.
HUH? RENNIE DOESN'T DO HOSPITALS.
RENNIE, IS IT?
WELL, I THINK YOU UNDERESTIMATE HIM. HE VISITED YOUR ROOM WHILE YOU WERE SEDATED. HE SEEMED QUITE EAGER TO CHECK THAT YOU WERE ALRIGHT.
HE?
I'M NOT HERE TO VISIT YOU, IDIOT...
NO BLOODY WAY...

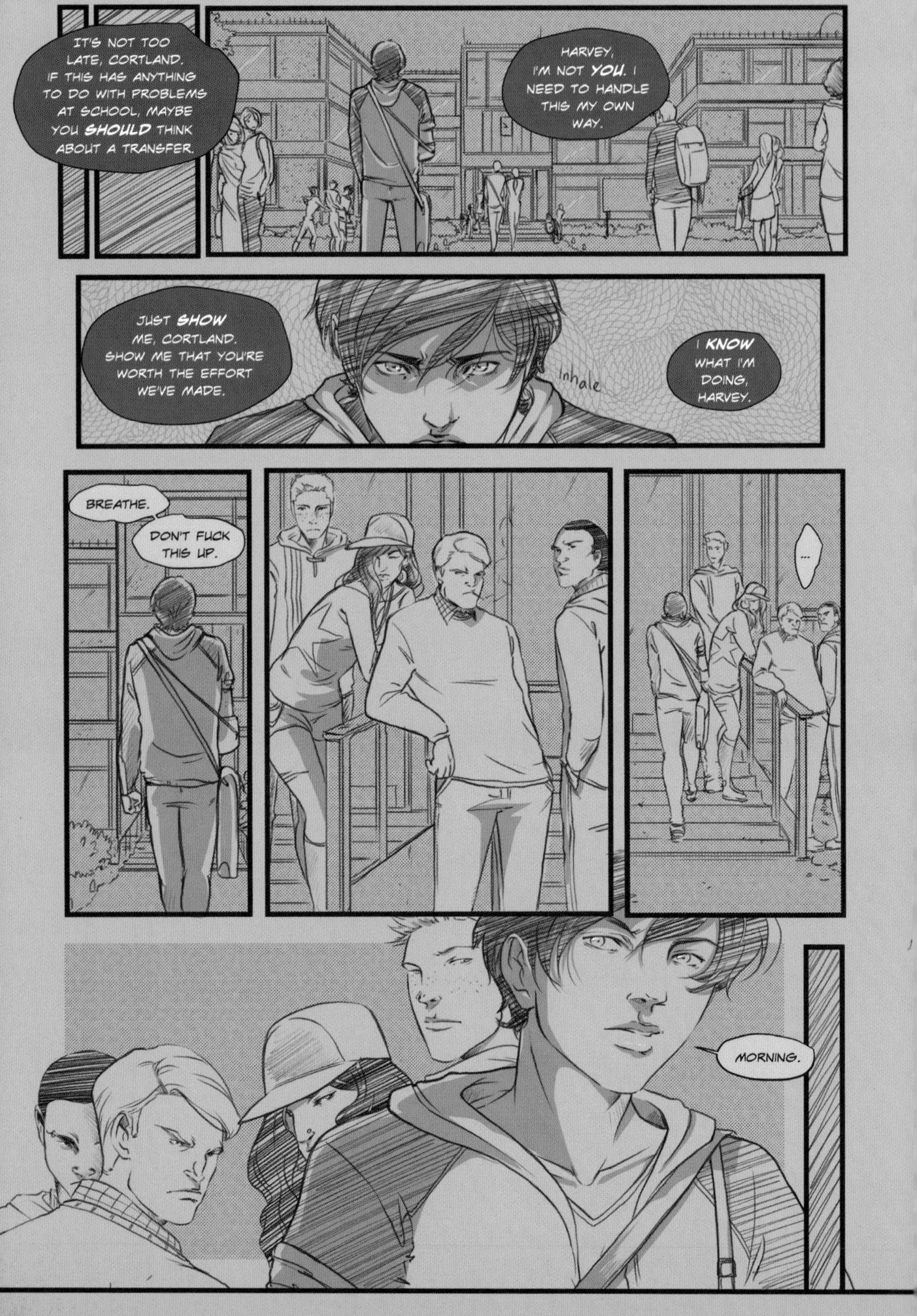
IT'S NOT TOO LATE, CORTLAND. IF THIS HAS ANYTHING TO DO WITH PROBLEMS AT SCHOOL, MAYBE YOU **SHOULD** THINK ABOUT A TRANSFER.
HARVEY, I'M NOT **YOU**. I NEED TO HANDLE THIS MY OWN WAY.
JUST **SHOW** ME, CORTLAND. SHOW ME THAT YOU'RE WORTH THE EFFORT WE'VE MADE.
inhale
I **KNOW** WHAT I'M DOING, HARVEY.
BREATHE.
DON'T FUCK THIS UP.
...
MORNING.

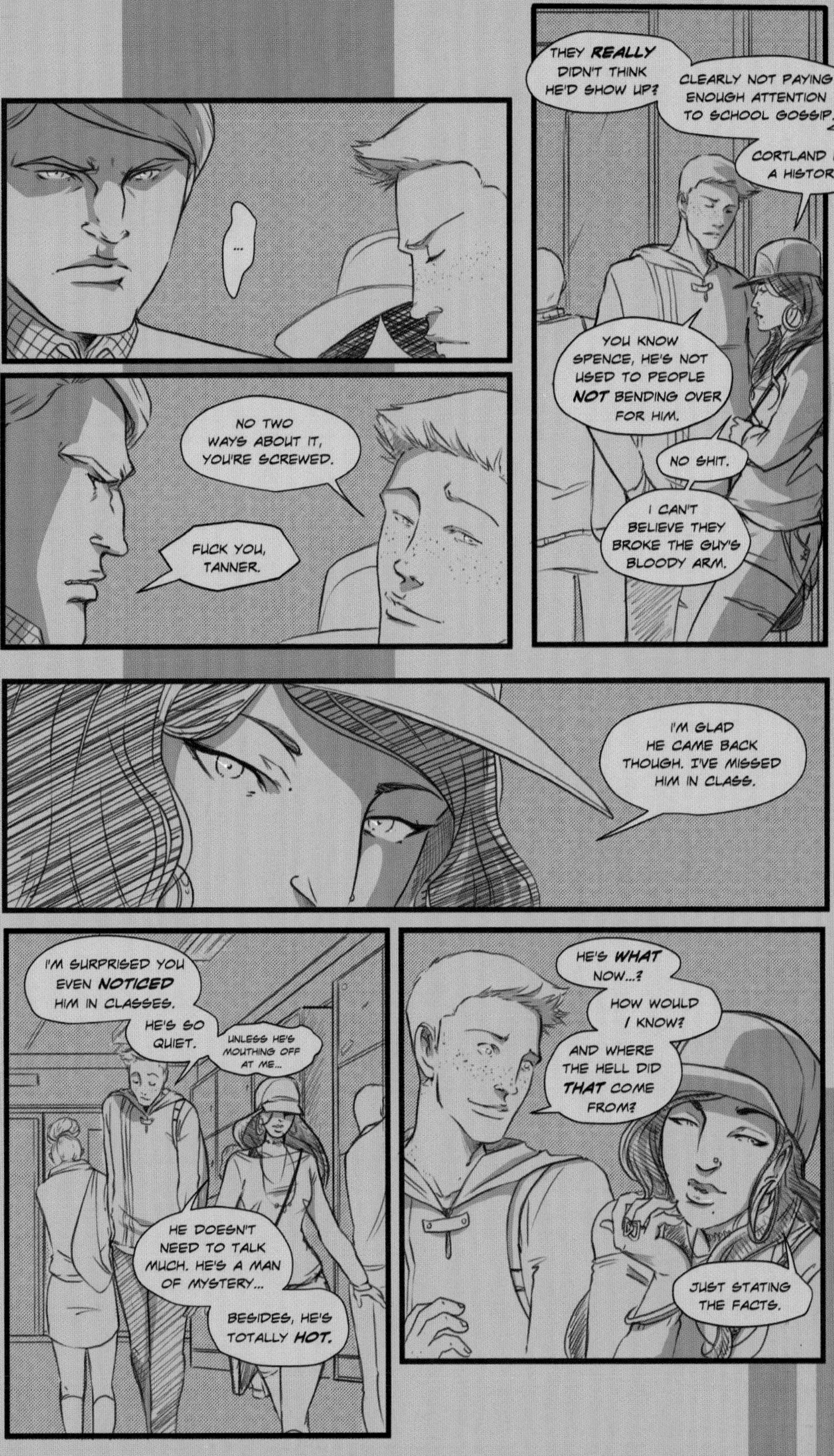
...
NO TWO WAYS ABOUT IT, YOU'RE SCREWED.
FUCK YOU, TANNER.
THEY REALLY DIDN'T THINK HE'D SHOW UP?
CLEARLY NOT PAYING ENOUGH ATTENTION TO SCHOOL GOSSIP.
CORTLAND HAS A HISTORY.
YOU KNOW SPENCE, HE'S NOT USED TO PEOPLE NOT BENDING OVER FOR HIM.
NO SHIT.
I CAN'T BELIEVE THEY BROKE THE GUY'S BLOODY ARM.
I'M GLAD HE CAME BACK THOUGH. I'VE MISSED HIM IN CLASS.
I'M SURPRISED YOU EVEN NOTICED HIM IN CLASSES.
HE'S SO QUIET.
UNLESS HE'S MOUTHING OFF AT ME...
HE DOESN'T NEED TO TALK MUCH. HE'S A MAN OF MYSTERY...
BESIDES, HE'S TOTALLY HOT.
HE'S WHAT NOW...?
HOW WOULD I KNOW?
AND WHERE THE HELL DID THAT COME FROM?
JUST STATING THE FACTS.

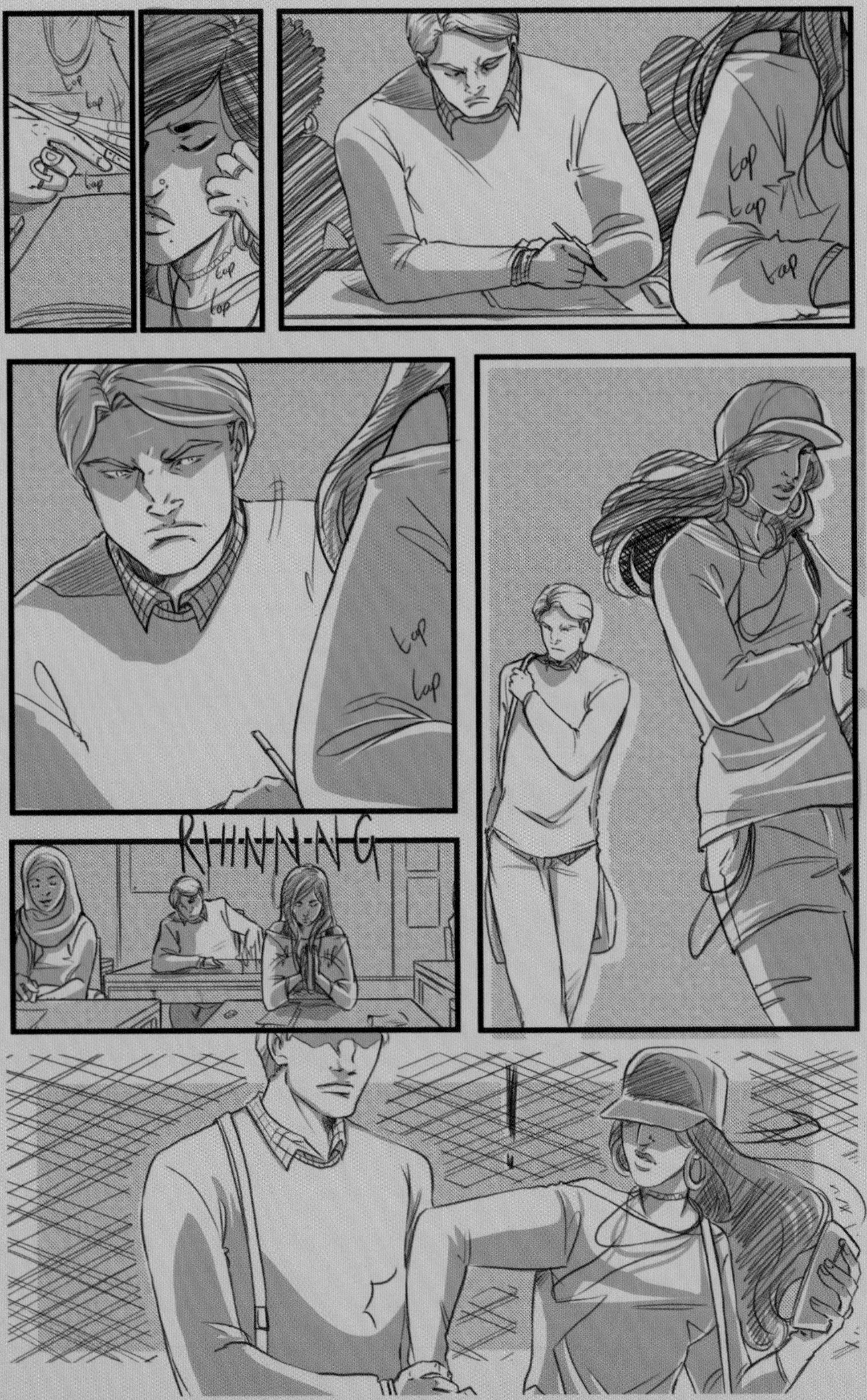

tap
tap
tap
tap
tap
tap
tap
tap
tap
tap
RIIINNNG

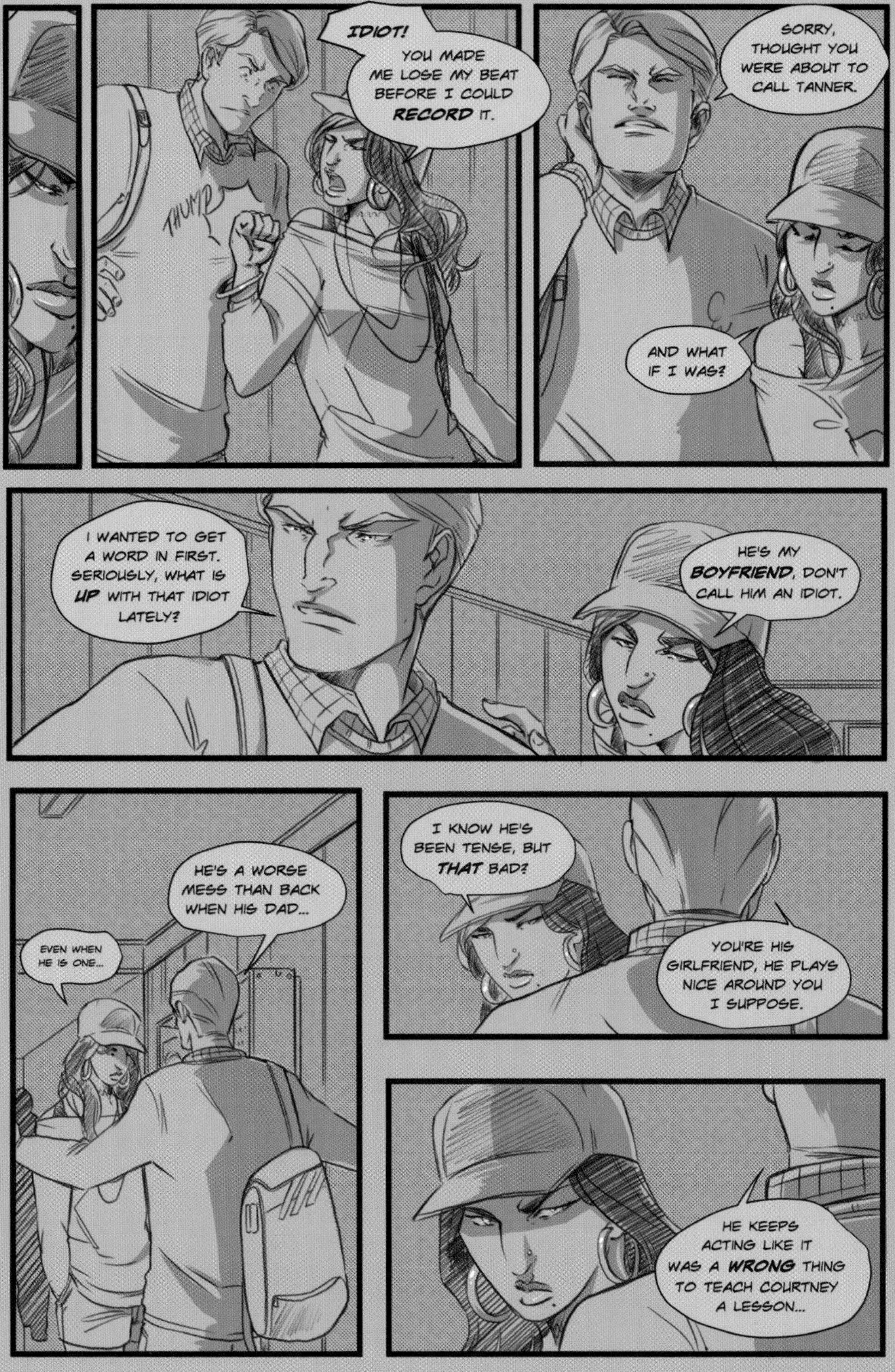
IDIOT!
YOU MADE ME LOSE MY BEAT BEFORE I COULD RECORD IT.
THUMP
SORRY, THOUGHT YOU WERE ABOUT TO CALL TANNER.
AND WHAT IF I WAS?
I WANTED TO GET A WORD IN FIRST. SERIOUSLY, WHAT IS UP WITH THAT IDIOT LATELY?
HE'S MY BOYFRIEND, DON'T CALL HIM AN IDIOT.
EVEN WHEN HE IS ONE...
HE'S A WORSE MESS THAN BACK WHEN HIS DAD...
I KNOW HE'S BEEN TENSE, BUT THAT BAD?
YOU'RE HIS GIRLFRIEND, HE PLAYS NICE AROUND YOU I SUPPOSE.
HE KEEPS ACTING LIKE IT WAS A WRONG THING TO TEACH COURTNEY A LESSON...

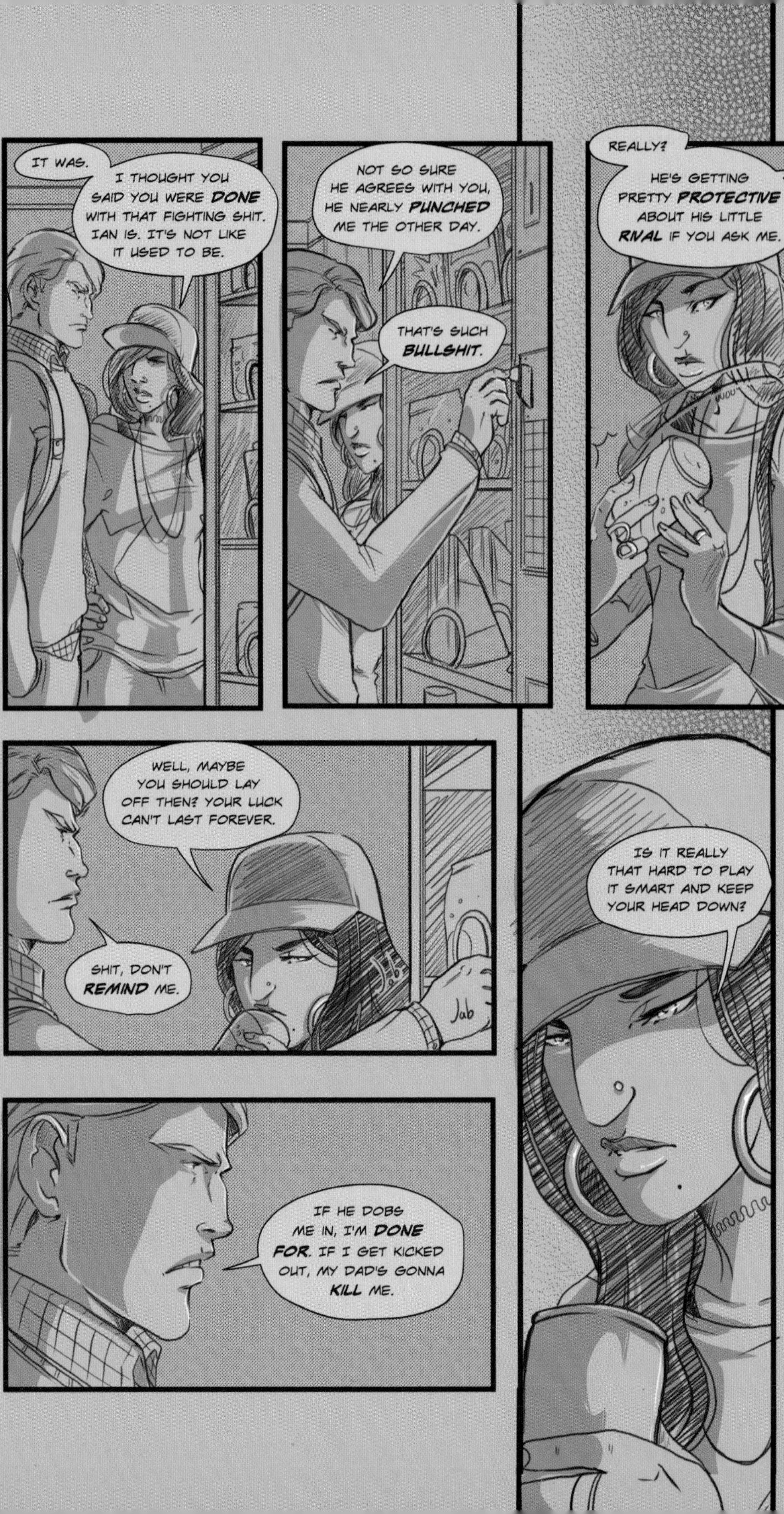
IT WAS.
I THOUGHT YOU SAID YOU WERE DONE WITH THAT FIGHTING SHIT.
IAN IS. IT'S NOT LIKE IT USED TO BE.
NOT SO SURE HE AGREES WITH YOU, HE NEARLY PUNCHED ME THE OTHER DAY.
THAT'S SUCH BULLSHIT.
REALLY?
HE'S GETTING PRETTY PROTECTIVE ABOUT HIS LITTLE RIVAL IF YOU ASK ME.
WELL, MAYBE YOU SHOULD LAY OFF THEN? YOUR LUCK CAN'T LAST FOREVER.
SHIT, DON'T REMIND ME.
IS IT REALLY THAT HARD TO PLAY IT SMART AND KEEP YOUR HEAD DOWN?
IF HE DOBS ME IN, I'M DONE FOR. IF I GET KICKED OUT, MY DAD'S GONNA KILL ME.

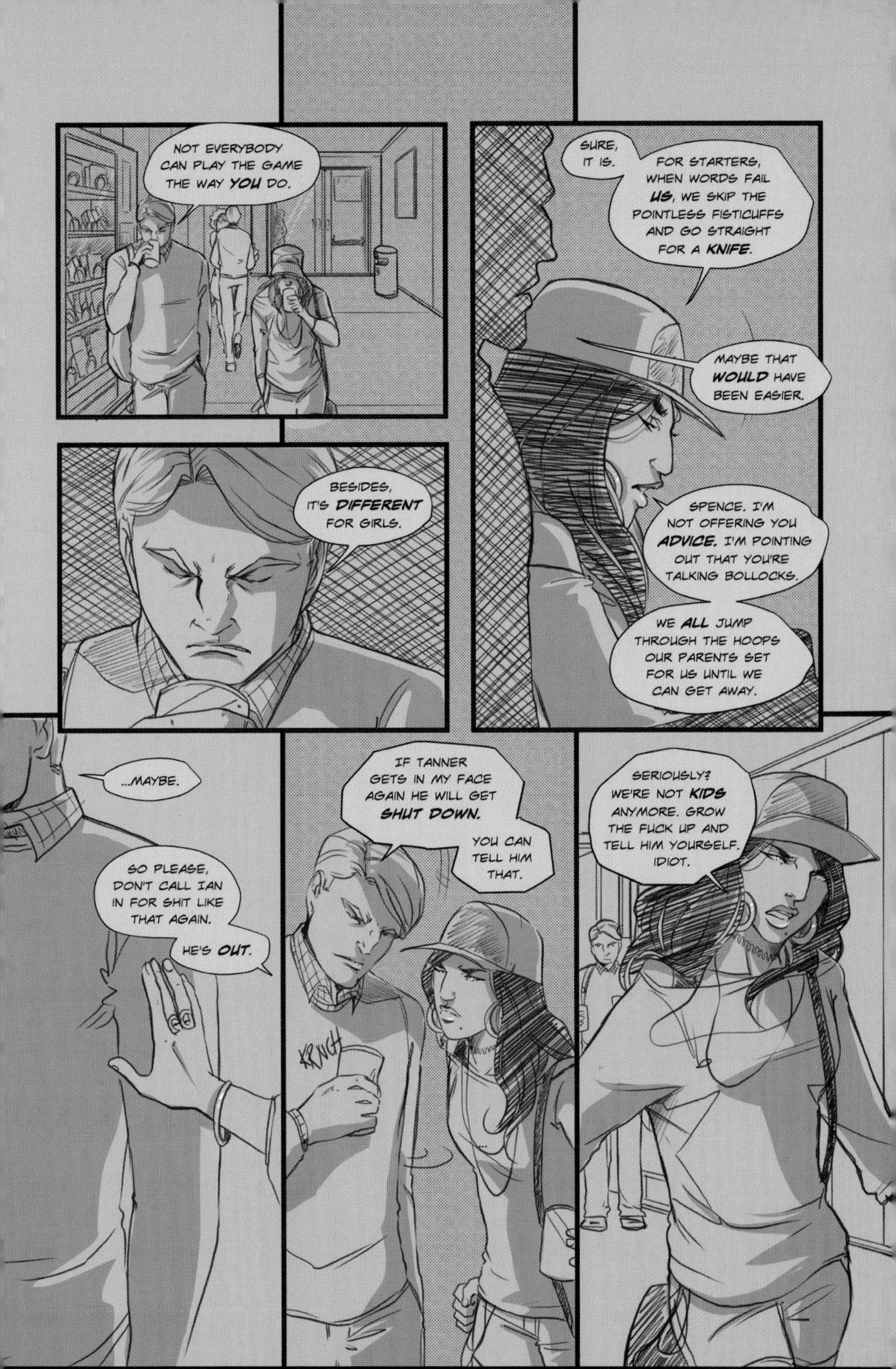
NOT EVERYBODY CAN PLAY THE GAME THE WAY YOU DO.
SURE, IT IS.
FOR STARTERS, WHEN WORDS FAIL US, WE SKIP THE POINTLESS FISTICUFFS AND GO STRAIGHT FOR A KNIFE.
MAYBE THAT WOULD HAVE BEEN EASIER.
BESIDES, IT'S DIFFERENT FOR GIRLS.
SPENCE. I'M NOT OFFERING YOU ADVICE. I'M POINTING OUT THAT YOU'RE TALKING BOLLOCKS.
WE ALL JUMP THROUGH THE HOOPS OUR PARENTS SET FOR US UNTIL WE CAN GET AWAY.
...MAYBE.
SO PLEASE, DON'T CALL IAN IN FOR SHIT LIKE THAT AGAIN.
HE'S OUT.
IF TANNER GETS IN MY FACE AGAIN HE WILL GET SHUT DOWN.
YOU CAN TELL HIM THAT.
KRNCH
SERIOUSLY? WE'RE NOT KIDS ANYMORE. GROW THE FUCK UP AND TELL HIM YOURSELF. IDIOT.

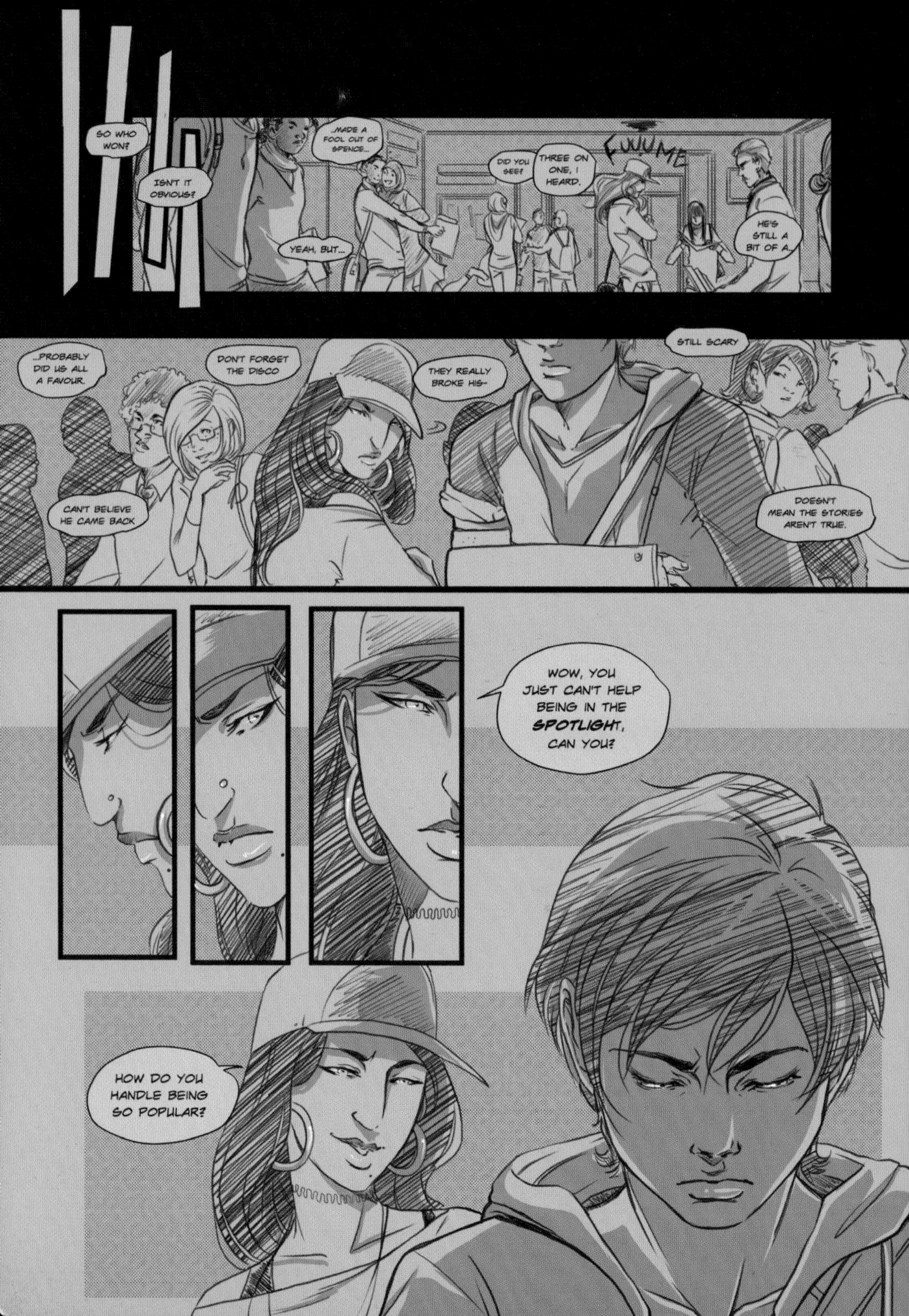
SO WHO WON?
ISN'T IT OBVIOUS?
..MADE A FOOL OUT OF SPENCE...
YEAH, BUT...
DID YOU SEE?
THREE ON ONE, I HEARD.
FUUUME
HE'S STILL A BIT OF A..
...PROBABLY DID US ALL A FAVOUR.
CAN'T BELIEVE HE CAME BACK
DON'T FORGET THE DISCO
THEY REALLY BROKE HIS-
STILL SCARY
DOESN'T MEAN THE STORIES AREN'T TRUE.
WOW, YOU JUST CAN'T HELP BEING IN THE SPOTLIGHT, CAN YOU?
HOW DO YOU HANDLE BEING SO POPULAR?

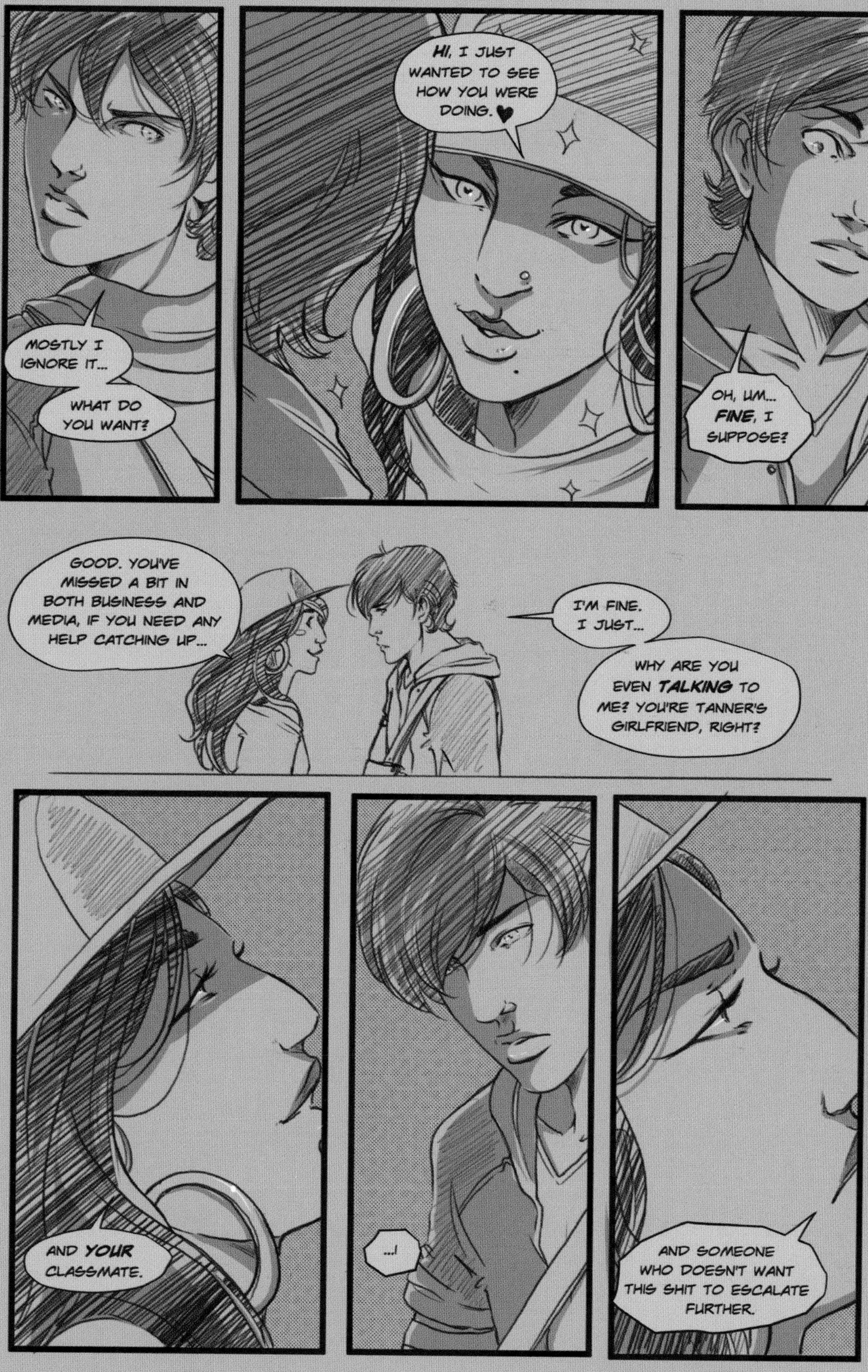
MOSTLY I IGNORE IT...
WHAT DO YOU WANT?
HI, I JUST WANTED TO SEE HOW YOU WERE DOING. ♥
OH, UM... FINE, I SUPPOSE?
GOOD. YOU'VE MISSED A BIT IN BOTH BUSINESS AND MEDIA, IF YOU NEED ANY HELP CATCHING UP...
I'M FINE. I JUST...
WHY ARE YOU EVEN TALKING TO ME? YOU'RE TANNER'S GIRLFRIEND, RIGHT?
AND YOUR CLASSMATE.
...!
AND SOMEONE WHO DOESN'T WANT THIS SHIT TO ESCALATE FURTHER.

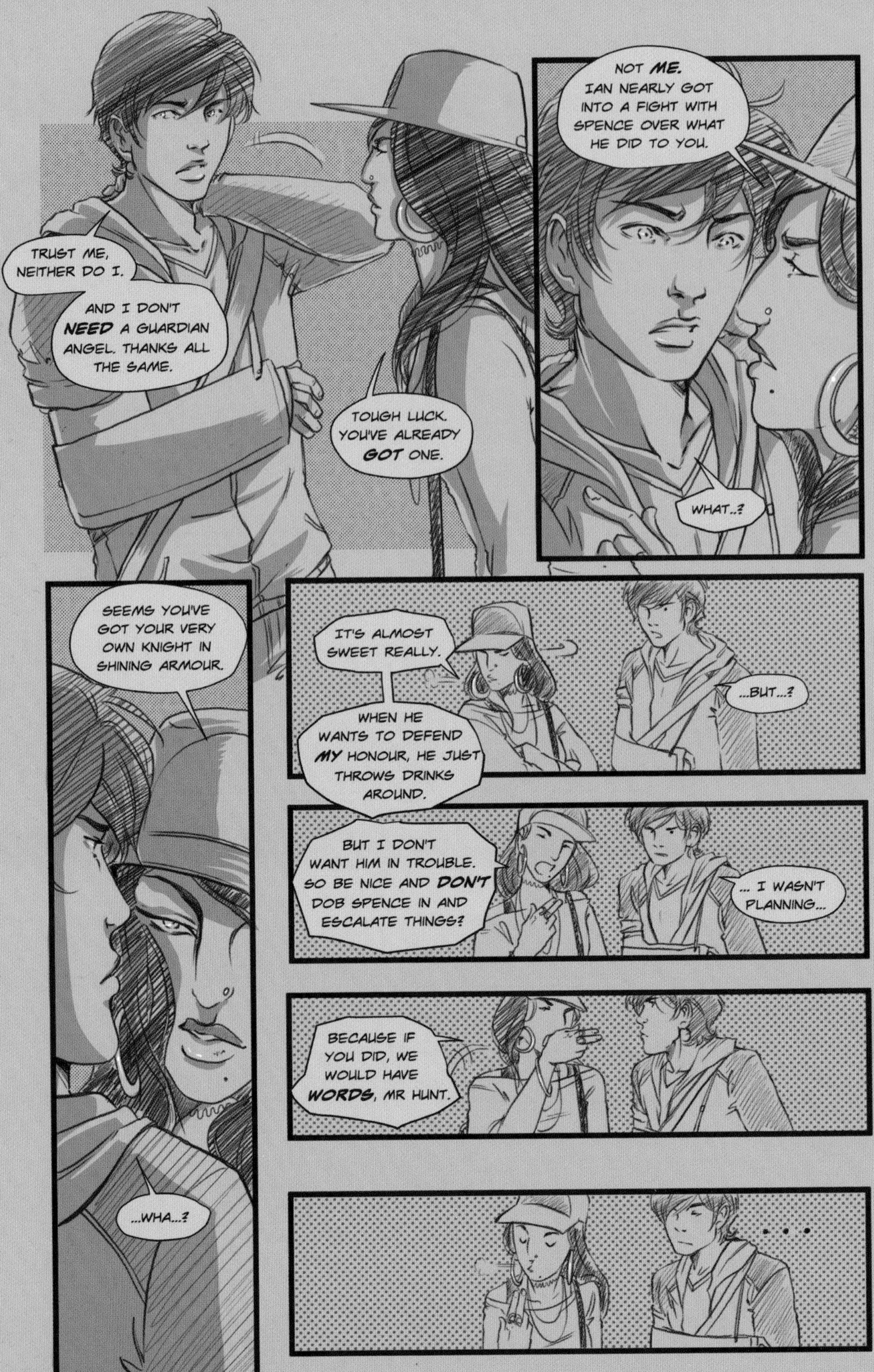
TRUST ME, NEITHER DO I.
AND I DON'T NEED A GUARDIAN ANGEL. THANKS ALL THE SAME.
TOUGH LUCK. YOU'VE ALREADY GOT ONE.
NOT ME. IAN NEARLY GOT INTO A FIGHT WITH SPENCE OVER WHAT HE DID TO YOU.
WHAT..?
SEEMS YOU'VE GOT YOUR VERY OWN KNIGHT IN SHINING ARMOUR.
...WHA...?
IT'S ALMOST SWEET REALLY.
WHEN HE WANTS TO DEFEND MY HONOUR, HE JUST THROWS DRINKS AROUND.
...BUT...?
BUT I DON'T WANT HIM IN TROUBLE. SO BE NICE AND DON'T DOB SPENCE IN AND ESCALATE THINGS?
... I WASN'T PLANNING...
BECAUSE IF YOU DID, WE WOULD HAVE WORDS, MR HUNT.
...

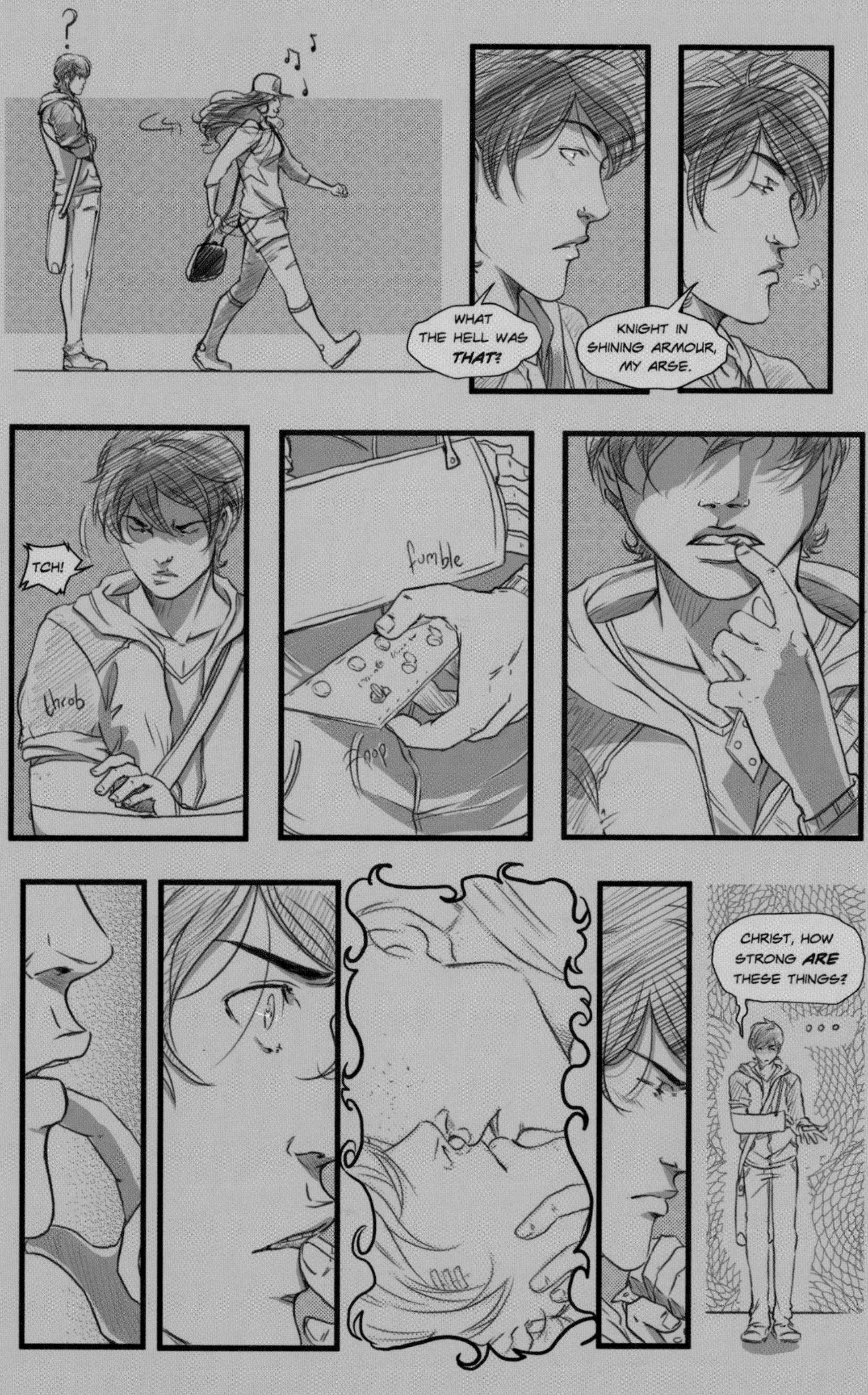
WHAT THE HELL WAS THAT?
KNIGHT IN SHINING ARMOUR, MY ARSE.
TCH!
throb
fumble
pop
CHRIST, HOW STRONG ARE THESE THINGS?
...

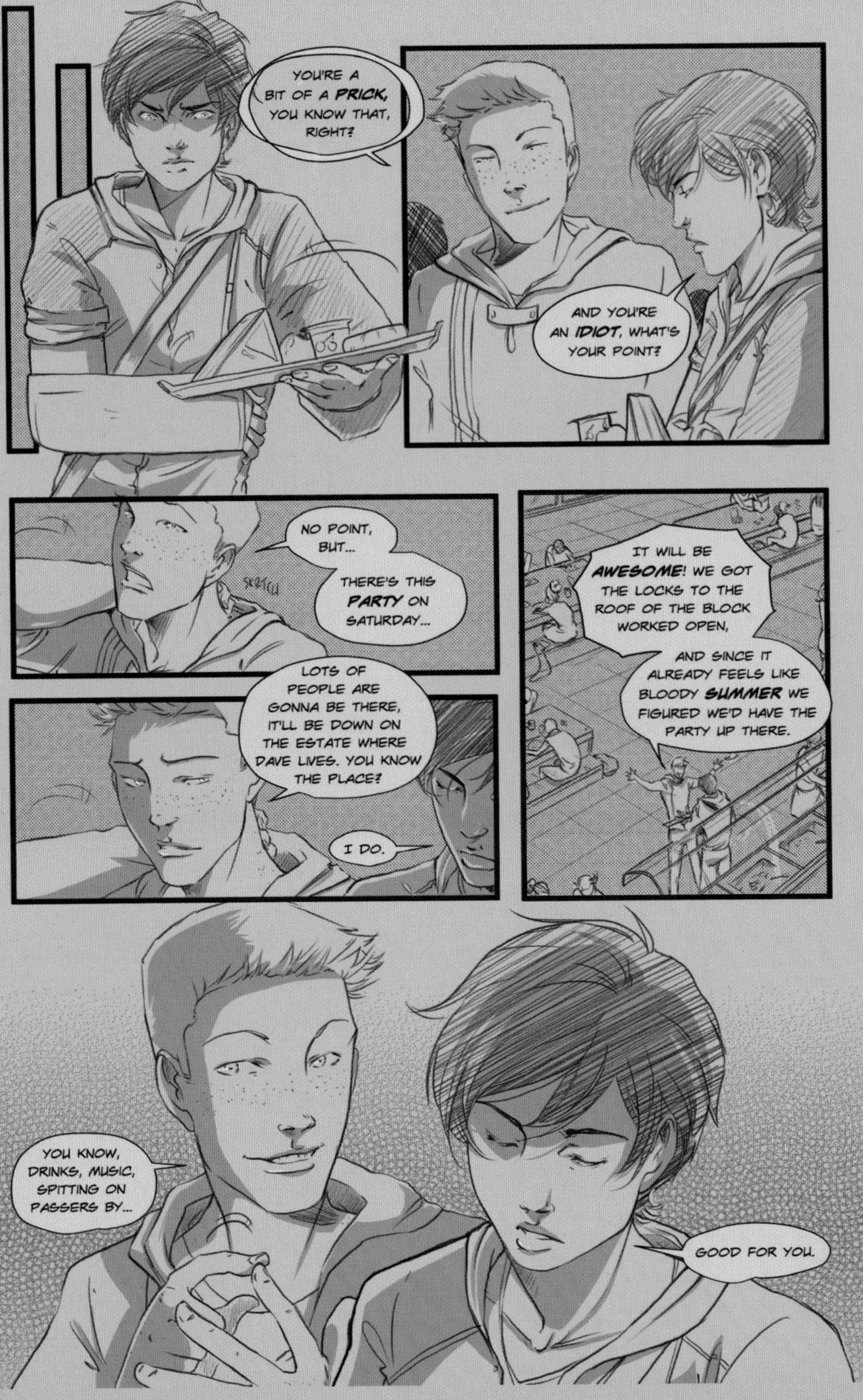
YOU'RE A BIT OF A PRICK, YOU KNOW THAT, RIGHT?
AND YOU'RE AN IDIOT, WHAT'S YOUR POINT?
NO POINT, BUT...
THERE'S THIS PARTY ON SATURDAY...
LOTS OF PEOPLE ARE GONNA BE THERE, IT'LL BE DOWN ON THE ESTATE WHERE DAVE LIVES. YOU KNOW THE PLACE?
I DO.
IT WILL BE AWESOME! WE GOT THE LOCKS TO THE ROOF OF THE BLOCK WORKED OPEN,
AND SINCE IT ALREADY FEELS LIKE BLOODY SUMMER WE FIGURED WE'D HAVE THE PARTY UP THERE.
YOU KNOW, DRINKS, MUSIC, SPITTING ON PASSERS BY...
GOOD FOR YOU.

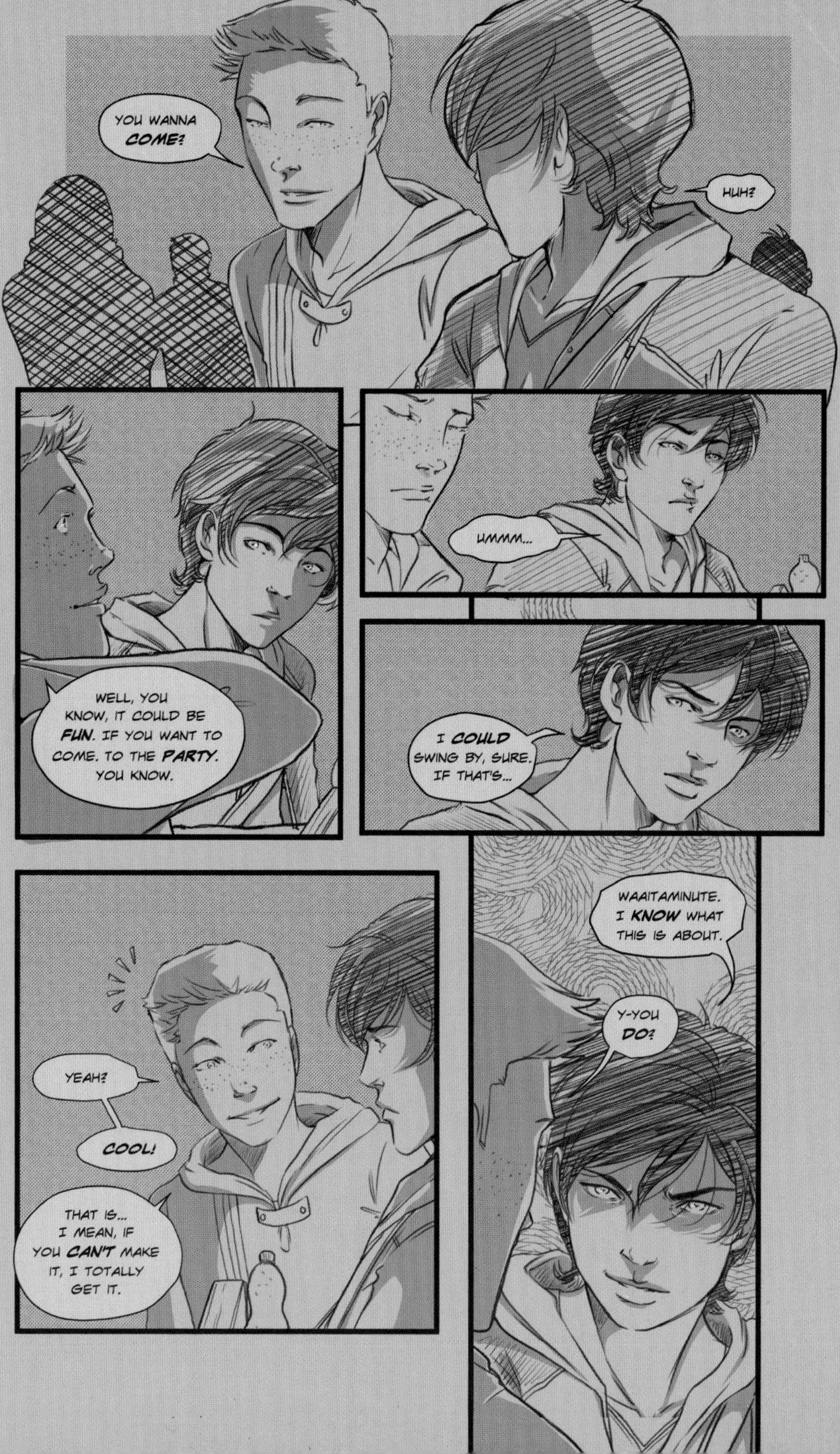
YOU WANNA COME?
HUH?
WELL, YOU KNOW, IT COULD BE FUN. IF YOU WANT TO COME. TO THE PARTY. YOU KNOW.
UMMM...
I COULD SWING BY, SURE. IF THAT'S...
YEAH?
COOL!
THAT IS... I MEAN, IF YOU CAN'T MAKE IT, I TOTALLY GET IT.
WAAITAMINUTE. I KNOW WHAT THIS IS ABOUT.
Y-YOU DO?

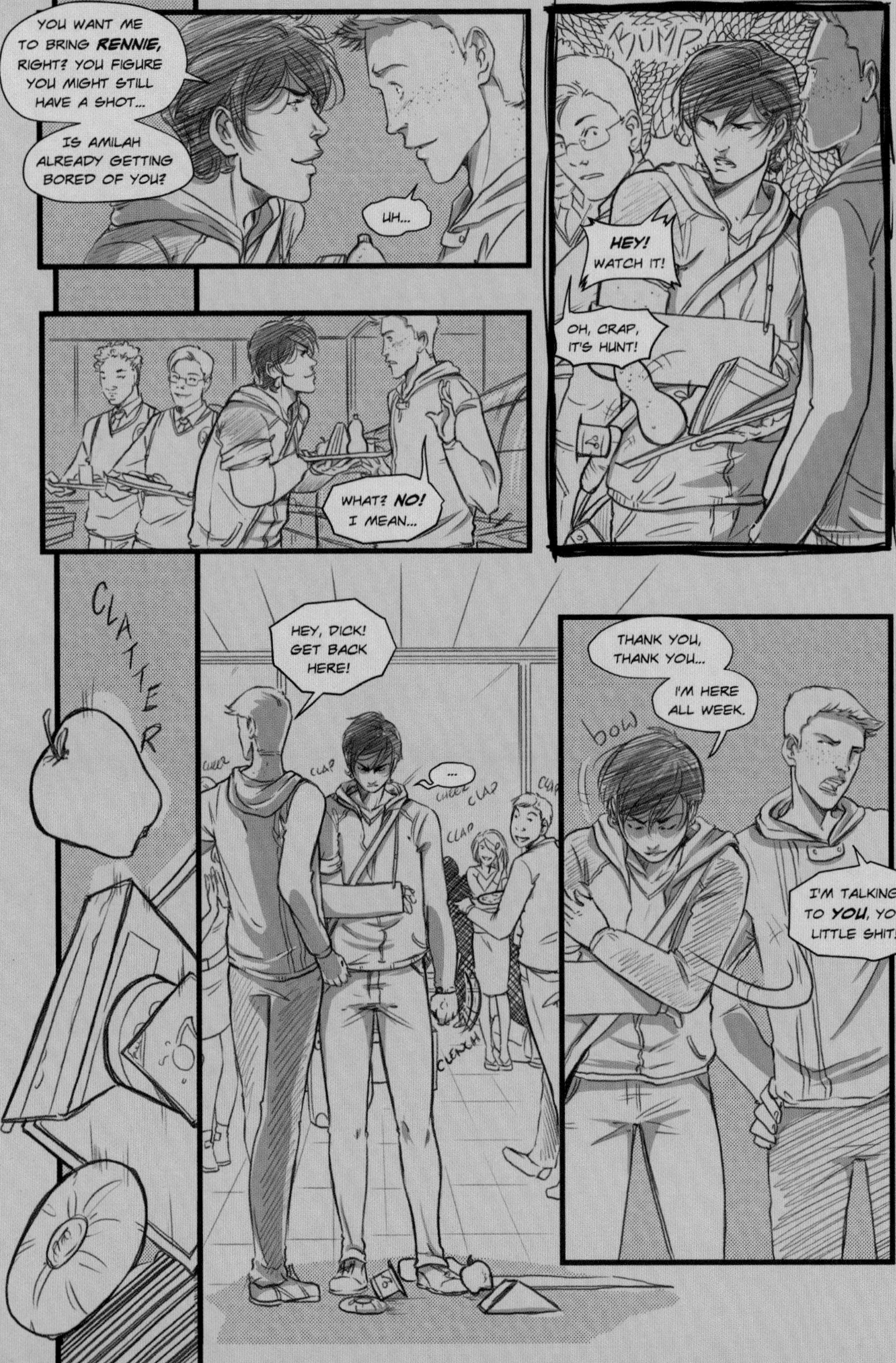
YOU WANT ME TO BRING RENNIE, RIGHT? YOU FIGURE YOU MIGHT STILL HAVE A SHOT...
IS AMILAH ALREADY GETTING BORED OF YOU?
UH...
WHAT? NO! I MEAN...
BUMP
HEY! WATCH IT!
OH, CRAP, IT'S HUNT!
CLATTER
HEY, DICK! GET BACK HERE!
...
CLAP
CLAP
CLAP
CLENCH
THANK YOU, THANK YOU...
I'M HERE ALL WEEK.
bow
I'M TALKING TO YOU, YOU LITTLE SHIT!

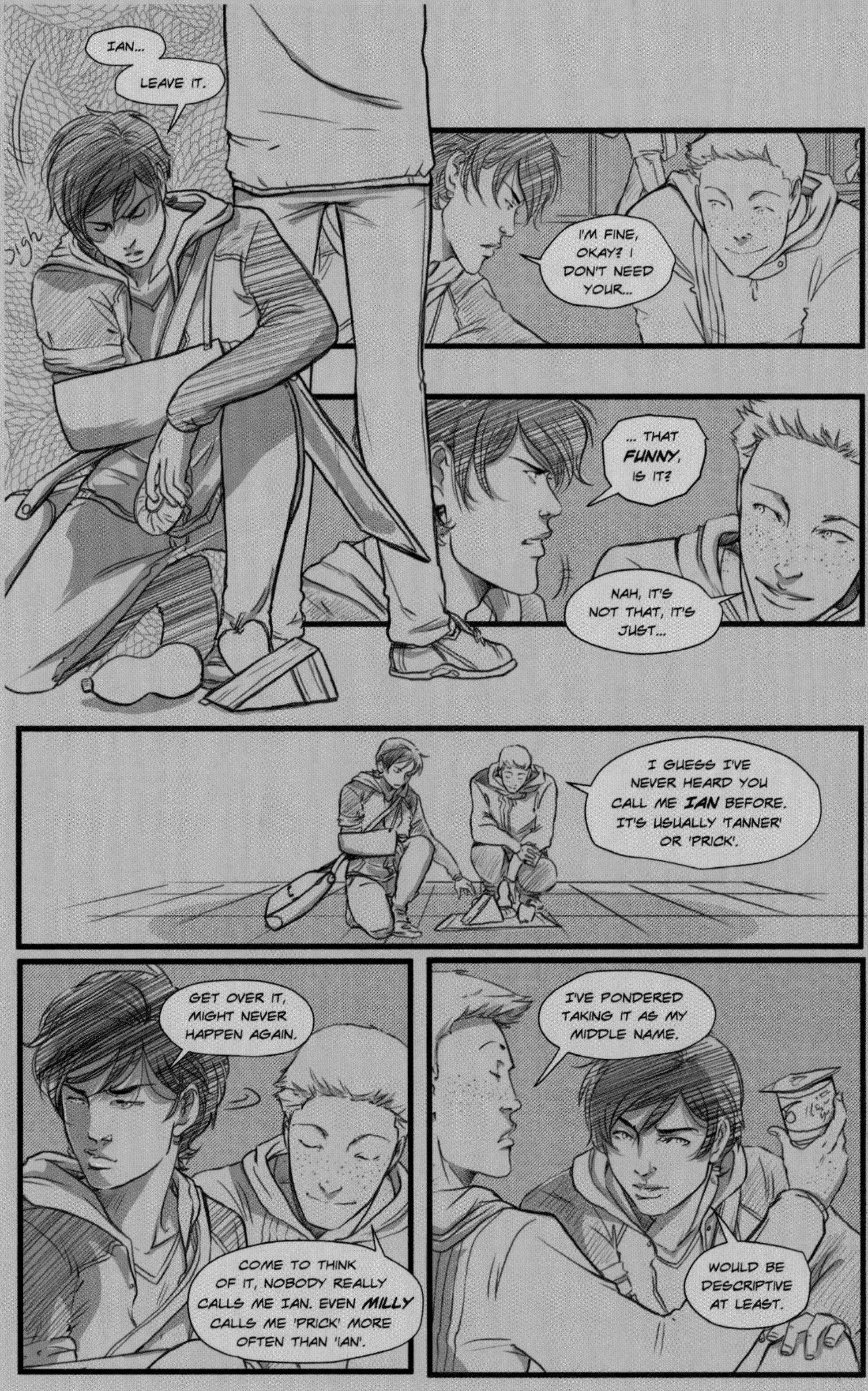
IAN...
LEAVE IT.
Sigh
I'M FINE, OKAY? I DON'T NEED YOUR...
... THAT FUNNY, IS IT?
NAH, IT'S NOT THAT, IT'S JUST...
I GUESS I'VE NEVER HEARD YOU CALL ME IAN BEFORE. IT'S USUALLY 'TANNER' OR 'PRICK'.
GET OVER IT, MIGHT NEVER HAPPEN AGAIN.
COME TO THINK OF IT, NOBODY REALLY CALLS ME IAN. EVEN MILLY CALLS ME 'PRICK' MORE OFTEN THAN 'IAN'.
I'VE PONDERED TAKING IT AS MY MIDDLE NAME.
WOULD BE DESCRIPTIVE AT LEAST.

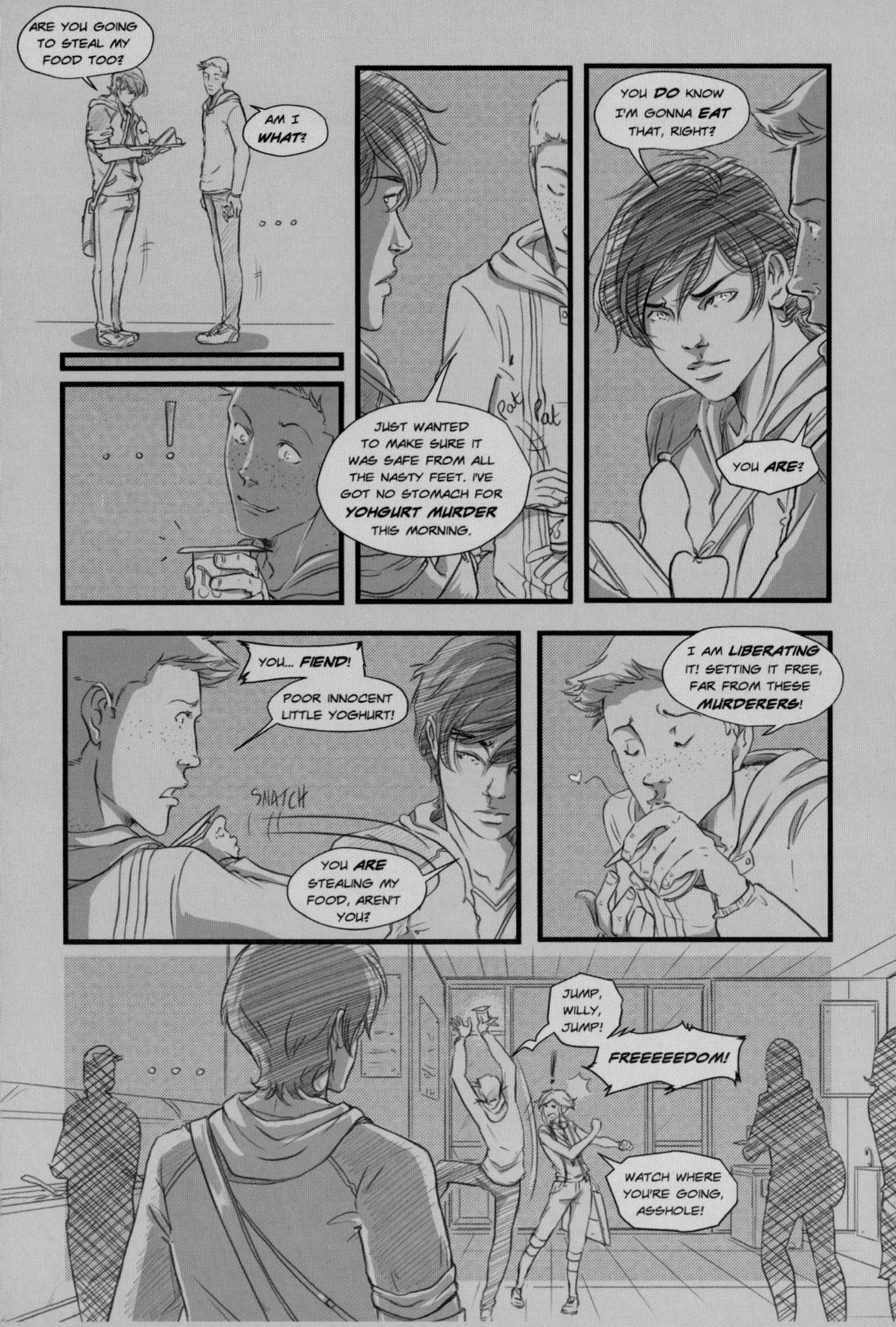

ARE YOU GOING TO STEAL MY FOOD TOO?
AM I WHAT?
...
...!
JUST WANTED TO MAKE SURE IT WAS SAFE FROM ALL THE NASTY FEET. I'VE GOT NO STOMACH FOR YOHGURT MURDER THIS MORNING.
PAT PAT
YOU DO KNOW I'M GONNA EAT THAT, RIGHT?
YOU ARE?
YOU... FIEND!
POOR INNOCENT LITTLE YOGHURT!
SNATCH
YOU ARE STEALING MY FOOD, AREN'T YOU?
I AM LIBERATING IT! SETTING IT FREE, FAR FROM THESE MURDERERS!
...
JUMP, WILLY, JUMP!
FREEEEEDOM!
!
WATCH WHERE YOU'RE GOING, ASSHOLE!

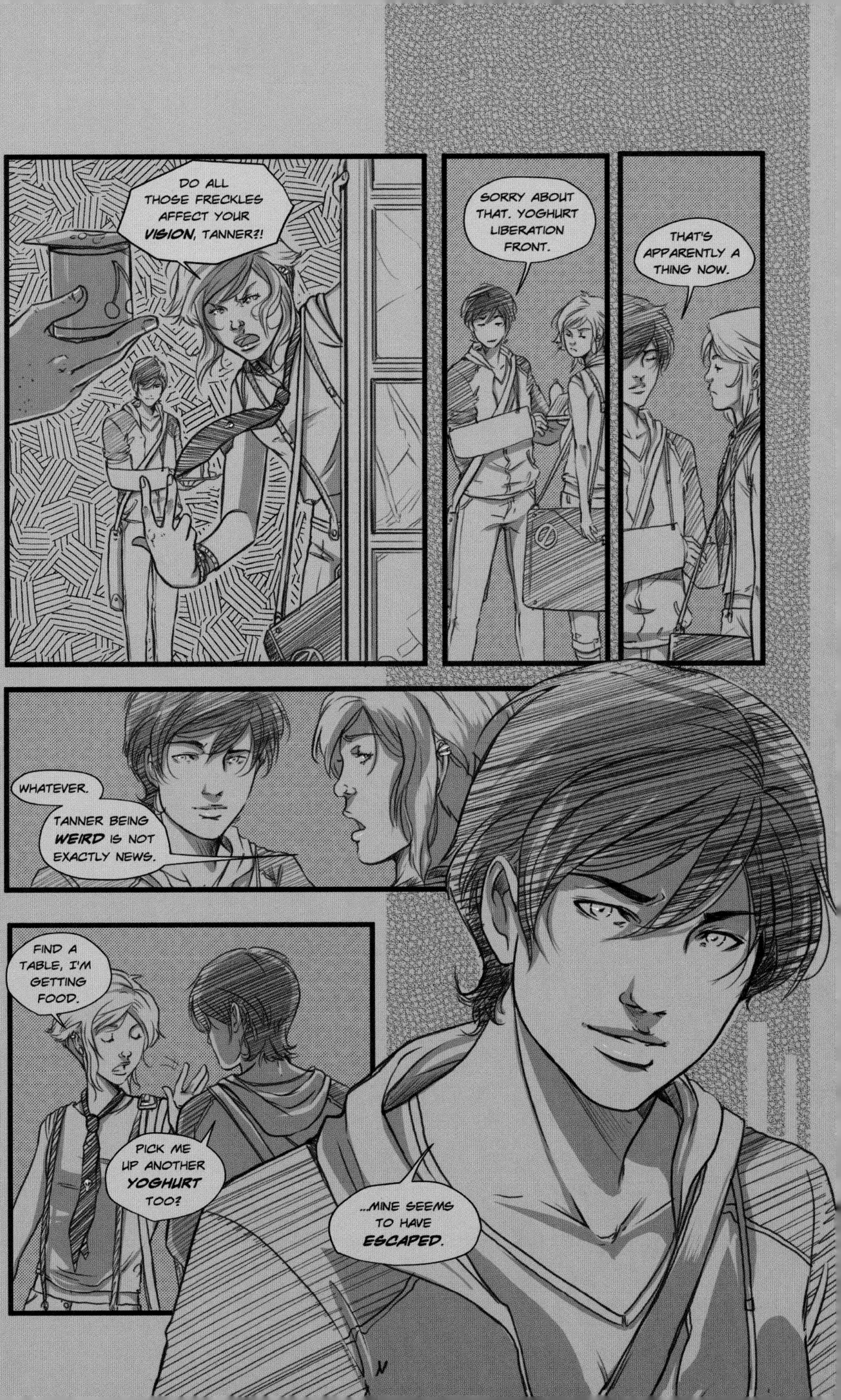
DO ALL THOSE FRECKLES AFFECT YOUR VISION, TANNER?!
SORRY ABOUT THAT. YOGHURT LIBERATION FRONT.
THAT'S APPARENTLY A THING NOW.
WHATEVER.
TANNER BEING WEIRD IS NOT EXACTLY NEWS.
FIND A TABLE, I'M GETTING FOOD.
PICK ME UP ANOTHER YOGHURT TOO?
...MINE SEEMS TO HAVE ESCAPED.

ISSUE 5

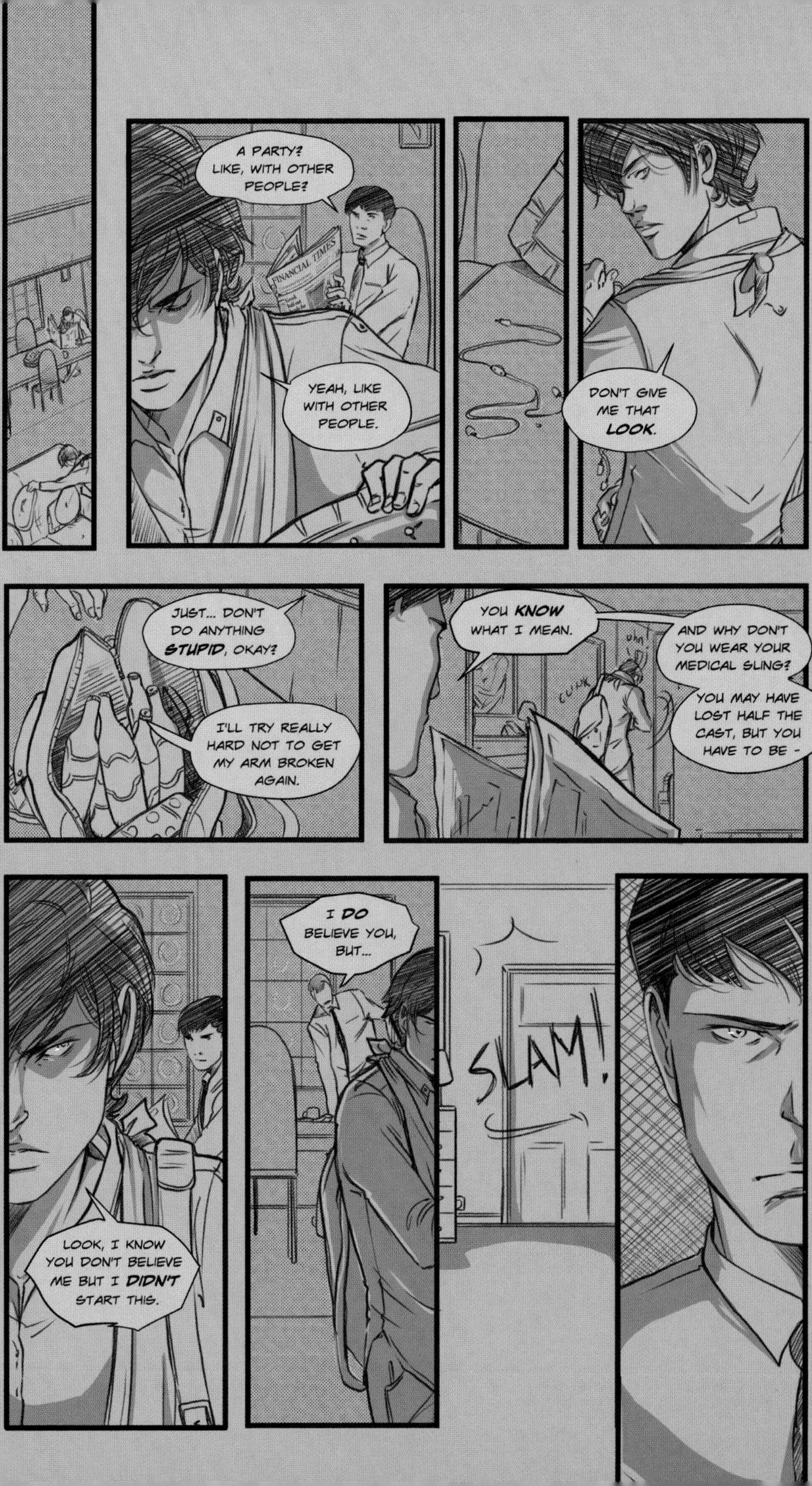
FINANCIAL TIMES
A PARTY? LIKE, WITH OTHER PEOPLE?
YEAH, LIKE WITH OTHER PEOPLE.
DON'T GIVE ME THAT **LOOK**.
JUST... DON'T DO ANYTHING **STUPID**, OKAY?
I'LL TRY REALLY HARD NOT TO GET MY ARM BROKEN AGAIN.
YOU **KNOW** WHAT I MEAN.
AND WHY DON'T YOU WEAR YOUR MEDICAL SLING?
YOU MAY HAVE LOST HALF THE CAST, BUT YOU HAVE TO BE -
LOOK, I KNOW YOU DON'T BELIEVE ME BUT I **DIDN'T** START THIS.
I **DO** BELIEVE YOU, BUT...
SLAM!

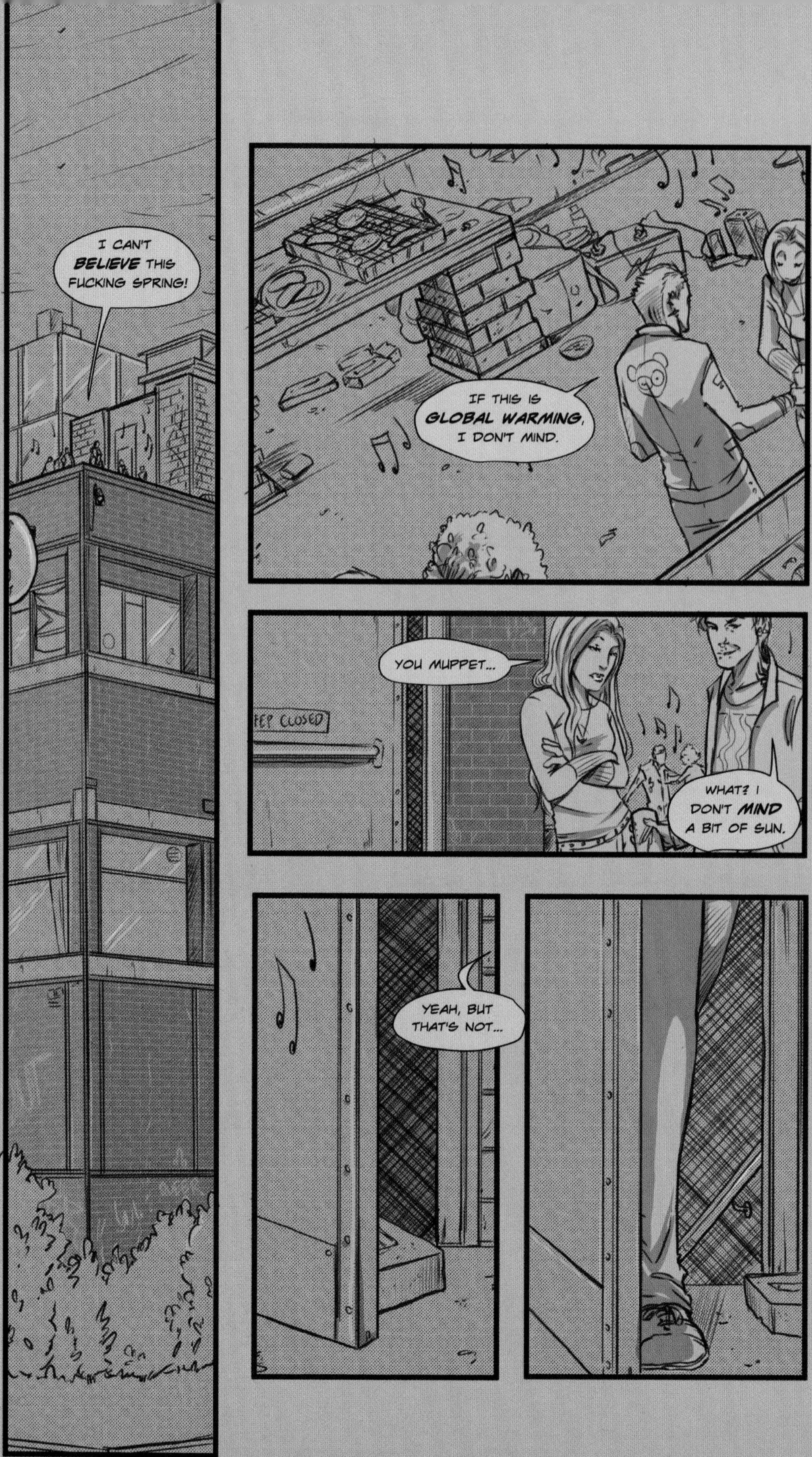
I CAN'T BELIEVE THIS FUCKING SPRING!
IF THIS IS GLOBAL WARMING, I DON'T MIND.
YOU MUPPET...
WHAT? I DON'T MIND A BIT OF SUN.
YEAH, BUT THAT'S NOT...

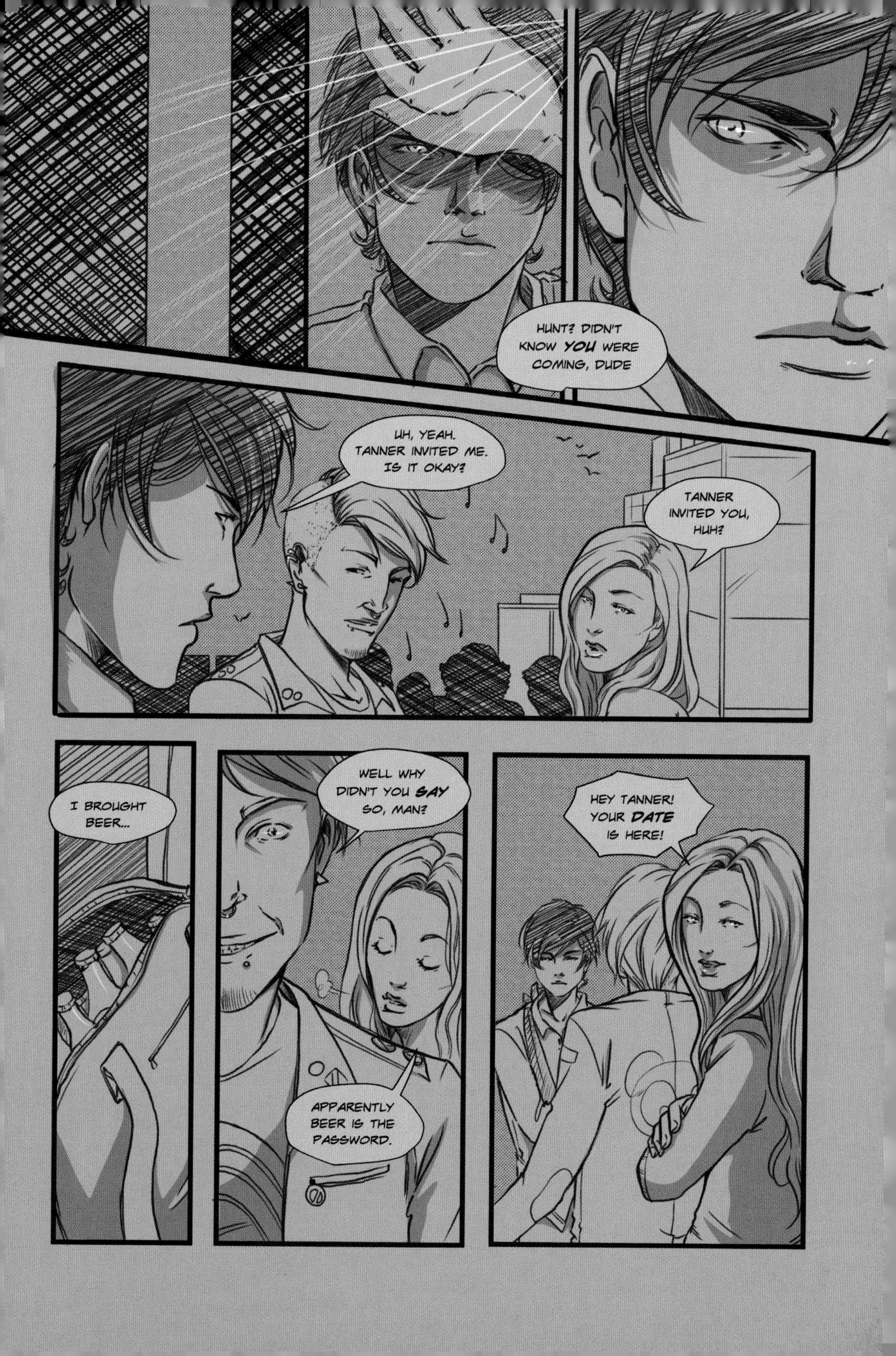
HUNT? DIDN'T KNOW YOU WERE COMING, DUDE
UH, YEAH. TANNER INVITED ME. IS IT OKAY?
TANNER INVITED YOU, HUH?
I BROUGHT BEER...
WELL WHY DIDN'T YOU SAY SO, MAN?
APPARENTLY BEER IS THE PASSWORD.
HEY TANNER! YOUR DATE IS HERE!

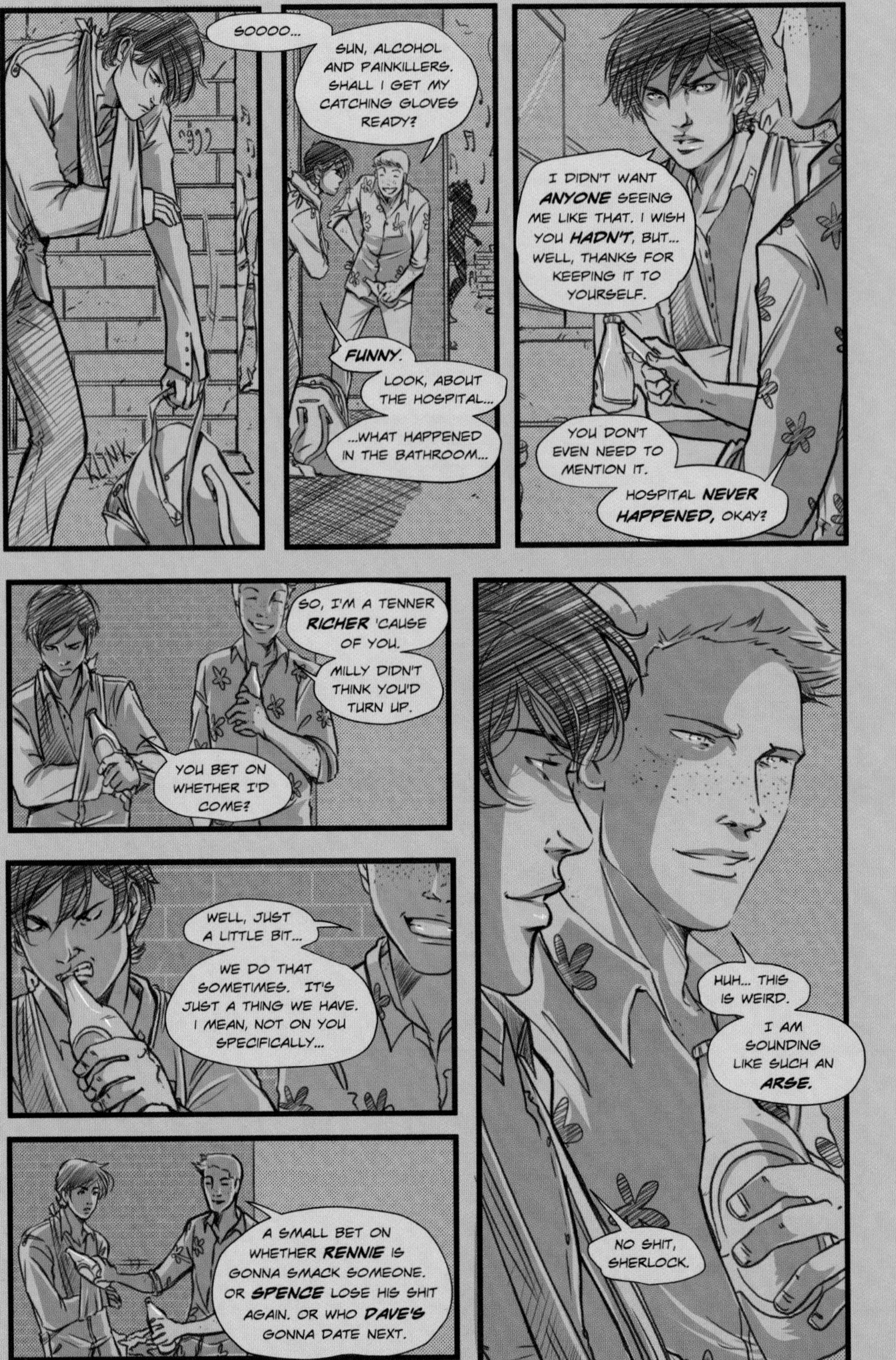
KLINK
SOOOO...
SUN, ALCOHOL AND PAINKILLERS. SHALL I GET MY CATCHING GLOVES READY?
FUNNY.
LOOK, ABOUT THE HOSPITAL...
...WHAT HAPPENED IN THE BATHROOM...
I DIDN'T WANT ANYONE SEEING ME LIKE THAT. I WISH YOU HADN'T, BUT... WELL, THANKS FOR KEEPING IT TO YOURSELF.
YOU DON'T EVEN NEED TO MENTION IT.
HOSPITAL NEVER HAPPENED, OKAY?
SO, I'M A TENNER RICHER 'CAUSE OF YOU.
MILLY DIDN'T THINK YOU'D TURN UP.
YOU BET ON WHETHER I'D COME?
WELL, JUST A LITTLE BIT...
WE DO THAT SOMETIMES. IT'S JUST A THING WE HAVE. I MEAN, NOT ON YOU SPECIFICALLY...
A SMALL BET ON WHETHER RENNIE IS GONNA SMACK SOMEONE. OR SPENCE LOSE HIS SHIT AGAIN. OR WHO DAVE'S GONNA DATE NEXT.
HUH... THIS IS WEIRD.
I AM SOUNDING LIKE SUCH AN ARSE.
NO SHIT, SHERLOCK.

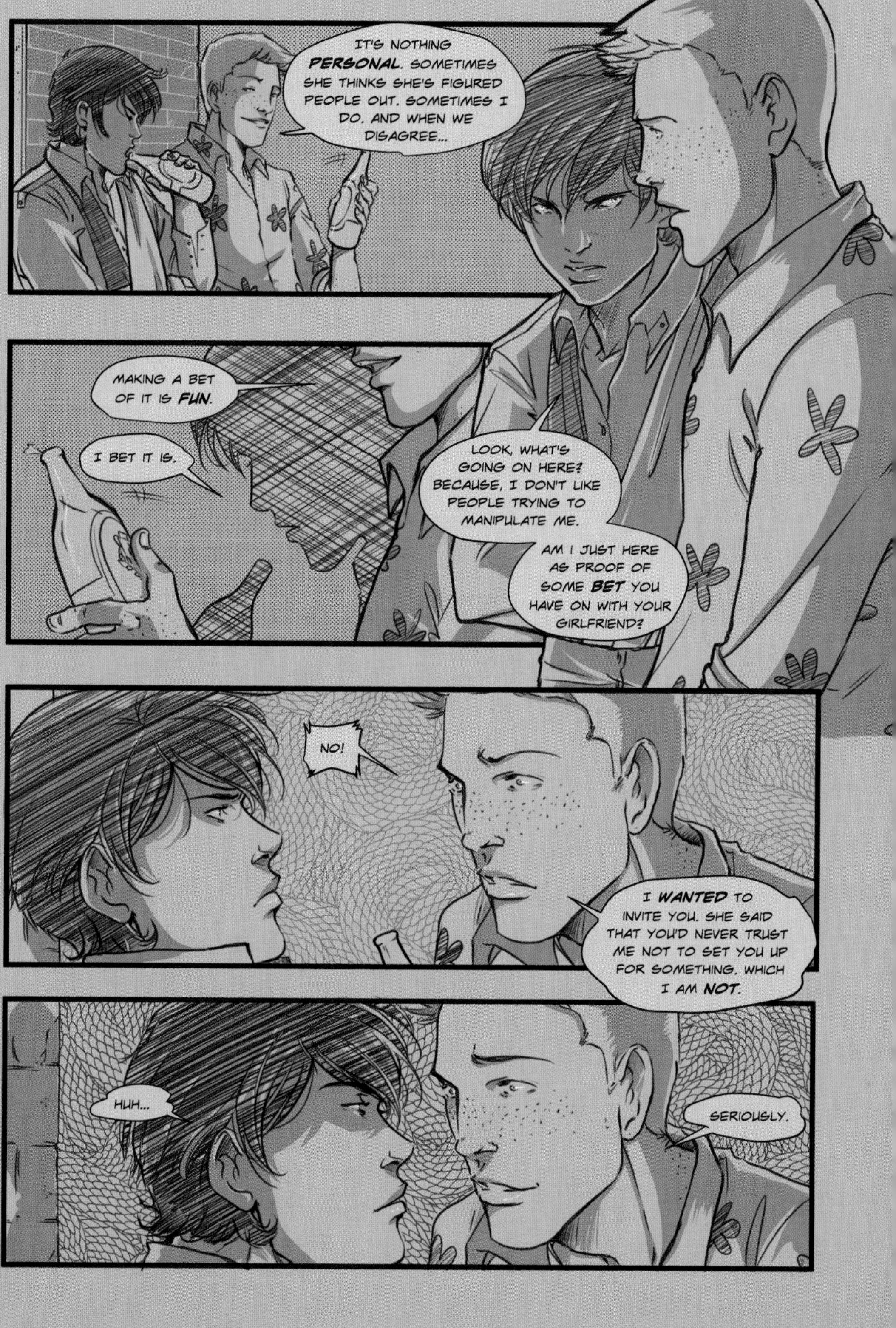
IT'S NOTHING PERSONAL. SOMETIMES SHE THINKS SHE'S FIGURED PEOPLE OUT. SOMETIMES I DO. AND WHEN WE DISAGREE...
MAKING A BET OF IT IS FUN.
I BET IT IS.
LOOK, WHAT'S GOING ON HERE? BECAUSE, I DON'T LIKE PEOPLE TRYING TO MANIPULATE ME.
AM I JUST HERE AS PROOF OF SOME BET YOU HAVE ON WITH YOUR GIRLFRIEND?
NO!
I WANTED TO INVITE YOU. SHE SAID THAT YOU'D NEVER TRUST ME NOT TO SET YOU UP FOR SOMETHING. WHICH I AM NOT.
HUH...
SERIOUSLY.

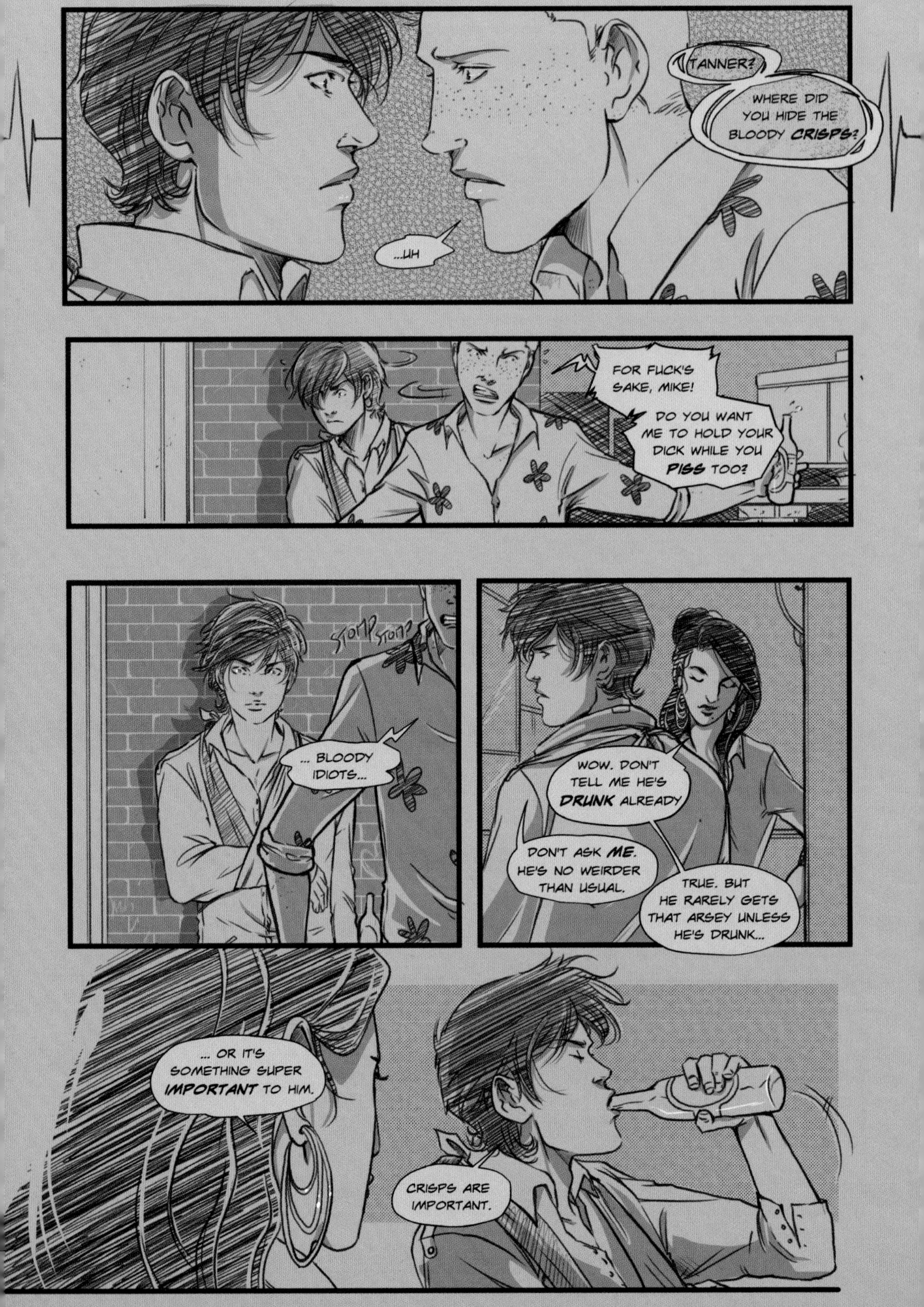
TANNER?
WHERE DID YOU HIDE THE BLOODY CRISPS?
...UH
FOR FUCK'S SAKE, MIKE!
DO YOU WANT ME TO HOLD YOUR DICK WHILE YOU PISS TOO?
STOMP STOMP
... BLOODY IDIOTS...
WOW. DON'T TELL ME HE'S DRUNK ALREADY
DON'T ASK ME. HE'S NO WEIRDER THAN USUAL.
TRUE. BUT HE RARELY GETS THAT ARSEY UNLESS HE'S DRUNK...
... OR IT'S SOMETHING SUPER IMPORTANT TO HIM.
CRISPS ARE IMPORTANT.

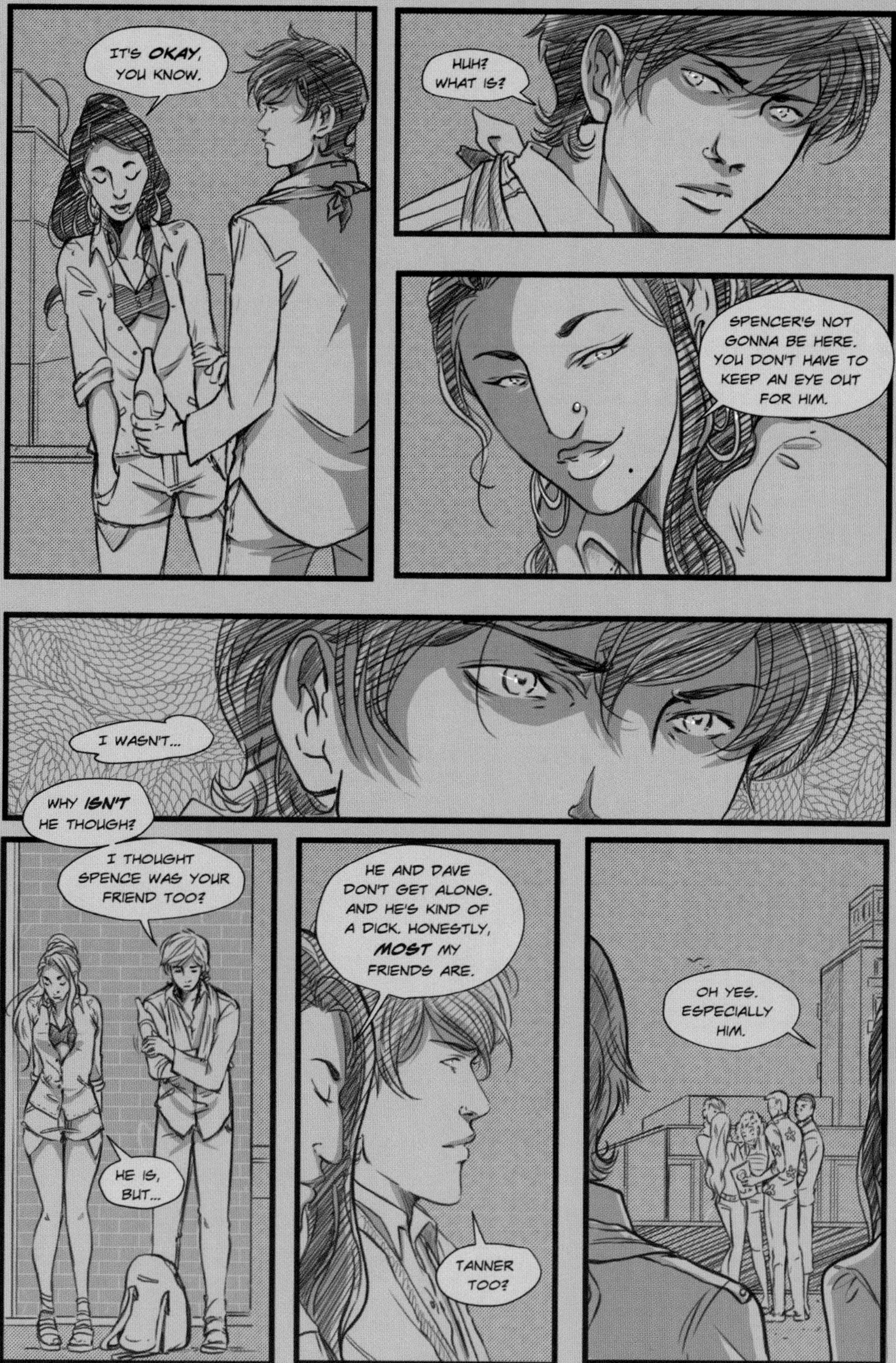

IT'S OKAY, YOU KNOW.
HUH? WHAT IS?
SPENCER'S NOT GONNA BE HERE. YOU DON'T HAVE TO KEEP AN EYE OUT FOR HIM.
I WASN'T...
WHY ISN'T HE THOUGH?
I THOUGHT SPENCE WAS YOUR FRIEND TOO?
HE IS, BUT...
HE AND DAVE DON'T GET ALONG. AND HE'S KIND OF A DICK. HONESTLY, MOST MY FRIENDS ARE.
TANNER TOO?
OH YES. ESPECIALLY HIM.

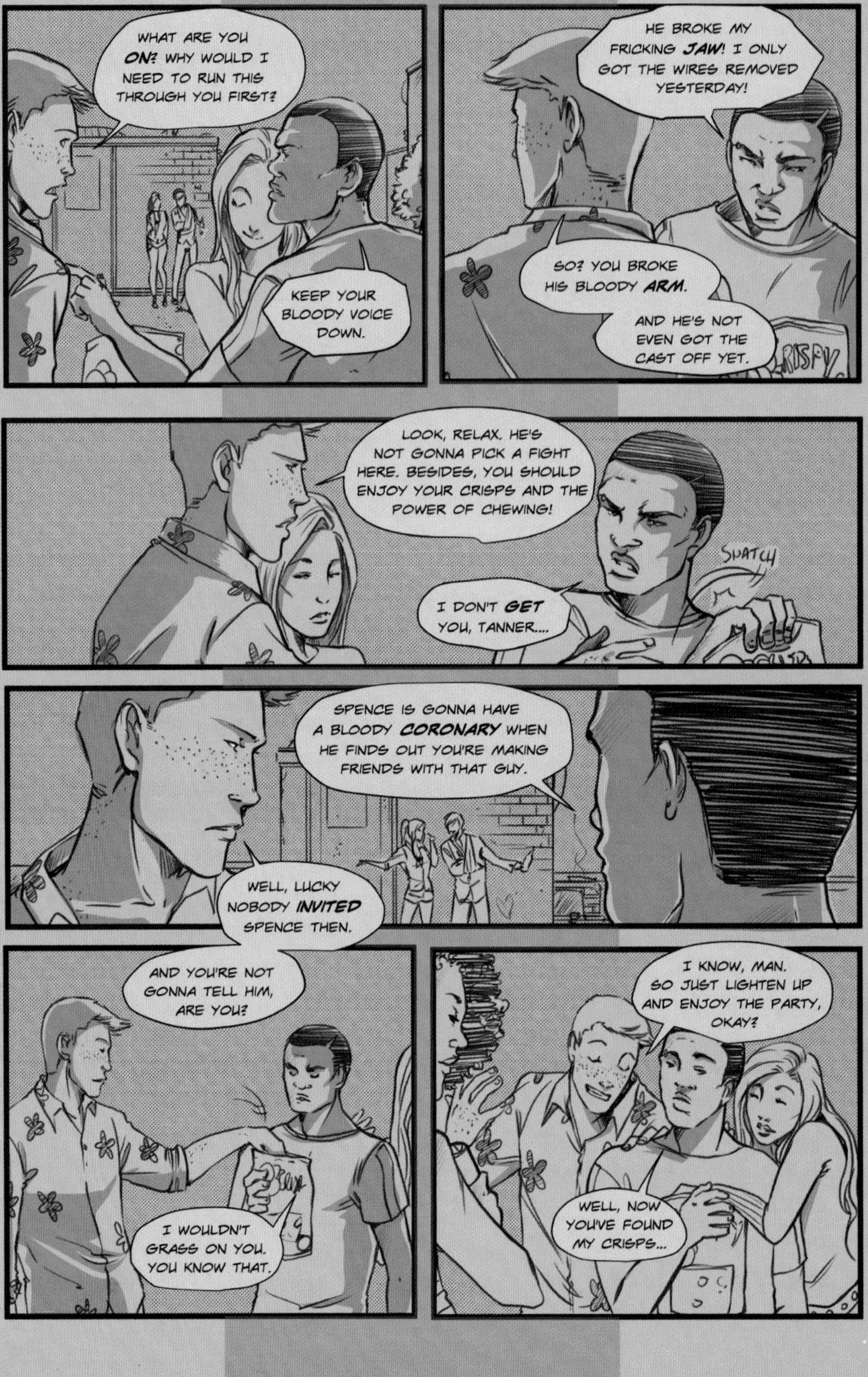
WHAT ARE YOU ON? WHY WOULD I NEED TO RUN THIS THROUGH YOU FIRST?
KEEP YOUR BLOODY VOICE DOWN.
HE BROKE MY FRICKING JAW! I ONLY GOT THE WIRES REMOVED YESTERDAY!
SO? YOU BROKE HIS BLOODY ARM.
AND HE'S NOT EVEN GOT THE CAST OFF YET.
CRISPY
LOOK, RELAX. HE'S NOT GONNA PICK A FIGHT HERE. BESIDES, YOU SHOULD ENJOY YOUR CRISPS AND THE POWER OF CHEWING!
SNATCH
I DON'T GET YOU, TANNER....
SPENCE IS GONNA HAVE A BLOODY CORONARY WHEN HE FINDS OUT YOU'RE MAKING FRIENDS WITH THAT GUY.
WELL, LUCKY NOBODY INVITED SPENCE THEN.
AND YOU'RE NOT GONNA TELL HIM, ARE YOU?
I WOULDN'T GRASS ON YOU. YOU KNOW THAT.
I KNOW, MAN. SO JUST LIGHTEN UP AND ENJOY THE PARTY, OKAY?
WELL, NOW YOU'VE FOUND MY CRISPS...

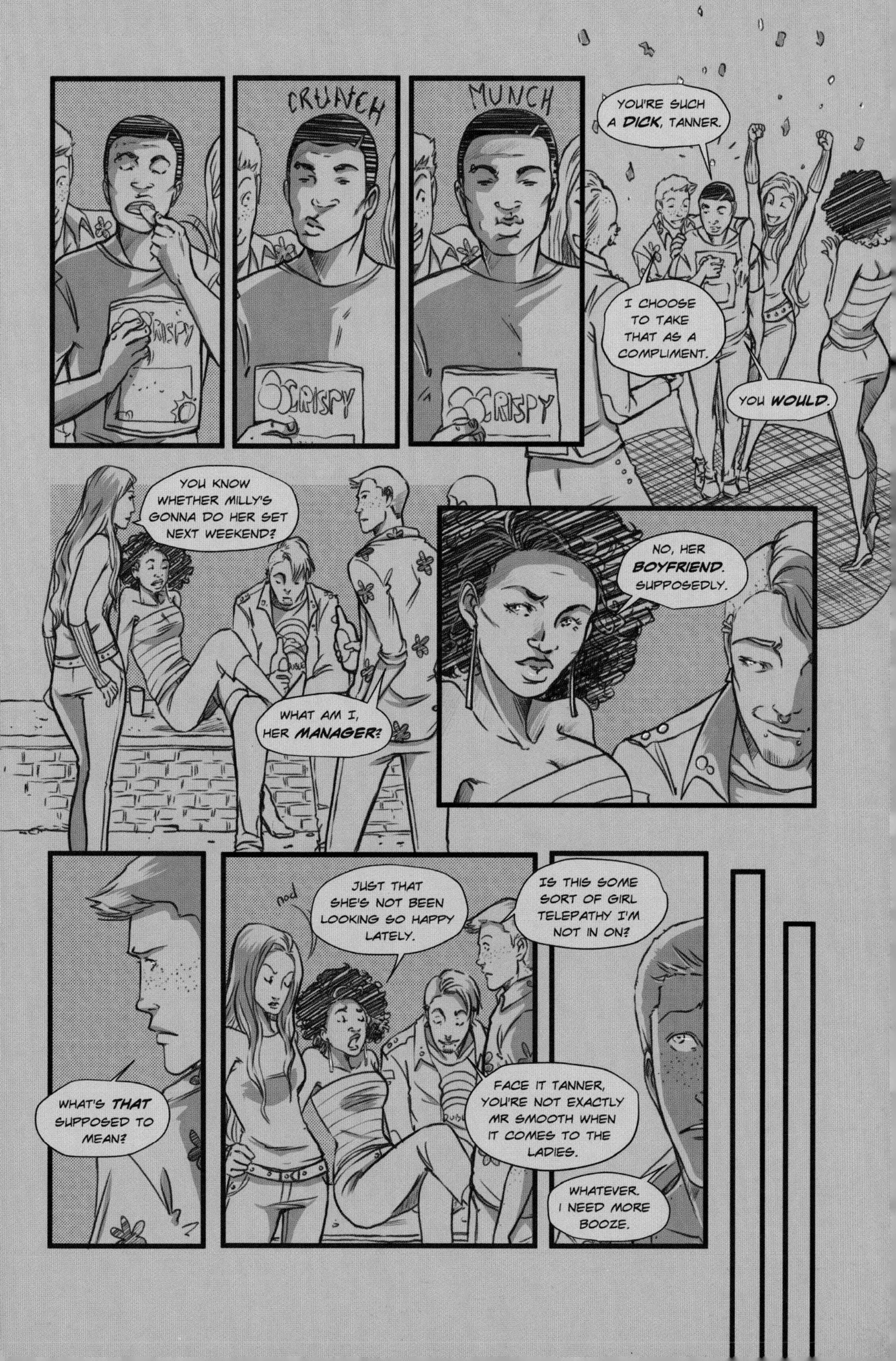

CRUNCH
MUNCH
CRISPY
YOU'RE SUCH A DICK, TANNER.
I CHOOSE TO TAKE THAT AS A COMPLIMENT.
YOU WOULD.
YOU KNOW WHETHER MILLY'S GONNA DO HER SET NEXT WEEKEND?
WHAT AM I, HER MANAGER?
NO, HER BOYFRIEND. SUPPOSEDLY.
WHAT'S THAT SUPPOSED TO MEAN?
nod
JUST THAT SHE'S NOT BEEN LOOKING SO HAPPY LATELY.
IS THIS SOME SORT OF GIRL TELEPATHY I'M NOT IN ON?
FACE IT TANNER, YOU'RE NOT EXACTLY MR SMOOTH WHEN IT COMES TO THE LADIES.
WHATEVER. I NEED MORE BOOZE.

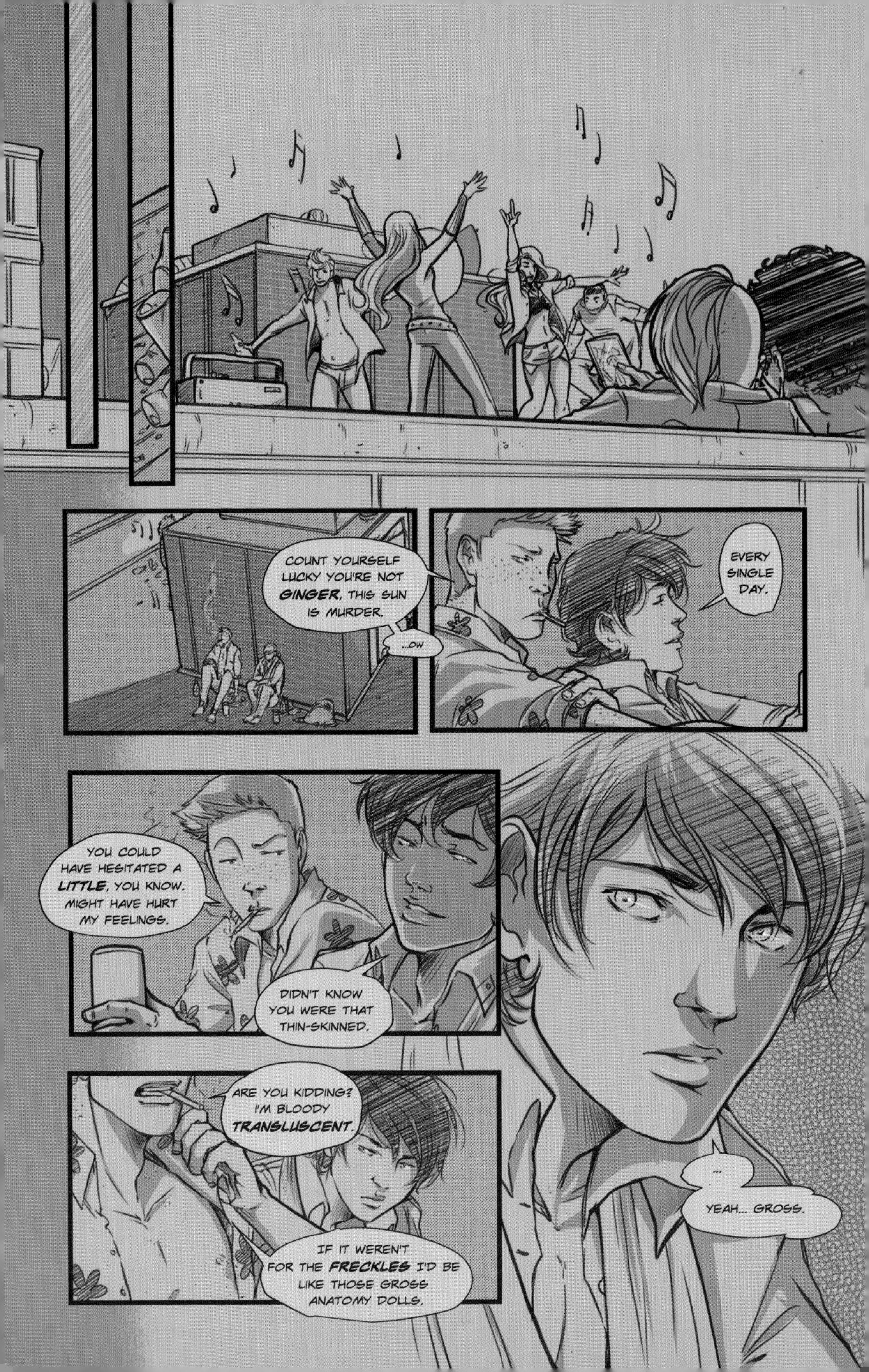
COUNT YOURSELF LUCKY YOU'RE NOT GINGER, THIS SUN IS MURDER.
...OW
EVERY SINGLE DAY.
YOU COULD HAVE HESITATED A LITTLE, YOU KNOW. MIGHT HAVE HURT MY FEELINGS.
DIDN'T KNOW YOU WERE THAT THIN-SKINNED.
ARE YOU KIDDING? I'M BLOODY TRANSLUSCENT.
IF IT WEREN'T FOR THE FRECKLES I'D BE LIKE THOSE GROSS ANATOMY DOLLS.
...
YEAH... GROSS.

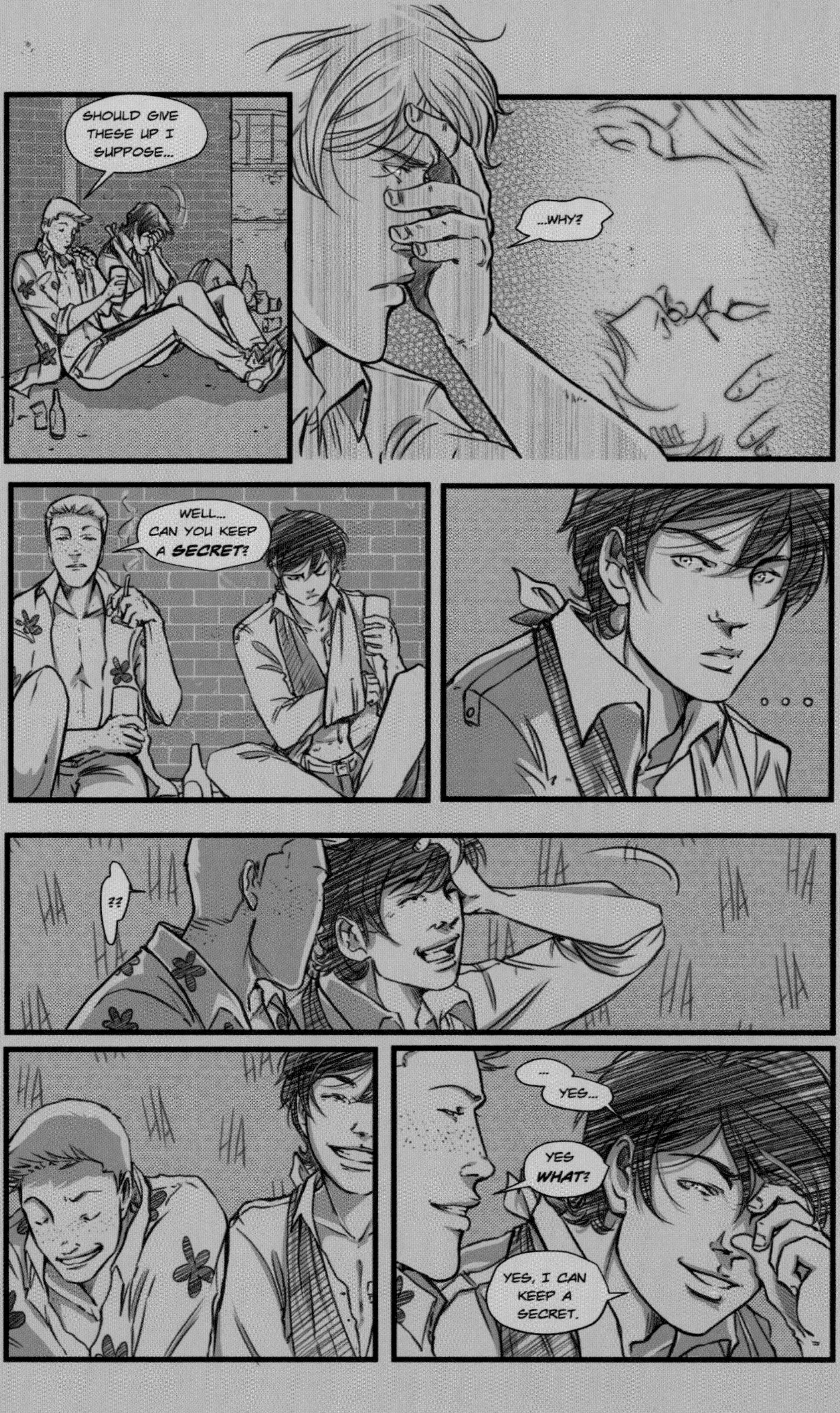
SHOULD GIVE THESE UP I SUPPOSE...
...WHY?
WELL... CAN YOU KEEP A SECRET?
...
??
HA HA HA HA HA HA HA HA HA HA HA HA
HA HA HA HA
... YES...
YES WHAT?
YES, I CAN KEEP A SECRET.

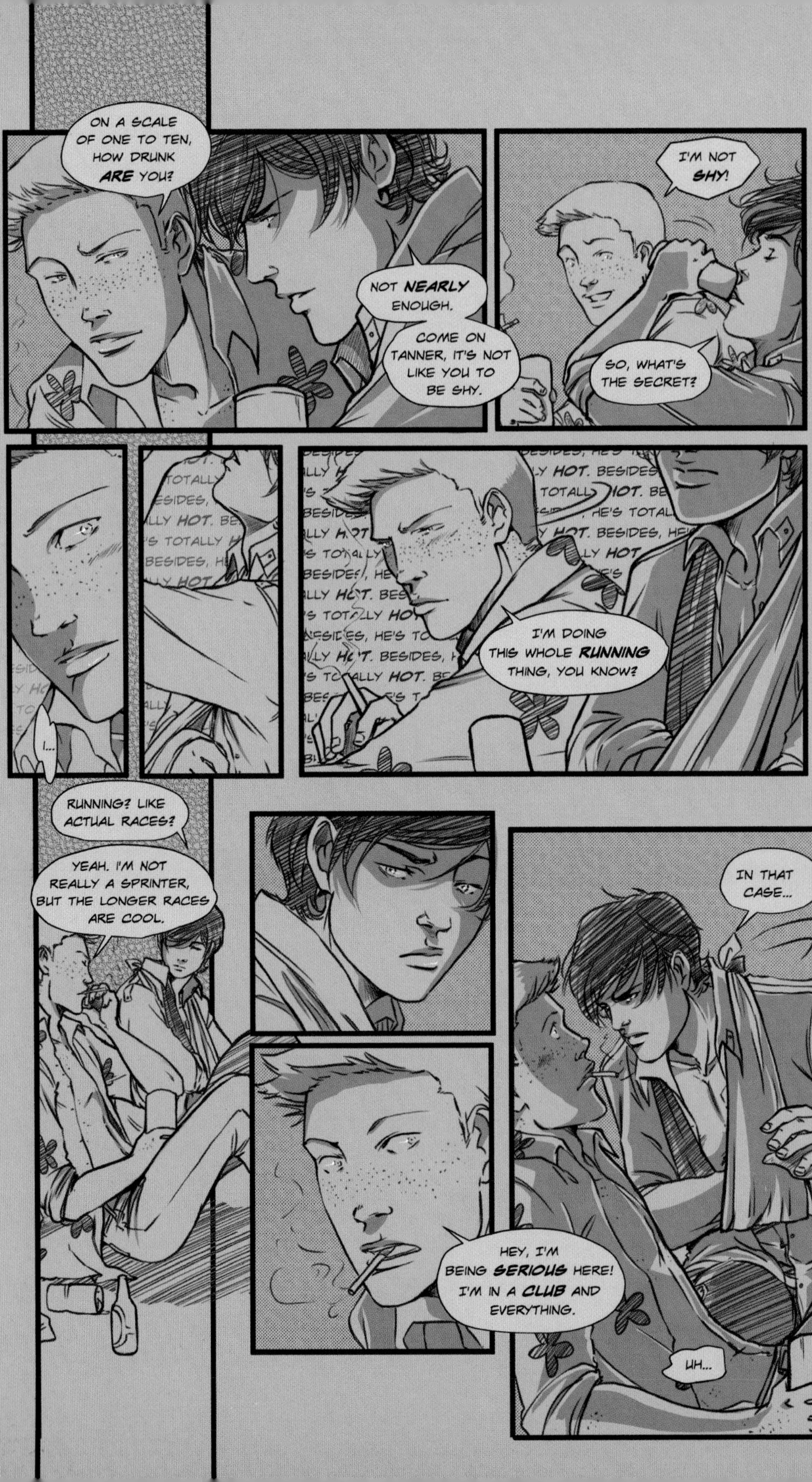
ON A SCALE OF ONE TO TEN, HOW DRUNK ARE YOU?
NOT NEARLY ENOUGH.
COME ON TANNER, IT'S NOT LIKE YOU TO BE SHY.
I'M NOT SHY!
SO, WHAT'S THE SECRET?
I...
HE'S TOTALLY HOT. BESIDES,
I'M DOING THIS WHOLE RUNNING THING, YOU KNOW?
RUNNING? LIKE ACTUAL RACES?
YEAH. I'M NOT REALLY A SPRINTER, BUT THE LONGER RACES ARE COOL.
HEY, I'M BEING SERIOUS HERE! I'M IN A CLUB AND EVERYTHING.
IN THAT CASE...
UH...

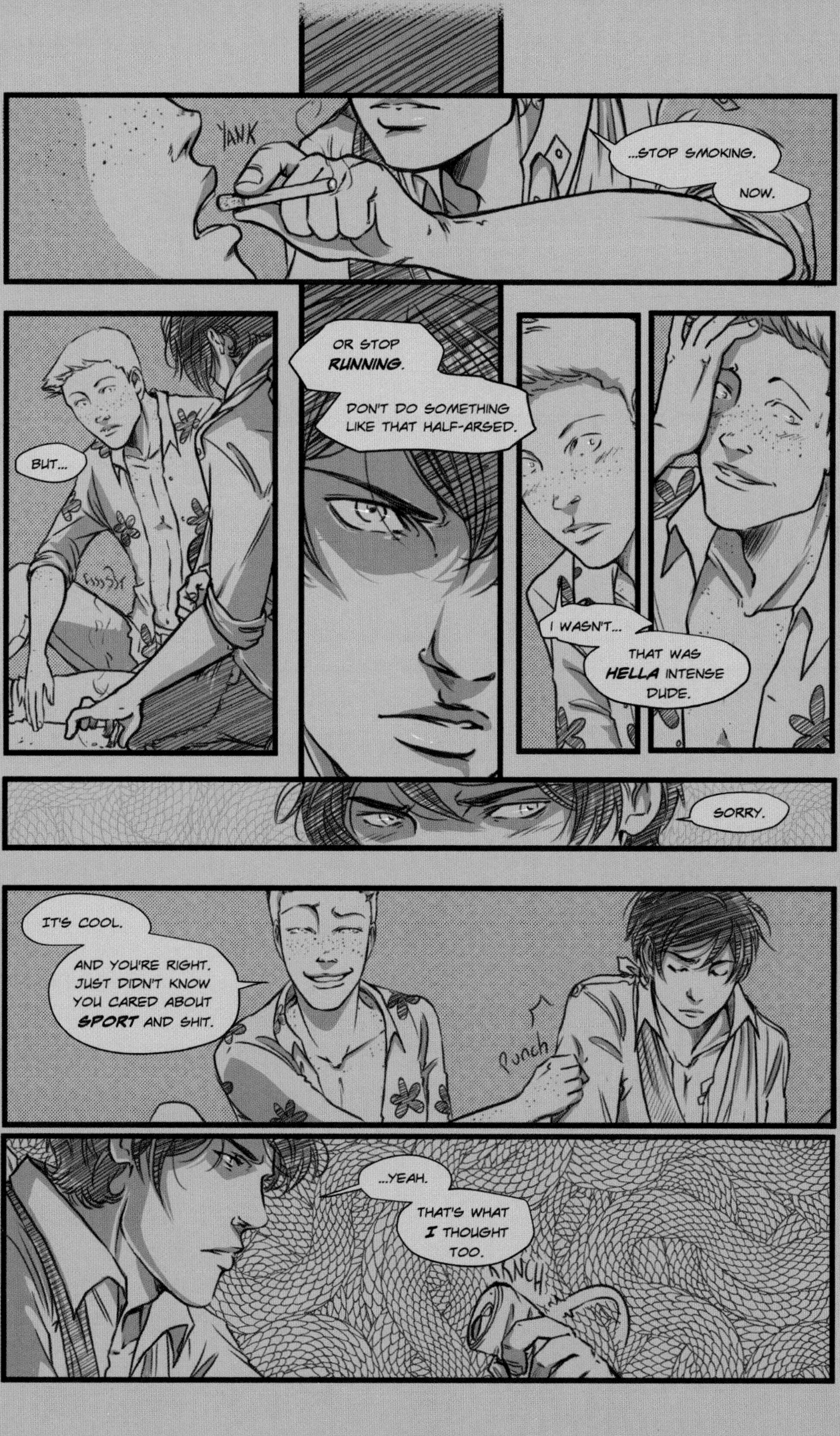
YANK
...STOP SMOKING.
NOW.
BUT...
OR STOP RUNNING.
DON'T DO SOMETHING LIKE THAT HALF-ARSED.
I WASN'T...
THAT WAS HELLA INTENSE DUDE.
SORRY.
IT'S COOL.
AND YOU'RE RIGHT. JUST DIDN'T KNOW YOU CARED ABOUT SPORT AND SHIT.
Punch
...YEAH.
THAT'S WHAT I THOUGHT TOO.

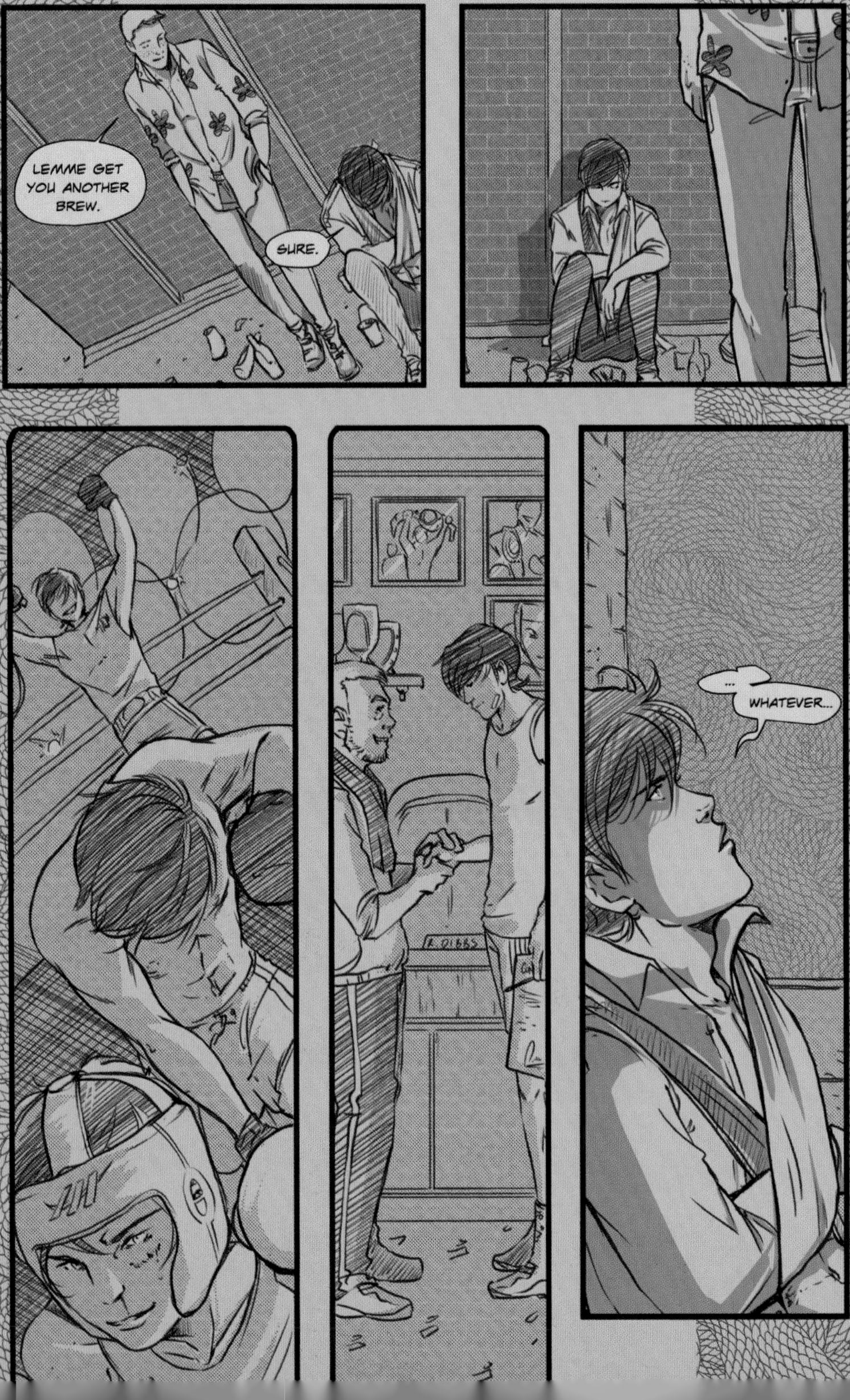
LEMME GET YOU ANOTHER BREW.
SURE.
... WHATEVER...

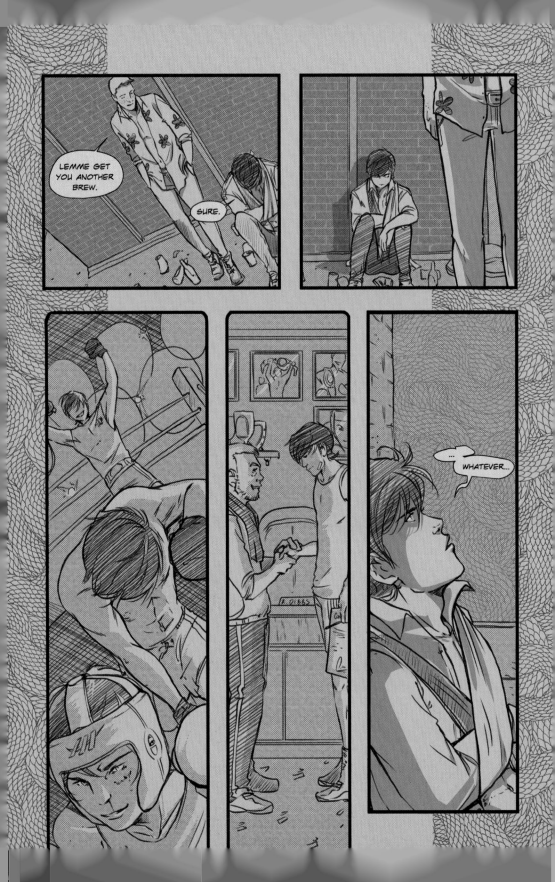

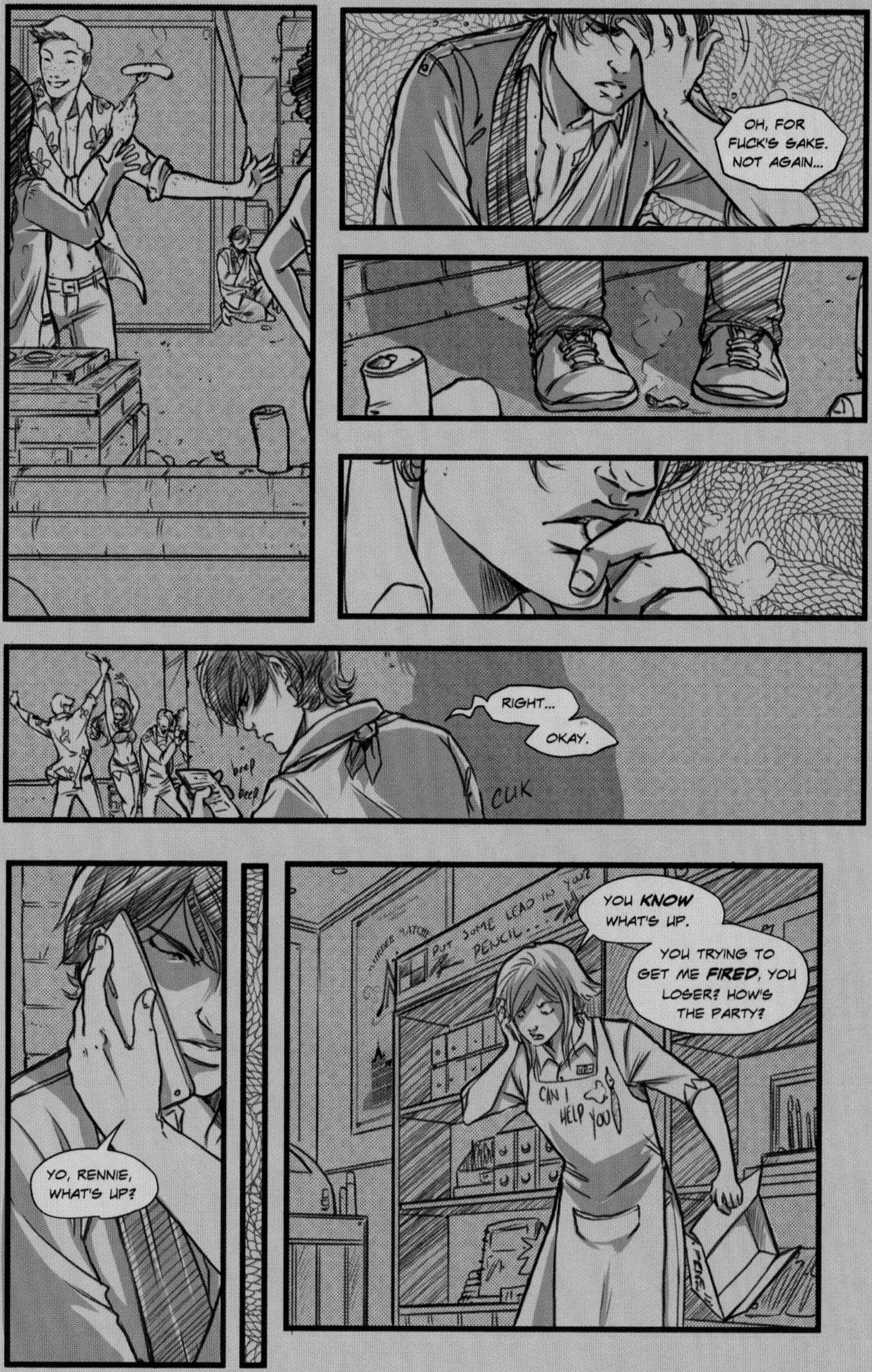
OH, FOR FUCK'S SAKE. NOT AGAIN...
RIGHT...
OKAY.
beep beep
CLIK
YO, RENNIE, WHAT'S UP?
PUT SOME LEAD IN YOUR PENCIL...
YOU KNOW WHAT'S UP.
YOU TRYING TO GET ME FIRED, YOU LOSER? HOW'S THE PARTY?
CAN I HELP YOU

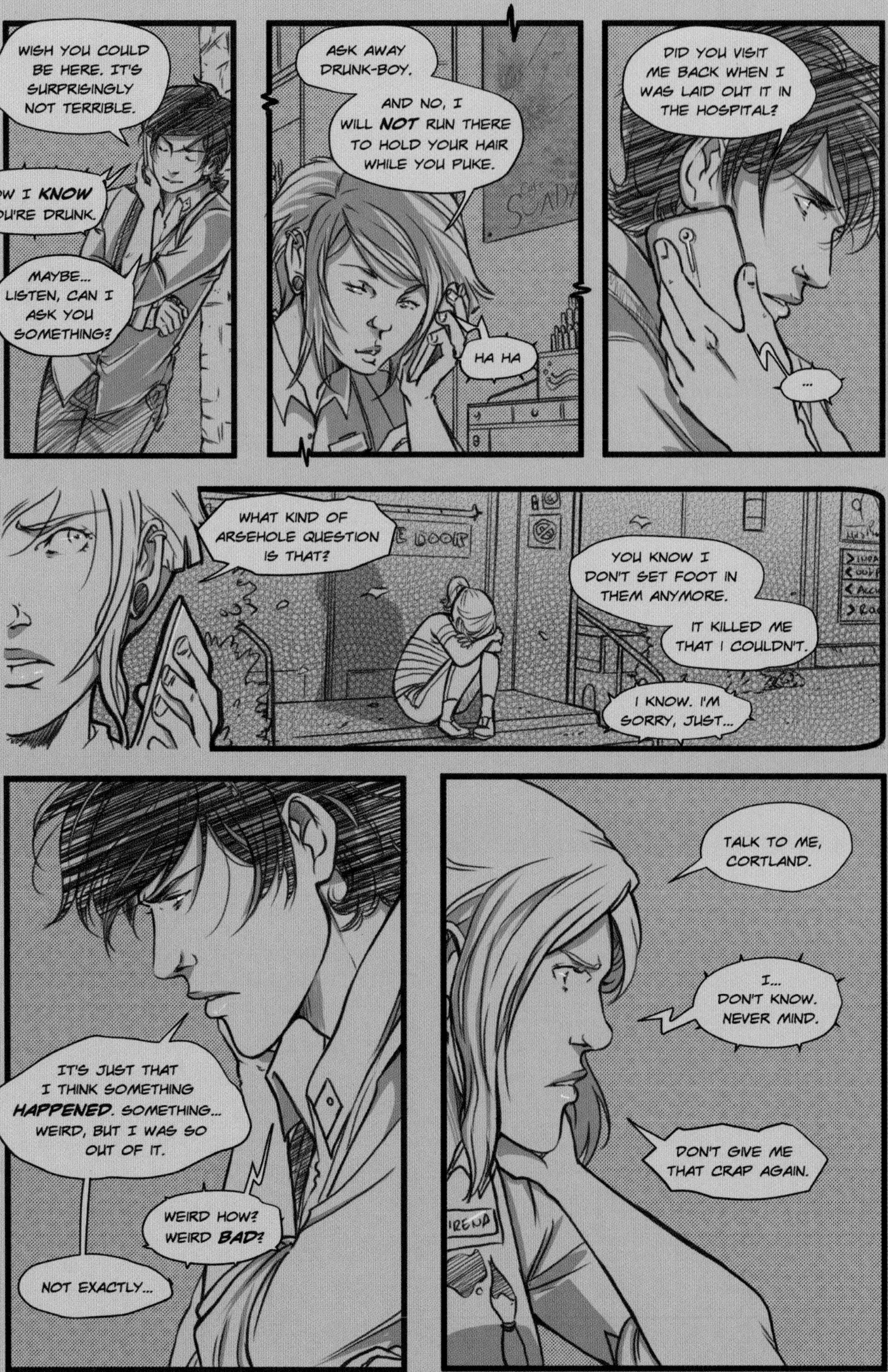
WISH YOU COULD BE HERE. IT'S SURPRISINGLY NOT TERRIBLE.
NOW I KNOW YOU'RE DRUNK.
MAYBE... LISTEN, CAN I ASK YOU SOMETHING?
ASK AWAY DRUNK-BOY.
AND NO, I WILL NOT RUN THERE TO HOLD YOUR HAIR WHILE YOU PUKE.
HA HA
DID YOU VISIT ME BACK WHEN I WAS LAID OUT IT IN THE HOSPITAL?
...
WHAT KIND OF ARSEHOLE QUESTION IS THAT?
YOU KNOW I DON'T SET FOOT IN THEM ANYMORE.
IT KILLED ME THAT I COULDN'T.
I KNOW. I'M SORRY, JUST...
IT'S JUST THAT I THINK SOMETHING HAPPENED. SOMETHING... WEIRD, BUT I WAS SO OUT OF IT.
WEIRD HOW? WEIRD BAD?
NOT EXACTLY...
TALK TO ME, CORTLAND.
I... DON'T KNOW. NEVER MIND.
DON'T GIVE ME THAT CRAP AGAIN.
IRENA

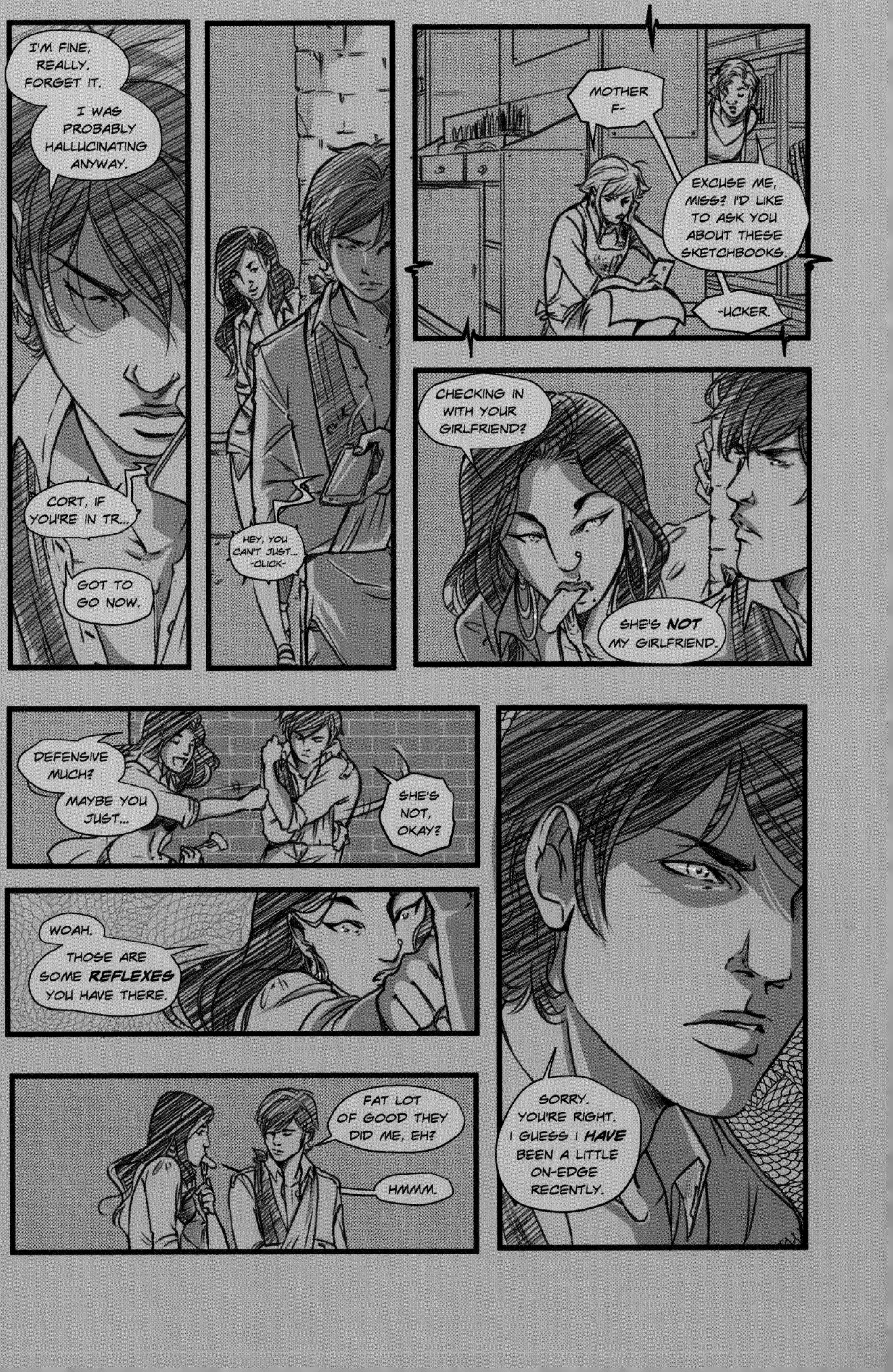
I'M FINE, REALLY. FORGET IT.
I WAS PROBABLY HALLUCINATING ANYWAY.
CORT, IF YOU'RE IN TR...
GOT TO GO NOW.
HEY, YOU CAN'T JUST... -CLICK-
MOTHER F-
EXCUSE ME, MISS? I'D LIKE TO ASK YOU ABOUT THESE SKETCHBOOKS.
-UCKER.
CHECKING IN WITH YOUR GIRLFRIEND?
SHE'S **NOT** MY GIRLFRIEND.
DEFENSIVE MUCH?
MAYBE YOU JUST...
SHE'S NOT, OKAY?
WOAH.
THOSE ARE SOME ***REFLEXES*** YOU HAVE THERE.
FAT LOT OF GOOD THEY DID ME, EH?
HMMM.
SORRY. YOU'RE RIGHT. I GUESS I ***HAVE*** BEEN A LITTLE ON-EDGE RECENTLY.

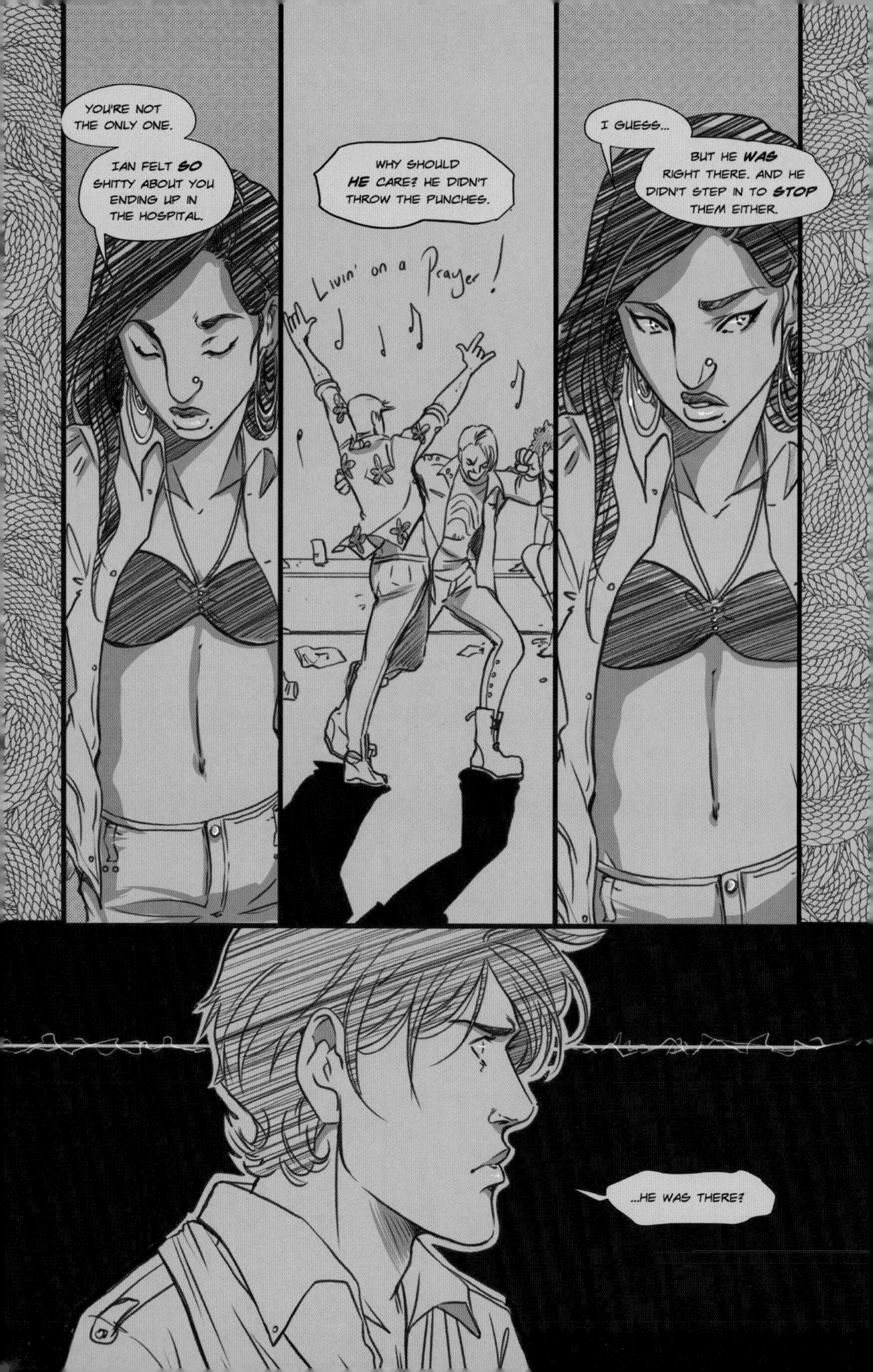
YOU'RE NOT THE ONLY ONE.
IAN FELT SO SHITTY ABOUT YOU ENDING UP IN THE HOSPITAL.
WHY SHOULD HE CARE? HE DIDN'T THROW THE PUNCHES.
Livin' on a Prayer!
I GUESS...
BUT HE WAS RIGHT THERE. AND HE DIDN'T STEP IN TO STOP THEM EITHER.
...HE WAS THERE?

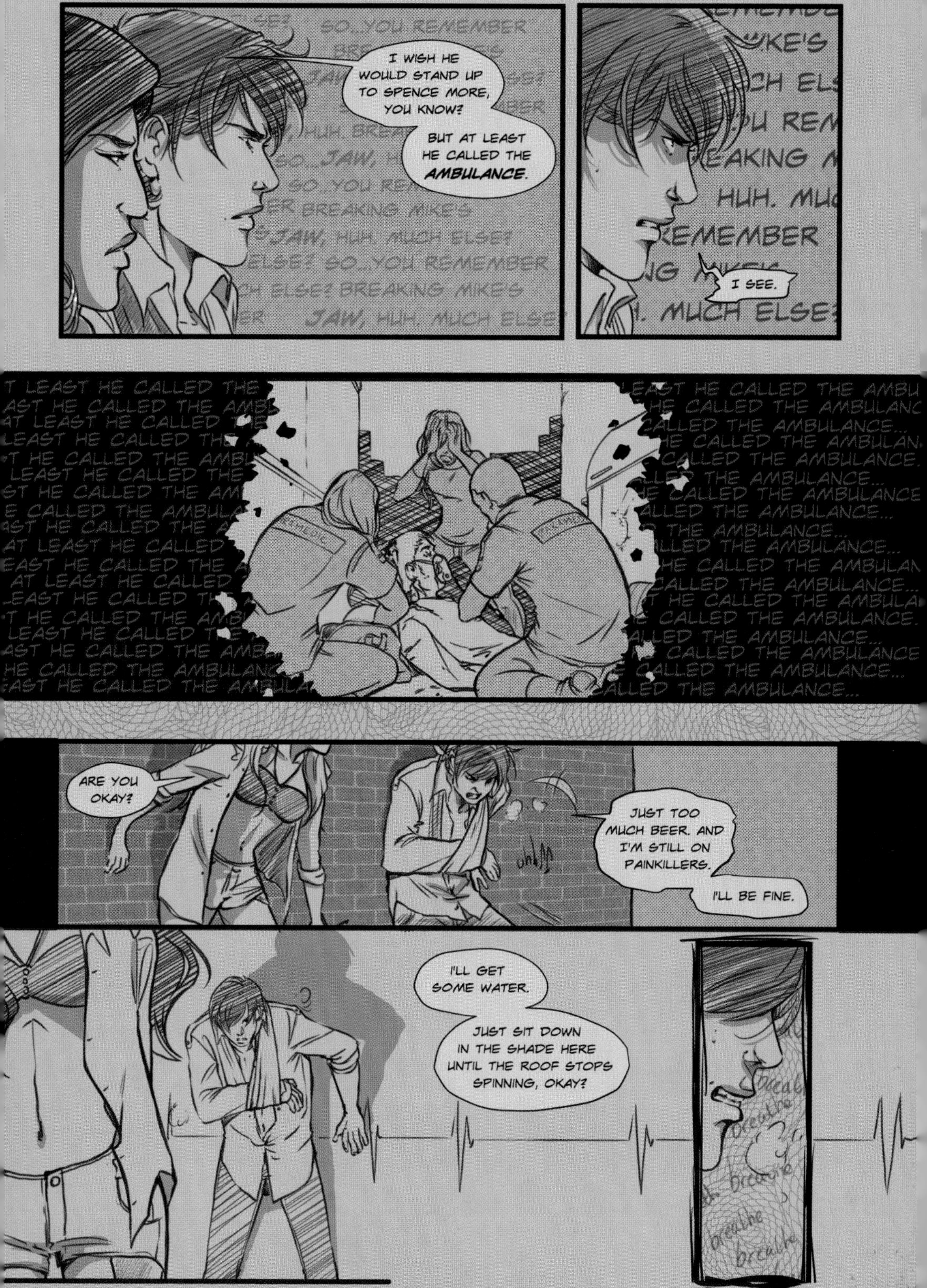
SO...YOU REMEMBER BREAKING MIKE'S JAW, HUH. MUCH ELSE?
I WISH HE WOULD STAND UP TO SPENCE MORE, YOU KNOW?
BUT AT LEAST HE CALLED THE AMBULANCE.
I SEE.
AT LEAST HE CALLED THE AMBULANCE...
PARAMEDIC
ARE YOU OKAY?
JUST TOO MUCH BEER. AND I'M STILL ON PAINKILLERS.
I'LL BE FINE.
I'LL GET SOME WATER.
JUST SIT DOWN IN THE SHADE HERE UNTIL THE ROOF STOPS SPINNING, OKAY?
breathe
breathe
breathe
breathe

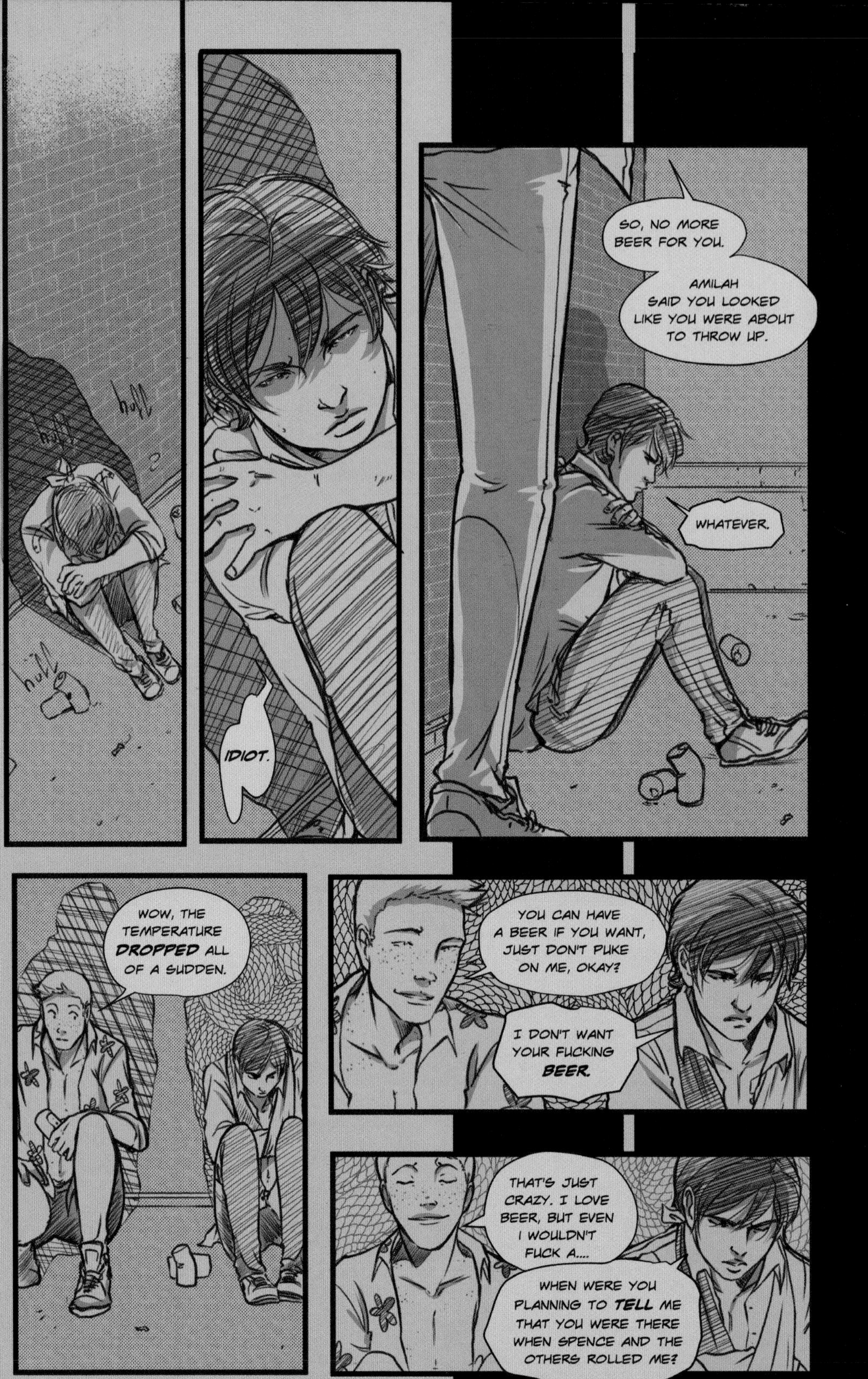
IDIOT.
SO, NO MORE BEER FOR YOU.
AMILAH SAID YOU LOOKED LIKE YOU WERE ABOUT TO THROW UP.
WHATEVER.
WOW, THE TEMPERATURE DROPPED ALL OF A SUDDEN.
YOU CAN HAVE A BEER IF YOU WANT, JUST DON'T PUKE ON ME, OKAY?
I DON'T WANT YOUR FUCKING BEER.
THAT'S JUST CRAZY. I LOVE BEER, BUT EVEN I WOULDN'T FUCK A....
WHEN WERE YOU PLANNING TO TELL ME THAT YOU WERE THERE WHEN SPENCE AND THE OTHERS ROLLED ME?

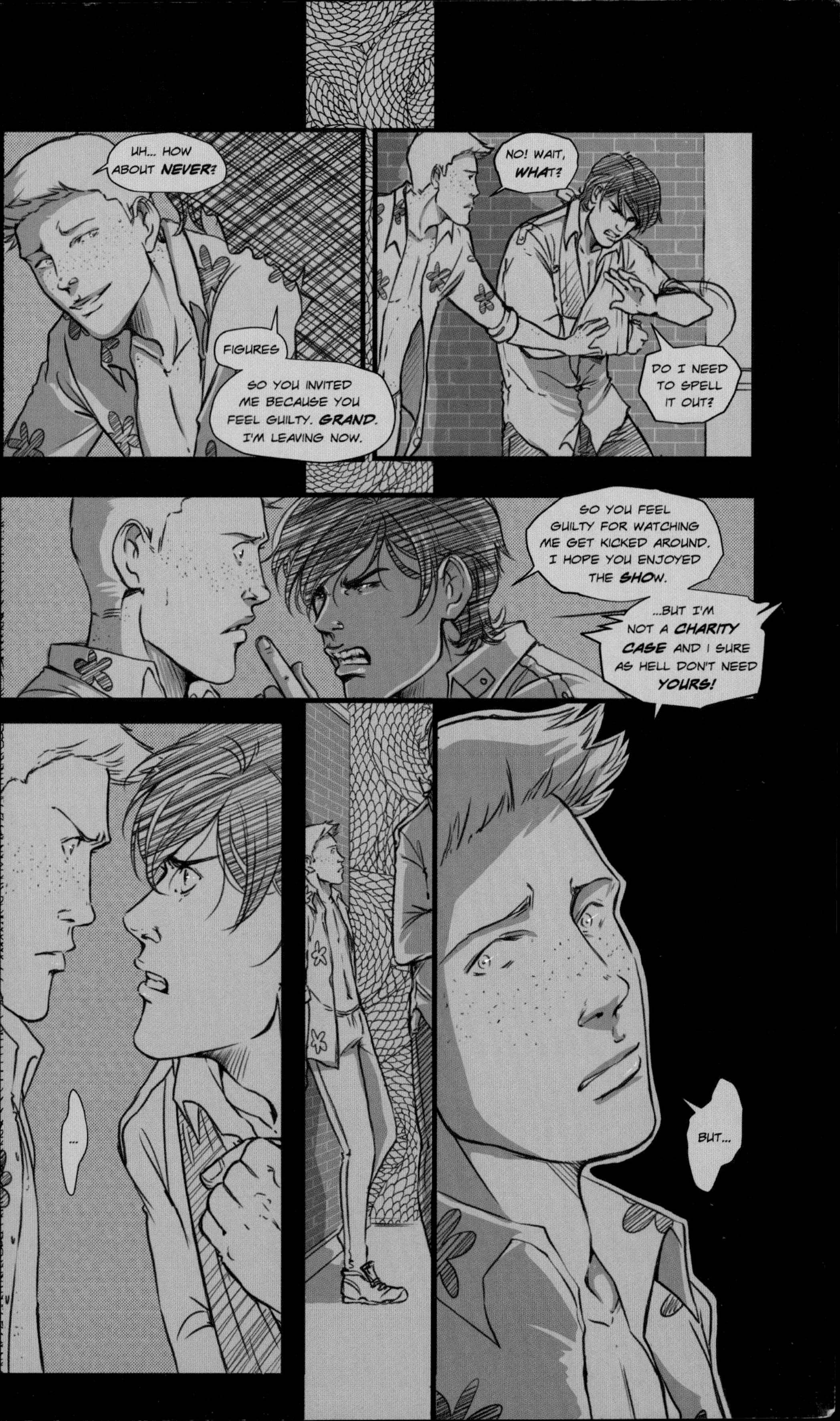
UH... HOW ABOUT NEVER?
FIGURES
SO YOU INVITED ME BECAUSE YOU FEEL GUILTY. GRAND. I'M LEAVING NOW.
NO! WAIT, WHAT?
DO I NEED TO SPELL IT OUT?
SO YOU FEEL GUILTY FOR WATCHING ME GET KICKED AROUND. I HOPE YOU ENJOYED THE SHOW.
...BUT I'M NOT A CHARITY CASE AND I SURE AS HELL DON'T NEED YOURS!
...
BUT...

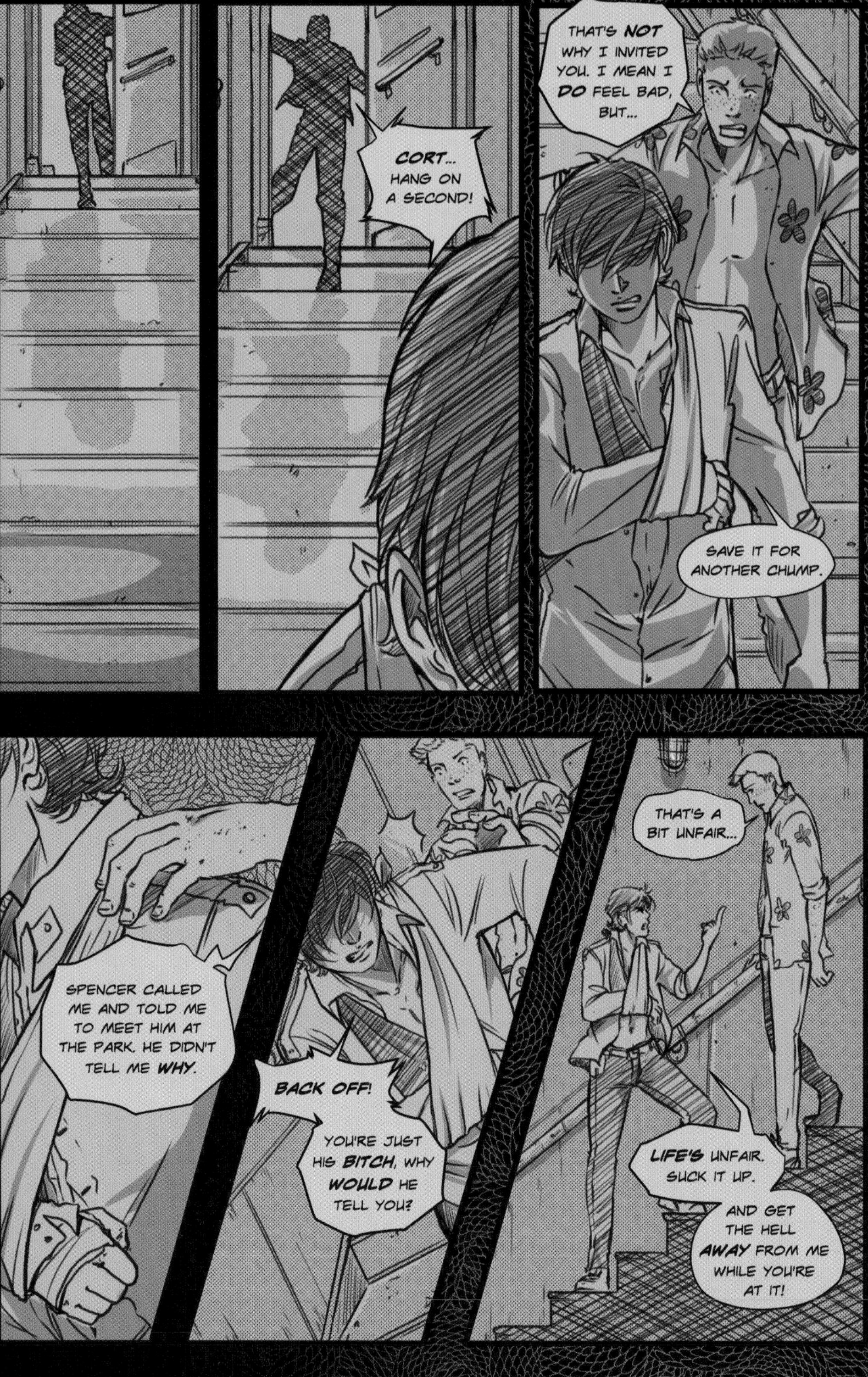
CORT... HANG ON A SECOND!
THAT'S NOT WHY I INVITED YOU. I MEAN I DO FEEL BAD, BUT...
SAVE IT FOR ANOTHER CHUMP.
SPENCER CALLED ME AND TOLD ME TO MEET HIM AT THE PARK. HE DIDN'T TELL ME WHY.
BACK OFF!
YOU'RE JUST HIS BITCH, WHY WOULD HE TELL YOU?
THAT'S A BIT UNFAIR...
LIFE'S UNFAIR. SUCK IT UP.
AND GET THE HELL AWAY FROM ME WHILE YOU'RE AT IT!

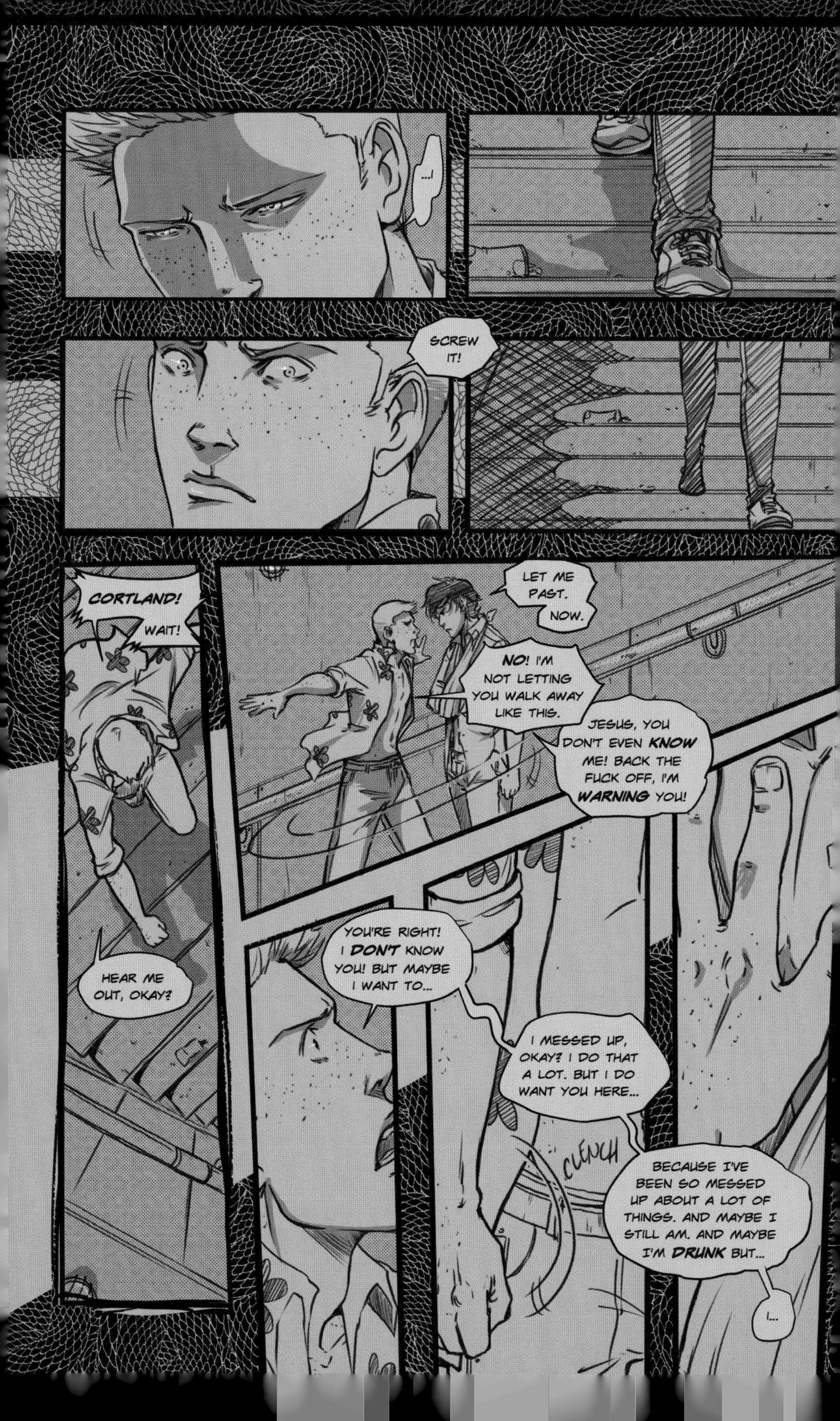
...!
SCREW IT!
CORTLAND! WAIT!
LET ME PAST. NOW.
NO! I'M NOT LETTING YOU WALK AWAY LIKE THIS.
JESUS, YOU DON'T EVEN KNOW ME! BACK THE FUCK OFF, I'M WARNING YOU!
HEAR ME OUT, OKAY?
YOU'RE RIGHT! I DON'T KNOW YOU! BUT MAYBE I WANT TO...
I MESSED UP, OKAY? I DO THAT A LOT. BUT I DO WANT YOU HERE...
CLENCH
BECAUSE I'VE BEEN SO MESSED UP ABOUT A LOT OF THINGS. AND MAYBE I STILL AM. AND MAYBE I'M DRUNK BUT...
I...

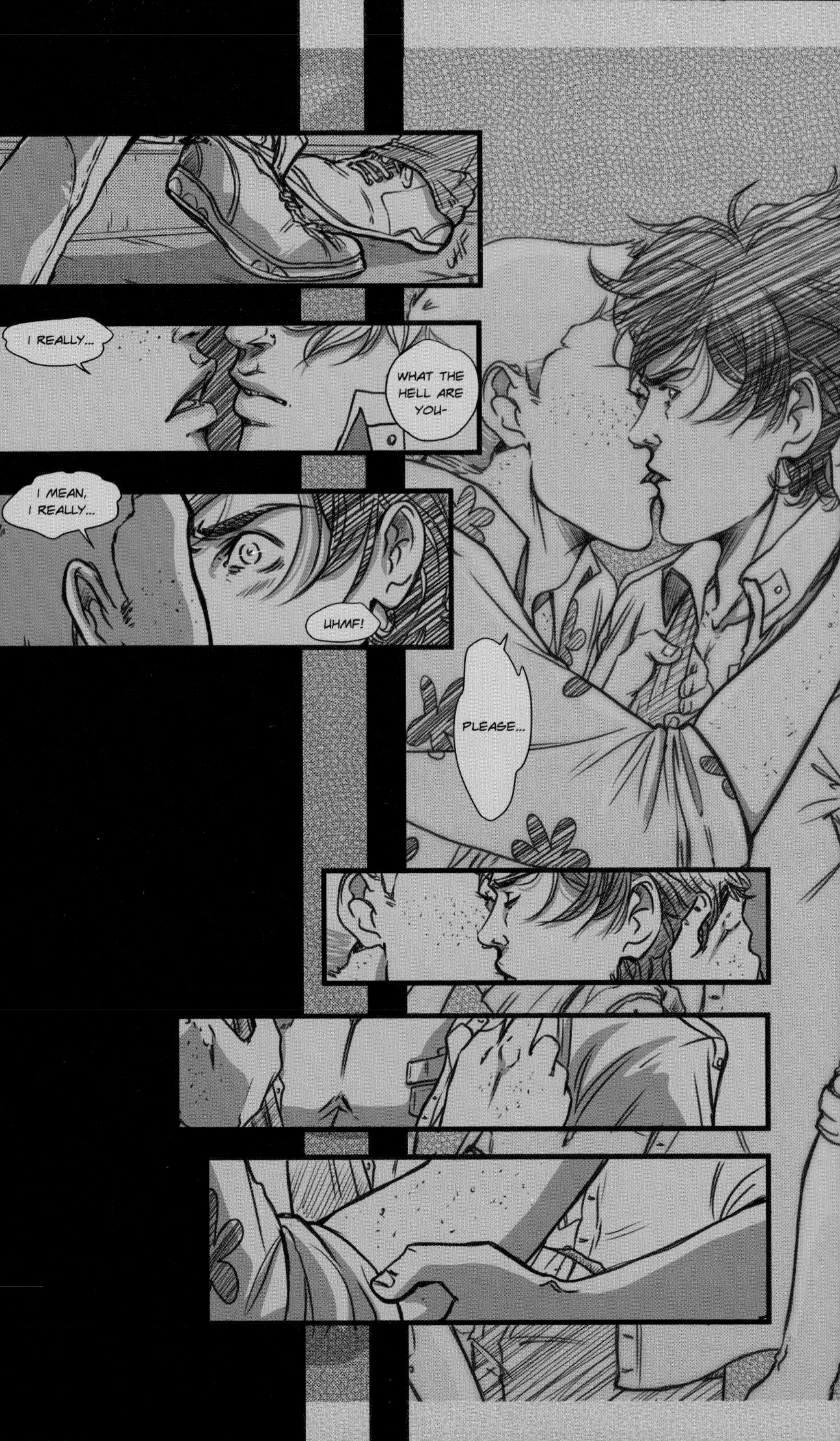
UHF
I REALLY...
WHAT THE HELL ARE YOU-
I MEAN, I REALLY...
UHMF!
PLEASE...

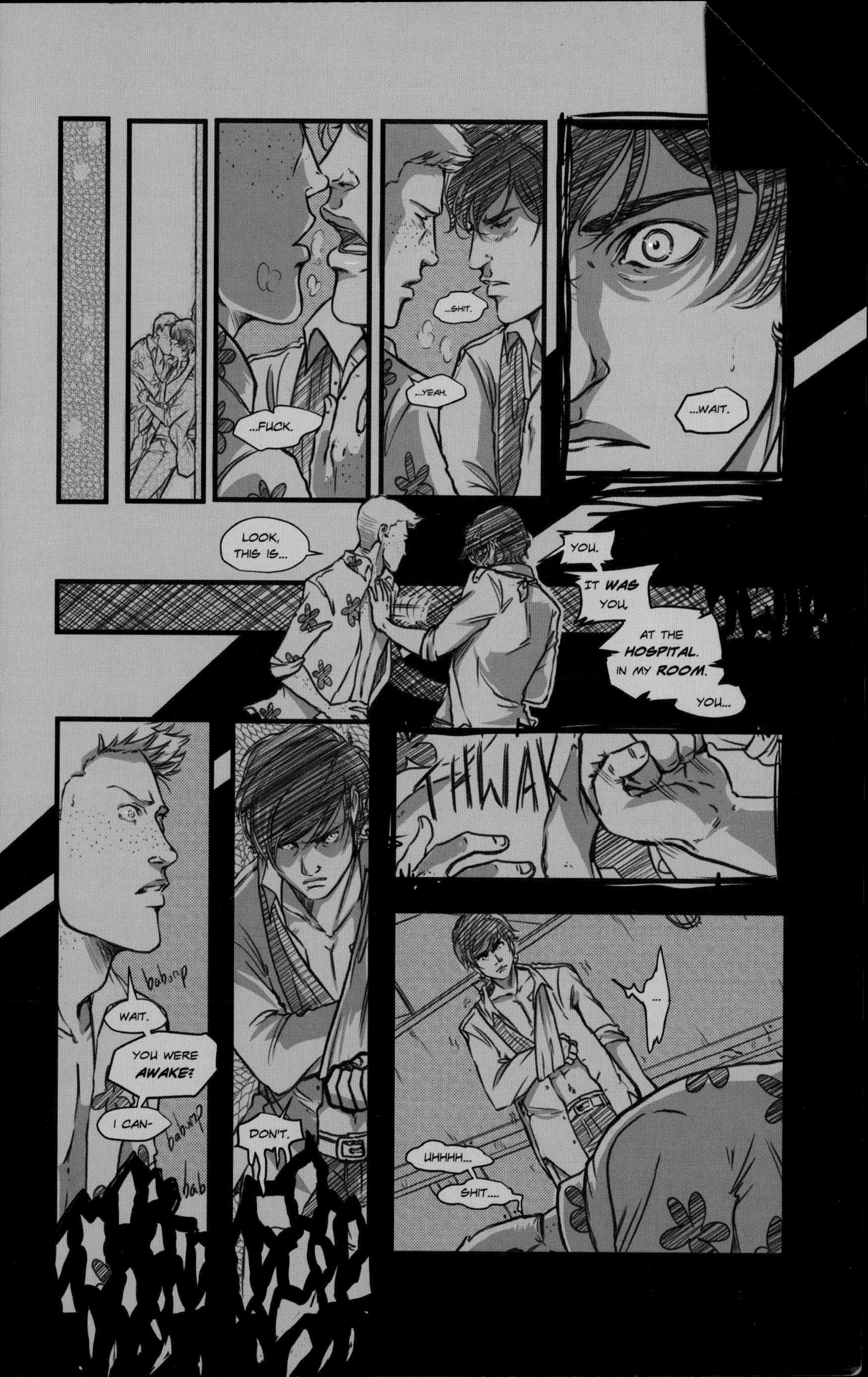

...FUCK.
...SHIT.
...YEAH.
...WAIT.
LOOK, THIS IS...
YOU.
IT WAS YOU.
AT THE HOSPITAL. IN MY ROOM.
YOU...
babump
WAIT.
YOU WERE AWAKE?
I CAN-
babump
bab
DON'T.
THWAK
...
UHHHH...
SHIT....

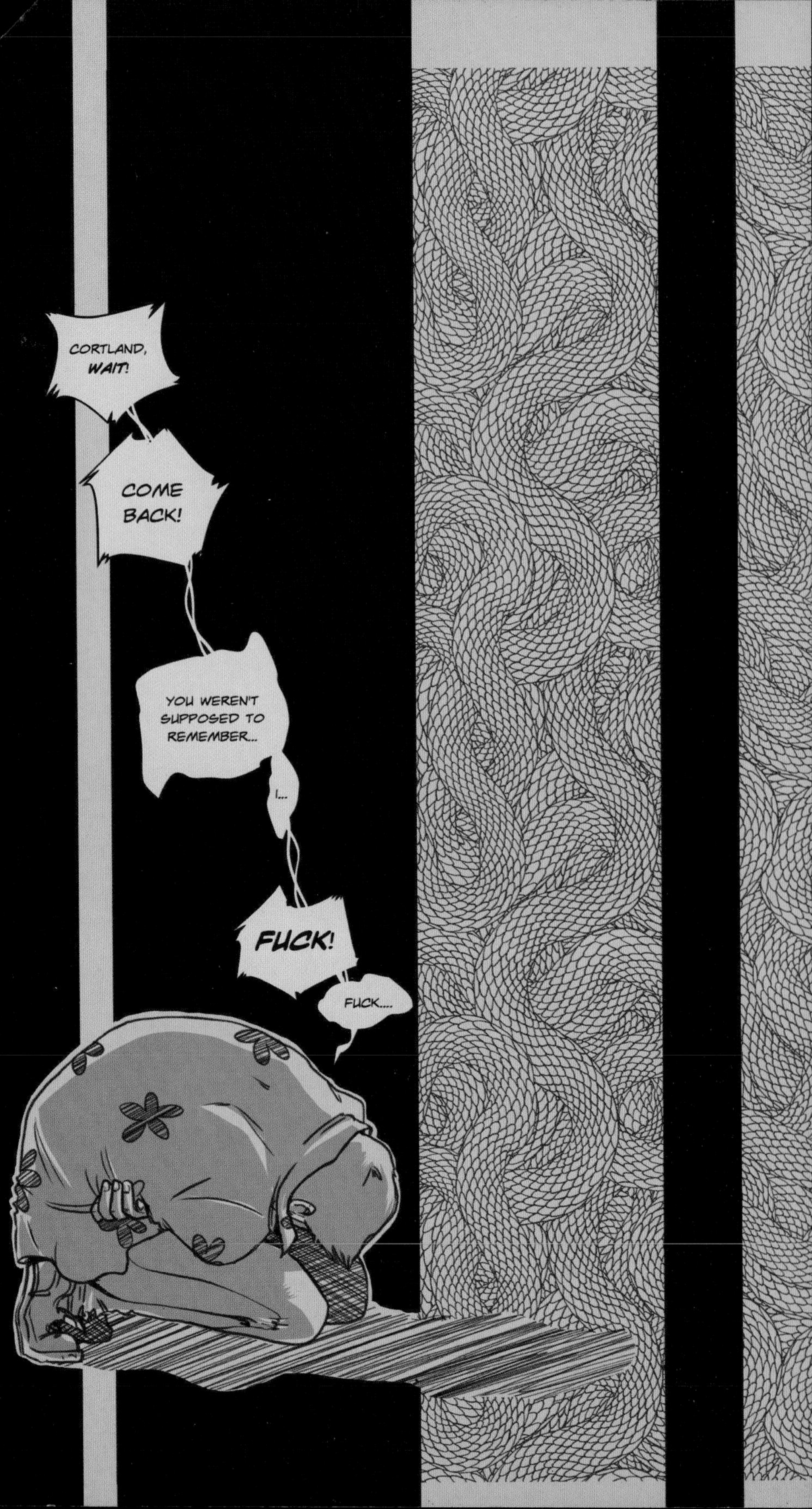
CORTLAND, WAIT!
COME BACK!
YOU WEREN'T SUPPOSED TO REMEMBER...
I...
FUCK!
FUCK....

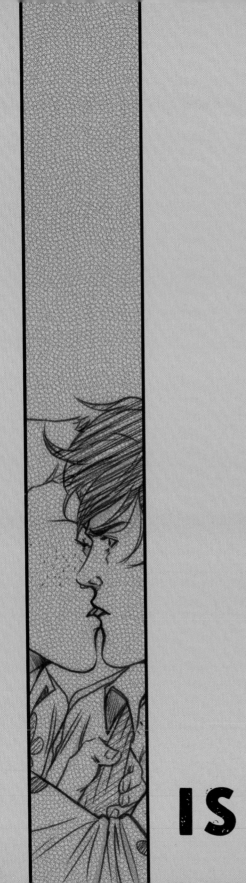

ISSUE 6

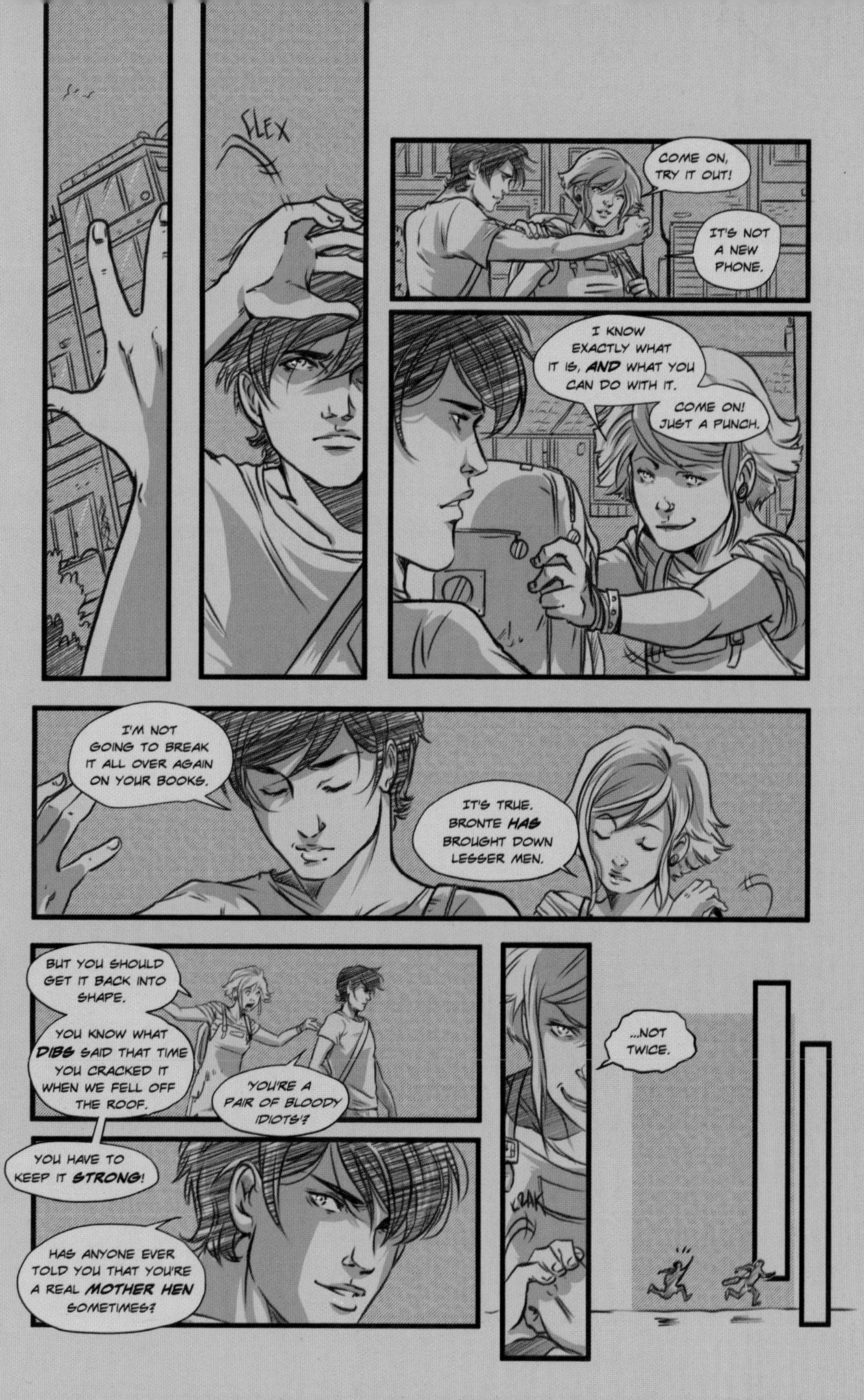
FLEX
COME ON, TRY IT OUT!
IT'S NOT A NEW PHONE.
I KNOW EXACTLY WHAT IT IS, AND WHAT YOU CAN DO WITH IT.
COME ON! JUST A PUNCH.
I'M NOT GOING TO BREAK IT ALL OVER AGAIN ON YOUR BOOKS.
IT'S TRUE. BRONTE HAS BROUGHT DOWN LESSER MEN.
BUT YOU SHOULD GET IT BACK INTO SHAPE.
YOU KNOW WHAT DIBS SAID THAT TIME YOU CRACKED IT WHEN WE FELL OFF THE ROOF.
'YOU'RE A PAIR OF BLOODY IDIOTS'?
YOU HAVE TO KEEP IT STRONG!
HAS ANYONE EVER TOLD YOU THAT YOU'RE A REAL MOTHER HEN SOMETIMES?
...NOT TWICE.
KRAK

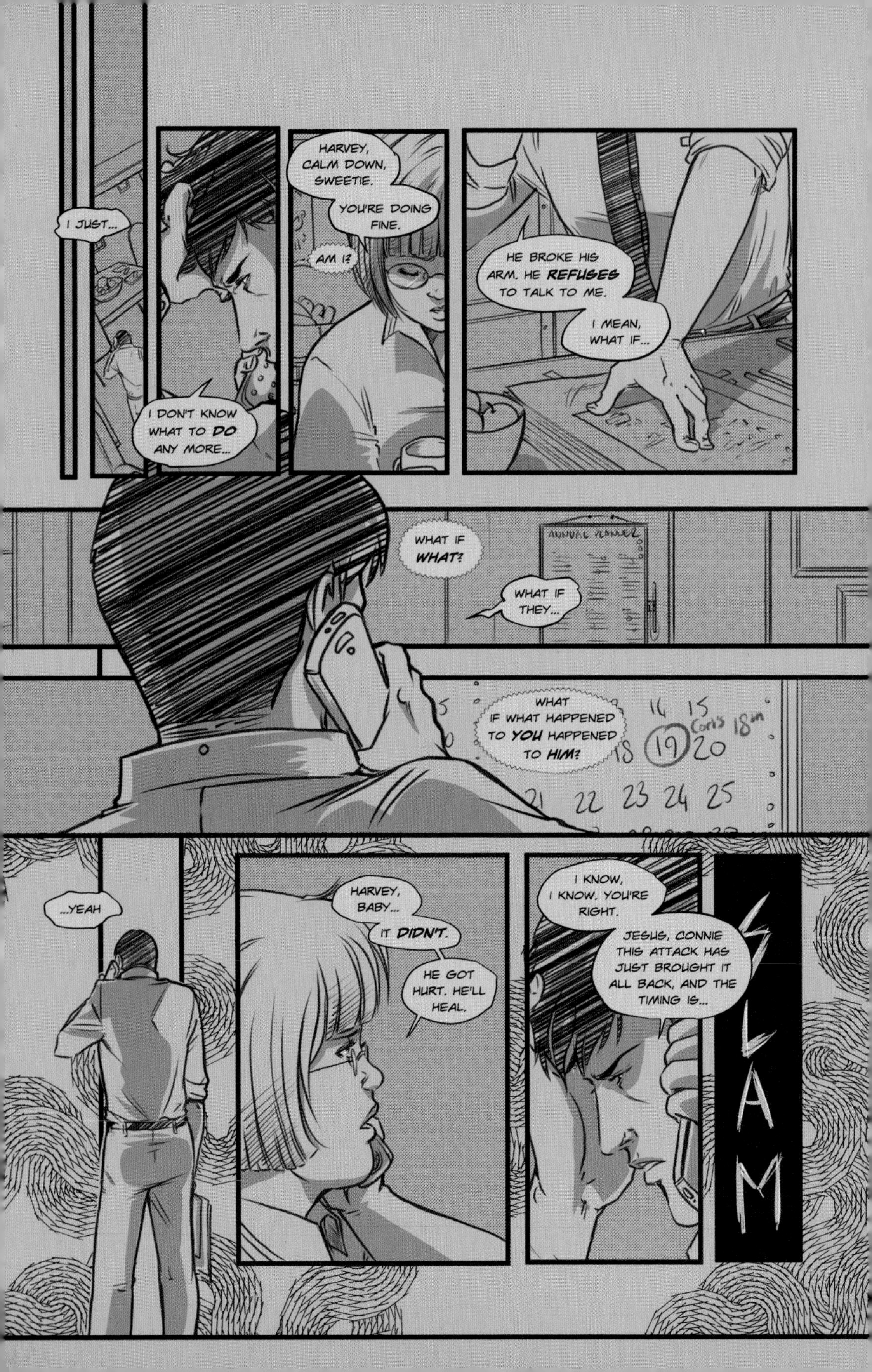
I JUST...
I DON'T KNOW WHAT TO DO ANY MORE...
HARVEY, CALM DOWN, SWEETIE.
YOU'RE DOING FINE.
AM I?
HE BROKE HIS ARM. HE REFUSES TO TALK TO ME.
I MEAN, WHAT IF...
WHAT IF WHAT?
WHAT IF THEY...
WHAT IF WHAT HAPPENED TO YOU HAPPENED TO HIM?
...YEAH
HARVEY, BABY...
IT DIDN'T.
HE GOT HURT. HE'LL HEAL.
I KNOW, I KNOW. YOU'RE RIGHT.
JESUS, CONNIE THIS ATTACK HAS JUST BROUGHT IT ALL BACK, AND THE TIMING IS...
SLAM

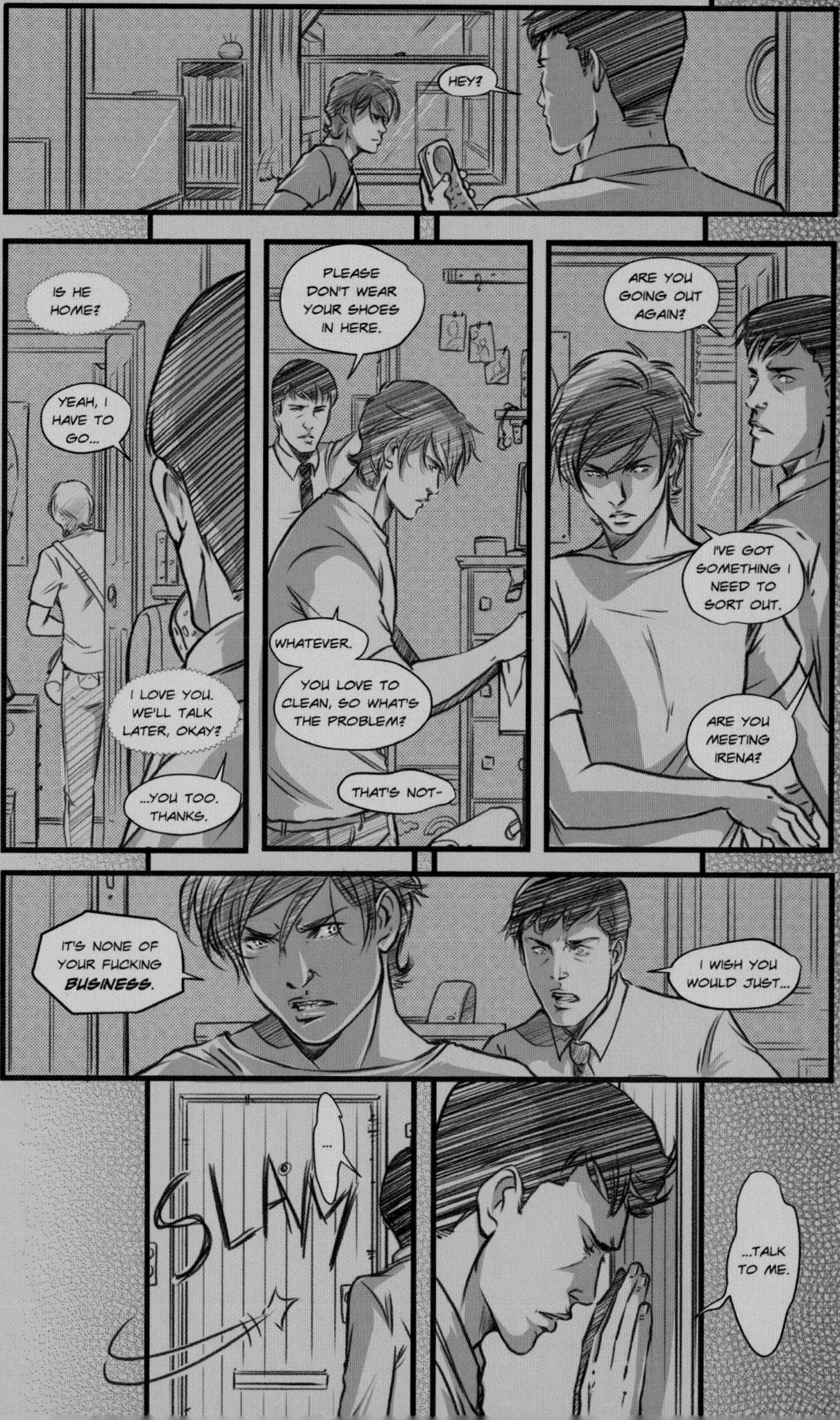
HEY?
IS HE HOME?
YEAH, I HAVE TO GO...
I LOVE YOU. WE'LL TALK LATER, OKAY?
...YOU TOO. THANKS.
PLEASE DON'T WEAR YOUR SHOES IN HERE.
WHATEVER.
YOU LOVE TO CLEAN, SO WHAT'S THE PROBLEM?
THAT'S NOT-
ARE YOU GOING OUT AGAIN?
I'VE GOT SOMETHING I NEED TO SORT OUT.
ARE YOU MEETING IRENA?
IT'S NONE OF YOUR FUCKING BUSINESS.
I WISH YOU WOULD JUST...
...
SLAM
...TALK TO ME.

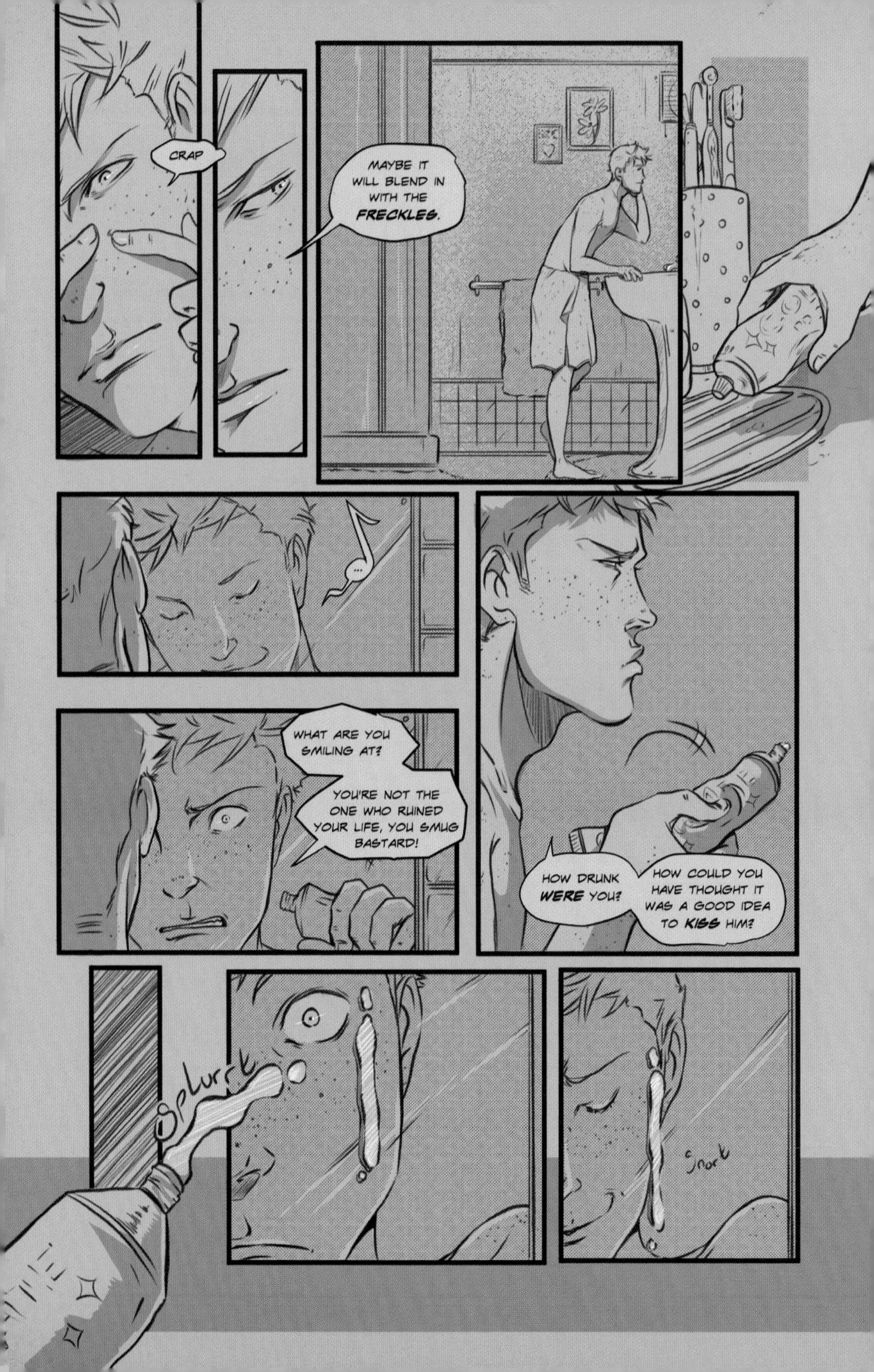
CRAP
MAYBE IT WILL BLEND IN WITH THE FRECKLES.
WHAT ARE YOU SMILING AT?
YOU'RE NOT THE ONE WHO RUINED YOUR LIFE, YOU SMUG BASTARD!
HOW DRUNK WERE YOU?
HOW COULD YOU HAVE THOUGHT IT WAS A GOOD IDEA TO KISS HIM?
Splurrt
Snort

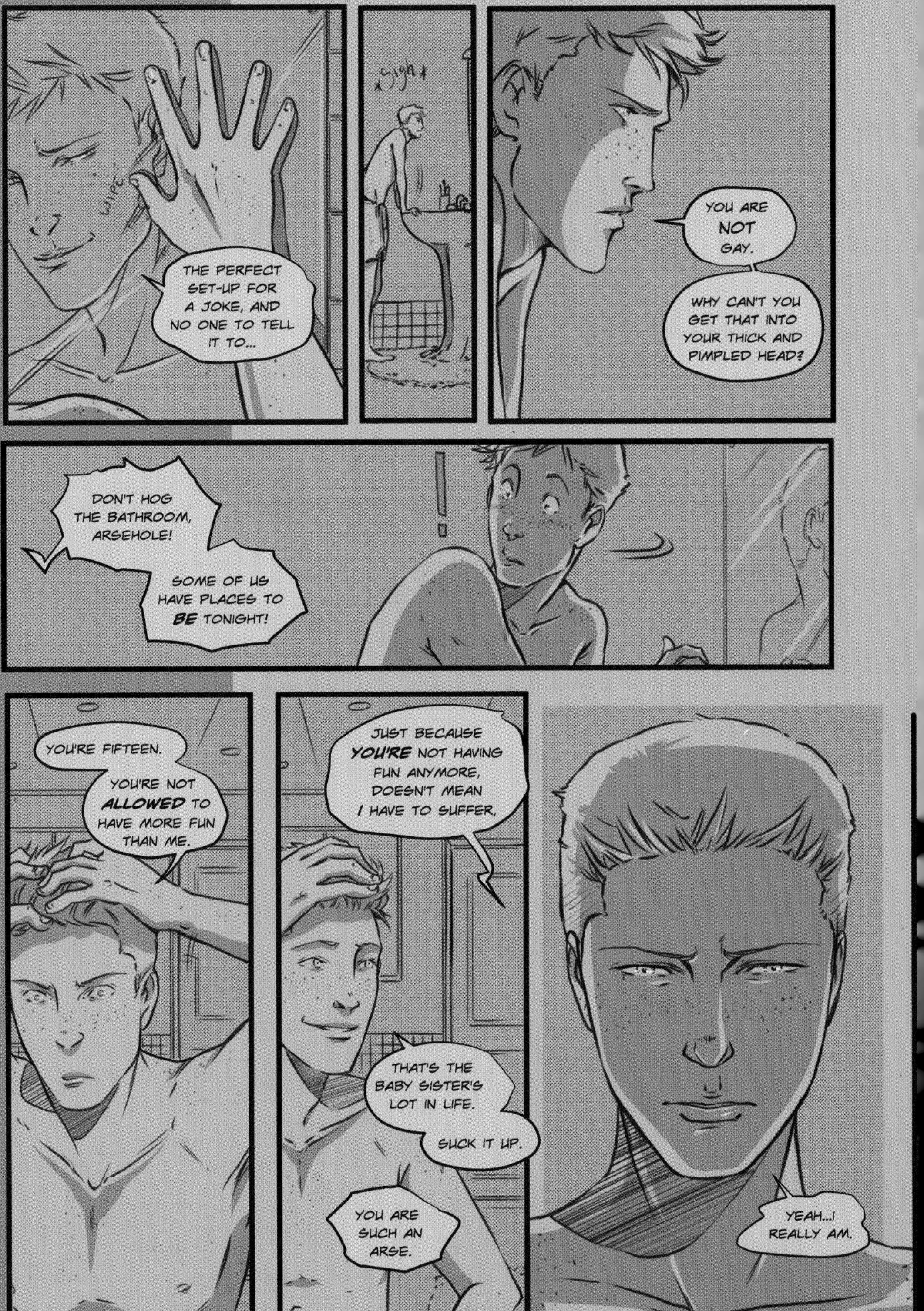
WIPE
THE PERFECT SET-UP FOR A JOKE, AND NO ONE TO TELL IT TO...
SIGH
YOU ARE NOT GAY.
WHY CAN'T YOU GET THAT INTO YOUR THICK AND PIMPLED HEAD?
DON'T HOG THE BATHROOM, ARSEHOLE!
SOME OF US HAVE PLACES TO BE TONIGHT!
!
YOU'RE FIFTEEN.
YOU'RE NOT ALLOWED TO HAVE MORE FUN THAN ME.
JUST BECAUSE YOU'RE NOT HAVING FUN ANYMORE, DOESN'T MEAN I HAVE TO SUFFER,
THAT'S THE BABY SISTER'S LOT IN LIFE.
SUCK IT UP.
YOU ARE SUCH AN ARSE.
YEAH...I REALLY AM.

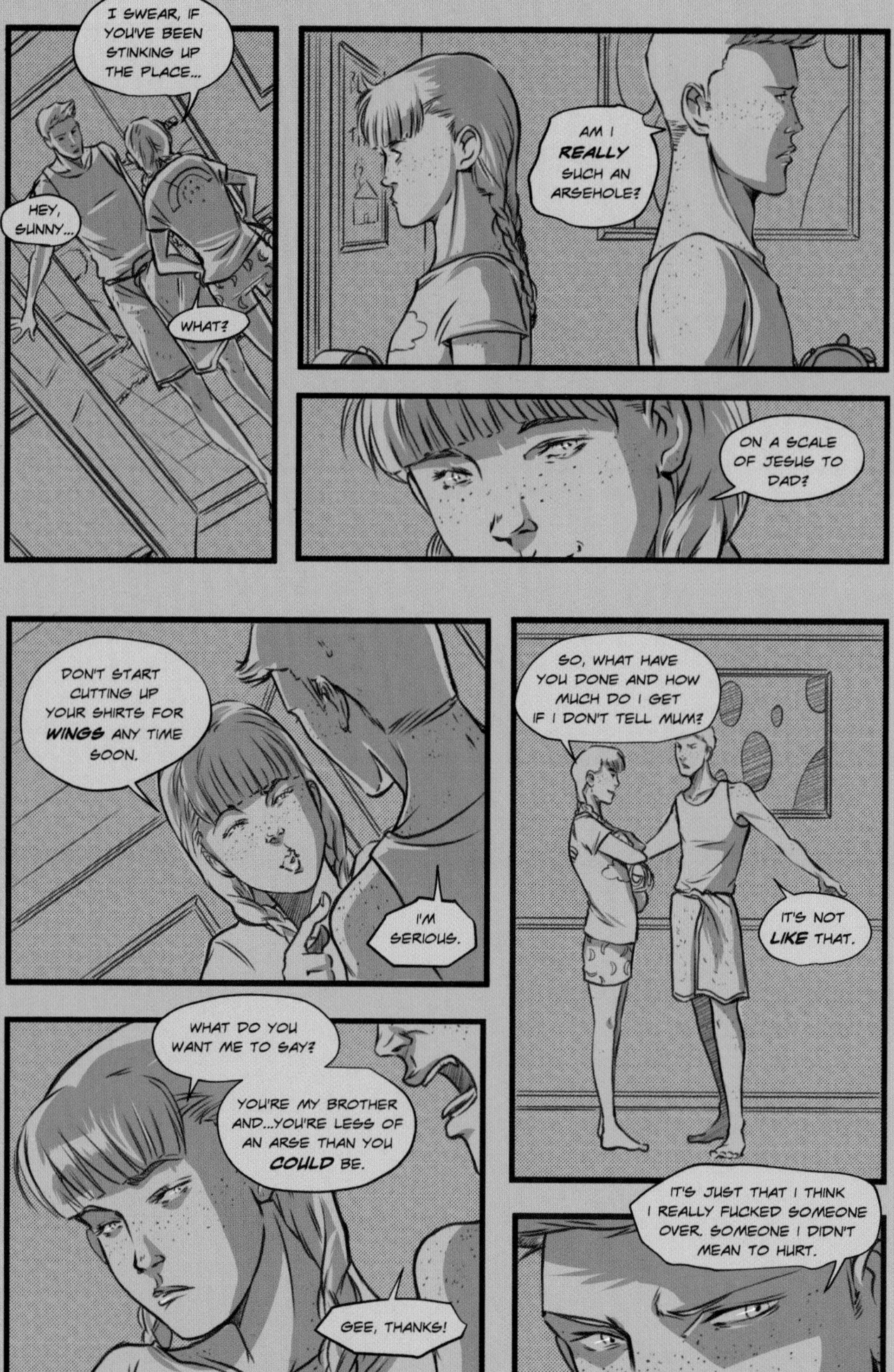
I SWEAR, IF YOU'VE BEEN STINKING UP THE PLACE...
HEY, SUNNY...
WHAT?
AM I REALLY SUCH AN ARSEHOLE?
ON A SCALE OF JESUS TO DAD?
DON'T START CUTTING UP YOUR SHIRTS FOR WINGS ANY TIME SOON.
I'M SERIOUS.
SO, WHAT HAVE YOU DONE AND HOW MUCH DO I GET IF I DON'T TELL MUM?
IT'S NOT LIKE THAT.
WHAT DO YOU WANT ME TO SAY?
YOU'RE MY BROTHER AND...YOU'RE LESS OF AN ARSE THAN YOU COULD BE.
GEE, THANKS!
IT'S JUST THAT I THINK I REALLY FUCKED SOMEONE OVER. SOMEONE I DIDN'T MEAN TO HURT.

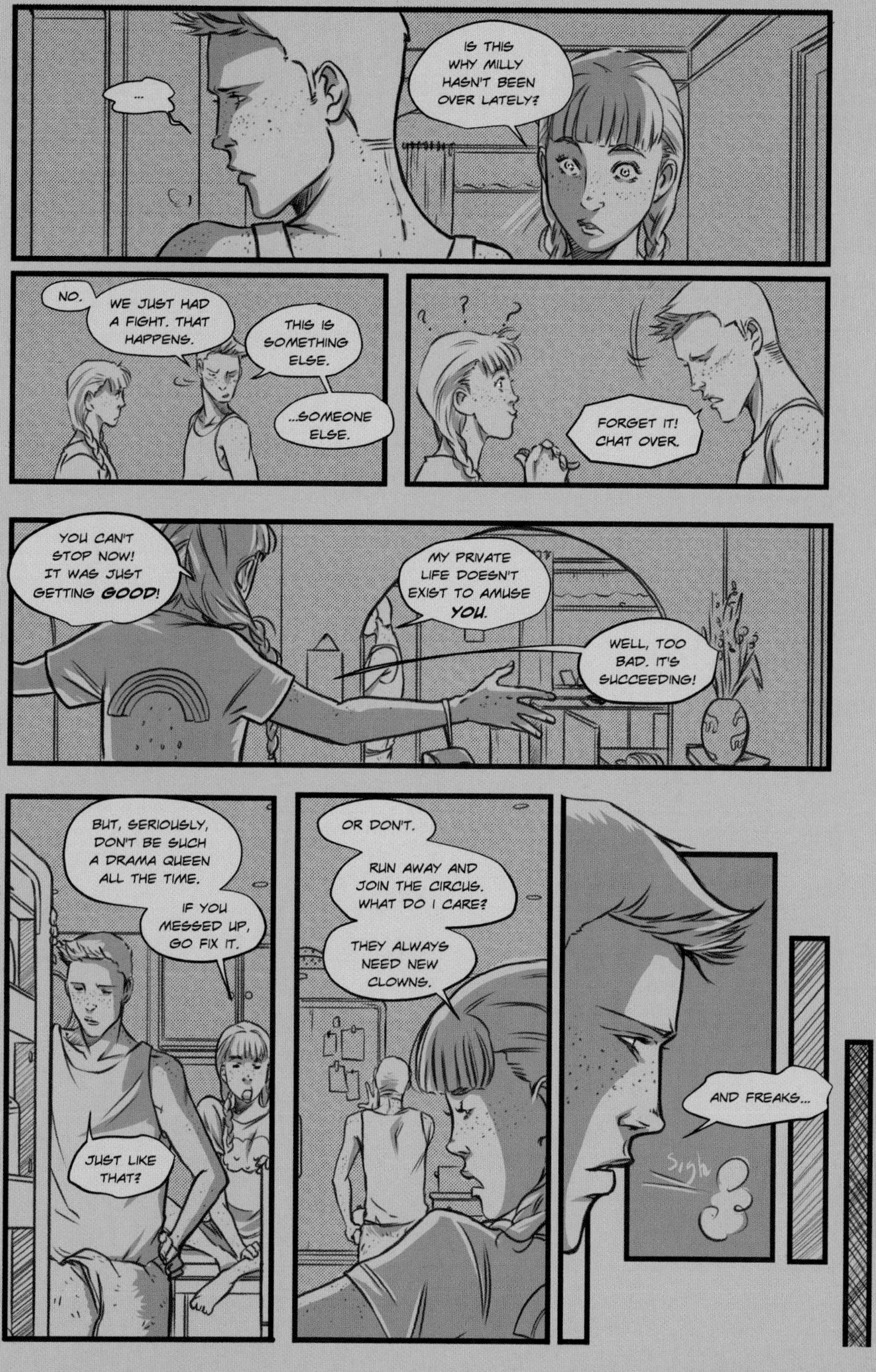
...
IS THIS WHY MILLY HASN'T BEEN OVER LATELY?
NO.
WE JUST HAD A FIGHT. THAT HAPPENS.
THIS IS SOMETHING ELSE.
...SOMEONE ELSE.
? ? ?
FORGET IT! CHAT OVER.
YOU CAN'T STOP NOW! IT WAS JUST GETTING GOOD!
MY PRIVATE LIFE DOESN'T EXIST TO AMUSE YOU.
WELL, TOO BAD. IT'S SUCCEEDING!
BUT, SERIOUSLY, DON'T BE SUCH A DRAMA QUEEN ALL THE TIME.
IF YOU MESSED UP, GO FIX IT.
JUST LIKE THAT?
OR DON'T.
RUN AWAY AND JOIN THE CIRCUS. WHAT DO I CARE?
THEY ALWAYS NEED NEW CLOWNS.
AND FREAKS...
Sigh

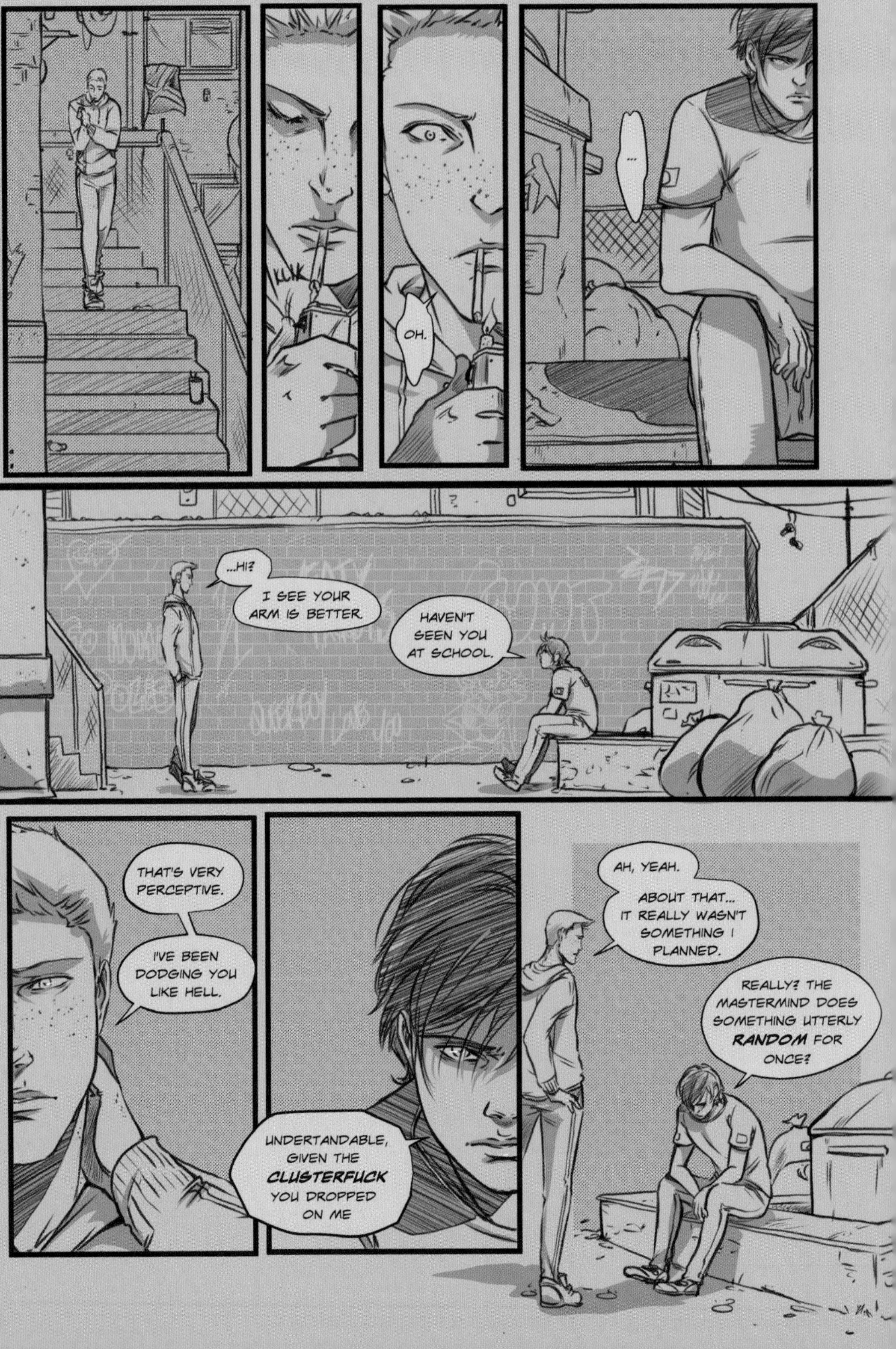
KLIK
OH.
...
...HI?
I SEE YOUR ARM IS BETTER.
HAVEN'T SEEN YOU AT SCHOOL.
THAT'S VERY PERCEPTIVE.
I'VE BEEN DODGING YOU LIKE HELL.
UNDERTANDABLE, GIVEN THE CLUSTERFUCK YOU DROPPED ON ME
AH, YEAH.
ABOUT THAT... IT REALLY WASN'T SOMETHING I PLANNED.
REALLY? THE MASTERMIND DOES SOMETHING UTTERLY RANDOM FOR ONCE?

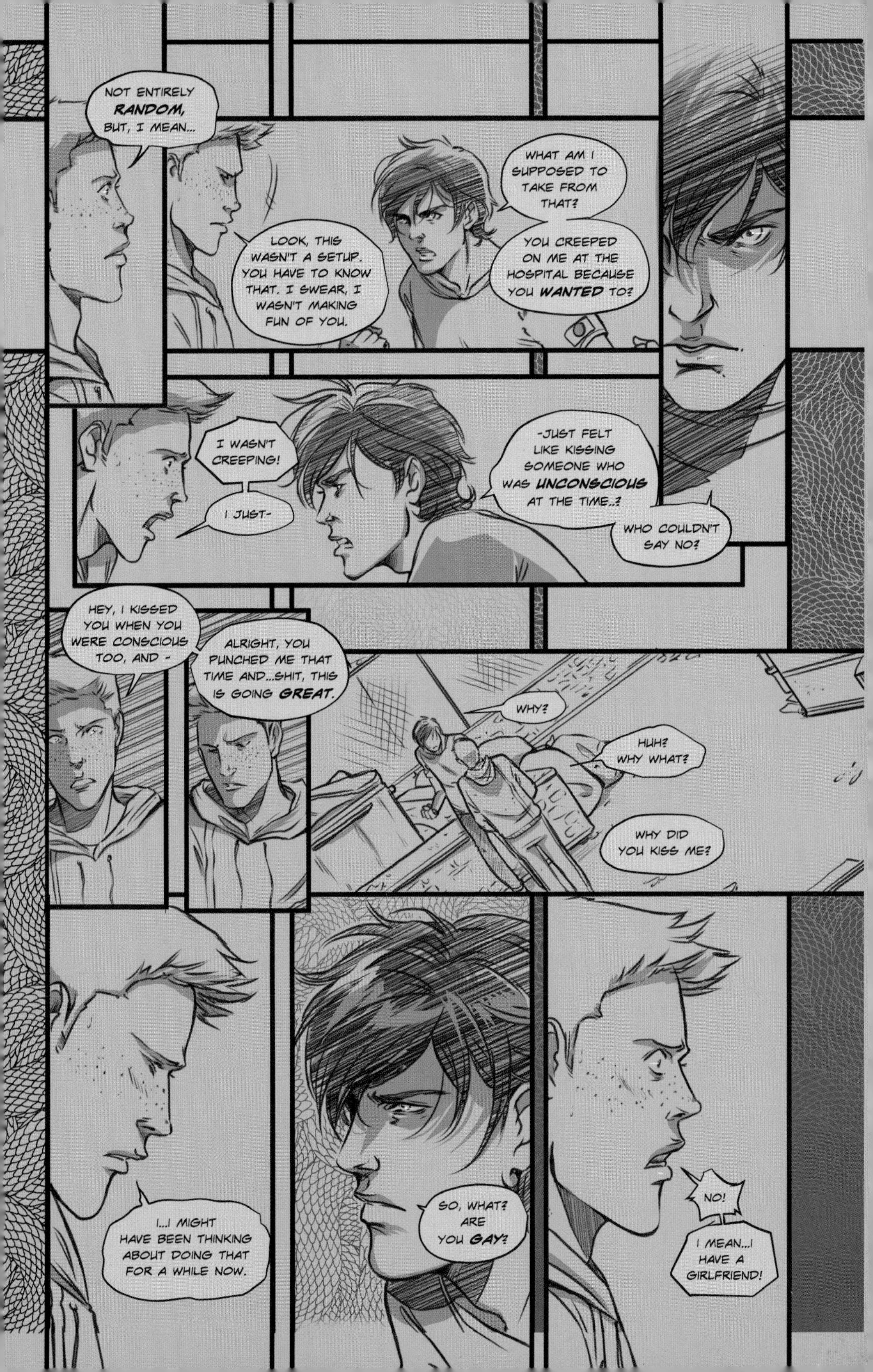
NOT ENTIRELY RANDOM, BUT, I MEAN...
LOOK, THIS WASN'T A SETUP. YOU HAVE TO KNOW THAT. I SWEAR, I WASN'T MAKING FUN OF YOU.
WHAT AM I SUPPOSED TO TAKE FROM THAT?
YOU CREEPED ON ME AT THE HOSPITAL BECAUSE YOU WANTED TO?
I WASN'T CREEPING!
I JUST-
-JUST FELT LIKE KISSING SOMEONE WHO WAS UNCONSCIOUS AT THE TIME..?
WHO COULDN'T SAY NO?
HEY, I KISSED YOU WHEN YOU WERE CONSCIOUS TOO, AND -
ALRIGHT, YOU PUNCHED ME THAT TIME AND...SHIT, THIS IS GOING GREAT.
WHY?
HUH? WHY WHAT?
WHY DID YOU KISS ME?
I...I MIGHT HAVE BEEN THINKING ABOUT DOING THAT FOR A WHILE NOW.
SO, WHAT? ARE YOU GAY?
NO!
I MEAN...I HAVE A GIRLFRIEND!

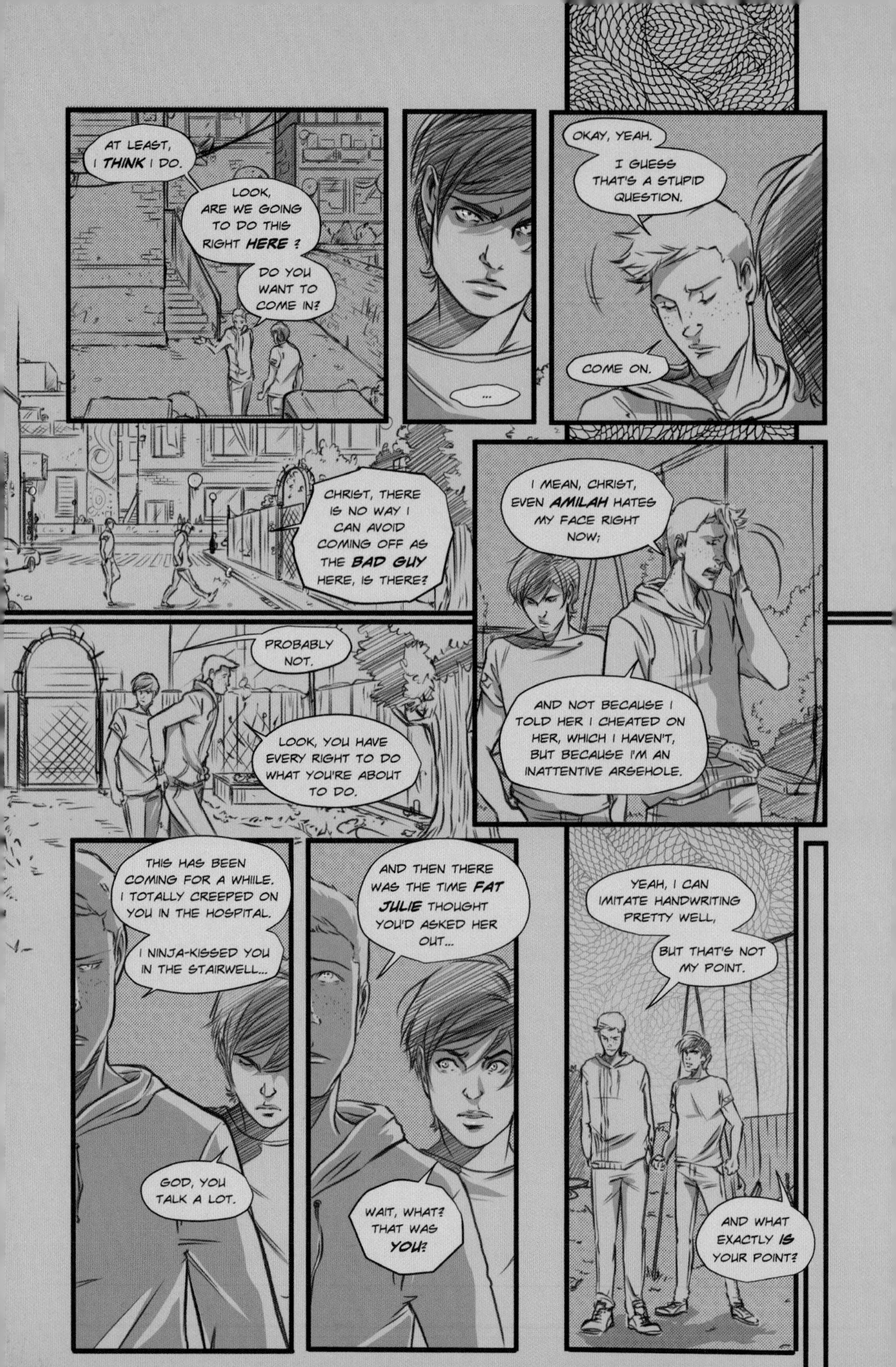
AT LEAST, I THINK I DO.
LOOK, ARE WE GOING TO DO THIS RIGHT HERE?
DO YOU WANT TO COME IN?
...
OKAY, YEAH.
I GUESS THAT'S A STUPID QUESTION.
COME ON.
CHRIST, THERE IS NO WAY I CAN AVOID COMING OFF AS THE BAD GUY HERE, IS THERE?
I MEAN, CHRIST, EVEN AMILAH HATES MY FACE RIGHT NOW;
PROBABLY NOT.
LOOK, YOU HAVE EVERY RIGHT TO DO WHAT YOU'RE ABOUT TO DO.
AND NOT BECAUSE I TOLD HER I CHEATED ON HER, WHICH I HAVEN'T, BUT BECAUSE I'M AN INATTENTIVE ARSEHOLE.
THIS HAS BEEN COMING FOR A WHILE. I TOTALLY CREEPED ON YOU IN THE HOSPITAL.
I NINJA-KISSED YOU IN THE STAIRWELL...
GOD, YOU TALK A LOT.
AND THEN THERE WAS THE TIME FAT JULIE THOUGHT YOU'D ASKED HER OUT...
WAIT, WHAT? THAT WAS YOU?
YEAH, I CAN IMITATE HANDWRITING PRETTY WELL,
BUT THAT'S NOT MY POINT.
AND WHAT EXACTLY IS YOUR POINT?

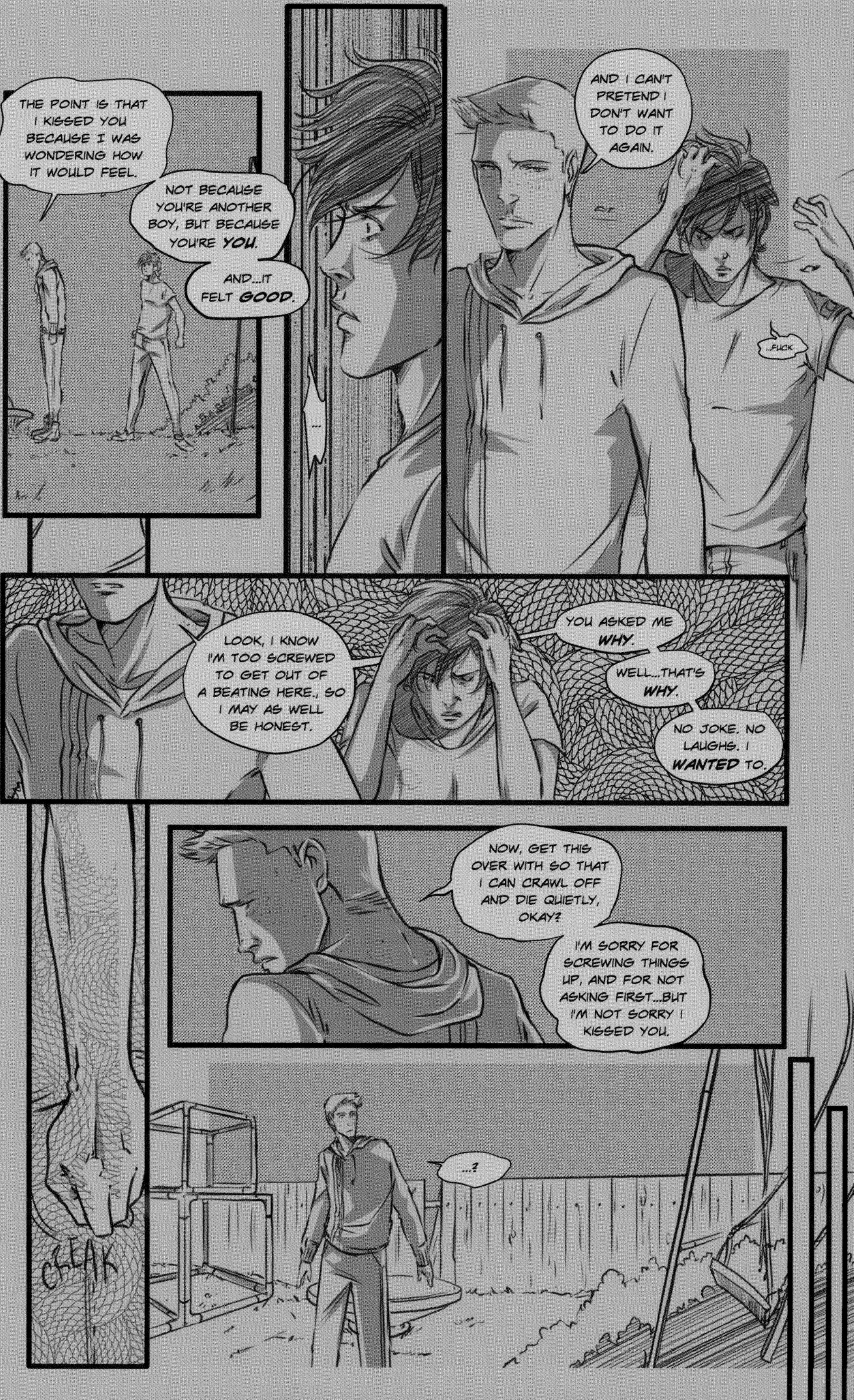
THE POINT IS THAT I KISSED YOU BECAUSE I WAS WONDERING HOW IT WOULD FEEL.
NOT BECAUSE YOU'RE ANOTHER BOY, BUT BECAUSE YOU'RE YOU.
AND...IT FELT GOOD.
...
AND I CAN'T PRETEND I DON'T WANT TO DO IT AGAIN.
...FUCK
LOOK, I KNOW I'M TOO SCREWED TO GET OUT OF A BEATING HERE., SO I MAY AS WELL BE HONEST.
YOU ASKED ME WHY.
WELL...THAT'S WHY.
NO JOKE. NO LAUGHS. I WANTED TO.
NOW, GET THIS OVER WITH SO THAT I CAN CRAWL OFF AND DIE QUIETLY, OKAY?
I'M SORRY FOR SCREWING THINGS UP, AND FOR NOT ASKING FIRST...BUT I'M NOT SORRY I KISSED YOU.
CREAK
...?

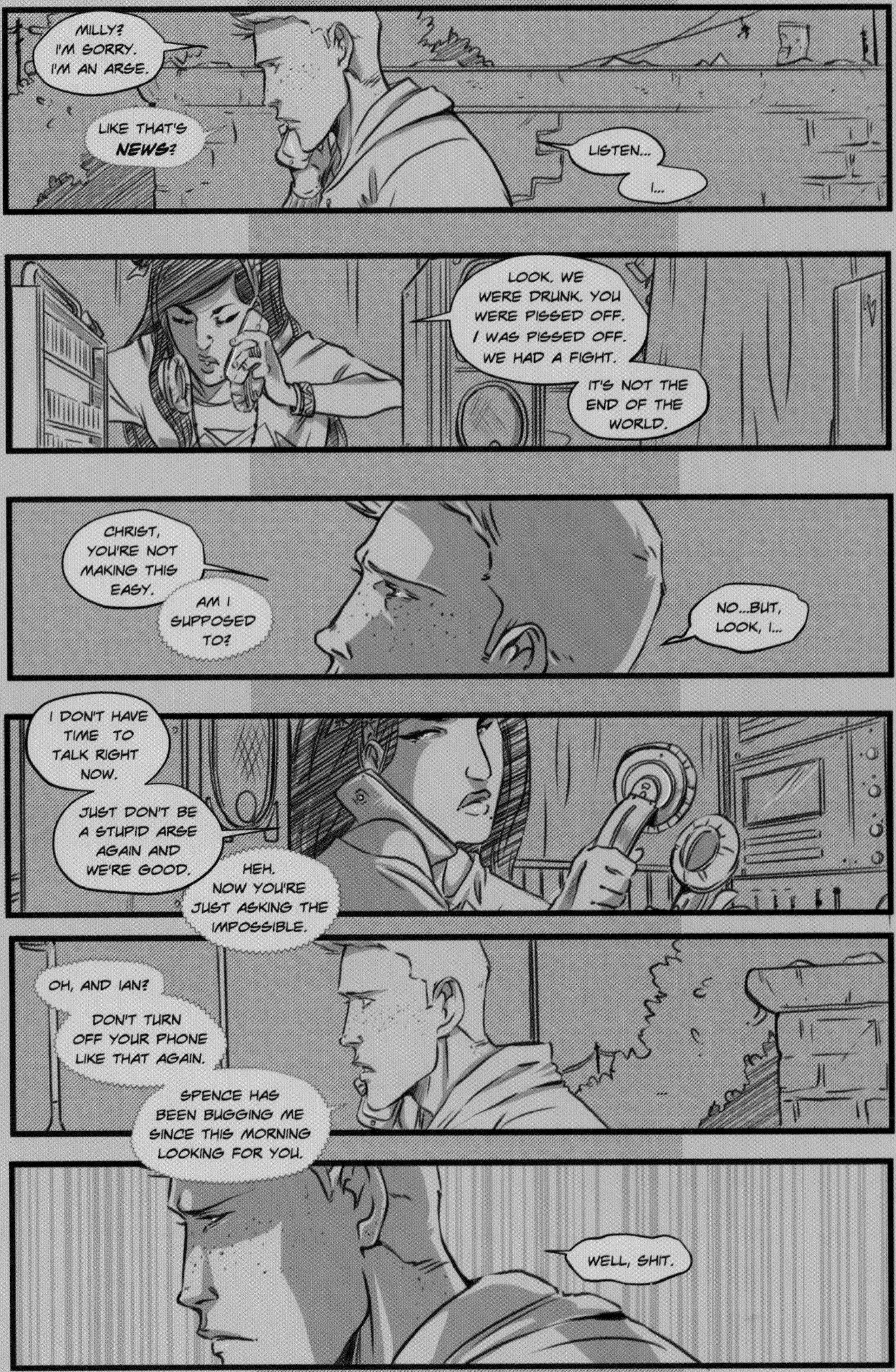
MILLY? I'M SORRY. I'M AN ARSE.
LIKE THAT'S NEWS?
LISTEN...
I...
LOOK. WE WERE DRUNK. YOU WERE PISSED OFF. I WAS PISSED OFF. WE HAD A FIGHT.
IT'S NOT THE END OF THE WORLD.
CHRIST, YOU'RE NOT MAKING THIS EASY.
AM I SUPPOSED TO?
NO...BUT, LOOK, I...
I DON'T HAVE TIME TO TALK RIGHT NOW.
JUST DON'T BE A STUPID ARSE AGAIN AND WE'RE GOOD.
HEH. NOW YOU'RE JUST ASKING THE IMPOSSIBLE.
OH, AND IAN?
DON'T TURN OFF YOUR PHONE LIKE THAT AGAIN.
SPENCE HAS BEEN BUGGING ME SINCE THIS MORNING LOOKING FOR YOU.
WELL, SHIT.

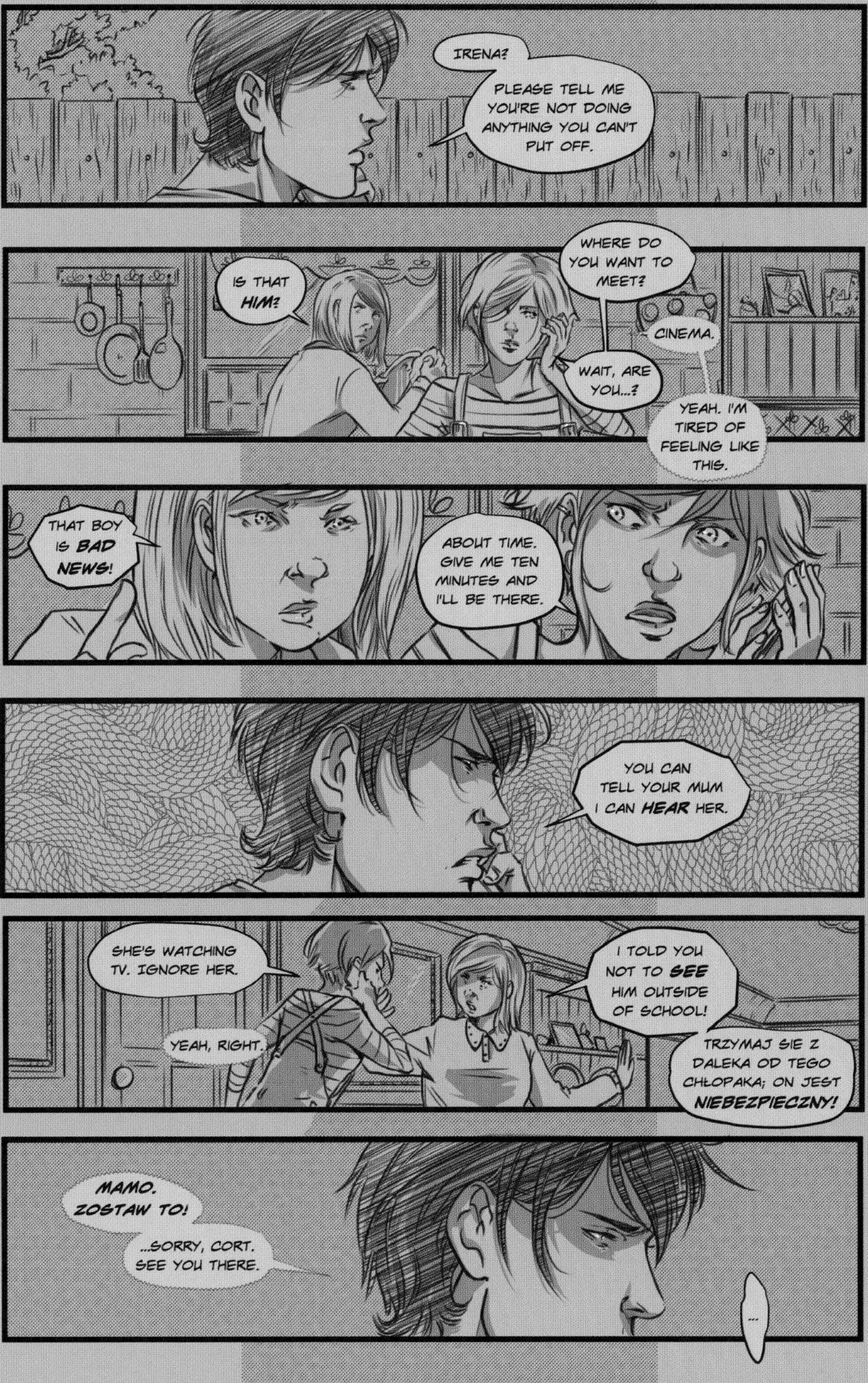

IRENA?
PLEASE TELL ME YOU'RE NOT DOING ANYTHING YOU CAN'T PUT OFF.
IS THAT HIM?
WHERE DO YOU WANT TO MEET?
CINEMA.
WAIT, ARE YOU...?
YEAH. I'M TIRED OF FEELING LIKE THIS.
THAT BOY IS BAD NEWS!
ABOUT TIME. GIVE ME TEN MINUTES AND I'LL BE THERE.
YOU CAN TELL YOUR MUM I CAN HEAR HER.
SHE'S WATCHING TV. IGNORE HER.
YEAH, RIGHT.
I TOLD YOU NOT TO SEE HIM OUTSIDE OF SCHOOL!
TRZYMAJ SIE Z DALEKA OD TEGO CHŁOPAKA; ON JEST NIEBEZPIECZNY!
MAMO. ZOSTAW TO!
...SORRY, CORT. SEE YOU THERE.
...

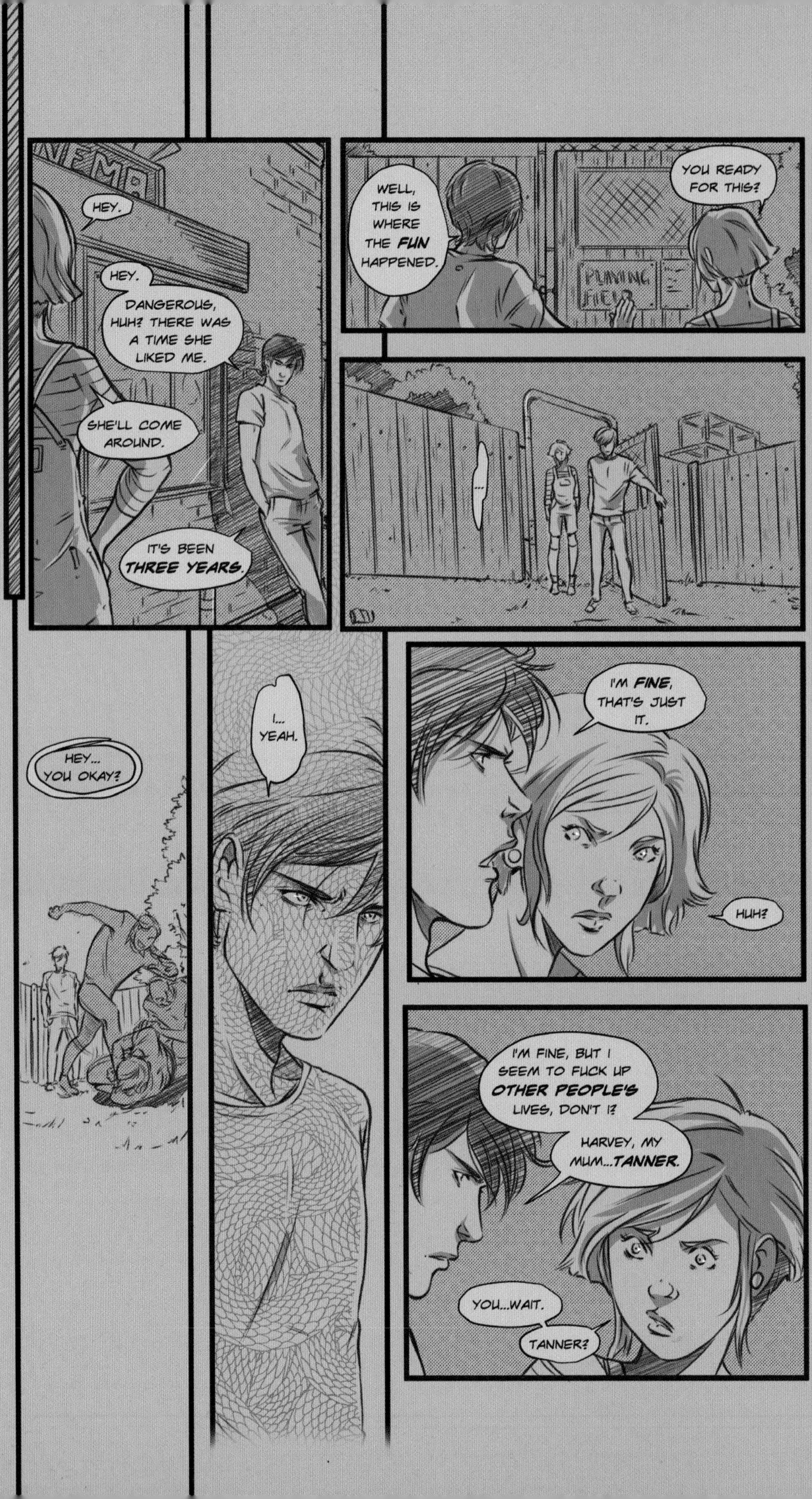
HEY.
HEY.
DANGEROUS, HUH? THERE WAS A TIME SHE LIKED ME.
SHE'LL COME AROUND.
IT'S BEEN THREE YEARS.
WELL, THIS IS WHERE THE FUN HAPPENED.
YOU READY FOR THIS?
...
HEY... YOU OKAY?
I... YEAH.
I'M FINE, THAT'S JUST IT.
HUH?
I'M FINE, BUT I SEEM TO FUCK UP OTHER PEOPLE'S LIVES, DON'T I?
HARVEY, MY MUM...TANNER.
YOU...WAIT.
TANNER?

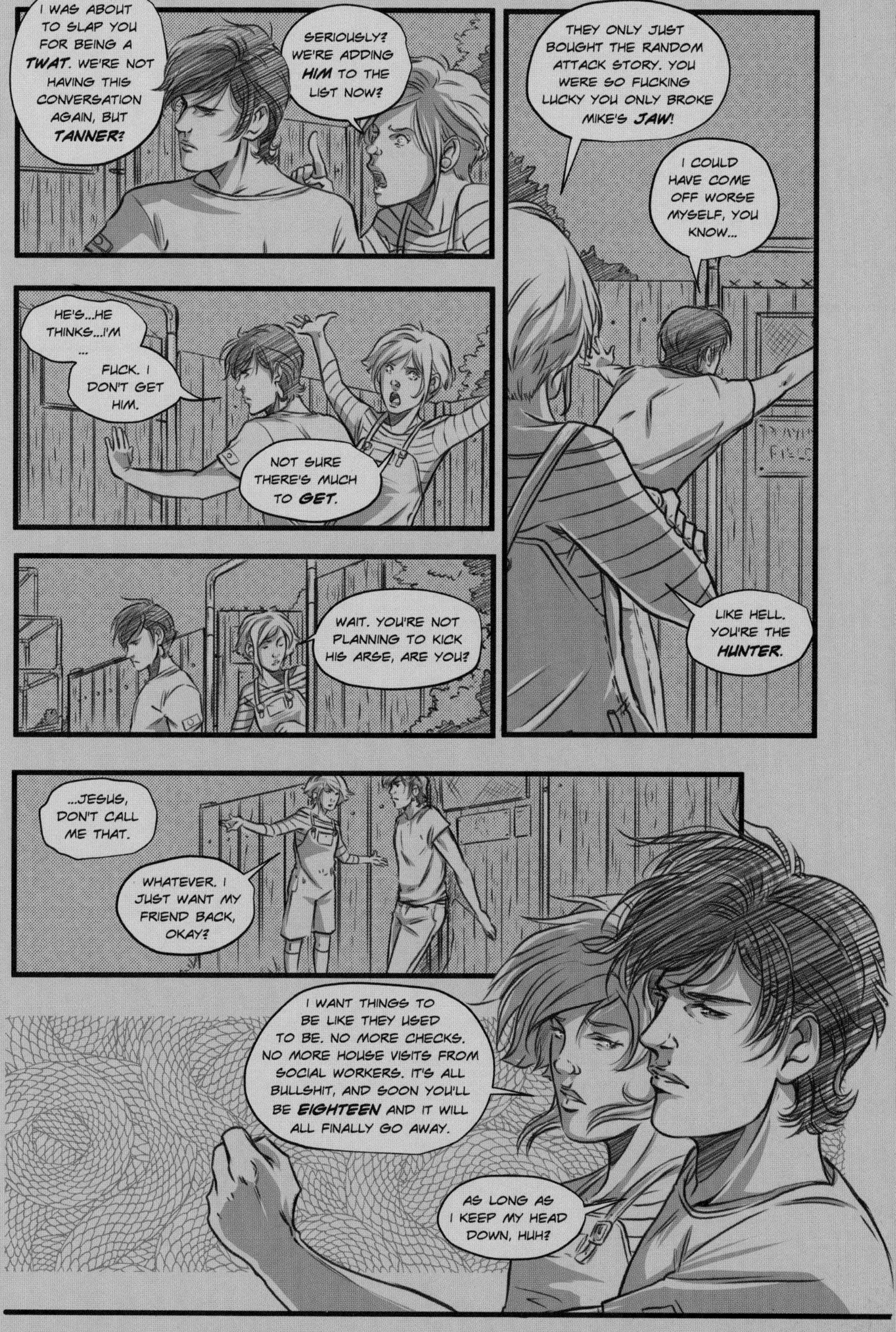
I WAS ABOUT TO SLAP YOU FOR BEING A TWAT. WE'RE NOT HAVING THIS CONVERSATION AGAIN, BUT TANNER?
SERIOUSLY? WE'RE ADDING HIM TO THE LIST NOW?
THEY ONLY JUST BOUGHT THE RANDOM ATTACK STORY. YOU WERE SO FUCKING LUCKY YOU ONLY BROKE MIKE'S JAW!
I COULD HAVE COME OFF WORSE MYSELF, YOU KNOW...
HE'S...HE THINKS...I'M ...
FUCK. I DON'T GET HIM.
NOT SURE THERE'S MUCH TO GET.
LIKE HELL. YOU'RE THE HUNTER.
WAIT. YOU'RE NOT PLANNING TO KICK HIS ARSE, ARE YOU?
...JESUS, DON'T CALL ME THAT.
WHATEVER. I JUST WANT MY FRIEND BACK, OKAY?
I WANT THINGS TO BE LIKE THEY USED TO BE. NO MORE CHECKS. NO MORE HOUSE VISITS FROM SOCIAL WORKERS. IT'S ALL BULLSHIT, AND SOON YOU'LL BE EIGHTEEN AND IT WILL ALL FINALLY GO AWAY.
AS LONG AS I KEEP MY HEAD DOWN, HUH?

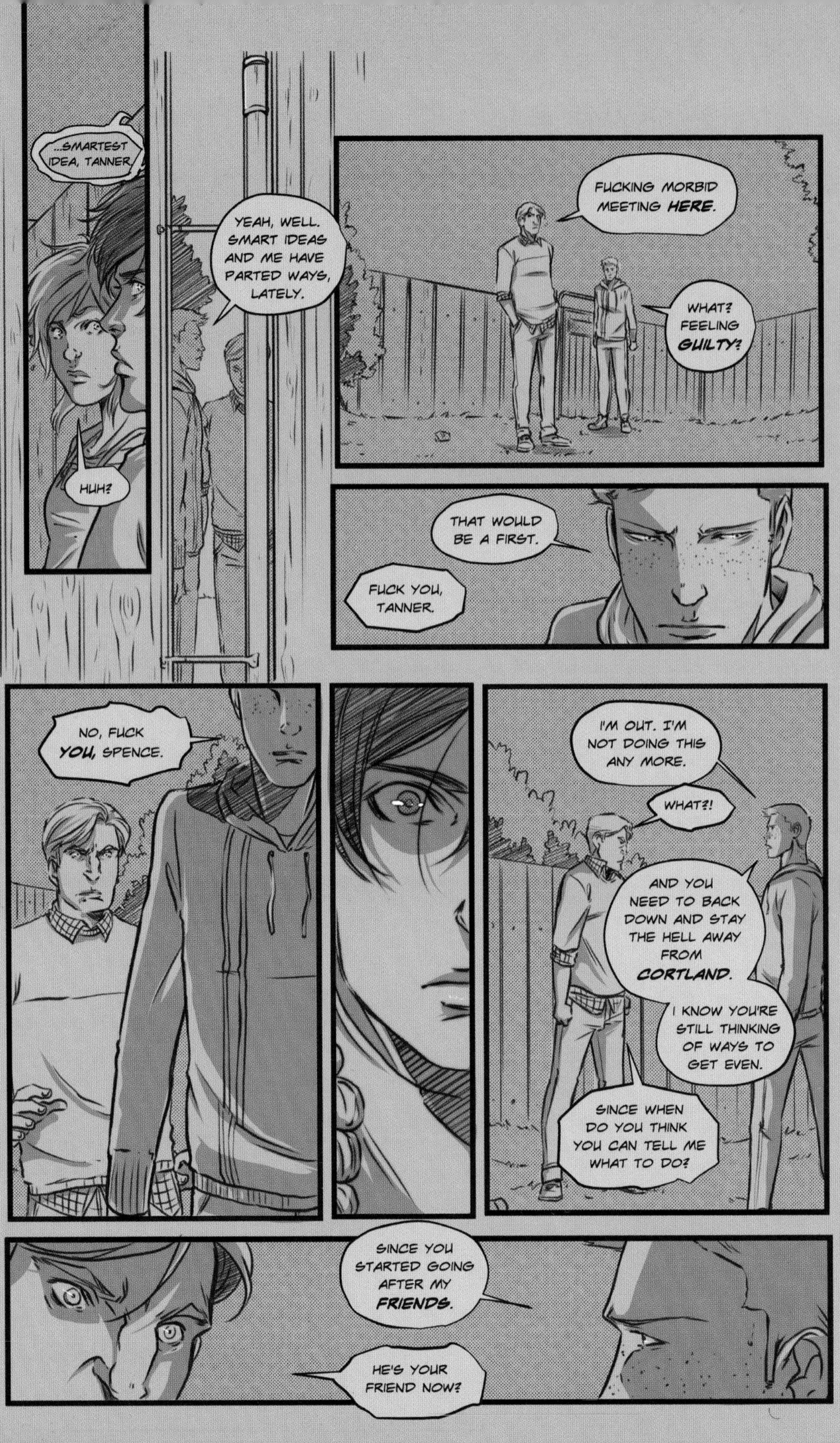
...SMARTEST IDEA, TANNER.
YEAH, WELL. SMART IDEAS AND ME HAVE PARTED WAYS, LATELY.
HUH?
FUCKING MORBID MEETING HERE.
WHAT? FEELING GUILTY?
THAT WOULD BE A FIRST.
FUCK YOU, TANNER.
NO, FUCK YOU, SPENCE.
I'M OUT. I'M NOT DOING THIS ANY MORE.
WHAT?!
AND YOU NEED TO BACK DOWN AND STAY THE HELL AWAY FROM CORTLAND.
I KNOW YOU'RE STILL THINKING OF WAYS TO GET EVEN.
SINCE WHEN DO YOU THINK YOU CAN TELL ME WHAT TO DO?
SINCE YOU STARTED GOING AFTER MY FRIENDS.
HE'S YOUR FRIEND NOW?

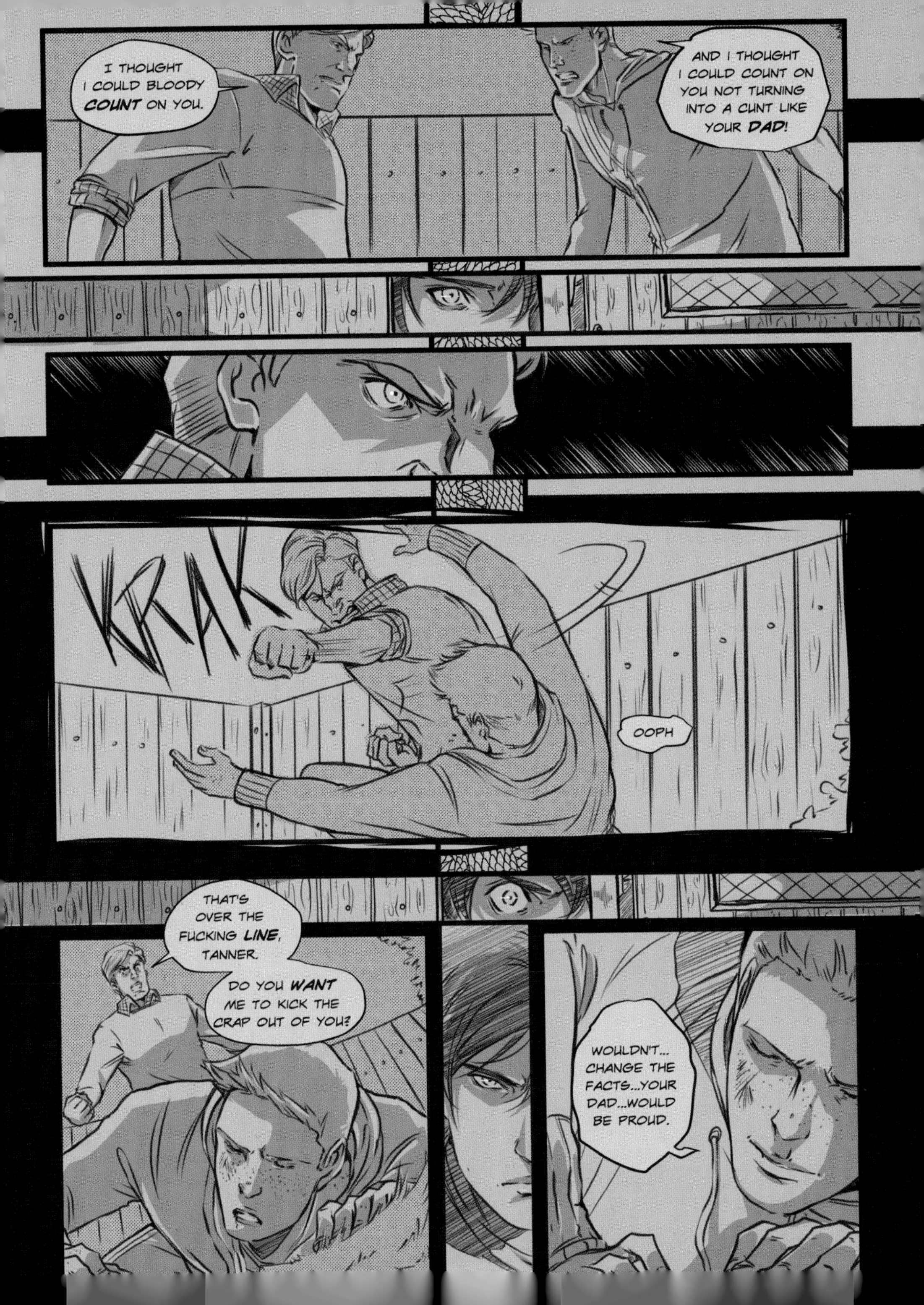
I THOUGHT I COULD BLOODY COUNT ON YOU.
AND I THOUGHT I COULD COUNT ON YOU NOT TURNING INTO A CUNT LIKE YOUR DAD!
KRAK
OOPH
THAT'S OVER THE FUCKING LINE, TANNER.
DO YOU WANT ME TO KICK THE CRAP OUT OF YOU?
WOULDN'T... CHANGE THE FACTS...YOUR DAD...WOULD BE PROUD.

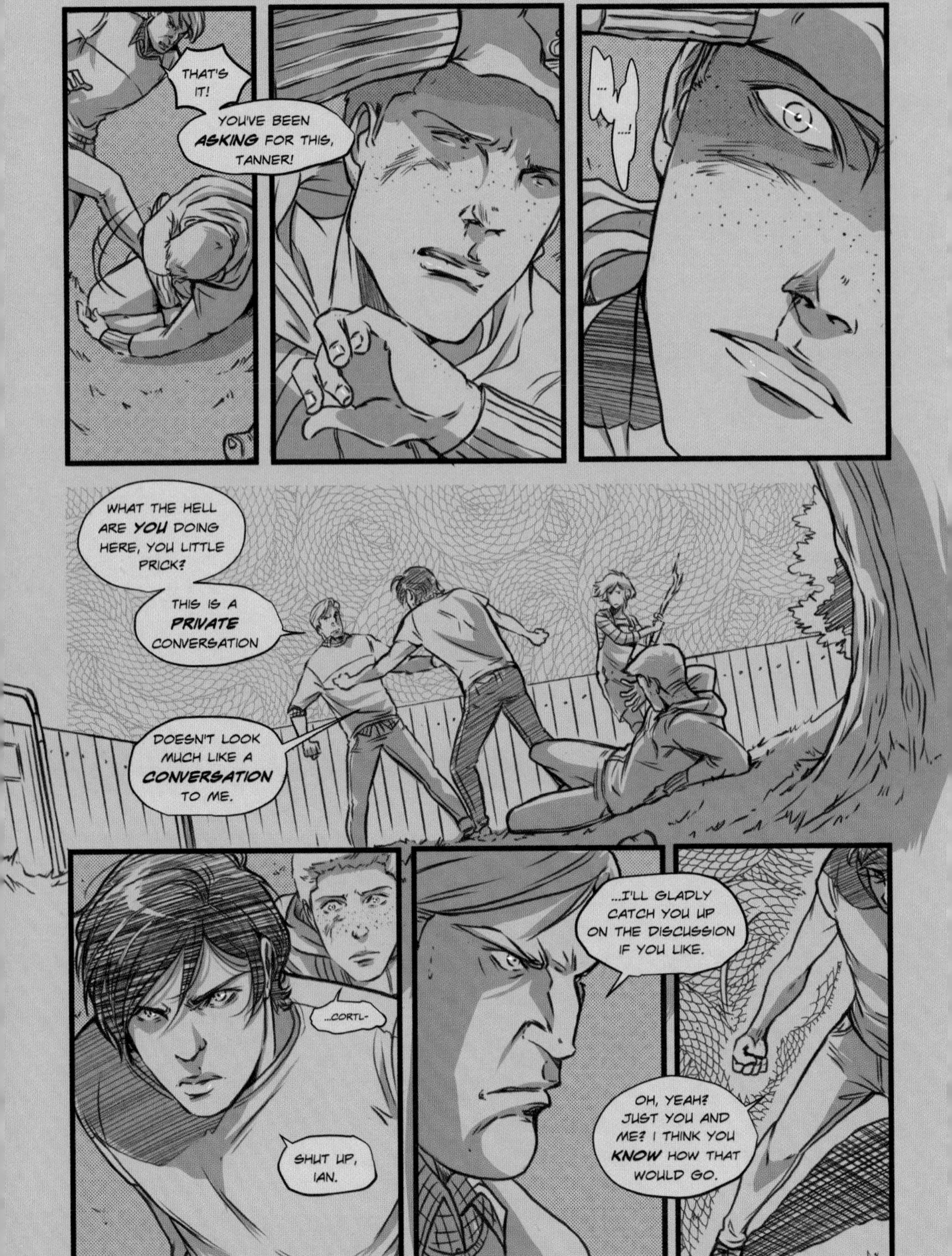
THAT'S IT!
YOU'VE BEEN ASKING FOR THIS, TANNER!
...
...!
WHAT THE HELL ARE YOU DOING HERE, YOU LITTLE PRICK?
THIS IS A PRIVATE CONVERSATION
DOESN'T LOOK MUCH LIKE A CONVERSATION TO ME.
...CORTL-
SHUT UP, IAN.
...I'LL GLADLY CATCH YOU UP ON THE DISCUSSION IF YOU LIKE.
OH, YEAH? JUST YOU AND ME? I THINK YOU KNOW HOW THAT WOULD GO.

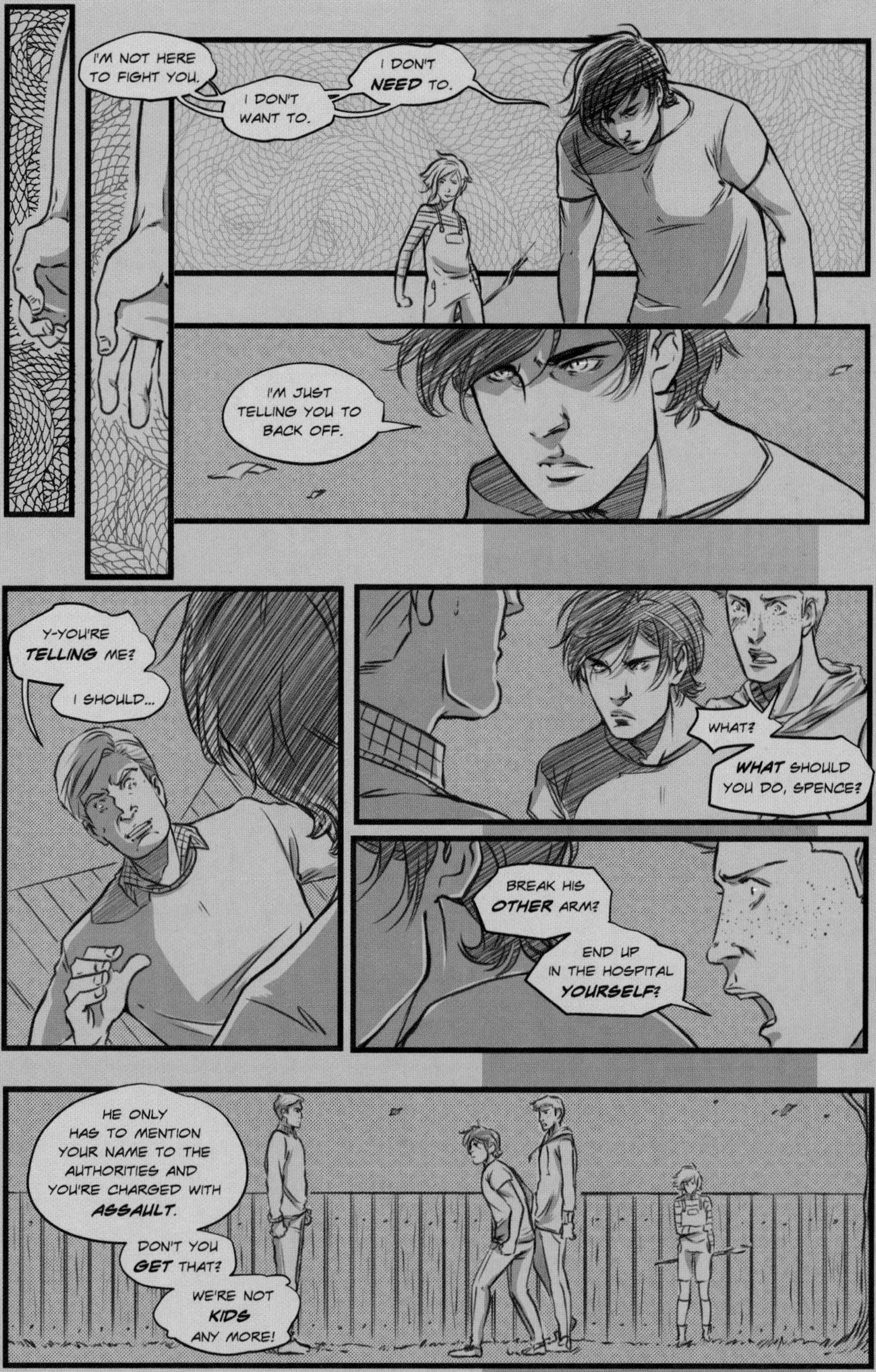
I'M NOT HERE TO FIGHT YOU.
I DON'T WANT TO.
I DON'T NEED TO.
I'M JUST TELLING YOU TO BACK OFF.
Y-YOU'RE TELLING ME?
I SHOULD...
WHAT?
WHAT SHOULD YOU DO, SPENCE?
BREAK HIS OTHER ARM?
END UP IN THE HOSPITAL YOURSELF?
HE ONLY HAS TO MENTION YOUR NAME TO THE AUTHORITIES AND YOU'RE CHARGED WITH ASSAULT.
DON'T YOU GET THAT?
WE'RE NOT KIDS ANY MORE!

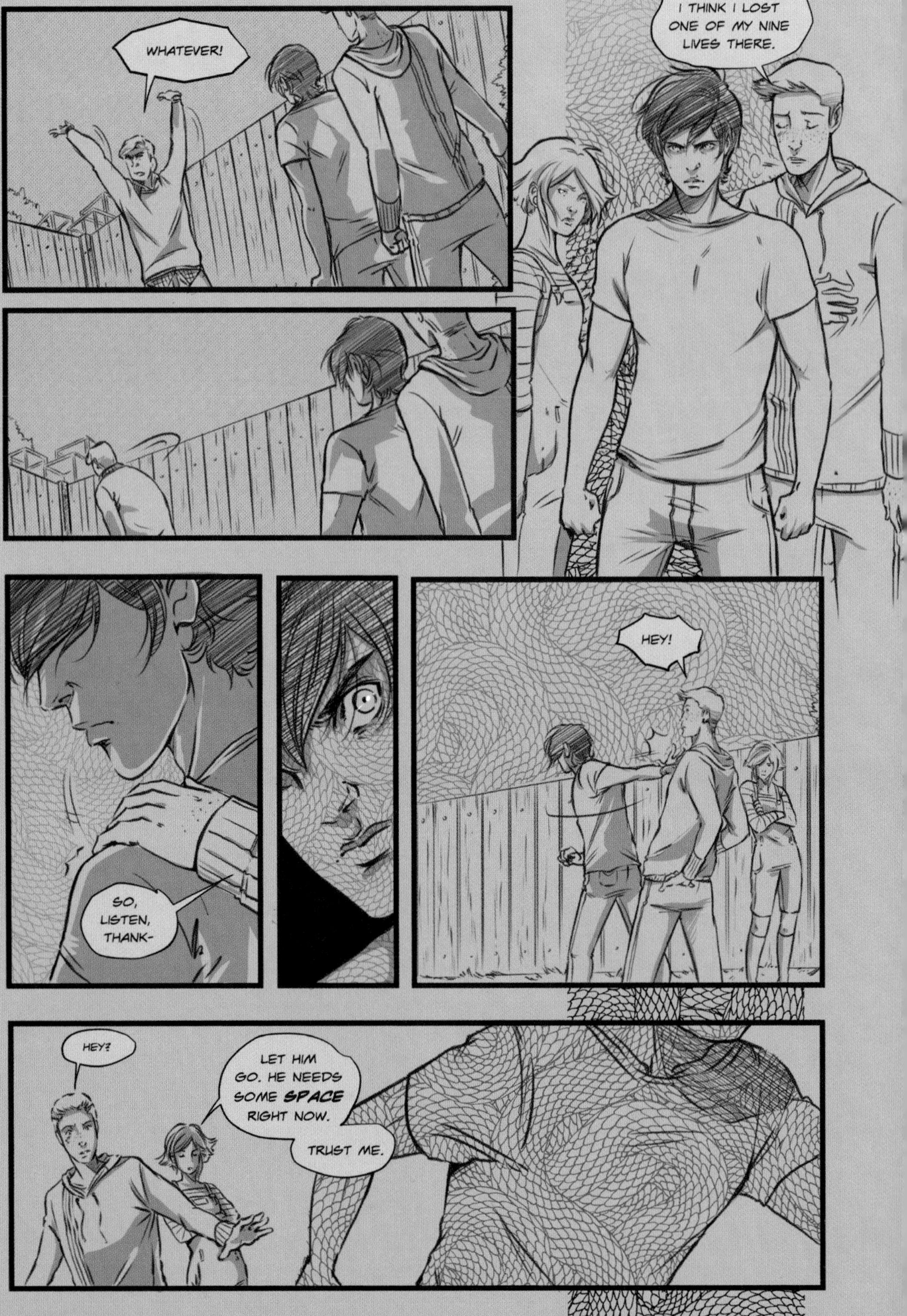
WHATEVER!
JESUS FUCK, I THINK I LOST ONE OF MY NINE LIVES THERE.
SO, LISTEN, THANK-
HEY!
HEY?
LET HIM GO. HE NEEDS SOME SPACE RIGHT NOW.
TRUST ME.

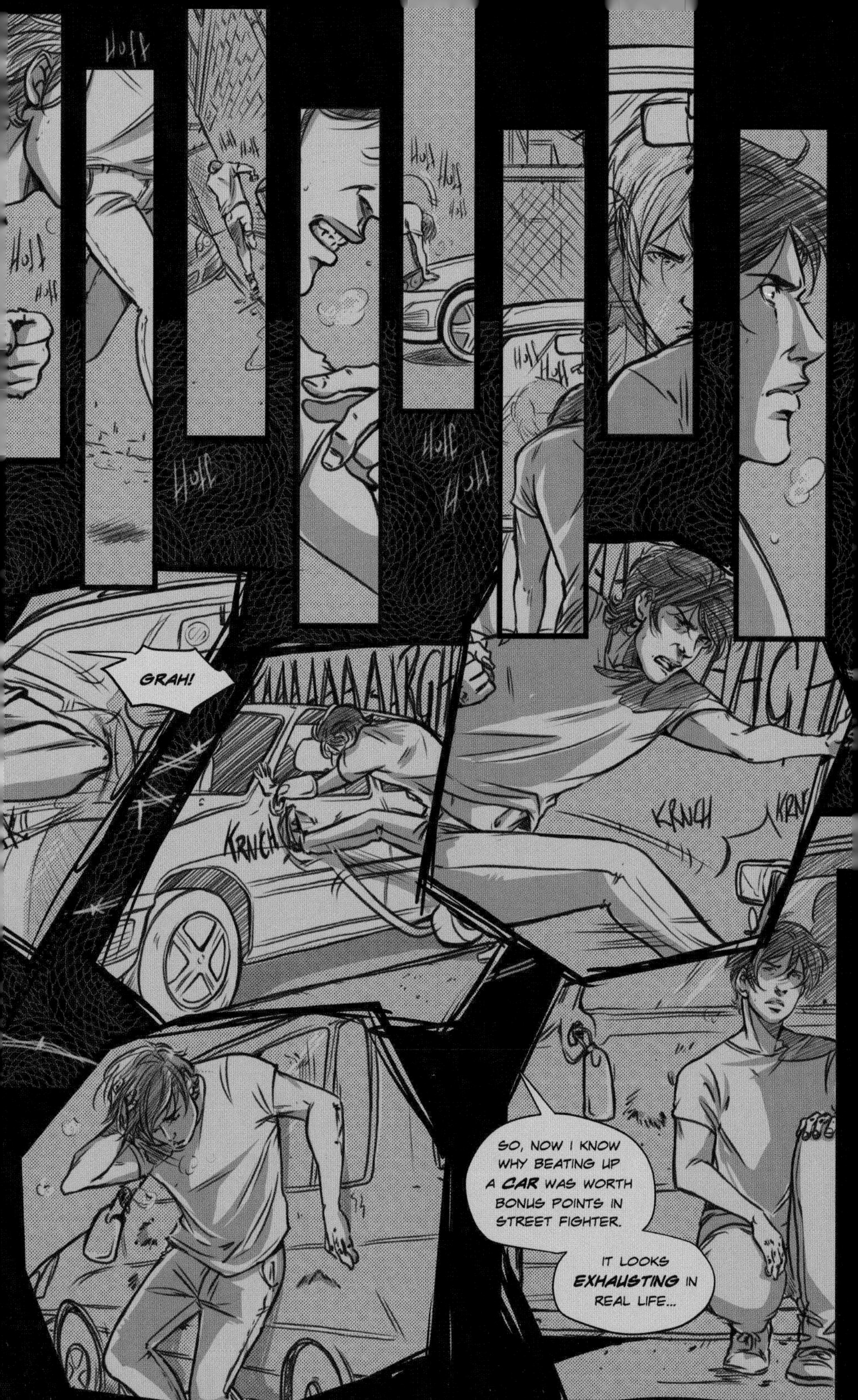
HUFF
HUFF
HUFF
HUFF
HUFF
HUFF
HUFF
HUFF
GRAH!
AAAAAAAAAAKGH
KRNCH
KRNCH
KRNCH
SO, NOW I KNOW WHY BEATING UP A CAR WAS WORTH BONUS POINTS IN STREET FIGHTER.
IT LOOKS EXHAUSTING IN REAL LIFE...

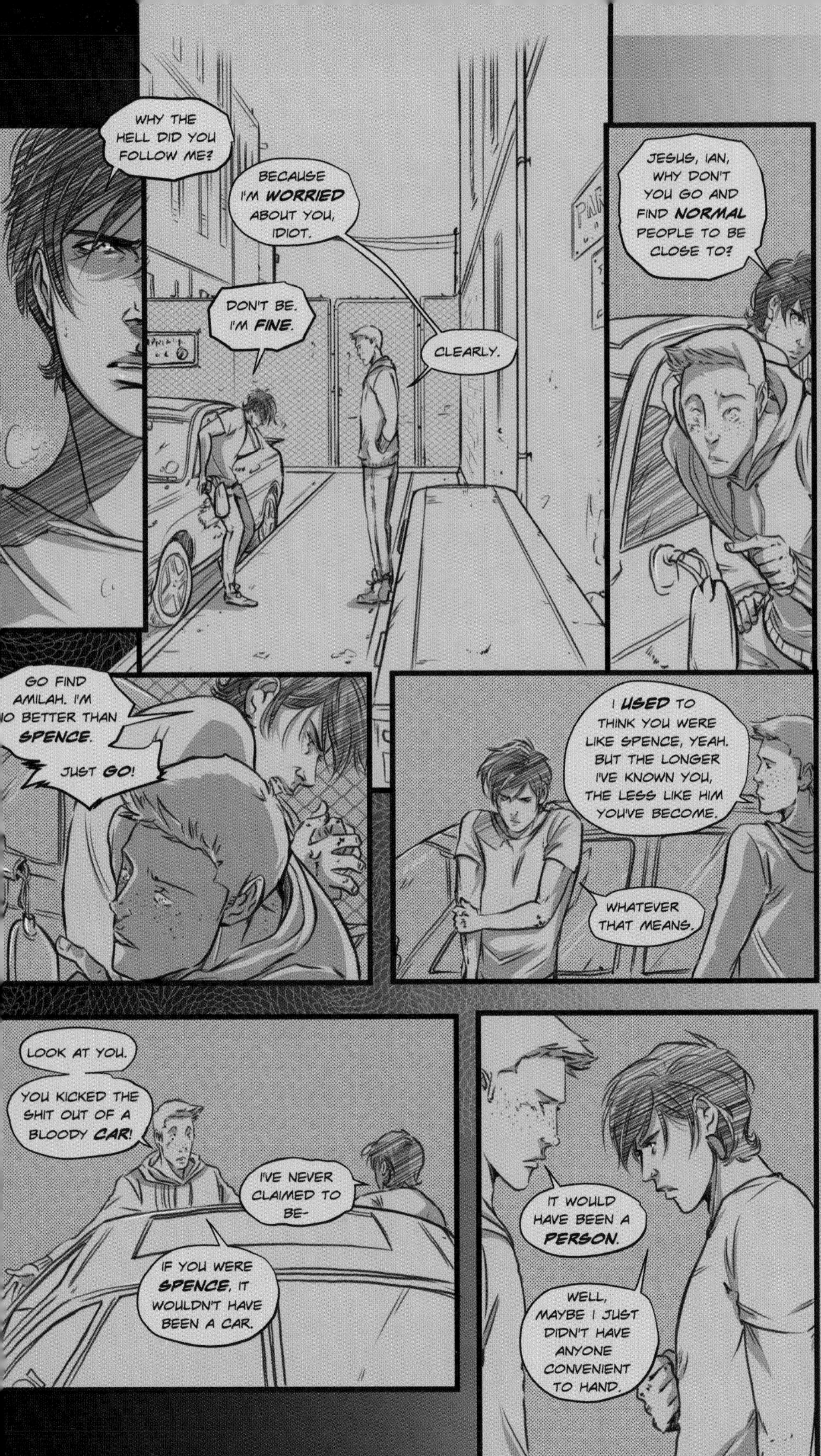
WHY THE HELL DID YOU FOLLOW ME?
BECAUSE I'M WORRIED ABOUT YOU, IDIOT.
DON'T BE. I'M FINE.
CLEARLY.
JESUS, IAN, WHY DON'T YOU GO AND FIND NORMAL PEOPLE TO BE CLOSE TO?
GO FIND AMILAH. I'M NO BETTER THAN SPENCE.
JUST GO!
I USED TO THINK YOU WERE LIKE SPENCE, YEAH. BUT THE LONGER I'VE KNOWN YOU, THE LESS LIKE HIM YOU'VE BECOME.
WHATEVER THAT MEANS.
LOOK AT YOU.
YOU KICKED THE SHIT OUT OF A BLOODY CAR!
I'VE NEVER CLAIMED TO BE-
IF YOU WERE SPENCE, IT WOULDN'T HAVE BEEN A CAR.
IT WOULD HAVE BEEN A PERSON.
WELL, MAYBE I JUST DIDN'T HAVE ANYONE CONVENIENT TO HAND.

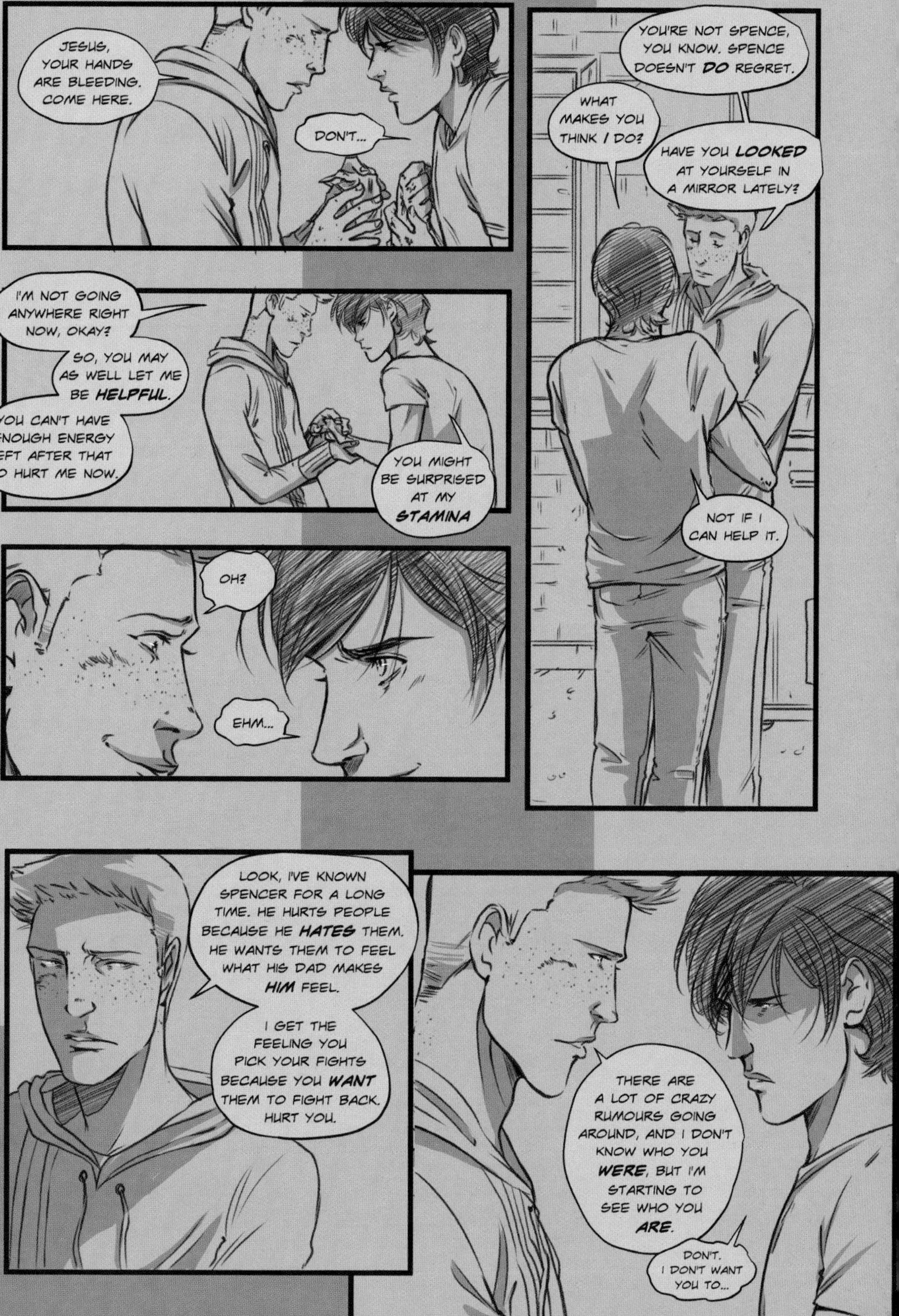
JESUS, YOUR HANDS ARE BLEEDING. COME HERE.
DON'T...
I'M NOT GOING ANYWHERE RIGHT NOW, OKAY?
SO, YOU MAY AS WELL LET ME BE HELPFUL.
YOU CAN'T HAVE ENOUGH ENERGY LEFT AFTER THAT TO HURT ME NOW.
YOU MIGHT BE SURPRISED AT MY STAMINA
OH?
EHM...
YOU'RE NOT SPENCE, YOU KNOW. SPENCE DOESN'T DO REGRET.
WHAT MAKES YOU THINK I DO?
HAVE YOU LOOKED AT YOURSELF IN A MIRROR LATELY?
NOT IF I CAN HELP IT.
LOOK, I'VE KNOWN SPENCER FOR A LONG TIME. HE HURTS PEOPLE BECAUSE HE HATES THEM. HE WANTS THEM TO FEEL WHAT HIS DAD MAKES HIM FEEL.
I GET THE FEELING YOU PICK YOUR FIGHTS BECAUSE YOU WANT THEM TO FIGHT BACK. HURT YOU.
THERE ARE A LOT OF CRAZY RUMOURS GOING AROUND, AND I DON'T KNOW WHO YOU WERE, BUT I'M STARTING TO SEE WHO YOU ARE.
DON'T. I DON'T WANT YOU TO...

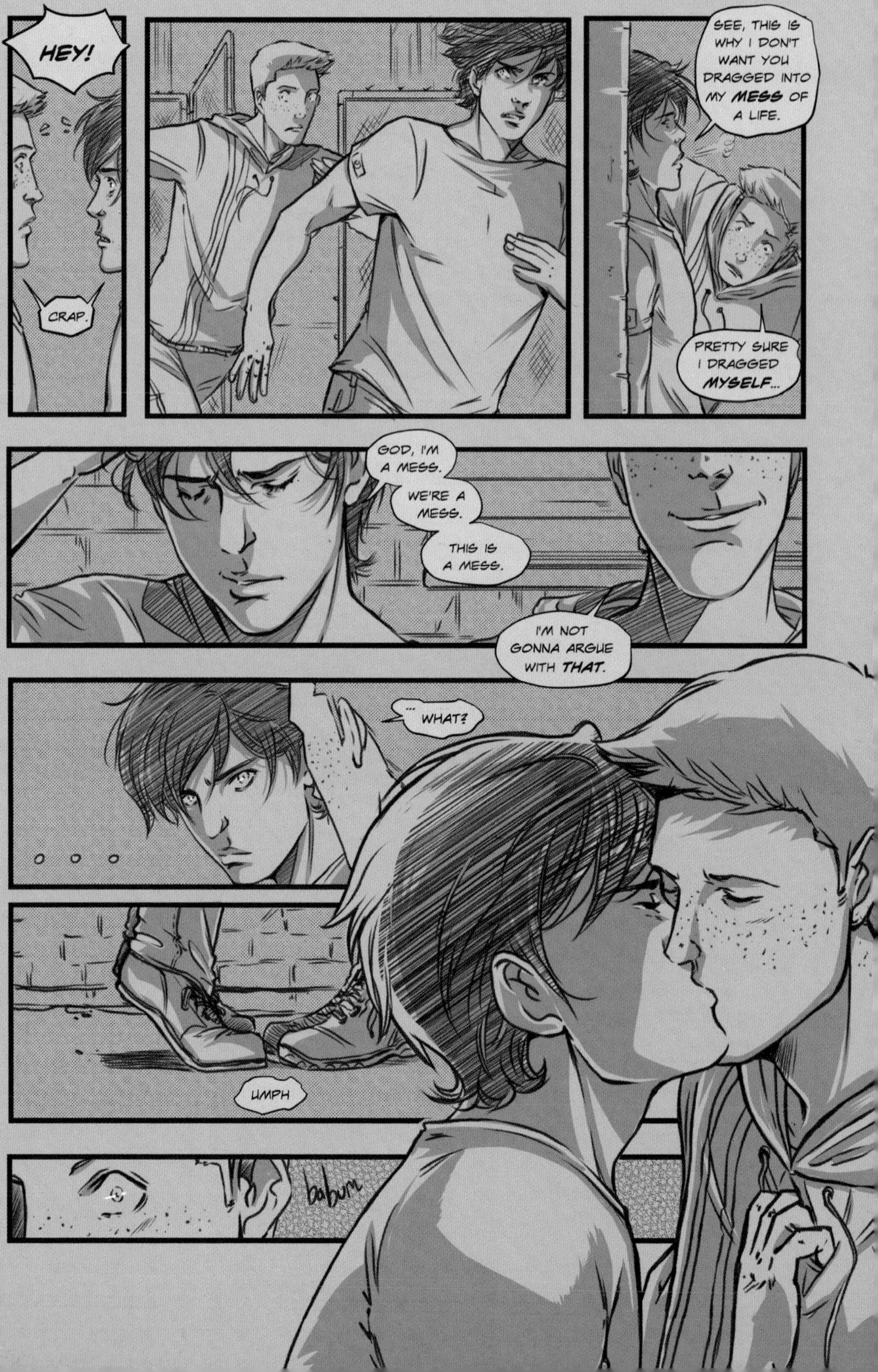
HEY!
CRAP.
SEE, THIS IS WHY I DON'T WANT YOU DRAGGED INTO MY MESS OF A LIFE.
PRETTY SURE I DRAGGED MYSELF...
GOD, I'M A MESS.
WE'RE A MESS.
THIS IS A MESS.
I'M NOT GONNA ARGUE WITH THAT.
... WHAT?
UMPH
babum

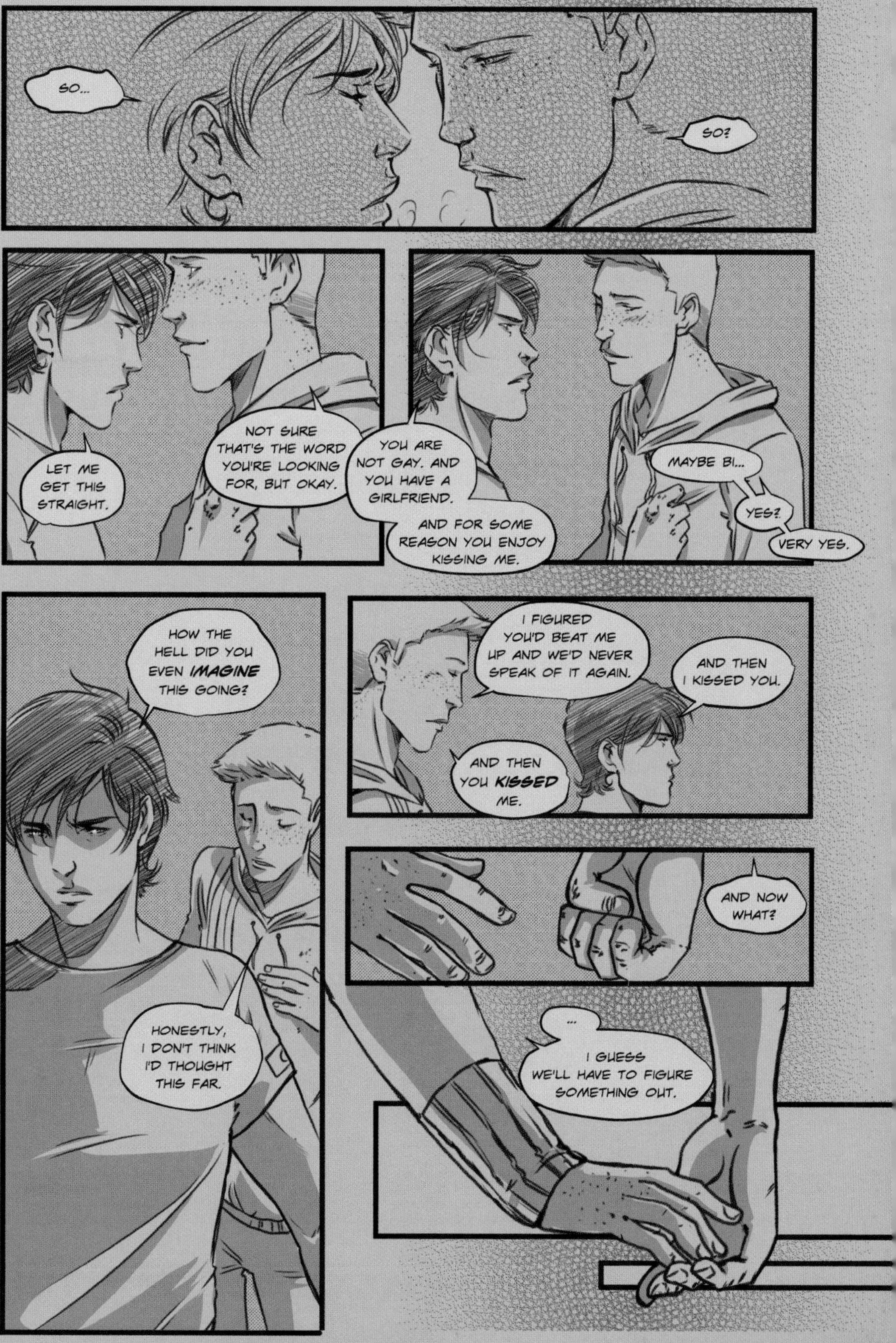
SO...
SO?
LET ME GET THIS STRAIGHT.
NOT SURE THAT'S THE WORD YOU'RE LOOKING FOR, BUT OKAY.
YOU ARE NOT GAY. AND YOU HAVE A GIRLFRIEND.
AND FOR SOME REASON YOU ENJOY KISSING ME.
MAYBE BI...
YES?
VERY YES.
HOW THE HELL DID YOU EVEN IMAGINE THIS GOING?
HONESTLY, I DON'T THINK I'D THOUGHT THIS FAR.
I FIGURED YOU'D BEAT ME UP AND WE'D NEVER SPEAK OF IT AGAIN.
AND THEN I KISSED YOU.
AND THEN YOU KISSED ME.
AND NOW WHAT?
...
I GUESS WE'LL HAVE TO FIGURE SOMETHING OUT.

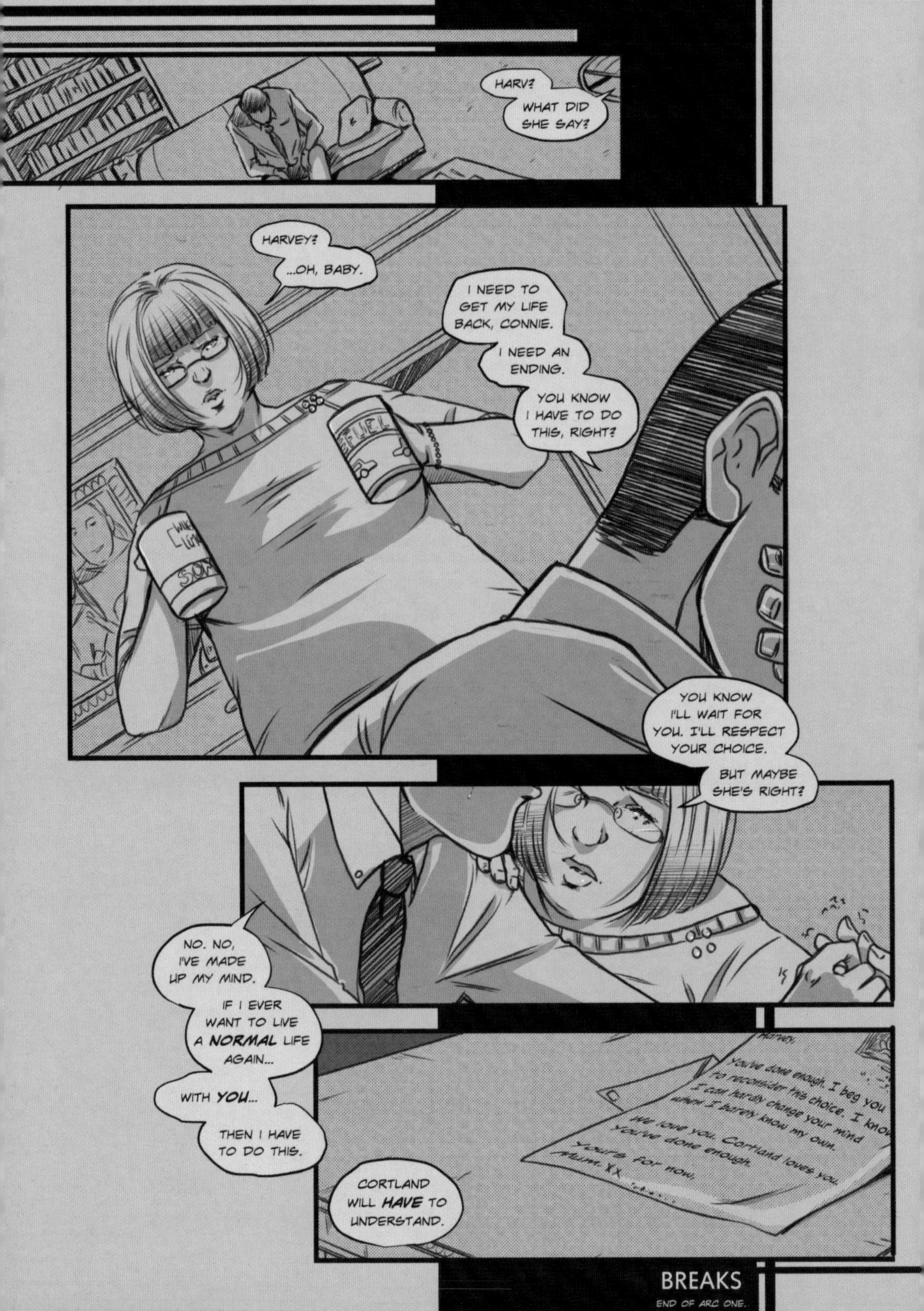
HARV? WHAT DID SHE SAY?
HARVEY? ...OH, BABY.
I NEED TO GET MY LIFE BACK, CONNIE.
I NEED AN ENDING.
YOU KNOW I HAVE TO DO THIS, RIGHT?
FUEL
YOU KNOW I'LL WAIT FOR YOU. I'LL RESPECT YOUR CHOICE.
BUT MAYBE SHE'S RIGHT?
NO. NO, I'VE MADE UP MY MIND.
IF I EVER WANT TO LIVE A NORMAL LIFE AGAIN...
WITH YOU...
THEN I HAVE TO DO THIS.
Harvey,
You've done enough. I beg you to reconsider this choice. I can hardly change your mind when I barely know my own.
We love you. Cortland loves you. You've done enough.
Yours for now,
Mum. Xx
CORTLAND WILL HAVE TO UNDERSTAND.
BREAKS
END OF ARC ONE.

The following, generous patrons have been supporting my
work with $5+ monthly donations on my Patreon campaign.
From $5-$50, these guys are **BREAKS** *legends!*
https://www.patreon.com/emmavieceli
(as of May, 2017)

Ariana Osborne (whose contribution was so generous that she
features in the comic as one of Dave's party guests!)
Benedict Durbin
Stephen Hamilton
Anna Tif Sikorska
Anu Harvey (one of the original DAH crew!)
Micaela B
Rebecca Strong
Nate Bee
Nekojita
Jamie McKelvie
Victoria West
Chaos-of-vinnie
Hana145
Susan Cook
Toria
Allycat99
Ben Templesmith
HE Cavanagh
R J Tysoe
Paul Cornell
Katy
Becky Cloonan
Kieron Gillen
Unevendays

They help make this comic happen and I am so, so grateful to
them. And to those backing me for $1 and $3 too - all of my
patrons are heroes to me!
Thank you.

Emma xx